WILD CARD BRIDE

"I'm making the best of a bad situation," Caleb growled. "Neither of us intends to be tied forever. But there's not a thing we can do about it right now. For tonight, Mrs. Logan, we're man and wife."

Libby gasped as he laid his hand against the side of her slender neck. His flesh was warmer than hers, his hand big and hard with calluses, so she felt fragile and even a little dizzy. "I won't sleep in this room with you, Caleb," she said with as much determination as she could muster.

He refused to release her, his hands making a tender frame for her face. "Libby," he whispered before he kissed her.

His mouth seemed to steal her breath. Desperately, she said, "I've said no. I'll scream!"

The reckless gleam in his eyes grew brighter. "Scream away," he advised.

WILD CARD BRIDE

JOY TUCKER

AVON BOOKS • NEW YORK

WILD CARD BRIDE is an original publication of Avon Books. This work has never before appeared in book form. This work is a novel. Any similarity to actual persons or events is purely coincidental.

AVON BOOKS
A division of
The Hearst Corporation
1350 Avenue of the Americas
New York, New York 10019

Special Printing: June 1993
First Avon Books Printing: October 1991

AVON TRADEMARK REG. U.S. PAT. OFF. AND IN OTHER COUNTRIES, MARCA REGISTRADA, HECHO EN U.S.A.

Printed in the U.S.A.

RA 10 9 8 7 6 5 4 3 2

For C. Edward Mannion,
Petaluma historian extraordinaire.
I love you, Daddy.

Thanks to Karl Kortum, Chief Curator, San Francisco Maritime Museum, and Alan Sorenson for sharing their expertise about steamboats, and to Perry Higman for information about horses and riding.

The Hounds of Portsmouth Square really did terrorize San Francisco in the latter days of the Gold Rush, and their exploits were ended by vigilante action in the 1850s. The individual Hounds in this story are entirely the product of my imagination, as are all the characters with the exception of General Mariano Vallejo and his family. His many descendants are a living part of California history.

Chapter 1

The roar that greeted Libby's first step onto the stage almost drove her back into the wings.

Mirrors behind the bar reflected the flames of a hundred candles. Smoke from at least as many cigars hung stationary in the air. The men who jostled among the deal tables blurred into a tide of red and blue shirts before Libby's startled eyes.

This wasn't the kind of theater she'd been led to expect.

After a moment's hesitation, she thrust out her chin and moved gracefully into position center stage. The roar grew louder as the candlelight fell directly on her tall, satin-clad figure.

Her pianist and manager, Aloysius Malloy, banged out an introduction on the tinny piano. The clamor faded. A monte dealer took advantage of the lull to shout, "Fellers! She may be purty, but a hand of cards is a healthier way to lose your gold dust! You won't have to fight off the other gents. You won't wonder what that itch is tomorrer morning. You can write to your wives back East with a clean conscience! So lay down your pokes right here! Monte, monte, monte . . ."

Threatening scowls from the patrons finally silenced the gambler. Libby took one more moment to draw her audience's attention to herself. Not, she thought wryly, that the effort was necessary. The way the men were staring at her breasts, milk-white against the screaming

1

scarlet of her gown and pushed into prominence by the ingenious corset beneath it, proved where their minds were.

Malloy had insisted she wear this low-cut dress. Malloy had promised her a triumphant concert before the music-thirsty miners flooding boomtown San Francisco. Now Libby had every intention of strangling Malloy.

Taking a deep breath that caused a kind of yearning groan to float through the room, Libby let out the first pure, round note of "The Lass of Roch Royal."

The ballad swooped up and down the scale, perfectly suited both to her tinkly high register and to the creamy lower range she could draw on at will. Her two-and-a-half-octave voice had supported her for two years from Canada to California. She'd sung in opera houses that had never heard an aria until she opened her mouth, in churches that boasted no steeples, in parlors, and in forest glades.

Never, until tonight, had she performed in a saloon.

She ended the song on a sweet, mournful note. Casting Malloy an unloving glance, Libby acknowledged applause with a deep curtsy. Her blond head cocked as though in rapt admiration while her accompanist struck a jangle of wrong notes. Inwardly seething, she drifted across the stage to lay her arm on the lid of the piano and hissed, "What's wrong? Are you drunk?"

"The keys stick," Malloy said out of the side of his mouth. He was perspiring.

Making a little business of shaking out her skirts, Libby smiled at the throng as he played the introduction again. She'd wondered about her own sanity when she'd allowed Malloy to choose the music for this program; now she admitted that his judgment had been superior. Even her hard-won nerve quailed at the thought of marching onto this dime-sized stage and breaking into Mozart. Of course, Malloy had had the advantage of knowing that Miss Elizabeth Owens, formerly of England where she'd been a pupil of the celebrated Giuditta Pasta, would be appearing in a taproom.

He fumbled another chord. In the resultant hush, someone yelled, "Let's hear 'The California Ball'!"

A few men laughed. Another shouted, "Aw, shut your filthy mouth and let the lady sing somethin' nice!"

"I want 'The California Ball'."

Libby couldn't make out her heckler in the sea of bearded faces. The insistent voice rose in a hoarse falsetto, bawling out the popular tune about a toothless hag and a pimp.

Half the audience shouted encouragement; the other half shouted to drown him out.

"We're losing them," Malloy muttered. "Nobody'll pay to listen to that caterwauling. You'd better give 'em what they want."

"You really *are* drunk. That song's indecent!" Libby answered furiously.

"You're not pretending you don't know the words, though, are you?" he asked unpleasantly. "And I presume Your Ladyship hopes to get paid?"

"Not for that! Play the Stephen Foster. Now."

Malloy took a huge gulp from the beer on the stand next to his sheet music and tried to coax a melody out of the recalcitrant instrument. Libby knew Malloy was right; she needed the money. Her heart thudding uncomfortably, she listened for a note in the discord that might serve for her opening.

Finally she chose one at random and filled her lungs with air. Her ribs strained against the confines of her corset, and her breasts swelled to half moons. From somewhere in the hubbub, she heard a soulful "Gawd, will you look at those?"

A hundred men in an enclosed space could make a considerable racket. Trained in the rigors of grand opera, Libby knew that she could almost equal it. As she began to sing, the audience began to fall silent. She felt a spurt of elation. More of them were listening to "Home, Sweet Home" than to each other . . .

"Damn it, that's not 'The California Ball!' " a rough voice exclaimed.

A grimy hand gripped the edge of the stage. Libby missed a note and stepped back hurriedly to avoid getting knocked over. Exchanging a wild glance with Malloy, she stood her ground and picked up the thread of the melody. "Be it ever so humble . . ."

Caleb Logan slammed his shot glass on the table and surged to his feet. Thrusting back a shock of black hair, he narrowed his dark eyes for another glimpse of the singer. He wanted a better look. His fancy had always been for fair women, and he hadn't seen one in months.

Even though he was a tall man, too many bodies filled the space between his table and the stage for him to see more than snatches of golden hair. Using his shoulders and elbows, he battled his way to the stage.

The fellow with the bawdy taste in music was on the stage, weaving an unsteady path near the footlights, kicking one candle in its reflective tin holder over the edge. Caleb ducked, but hot wax splashed on his neck.

"Hey!" he protested. "What are you trying to do? Set the place on fire or just horn in on the little lady's song?"

The drunk grunted a curse. The prospect of a fight sobered Caleb enough so that he vaulted onto the stage. He heard the monte dealer's professionally bored voice following him. "Odds on the tall dude in the brown coat. Get your bets down . . ."

"Stand back," he told the singer. "I'll get rid of him for you."

She glared at him and sang louder.

The drunk stumbled forward, his fist cocked low. Caleb's quick reflexes saved him from being hit, but his assailant's rush carried the drunk several steps beyond where he had been standing. In the curious sloweddown time of a scuffle, Caleb turned and still had an opportunity to study the saloon singer up close.

Despite her tawdry setting, she seemed made for

moonbeams and starshine. She shone. Hair like spun sugar glistened in the flickering light, and her youthful features were cameo-perfect even under the strain of singing in the middle of a brawl.

A plan jumped full-blown into his brain.

He couldn't give it the long, careful consideration it deserved because the other man had circled and was aiming a roundhouse swing. Caleb dodged, but with his gaze still riveted to the line of shadow between the singer's white, upthrust breasts, he wasn't quite fast enough. A wallop caught the side of his neck. The blow hurt. Pain cleared away another layer of the alcohol-induced fog from his head. Caleb moved in with confidence, grabbing his opponent's arm and spinning him around. Finally Caleb pushed him away.

As the drunk staggered toward the back of the stage, Caleb's eyes returned to the golden-haired singer. She really was a beauty. Full of grit, too.

Mesmerized by so much pale loveliness and stubborn spirit, Caleb said seriously, "I want you to be my wife."

She paused long enough to snap, "Get off the stage. And take the other ruffian with you!"

Losing no more than a beat, she soared back into the song.

Caleb waited till she broke off for a breath and repeated, "I need a wife. And you'll do just fine."

She simply swept by him, opening slender arms to the crowd on the floor. Caleb wasn't used to women who ignored him. Besides, she'd gone by so fast that he hadn't been able to decide what color her eyes were. Some cool color, blue or gray, he thought. He stepped around her to find out.

The noises from the audience changed from catcalls to shouted warnings. He swiveled just in time to receive a butt on his belt buckle from his opponent's head. His sense of balance, developed years ago at sea, kept him on his feet, but the whiskey he'd drunk threatened to erupt from his abused belly.

The blow seemed to daze its instigator more than Caleb. The man subsided slowly to the boards, croaking, "Gonna sing 'The California Ball.' "

"Oh, no, sir, you are not," retorted the singer. Her bell-shaped skirt swishing angrily, she marched to the piano and lifted the heavy glass mug that rested there. "Remove yourself. Yourselves. Both of you. This instant."

The crowd screamed its approval.

"Hold on here," Caleb said, keeping a wary eye on the mug while he hoisted his opponent by a limp arm and draped him over one shoulder. "I came to your rescue. You don't need to do anything hasty." He tried a grin he'd been told often enough was irresistible.

Shouting *"Oooh!"* she threw the mug.

A geyser of beer splashed over Caleb's good coat, but he could hardly complain because the mug itself struck the other man's head with deadly accuracy. Apparently his lady had a temper. He liked that.

"Nice aim for a female," said Caleb.

The audience went wild, whistling and bellowing and stamping boots on the dirty floor until the whole place shook. Caleb figured he'd better get off the stage before the singer's admirers tore him apart.

"Remember what I told you," he said, strolling into the dark little area behind the curtain.

Libby let out a slow gasp of relief as the polite drunkard carried the obnoxious drunkard into the wings. Did every man in San Francisco drink to excess? What had he said at the end? Remember . . . oh, about marrying him.

Marriage was the last thing on her mind. She faced Malloy.

"Done heaving the crockery about now, are we, darlin'?" he asked silkily over the noise of the saloon patrons.

"Certainly," she stated. "When have you ever seen me do such a thing? I believe our next selection is also by Stephen Foster."

By now the audience loved her. The wild response built after every song she sang until she concluded her encore with a helpless gesture at her burning throat. The din was thunderous. Even though Libby wasn't sure if the loud appreciation was for her voice or her show of spirit or the red dress she was wearing, she couldn't help but be touched by it.

She laughed out loud, tossing back her head with no care for the cornsilk hair piled so elaborately in puffs and ringlets. Coins rained at her feet, and even a small pouch that might be filled with gold dust.

Malloy scrambled after the booty, allowing Libby to sidle out of sight. Exhaustion hit her as soon as she reached the privacy of the wings. Stubbing her toe in its soft evening slipper, she would have fallen if a bony hand hadn't caught her elbow.

"By the Lord Harry!" exclaimed the proprietor. "Never would have dreamed you could sing like that!"

Libby blinked to clear her smoke-blurred vision. The man was thin, except for a burgeoning pot belly. Carefully, she shook his hand off her. "What did you imagine I was going to do instead?" she asked. He looked disconcerted, and she added, "Never mind. I would sincerely prefer not to know."

Pressing so close she could smell spirits on his breath, he murmured, "You must be all tuckered out. There's a real comfortable settee in my office where you could, ah, rest a spell."

Theatrical life had taught Libby how to deal with invitations to "ah, rest," so she smiled sweetly and said in her most clipped British accent, "Thank you ever so much. But as Mr. Malloy perhaps explained to you, I have other arrangements."

His lips set in an affronted expression. "Suit yourself. That fancy man of yours done picking up the two-bit pieces?"

Long ago, when she'd set out to earn her fare home to England, she'd decided it wasn't worthwhile to notice the insults of people she intended to know for as short a time as possible. But it was hard. A good reputation meant something to her. "I'm sure as soon as—oh, Mr. Malloy!" Despite her exasperation with the pianist, she turned to Malloy in relief as he limped off the stage, clutching a hat full of coins. "Have we done well?"

"Rich, darlin', we're rich!" Malloy's jubilation was short-lived. Libby plucked the hat from his grasp, folding the brim to create a makeshift purse. She tucked it under one arm. Malloy protested, "You don't need to do that!"

"Indeed, I do, Mr. Malloy. You remember the terms of our agreement?" Sometimes she felt like Aloysius Malloy's nanny or—God forfend—his mother. Inclining her head regally to the saloon owner, she added, "I shall sing for you again on Monday."

He blustered toward her back, "This—this—Malloy said you'd perform for a week! What about tomorrow?"

Libby didn't pause. "Tomorrow is the Lord's day, sir. I'm sure your patrons will understand. Good evening."

Limping rapidly beside her, Malloy urged, "Just for once, couldn't you—"

"No, I couldn't," said Libby flatly. "You know I don't sing on Sundays. Especially not in taprooms!"

Malloy muttered, "Holy Mother of God."

"I doubt she's going to be on your side in this discussion, Mr. Malloy," said Libby as they left the saloon. Their heels rang on wooden planks a perilous few feet above liquid mud flats. This portion of Sansome Street, buildings and all, sat on a pier above the bay. "May I ask if that was your idea of a prestigious concert hall?"

"Now, acushla—"

"Don't blarney me!"

"You said you needed to make quick money," he pointed out sullenly. "We made it tonight. If you wanted to stun them with your trills in the Jenny bloody

Lind Theater, we'd have had to wait forever. My way, by next Saturday your share will be more than enough for passage to England—if there's a ship with the crew to lift anchor.''

She turned to study him, a daring thing to do on the unrailed walkway, especially since clouds spread a thick blanket over the April night sky. The two of them were merely walking from the back of the saloon to the main entrance of the adjoining hotel, but darkness and un-certain footing made long minutes of a trip that should have taken seconds. For a moment, however, she forgot that they stood on creaky planks above pilings sunk in shifting ooze.

''What on earth are you talking about?''

He burst into overloud laughter. ''Didn't you look around the harbor this afternoon?''

Weeks on California's mud-paved roads had left Libby disinclined for sightseeing. ''After we got to town this morning, all I did was sleep,'' she admitted. ''When I woke up, I drank some soup the waiter brought to my room and then you and that—that female arrived with these clothes.''

Accompanying Malloy had been a brassy middle-aged woman Libby had had no difficulty identifying as an extremely soiled dove. Libby knew all too well that the extent of her decolletage often had an effect on the size of her earnings, so she had allowed the impromptu maid to strap her into the gown with its scandalous underpinnings. Both were more daringly constructed than anything she'd ever worn before.

''Besides,'' she said, ''this doesn't seem to be the kind of town where a lady should go strolling about without an escort.'' Torches flared at the hotel en-trance, and Libby saw Malloy's chest puff out. ''Even yours,'' she added gently.

His brightly colored waistcoat deflated. ''You've got a bitter tongue, woman,'' he said. ''Don't you know what the Bible says about vicious females?''

"Better than you, probably," she answered serenely. "My uncle is a vicar. Church of England."

The Irishman glared.

"Ah, yes, your famous uncle, the vicar. I'm sure he's proud to know how his niece is keeping herself these days."

"I at least try to be a lady," Libby said pointedly. She looked up and down the street. There were other hotels on the waterfront, and noise and light spilled from them, but most of the pier was very dark. If ships drifted at anchor at the harbor end, she couldn't see them.

"Throwing mugs of beer?" he taunted.

"I had ample provocation. And I wasn't the one drinking it. If I'd known two years ago what your propensities are for the stuff—"

"Don't be forgetting your own circumstances. It's not every man who'd be willing to travel the whole blamed West playing second fiddle to you, my dear. Especially considering you've turned out to be miserly with the purse strings."

This was old ground in their frequent quarrels. "You understood from the start who would control the money, and don't try to pretend you didn't."

"You always have to be right," he grumbled.

"No, no," she assured him. "I make mistakes quite often. For example, once I thought you retained the remnants of a decent upbringing. But I'm more than willing to admit I was wrong. You've obviously outgrown it."

A wary expression replaced Malloy's grimace. "Now, why would you be saying that, darlin'?"

"You mean besides the fact you contracted for me to sing in a saloon? There was money missing from the kitty again this morning. I suppose it's gone?"

His silence answered her.

"You know," she continued after a moment, "I don't know if you're venal and devious because you drink, or if you drink because you can't stand yourself. Come along, we can't stand in the doorway all night. I want to count our profits.''

If they were really going to make enough money to send her home, she told herself, she'd sing hosannas to his departing back.

The thought of returning to normal life made her treat him to her prettiest smile. ''You may come up-stairs.''

Ironically, he offered her his arm. Daintily, Libby took it, aware that they were providing a show for the denizens of the lobby. She reluctantly accepted that the perception Malloy shared her room created a safeguard she didn't dare dismiss. A woman without a protector was fair game to too many men in this year of grace 1852. As it happened, Malloy's habits furnished their own kind of protection. He desired no mistress except the bottle.

His allotment of male vanity survived intact, how-ever. The expression under his straggly beard was pleased enough to fool anyone pondering the exact con-ditions of their partnership as Libby preceded him up the stairs.

She produced the key from a pocket hidden in the folds of her skirt.

''I'll hold the hat,'' Malloy offered.

Libby gave him the key instead. ''Perhaps not,'' she said.

Shrugging philosophically, Malloy unlocked the door and stood aside so she could enter first. Pausing to gather up the voluminous skirts of her gown and avoid catching them on splinters from the narrow doorjamb, Libby peered idly down at the lobby.

The rooms for hire opened off a mezzanine visible from the floor below. Customers overflowing from the saloon filled the lobby. Packed shoulder to shoulder, they scarcely varied in their customary miner's shirts—except for one particular set of shoulders that rose above the others, broad and stiff in a brown suit coat.

''Oh, no,'' she said involuntarily.

Malloy's eyes widened. "Trouble?"

"No. That is—no," answered Libby, wondering why a quick, hot shiver had touched her spine at the sight of that distinctive, almost well-tailored coat. "It's one of those barbarians who jumped onto the stage."

He squinted down. "Ah. The gallant johnny who wants to marry you. Brave lad. Will you be taking him up on it?"

"Don't be absurd. I haven't spent two years working my way toward San Francisco to give up my chance of getting to England now. He was foxed, that's all."

Nevertheless, she spent another moment returning the stranger's stare, trying to distinguish whether his eyes could be as bright and reckless as she remembered them.

They were. Just now they narrowed slightly above a masterful nose and a clean-shaven, thin-lipped mouth that didn't leer or sag as so many men's did. He no longer grinned at her with the maddening charm that had driven her to throw Malloy's mug at him; his lips were tight with anger, or perhaps disapproval.

Libby's soft lips pressed together in a similar expression. The tug of interest she felt formed a distraction she could do without. It was time to count the night's take. Every penny would buy another small piece of her ticket away from the crudity and emptiness and frightening, larger-than-life grandeur of America. Her breath came quicker at the thought.

Turning abruptly, she swept into her room. Malloy closed the door and leaned against it before she dumped the contents of his hat onto the straw mattress.

Libby gasped. If there were pennies or two-bit pieces in the shining mound, her dazzled eyes couldn't separate them. American gold eagles glittered next to Mexican, Canadian, and English coins.

"How much?" she asked reverently.

Malloy smirked. "More than two hundred dollars, if the foreign stuff is worth anything here. I think it is;

there's not enough American mintage in circulation yet to crowd the other money out.''

"I should flail you alive for sending me to sing in front of that assemblage of topers. Just because you have a natural affinity for saloons doesn't mean I do.'' She picked up a twenty-dollar gold piece and bit it delicately. The metal held its shape. "However, I suppose I can't argue with the results.''

Malloy inched forward. "I'll just be taking a little advance then . . .''

Libby sifted through the pile and chose a silver dollar.

Malloy wrinkled his face in distress. It wasn't an unhandsome face, Libby thought, just unconvincing.

"Prices are inflated to the sky. This won't buy anything at all,'' he protested.

Sighing, she handed him another dollar. "And now I'd like the pouch, please.''

Malloy's smile showed all his teeth. "What would you be talking about, darling'?''

"A leather pouch, deerskin, I think, with Indian beadwork on it. Quite pretty. It was, oh, about three feet to the right of that broken-down piano. Don't make me ask twice, Mr. Malloy.''

Her implacable tone induced Malloy to bring the pouch out of its hiding place inside his shirt.

It weighed an ounce or more, Libby estimated, balancing the tiny bag on one palm. After peeking within by the light of the lantern, she carefully pulled the drawstrings tight again without removing any of the contents. The precious yellow dust was too easy to spill.

"I'm ashamed of you, Aloysius Malloy," she said, half seriously. "Surely somewhere you've heard that stealing is a sin.''

His agate eyes, some color between green and brown, darkened with hatred. "I've had about enough of your sermonizing, Libby Owens. Two bloody years of it. Did no one ever tell you to take care not to push a man too far?''

"When I meet a real man, I'll take every care," she promised flippantly, but her own eyes widened at the expression in his.

"Dear God, deliver me from this bitch," he whispered.

"Amen," Libby agreed. She'd never considered Malloy worthy of fear before, but now a metallic taste coated her tongue. A strongly developed instinct for survival kept her words measured and calm. Moral ascendency had always been the best weapon to control Malloy. "I think the end of the week will mark the parting of our ways. You've tried to cheat me for the last time."

"Give me my half now!"

"Oh, no. I'd never see you again. Who would play the piano? We're both under contract, remember? So we'll have our triumph at—what is the name of this abysmal establishment?—and we can quit each other wealthier and wiser a week from today. You can drink yourself into a stupor then."

His fist clenched, white-knuckled, around the two dollars. "I need more until Monday," he muttered.

Libby felt tired and shaken, at the end of her patience. "No. You've got your bed here at this—hotel, for want of a better word. Since rooms are the only direct payment you managed to get for us from that unappealing man, you might as well use yours instead of lying senseless in some alley. Take your meals downstairs. I'll pay for them." Exasperated concern crept into her tone. This worthless creature was the only human being she'd seen from one day to the next for twenty-four months. "You'd be better off with some food in you, anyway."

"Spare me the temperance lecture!" He flung out of the room, slamming the door so hard it failed to catch and crashed back against the flimsy wall.

Wincing, Libby closed it, noticing as she did that the key was missing. A quick search didn't reveal it. The lock it fit was large, apparently hand-turned and of local manufacture. Losing the key didn't really alter her safety. Even assuming the lock would hold against a determined assault—and Libby wasn't foolish enough to make any such assumption—the hinges bolting the slab of uncured redwood upright in its frame would buckle at the least pressure.

The key itself was of no importance. The fact that Malloy probably had it was. With his thirst exacerbated by temper, the Irishman might well try to sell her for the price of a drink.

Frowning, Libby dragged the bedstead across the doorway before attacking the tiny buttons at the back of the gown. A frank moan of contentment escaped her as she loosened her stays. Her full breasts resumed their normal shape.

The corset was a hellish contraption, but it had served its purpose tonight. Two hundred dollars, plus whatever the gold dust might be worth.

"Elizabeth," she said to herself, "you're going home."

Even with its hard mattress, the bed beckoned, but Libby had one more task to perform before she could sleep. From a round-topped trunk she withdrew a small oval sewing kit. Clad in her pantalets, she sat cross-legged on the floor and began unpicking the hem of her least favorite dress. As she knew from experience, creating an individual pocket for each coin was a time-consuming task. But she didn't want suspicious clankings to arouse the curiosity of a would-be thief. And since all of the banks would be closed until Monday, her riches had to be hidden somewhere.

Caleb's shoulders relaxed as he watched the piano player hurl himself down the stairs. The man's uneven gait didn't seem to slow him down. In fact, he acted as if all the demons in hell were waiting for him back in the saloon singer's room. Caleb was interested in only one demon—the girl with the face of an angel and the body of a succubus in a flame-red dress.

It occurred to Caleb that he might have had too much to drink. He didn't usually indulge in strong liquor—or poetry, for that matter. He'd certainly never wrestled a drunk off a stage before. As for chasing a waterfront woman who already shared a room with a man, only yesterday he would have snorted in derision at the thought.

But yesterday he hadn't seen a woman so beautiful and mettlesome that she put wild ideas into his head.

A hoarse chuckle sounded from the vicinity of his shoulder. "Liked the looks of our songbird, did you, buck?"

Caleb glanced down at a meager fellow who nevertheless carried a belly that would have done credit to an expectant mother eight months gone. "Do I know you?" he asked.

The man smiled. "I own this hotel and the saloon next door."

Caleb allowed his gaze to travel around the lobby's sparse appointments. Iron kettles served as spittoons. The chairs lined up against the walls were clumsy things hammered together from local wood; a scarred oak desk was the only considerable piece of furniture.

"You're a fortunate man," Caleb said, straight-faced.

"Done pretty well. Parlayed a little strike six months ago into this place. Hell of a lot easier than freezing my feet and burning my butt bent over panning for gold in the Coloma."

Caleb had heard more than he wanted about the cold water and sweltering sun that plagued prospectors working the ore-rich bottom of the Coloma River. "Good for you," he said, trying to turn away.

"Now, here I got all the comforts of home, *if* you follow me, buck." The owner leered up into Caleb's face, which went still. "You don't have to want for a real bed and something soft to fill it when you take the urge. I got some girls—"

"No, thanks."

"Real nice girls," he persisted. "Friendly. Accommodating, if you got a particular taste. Sixteen dollars to sit at your table, rising to two hundred for a whole night's pleasure. Won't beat the price anywhere in town.''

Caleb's distaste grew. "Sounds dear to me for a case of head lice.'' Not to mention the other contagions prostitutes were passing from miner to miner faster than gold fever. "I've got business upstairs."

Following his gaze, the owner laughed coarsely. "Don't expect much joy of Miss Lah-Di-Dah Libby Owens. She's got other arrangements."

So that was her name. Caleb didn't miss the note of malice in the man's voice and had no trouble interpreting it as disappointment. So she'd turned the saloon owner down. His certainty that Libby Owens was perfect for the plan he'd devised hardened to conviction. Of course, he wasn't green enough to imagine a saloon singer chaste, but any pretensions she had to exclusivity would suit him very well.

Without bothering to answer, he strode eagerly up the stairs.

Chapter 2

Libby froze at the peremptory knock. Coins littered the frayed blanket that covered her bed. Don't panic, she thought, scooping up the loose money as quietly as she could and wrapping the gown around it. Desperately, she searched the barren room for a safe hiding place.

With a sudden crow of amusement, she went to the lidded chamber pot and stuffed the rolled material inside. It was reasonably clean—she'd made the waiter who'd brought her soup earlier in the day empty and rinse it—and the thing might be overlooked.

The knock sounded again. This time the knob turned and the redwood plank banged into the frame of the bedstead.

There was a pause, then the clearing of a male throat. "Libby Owens?"

"Go away," she replied.

"Miss Owens," her tormenter continued, "I have a proposition for you. My name is Caleb Logan—"

Libby interrupted, "Mr. Logan, did you happen to hear me sing tonight?"

"Yes, very nice. Matter of fact, I got rid of the drunk for you."

Not you again, Libby thought. "Would you like to hear how loudly I can scream?"

"You don't need to do that," the deep voice said

swiftly. "What I have to say could be to your advantage."

As Libby hesitated, the bed screeched an inch across the floor in response to the force being exerted from the other side of the door. Quickly, she lay facedown on the mattress, trying to make herself as heavy as possible to add weight to the barrier.

It was barely feasible, she supposed, that the barbarian had something legitimate to offer. At any rate, the hotel was full of people, and she felt at least fairly sure some of them would come to her rescue if she decided to call for help.

"To my advantage?" she repeated with delicate sarcasm, sitting up. "I should warn you, I'm not accepting any proposals of marriage tonight."

"My proposal is strictly business."

Libby mulled that over. "What is your business, sir?"

"Personal business. If you'd open up, we could talk in private."

Libby made a face. Just another man who assumed she was a whore.

"Do you know a Mr. Malloy?"

"No."

"That's something, anyway," she murmured. Come to think of it, if Malloy had sold the key, the purchaser would hardly be as patient as this Caleb Logan outside her door.

"Beg pardon?" he asked.

"Never mind," she answered. "Tell me, just how inebriated are you?"

He sounded as if he were smiling. "You remind me of my sister. To be frank, yes, Miss Owens, I've taken a drink or two. But, no, Miss Owens, I'm not *inebriated*. Wouldn't make any difference in what I had to say to you if I was."

"Perhaps not," she said, looking down at her bare breasts. A blush was spreading across the firm flesh, and for some reason, as the stranger's baritone vibrated through the crack between door and frame, her pink nipples had contracted. She snatched a corner of the blanket to hold over them. "However, it's late and I'm not prepared to receive visitors at this hour."

To her surprise, he capitulated at once. "I apologize for calling so late." His sudden, grand formality seemed so absurd under the circumstances that Libby choked back a hysterical giggle. "Let's talk tomorrow."

"Tomorrow is the Sabbath," she countered. "I don't transact business on Sunday."

Despite her distrust of men who hopped onto the stage and grinned at her, she found herself recalling his brash charm. The timbre of his voice conveyed reassurance. However, the fact that he still leaned against her door did not.

"The Sabbath?" His already low tones deepened further with disbelief. "You mean *church*?"

He made it sound as if the Whore of Babylon wanted to go to morning service. Libby considered. Churchgoing hadn't formed part of her plans because she'd previously lacked an escort to get her there. She knew better than to try to coerce Malloy while the bottle had hold of him. But Mr. Logan might be put to good account . . . and paid back a little for his offensive incredulity. A slow, mischievous smile brightened her face.

"Of course I mean church," she said.

"Tomorrow is the only day I have free. I leave Monday on the steamer *Red Jacket*."

"Indeed." Libby's mind raced. Another of Malloy's lies; ships must be coming and going from the bay after all. "Then perhaps your proposition isn't as important as you thought."

"You're wrong," he said flatly. "It's important. At least to me."

Morning service, she thought, scarcely hearing him. It sounded like heaven. It sounded like England.

She stayed mum so long that he said, "Miss Owens?

I know she can't have gone anywhere," he added, as if to himself.

Trying not to laugh out loud, Libby thought he must be more than slightly intoxicated. Her experience with Malloy had left her skeptical about men who imbibed, but the fact remained it was Saturday night in San Francisco, and if there existed a man in town who hadn't had something to drink, she hadn't met him yet. Perhaps she should reserve judgment on Caleb Logan.

But if she took pity on him and dropped the subject, she wouldn't be able to go to church.

And suddenly going to church seemed like the most important thing in the world.

"Mr. Logan? I would be willing to listen to your proposition. Tomorrow. *After* church. There must be an Anglican congregation in a city this size."

She could hear his resigned sigh through the door. "Matter of fact . . ."

It was almost midnight by the time Logan had abandoned his post and Libby had finished sewing the last of the evening's profits into the hem of her skirt. Libby yawned and curled up under the blanket.

Sleep eluded her. Her uninvited visitor posed a fascinating conundrum. What could he have to suggest, since he seemed to have given up the idea of marriage? Not that it mattered to her, she assured herself. She remembered him as handsome, but he could be the Adonis of the West and he wouldn't distract her from the goal that had obsessed her for two grueling years.

Potent images of England drifted behind her closed eyelids. Thatched cottages and hedges higher than her head. An ornamental lily pond gray under a gray sky. Chinese wallpaper in the morning parlor where she practiced her scales. A civilized country where everybody knew his place—and if he lost his place, then he immigrated to the New World, she thought wearily.

Her shoulders were cold. Pulling the blanket higher,

she rolled over and gazed into the half darkness left by the shuttered lantern.

"Oh, Papa," she whispered. "Why did you have to think you understood finance? And why couldn't you keep Maman from the card tables?"

Pictures from the more recent past assaulted her. A cabin that she, Papa, and Maman had built with their own hands—with chinks of daylight coming through the walls because somehow the wattle of muddied straw wouldn't stick properly between the massive, rough-hewn logs. Everlasting pine forest always threatening to engulf them. Pennies holding down Papa's and Maman's eyelids in death. The stares—sympathetic, appalled, embarrassed—of their woodland neighbors when her voice broke shamefully as she tried to sing her parents one last song before the moist Canadian earth took them from her forever.

Furious with her thoughts, she sat up and hugged her knees to her chest. Tears were useless. Self-pity had become an indulgence far beyond her pocketbook.

San Francisco was a port city with ships in the harbor. She had to be strong to manage Malloy, dazzling to charm the price of a fare to England out of men like the ones who'd cheered for her tonight.

Caleb Logan at least provided a distraction. Whatever his motive for seeking her company, he was making it possible for her to venture along the city's dirt thoroughfares tomorrow. Without him, she'd have had to spend the next seven days a prisoner in the hotel, with interludes in the taproom. That prospect was horrid enough to inspire a warmth of relief that gradually lulled her into a relaxed drowsiness.

She would have to try to be nice to him, she realized as her thoughts lost coherence. And when dreams filled her sleep, they were all of reckless dark eyes and a bold smile full of charm.

Libby woke to find the other buildings on the pier invisible behind dense fog. Tendrils of the damp white stuff curled inside the instant she opened the shutters, bringing the raucous cry of gulls and the smell of the sea. Prickling with gooseflesh, she performed her morning ritual; using the convenience, sponging her body with tepid water, brushing her teeth, braiding her hair.

When she felt tidy, she began the arduous undertaking of dressing like a lady without assistance.

After pulling on a chemise, she tied herself into a corset—her own, not the instrument of torture she'd worn last night. Then came layer after layer of petticoats, one of them stiffened with crinoline. Finally, her movements slightly constricted although she'd decided to spare herself really tight lacing this morning, she struggled into a bottle-green merino walking dress with tan velvet trim at the collar and cuffs. No doubt the cut had been outmoded for five years in London, but she didn't think the latest styles would be a burning issue here.

Producing an uncrushed bonnet, however, presented a different problem. She always packed carefully; after all, the right clothes, the residue of her privileged life as the pampered daughter of an English gentleman, added stature to her claim to operatic splendor. The merino wool did show a crease here and there, but not too noticeably. Unfortunately, a bonnet of shirred and corded silk she'd hoped to wear with it had worked its way to the bottom of the trunk and needed a good pressing she didn't have time to give it.

With a sigh, Libby finished her ensemble by tossing a long piece of beige lace over her coronet of braids and down her back. Since the hotel didn't provide a looking glass, she could only hope her face didn't betray any effects of her disturbed rest, or that Mr. Logan's standards weren't high.

Pulling cautiously, so the strain wouldn't cause seams to part under her arms, Libby manhandled the bed into its original position. The silver watch pinned to her bodice told her it was time to go downstairs.

At the last moment, she hesitated and drew the shutters closed again. The bar furnished as a latch was hardly more than a stick, but she clicked it into place anyway. A woman who was alone for all intents and purposes, and who had valuables to hide, couldn't be too careful.

Tripping lightly through the door, she could almost hear her mother's brisk, French-accented admonitions. *Small, even steps, Libby. You must float, float like a swan.* She might be almightily sick of it, but once again Libby Owens was going on display.

Caleb's eyes narrowed as the Owens woman stepped onto the balcony. He'd woken to a thundering headache and the dim knowledge that he'd made a fool of himself. It had taken repeated applications of cold water to sluice some sense back into his brain. Once the brief flashes of memory settled into an image of himself lounging against some saloon girl's door as he bargained with her within earshot of every saddle tramp and down-on-his-luck prospector using the flea-ridden hotel, he groaned aloud. So much for washing his troubles away with coffin varnish. The plan that had seemed so goddamned clever last night looked asinine in the foggy light of early morning.

Not that the idea itself was so bad. But it required a real lady. No saloon girl could possibly carry it off.

The woman must have agreed to meet him, though. Somewhere amid the whiskey fumes drifted the echo of her warm, rather husky voice saying, "Nine o'clock in the morning, then."

He had felt a niggling curiosity as to whether the singer could possibly be as alluring as he'd thought. Cursing himself mildly, he had gotten shaved and dressed and down to the pier on time.

She glided to the rail in tight-buttoned shoes, a dignified barque with all her sails unfurled. Her wide eyes met his. Damn, what color were they, anyway? Recognition and something else flashed between them.

Caleb felt as if a fist had slammed into his middle.

He shook his head sharply to rid himself of the sensation. He had to be mistaken. She couldn't have looked at him with delight and . . . desire, because in the next moment her gaze coolly traveled on until it reached the desk.

"Clerk! I say, clerk!"

Her imperious tones, very British, carried without effort. The desk clerk bobbed up out of his chair. "Yes, er, ma'am?"

"I seem to have mislaid the key to my room. Is there another I could use, please?"

"Uh, sure. All the keys fit all the locks. Get you fixed up in a jiffy."

Her Majesty looked slightly thunderstruck, Caleb thought. Some sort of genuine emotion softened the rose-petal mouth, but only for an instant. Then the lovely face regained its haughty expression as she waited for the clerk to deliver a key into her silk-mittened hand.

She turned the key in the lock herself and slipped it into the reticule hanging from her wrist, before bestowing a coin and a smile on the clerk. "I would quite appreciate it if you could make sure no one—*no one*—goes into my room. All my things, you understand—"

"Yes, ma'am!"

As if it were only her due, she led the way downstairs. The clerk followed like a puppy frisking at the heels of an adored mistress.

At the bottom, she cast Caleb a glance he decided couldn't be anything but dubious; in another woman, he would have described it as shy, but her self-assurance seemed too complete to have room for timidity. In response, he moved forward.

"Mr. Logan." She offered her hand.

Caleb wondered sourly if he was expected to kiss it. Something about her queenly bearing raised his hackles. Did she maintain such a regal distance from the piano player she allowed into her room? She hadn't let Caleb get past the door.

A purely male fit of pique made him grasp her hand for a firm shake. He felt surprise when she responded with a nearly manlike pressure. Examining her openly, he said, "I didn't . . . expect you."

Delicate brows, darker than her glorious hair, rose. "No? Did I mistake the time?"

"It's not that. You're prompt all right."

A sudden smile, completely unlike the one she'd doled out to the clerk, warmed the perfection of her features and created a dimple beside her tempting mouth. The grand lady dissolved, and in her place sparkled a young woman in her early twenties. "Thank you for not saying what an unfeminine trait promptness is."

"Believe me, I wouldn't dare call you unfeminine."

Her eyes still smiled. They weren't blue or gray, but a clear, lustrous green between thick lashes. "Mr. Logan, I wasn't fishing for a compliment, really. I just meant most men wouldn't be able to resist the temptation to trot out some hoary chestnut about the eternal unpunctuality of women."

"I'm not most men."

Libby's heart beat fast, although its first, unexpected bound at the sight of him had subsided.

"N-no," she said uncertainly. When his dark eyes, hard and alive, fixed on her and his bass voice mellowed to a soft rumble, she had to agree. No woman would ever mistake him for any other man.

As she'd recalled, he stood taller than she did, which pleased her; so many men didn't. Muscle bulked in his shoulders and long legs, but a certain looseness in his clothing that she'd taken for a deficiency in California tailoring might as easily have been caused by a recent loss of flesh. His features were bold and arrestingly irregular, dominated by a strong nose and too sharply chiseled jaw that should have made him unhandsome, but didn't. Although no one would call it a classic face, it had a masculine cleanness of line that struck her now with double force. A devil with the ladies—when he wanted to be, she thought, for the charm he'd spent on her during their few moments on the stage had vanished. In its stead he gave off a much more potent and dangerous sense of unhumbled masculinity. And her heartbeat still raced.

"Will it take us long to get to the Church of England service?" she asked, a trifle breathlessly. "Oh, you call it Episcopal in America, don't you?"

He stared at her with disbelief. "Church," he repeated.

"Surely you remember?"

"No," he told her bluntly. "Can't say that I do."

Her nostrils flared slightly at his tone. "I see. You really were inebriated last night, weren't you?"

"I must have been booze-blind. Just what did I say, anyway?"

"That you would escort me to services, and in return I would allow you to tell me your—proposal is the word you used."

"Set a value on yourself, don't you?" he asked.

She shrugged and lifted her chin proudly, revealing the lovely outline of her throat. Caleb discovered he wouldn't mind spending time with her, no matter how she'd earned the costly clothes she wore, but . . . church?

Her jaw jutted with determination. Mulish, Caleb thought. And downright beautiful.

"You win," he said, feeling ridiculous. "Church, by God. We'd better get going. Our San Francisco streets aren't exactly easy on ladies' feet."

They stepped into a world of swirling white cloud, populated by ghosts. She leaned against him, clutching his arm.

"Oh, my goodness," she exclaimed.

Caleb decided it would be interesting to see how convincing this strange saloon girl could be in her imitation of respectability. She might fit into his plan after all. "The fog will be rolling into the ocean any time now. A few hundred yards and we should walk out of it. You'll see."

Libby could feel his muscular arm under his sleeve and smelled bay rum. Papa and Uncle Adelbert had always smelled of bay rum.

Knowing that a stumble could cost them a dunking in the rankly stinking mud flats, Libby retained her grip on his arm and matched him stride for stride. Her small core of hurt pride dwindled, and she felt a slightly pleasurable guilt at stretching her legs. The closer she approached embarking for home, the more often injunctions from her childhood came back to haunt her. *You are too tall,* chérie. *You have the good bosoms,* her mother had said with the French frankness that had devastated Libby as she blossomed into womanhood, *so men will look at you. But you must stop looming over them.*

Height had turned out to be an advantage on the stage, and none of the men who stared at her hungrily as she toured the West seemed to mind whether she loomed. Caleb Logan didn't appear repulsed, either. Libby decided to enjoy herself.

"I do admit to some womanly curiosity," she said. "You said earlier that you found me unexpected. May I ask in what way?"

He seemed to consider before he replied. "Let's say you keep a fellow guessing."

"I won't strain your tact by asking what you mean," Libby said ruefully. "Honestly, I didn't know my accompanist had arranged for me to sing in a public house until it was too late to do anything about it. And that dress . . ."

So suddenly that she rocked on her heels, they burst through the edge of the fog into sparkling sunshine. Caleb stopped, too, and looked at her with a grin hovering at the corners of his mouth. Libby bit her lip. Mentioning the red dress had been a mistake; his dark eyes flicked over her bosom in a way that made her feel that the dependable green merino was both too tight and too warm. Now he'd be sure she belonged in a saloon.

Calculation tempered Caleb's amusement. No doubt about it, Libby had laced herself differently this morning. Her tall figure retained its agreeable curves, but now they were elegant rather than flashy. Both incarnations were highly desirable, and he began to contemplate what it would take to oust the piano player from her bed. Miss Libby Owens was a charming package. Precisely the sort of package he could use to make his plan succeed.

Mixing pleasure into this particular business had a sort of rough justice about it. In fact, given the nature of the business and Libby's ripe attractions, Caleb thought he would have to be odd *not* to take his pleasure where it came.

Yet, in her high-necked gown she managed to present the appearance of a decent young lady, as much as—as his own sister did.

He caught at his thoughts. He said, "Yes? You were saying?"

Libby devised and disgarded several gambits. "Did I look very terrible on the stage?" she asked candidly.

Caleb's grin broadened, banishing the hint of speculation but not reaching his eyes. His eyes never smiled, she realized. "About a hundred men thought you looked damned good."

Libby stiffened and withdrew her hand. "Must you be crude?"

"It was a compliment."

"I beg to differ. It may be that I am unlike the other ladies you know. I object to swearing. And I prefer compliments that aren't veiled insults."

His brows rose skeptically. But he said, "I'll remember that."

A breeze lifted the veil from her braids. She captured it with a small exclamation and draped it once more. Realizing that dirt now muffled their footsteps, she said, "Is it very far to the church?" Resentment kept her tone cool.

"Another few steps. If I'd thought of it, I could have

bespoken a carriage from a livery stable. At least we have sidewalks in this district.''

"Very citified," she agreed stiffly, stepping up from the street. The lace blew free again. Caleb caught it mid-air and deftly arranged the folds over her hair. His knuckles brushed her forehead.

"Pretty mantilla," he said with a blend of mockery and frank male approval that unsettled her. "Is that the right kind of compliment?"

Her cheeks burned. "Yes, thank you," she replied as calmly as she could. "But I—I don't know that word."

"Mantilla," he repeated. He let his hands fall; she wondered if he'd felt the heat his touch had generated in her skin. "It means lace scarf. All the Spanish ladies around here wear them."

"I'm in style, then. That's comforting."

"You haven't seen them before? Where are you from?" he asked.

"Originally? England. Near London. A village called Little Paddocks."

"Miss it?"

"Unbearably," she said truthfully.

Startling her, Caleb said, "Here's the church."

"It's not St. George's, Hanover Square, is it?" Libby commented.

A brick propped open the door to J. Klein's New York Store. Caleb stood aside so Libby could enter. "Not all congregations have permanent sites yet."

The man behind the counter wore a red beard curling wildly to his waist and a shiny black skullcap over an otherwise bald head.

Caleb bent down to murmur, "Don't worry, Mr. Klein is very broad-minded."

"Is he?" she asked in awe.

"Yes. He's also one of my customers. That's how I know the Episcopalians meet here. How are you, Jacob?"

"Caleb, my friend! You have discovered religion!

And you bring me a good woman! Where have you found such a jewel?'' The bearded man gazed at Libby soulfully. ''You must know that good women eschew San Francisco. They do not like the trip around the Horn. And if they were to come, they would not like the rats, the dirt, the swearing in the streets. Even my Sarah tells me to go to California, make my fortune, come back when I am richer than her papa. In the East, they think every geyser is a fountain of gold.''

''In the North, too,'' Libby said. ''I sympathize, Mr. Klein.''

''Ah, but with me or my Sarah?''

''Both!'' she told him, and he gave a booming laugh.

''Service started, Jacob?'' asked Caleb.

''The priest just arrived.''

Caleb paused a moment to ask, ''No visit yet from the Hounds?''

''Not yet,'' said Mr. Klein, the round face above the beard puckering.

''Have you decided what you're going to do?''

''I do not know, my friend. I do not know. And you?''

''The Hounds aren't any business of mine. There's enough to keep me busy up north.''

Libby glanced from one to the other, unable to follow the conversation. Did the city have a problem with dogs?

The upper story formed one large room, filled with straight-backed chairs. No sooner did the clergyman see Libby take an inconspicuous seat toward the rear than he dashed toward her.

''I'll call on biblical precedent and insist that the last shall be first. Please come sit in the front row. That way I won't have to preach to the backs of my congregation's heads.'' He leaned forward with a twinkle. ''And I'll have a nice view of you myself!''

The service was briskly paced, the sermon a rafter-shaking denunciation of gambling.

''It makes the angels weep,'' shouted the minister

impressively, "to see your hard-earned gold disappear into the monte dealers' pockets when God's house is still located above a general store."

It took time to wend their way outside after the last amen. Libby's hand throbbed slightly from the dozens of enthusiastic shakings it received.

"Are you uplifted?" asked Caleb as they stepped into the sunshine. "What did you think?"

"One gets used to—to people"—she meant men— "being so friendly. It's because they don't see a woman very often."

"I was talking about the sermon," he told her.

"Oh." Libby could see her mother's plump white hands, shuffling cards with blinding speed. "He's right," she said vigorously. "Gambling's an affliction on the human race."

The strength of her distaste made Caleb look at her closely. "Never take a little flutter?"

"Never!" She felt anxious to change the subject. "Thank you for bringing me. I wouldn't have been able to find this place by myself, even if I wanted to walk out alone."

"You're wise to stay off the streets. A year ago, a woman—if there'd been one to find—would have been safer here than in New York or Boston. Times have changed. The richest strikes have all run out, and disappointed men get mean. The jackals and johnny-come-latelies who think they got cheated out of easy pickings prey on anyone in their path. They—well, never mind. You wouldn't be interested."

"Yes, I would," Libby said indignantly. "I am not a brainless doll, Mr. Logan."

"Not brainless, no." He frowned at her thoughtfully. She'd been demure as a nun during church. Now was as good a time as any to find out if the lady ate with her knife. "I'm hungry. Want a bite to eat?"

"That would be most welcome."

"The Georgius is close. Do you like salmon?"

"I'll eat *anything* that isn't salt pork and beans," she

said with such heartfelt fervor that his expression lightened.

"The pioneer diet can get tiresome," he agreed. "This way, then."

A short walk through a neighborhood that boasted brick and iron-front structures brought them to a large building with a handsome facade. Inside, the manager greeted Caleb by name. They were whisked into the dining room and seated with flattering dispatch.

Libby did full justice to her meal. None of the food was prepared with imagination, but the boiled salmon and tender greens were fresh and hadn't been reduced to the mush she'd come to expect in American hostelries.

Caleb watched her intently. He picked at his own fish, but his bright, unreadable eyes followed each morsel from her fork to her mouth, and then dwelled on her lips as she chewed more and more slowly under the weight of his gaze. His level stare made the simple act of eating oddly intimate. She became aware of the pleasure of each soft motion of her own lips, of the strength and evenness of her teeth as they opened and closed, of the hot, sweet, smoky flavor of the tea swirling over her tongue. She tried to look away and couldn't. By the time she left the last small, precise bite of tangy bread on her plate for politeness' sake, she'd grown so flustered that her napkin slipped from her fingers to the floor.

Approaching with a fresh pot of tea, the waiter picked up the square of linen and handed it to her. She thanked him in a hushed, unsure tone and looked at Caleb. "I don't know what's the matter with me. I'm not usually clumsy."

"Don't apologize." Satisfaction made his eyelids sleepy. "Your table manners are very good."

"Thank you," she said, recovering her composure. Sweetly, she added, "I do try to remember not to put my elbows on the table or wipe my fingers on the tablecloth."

"I can see that."

"But I didn't expect to get tea when I asked for it. San Francisco has the most startling amenities." She glanced around the room as she spoke. Crystal chandeliers, their candles unlit at this time of day, hung above their heads. The plaster walls were painted and a Turkish carpet covered the floor.

"Wealth buys comfort, Miss Owens. It buys all sorts of things." He gave her another straight stare, like a man gauging the price of an object he intended to own.

It was the look of someone who generally got what he wanted. She felt a stir of alarm. "I am not for sale, Mr. Logan."

Ignoring her soft-spoken comment, he continued, "Five years ago you might have had trouble tracking down anything as exotic as tea from China in this part of the world." His absorbed gaze didn't falter, but he added prosaically, "There's dessert. Some form of dried apple pie, probably. Want any?"

She nodded and sipped her tea before forcing herself to relax in the cane-backed chair. If he was willing to steer the conversation in a safer direction, she'd happily follow his lead. "You've lived in California a long time?"

" 'What did I do in the States?' " he quoted the song. "I'm practically an old California hand for a gringo. I come from Boston. Shipping. Made landfall in Monterey, and I—well, I fell in love, I guess."

The tea tasted acid suddenly. Libby swallowed painfully.

He went on, "The minute I set foot on that rocky beach, I knew I was done sailing. Happily for me, a couple of the old Mexican families were selling off their land grants. So now I grow the cabbage you just ate, among other things."

"Really?" Libby set her cup down carefully. "Does your wife like being married to a farmer?"

"Rancher," he corrected. "Most of the land's in cattle. Tan the hides and sell the meat. But the vegetable fields are booming. We supply the markets and a lot of the hotels here in the city. Just expanded the lumber mill . . . And I'm not married.''

"No? You said you fell in love . . ."

"With California," he said.

"I see." To hide the fact that her spirits suddenly rocketed, Libby asked, "What is the plan you intended to tell me about?"

He spread his hands on the table. The white cloth contrasted with his tanned, callused fingers.

"I told you once already. I want you to be my wife." He shrugged. "I figure for about two months."

Chapter 3

She's magnificent, he thought. The soft pink in her cheeks darkened to dusky rose, and her emerald eyes snapped. However far down life had brought Libby recently—and he was beginning to think it possible she'd fallen from the social equivalent of a great height—there was no doubt she looked every inch a lady. A very angry, deeply insulted lady.

"Mr. Logan," she said with alarming precision. "I think you must have misunderstood the kinds of services I'm willing to provide for hire. I sing."

"Let me explain—"

"Possibly you were misled by finding me in circumstances that—that—I won't go into it again. However, I can assure you I'm not a harlot."

"The arrangement was going to be more in the line of a theatrical performance."

"I don't engage in *amateur* theatricals," she flashed back.

Every whore Caleb had ever heard of could carry on for hours about her unstained virtue. Not that he thought Libby a whore. Well, he qualified, certainly not a common one. Not common at all. But did she expect him to ignore the facts that she sang in a saloon and welcomed the piano player into her room? Did she think he was stupid? Harshly, he said, "But you do entertain men in your bedroom."

His impatient words drove every drop of color from

36

her face. She looked so stricken that he reached out to catch her in case the pallor led to a faint. The green fire in her eyes stopped his hand in midair.

"Not you, if you recall," she said firmly.

"Don't misunderstand me. I don't care how many men friends you've had." Didn't he? He wondered. The thought of this genteel English showgirl, with her delicate beauty and quick intelligence, lying down for just any man . . . It made him feel angry and restless, spoiling for a fight. "But get this clear. As long as you work for me, you're mine. You belong to me."

"I don't belong to anyone. I keep myself, Mr. Logan. I'm not kept."

Hell, maybe she loved the piano player. Caleb scowled. If she felt an attachment to the weedy pilgrim, it would complicate matters. But it wouldn't make them impossible. "You can lower the battle flags. I don't force women."

As clearly as if he'd said it aloud, Libby heard, *I don't need to.* They must swarm after him like wanton bees, hungry for the nectar of his deep, intimate voice and rare smile, she thought sarcastically.

Normal color had seeped back into her cheeks and lips as her unreasoning hurt at the way he'd spelled out his opinion of her had gradually returned to anger. "Then you won't mind taking me back to my hotel. Now, please."

"I'd rather talk to you."

He leaned forward and suddenly smiled with all of his charm. The fine hairs along Libby's arms brushed up, as if she were in the presence of danger. Caleb *was* dangerous to her, she realized. She responded to him too much, and if she had any sense at all, it would frighten her.

"Have you decided to try cajolery?" she asked coldly. "It won't work. My person is not for sale. Under any circumstances. I'll quite understand if you don't care to escort me any longer. Perhaps the management can spare someone to—"

His smile and easy, confiding air disappeared, leaving him looking grim and, yes, frightening.

He swore softly, then stood up. "All right, Miss Owens. I'll take you back to Sansome Street. But I'm not giving up."

They walked in tense silence for two blocks before Libby noticed he wasn't taking her back the way they had come. She balked. "Where are we going?"

His black brows drew together. "The livery stable. I thought you'd rather ride than walk any farther in those shoes."

"Oh." Caleb's considerate offer disconcerted her. Her shoes did feel tight. She wished he'd just be a villain and spare her the trouble of figuring him out. Big shoulders in a fine wool coat and the smell of bay rum had seduced her into liking him for a few hours. Dear Lord, she'd gotten tired of the lonely, traveling life, without friends—without even enemies, unless she counted Malloy. She thought of the proper young lady she'd been once upon a time, and silly tears welled up in her eyes. Her virtue remained untouched, but Caleb had just stolen the last of her innocence.

Since he couldn't think worse of her, she might as well bring up a question that had been gnawing at her. "Why did you say you wanted a wife," she asked slowly, "when you meant mistress?"

He looked down at her, and she saw a different gleam in the brightness of his dark eyes.

"I've decided I want you to be both. And that, little lady, is a compliment." His laugh grated on her.

"I don't know what you're talking about."

"I want a wife to make my sister happy. And I want you because—well, hell, you must know you stir a man's blood." When he smiled knowingly down at her, she felt once again that disturbing mixture of scorn and hunger.

Underneath the confusion of emotions Caleb roused in her flickered a heady satisfaction that Libby tried not to think about.

"What do you mean, a wife to make your sister happy? For two months?"

"My little sister would like to see me married. Julia frets." He added roughly, "She's dying. Her heart's giving out. Here's the livery."

Shock held Libby motionless as he strode through the double doors. Hiring a wife had to be the most ridiculous scheme she'd ever heard of, but at least the reason for it explained his quick changes of mood. Less tolerable remained his firmly fixed notion that she would fall in with his plan, and into his bed.

Still, she felt herself softening toward him. Much could be forgiven a grief-stricken brother. She tried to imagine what he would be like as a brother and couldn't, not really. Although she was an only child, she was sure that whatever feelings Caleb woke in her, they weren't those of a sister. Every move he made left her more aware of his confident, masculine grace and arrogant assurance.

A curious little ache settled under her rib cage at the thought of bidding him goodbye. Pausing inside the doors, she studied him as he spoke to the hostler. His black hair was combed without any pretensions to style, and a lock fell over his forehead. A tiny muscle pulled down one corner of his mouth when he smiled.

She wanted to brush back his hair, smooth the pain out of his crooked grin, touch . . .

She refused to think such thoughts anymore. Caleb Logan wasn't going to charm or intimidate or coax her into abandoning her own plans to sail away from America.

Her palms in the silk mittens felt wet. She rubbed them surreptitiously together. Perhaps the unwontedly rich meal had brought on a colicky fit. The cramp trapped inside the metal bands of her corset certainly resembled colic.

The homely diagnosis calmed her.

Libby suffered a different kind of shock at the incredible amount of money he paid in advance to rent a weatherbeaten gig. She stood next to Caleb, watching the hostler begin to harness a dispirited-looking gelding between the traces. Another man entered the stable and swaggered over to the liveryman.

"Are you sure?" she asked. "About your sister?"

"Rheumatic fever."

"It's not always fatal."

"I had a doctor for her. Leech on his way to the goldfields. He made a little detour."

"I'm sure he did," Libby murmured, glancing up at his grim profile and wondering at the means he'd used to persuade the doctor to come to his ranch. "If Miss Logan is still feverish—"

"Oh, she's cured of the fever. But it did something to her heart. The doctor said it happens that way. We've had a hell of a time keeping her from overtaxing her strength. She's strong-willed, my little sister. Smart as a whip, too. I can't believe . . ."

"I'm so sorry," offered Libby, feeling her words were inadequate. Caleb looked unreachable again.

Abruptly, he walked away.

Whatever his feelings, he evidently preferred not to share them with her. Fair enough. They were little more than strangers. Swallowing an unaccountable lump in her throat, Libby eased her back and stretched discreetly, careful not to bump against a bucket of water by the door. At least after this week she'd never have to ride a mule again. Her body still mutely protested months of hard traveling.

A heady aroma of leather and horse filled the stable. Papa had loved his horses and she had loved Papa, so the smell of horses had been part of her life until the money, and thus the horses, had disappeared. She stood thinking determinedly of England, trying not to listen to the increasingly acrimonious exchange going on by the buggy. She couldn't ignore it, however, when the liveryman shouted at the newcomer, "I told you, that's all I have to give you. We have a deal! You go back to Portsmouth Square and bleed some other sucker white—"

A swift blow below the stomach doubled him to his knees.

Libby stared, appalled. After a stupefied moment, she reached for the bucket and heaved its contents in the direction of the fight. Caleb had been inspecting the other cobs; she heard him say, "Oh, for God's sake!" and then he was in motion. The glittering arc of water blinded the two combatants long enough for Caleb to clutch a handful of soaked flannel and jerk the attacker off his feet.

Sparing no more than a glance at the bully who'd started the fracas, Libby knelt by the liveryman.

He was a pitiable sight. Drenched and shivering, arms and legs drawn up around his vulnerable midsection, he crouched in the muddy straw, sobbing. When Libby crooned something in an attempt to soothe him, he cried out, "Leave me alone! Gawd, look what you done, the two of you! Now the Hounds'll never let me be . . . all your fault . . ."

Sopping skirts clung to her calves as Libby sprang up in disgust.

"Oh, please don't thank us," she said crisply. "Naturally, we wouldn't expect gratitude for a little favor like saving you from a beating."

Caleb interrupted, "The drowned weasel has a point."

At Libby's questioning glance, he stared at her hard and quickly shook his head. Then he indicated the man in his grasp as if to remind her of his presence.

She felt her face go rigid with astonishment . . . and disappointment. The attack had been unprovoked, inexcusable. Libby couldn't see what any of them might have to fear from the person who cawed for breath as Caleb's fist tightened a final time before he allowed the man to drop to the straw.

"Damned if it isn't your singing rival from last night. Up on the stage."

Libby gasped. "You're right! Why did he hit this man?"

"What we have here," he explained, "is a kind of animal new to the coast. This specimen is one of the Hounds of Portsmouth Square. Aren't you?" A toe in the ribs brought a moan from the recumbent figure. "Australians, most of them. They've gone into business. Providing protection."

She looked from the liveryman to the Hound to Caleb. "From what?" she asked.

"From themselves. They're blackmailers. San Francisco doesn't run according to law and order."

"My father would have given a fellow like this a lordly thrashing and sent him on his way. You dealt with him easily enough last night." Some of Libby's disillusionment edged her voice. "It's wrong to allow such vermin to believe they have the upper hand. It only encourages them."

"That's an attitude the San Franciscans would like to take." He shrugged, disassociating himself from the problem. "I didn't know who his business associates were last night. A good caning today would only make things worse. Unfortunately, the Hounds are powerful. They hold grudges, and none of them that I've ever heard of has much in the way of a sense of humor. Probably can't afford it in their profession." He fingered his jaw. "The sensible thing to do would be to kill him right now."

A squawk indicated that the Hound was more alert than Libby had thought. The hostler began to look more cheerful.

"Caleb Logan, if you think for one minute—"

"We'd have to hide the remains, of course," said Caleb with complete seriousness. "There's the bay. Or a couple of places being leveled off with nice, soft fill. The main stumbling block is that our friend who runs the stable here would have to be able to convince the Hounds he hadn't been visited today."

"Mr. Logan!"

He cursed silently. Who would have thought a young woman who knocked around a saloon could be so squeamish? That was genuine indignation she radiated, no doubt about it. Could be he really was daft to want to bring her back to the ranch and Julia. Libby Owens was a complicated creature. And his life was already complicated as it was.

He didn't want any Hounds in it, either. Since most of his business interests were located to the north, he'd never had a run-in with the denizens of Portsmouth Square, and he'd as soon avoid a major one if he could. Not that he'd turn tail if it came to that, but he'd learned early in life to pick and choose his fights. No, the best, most logical choice would be to grind this piece of Portsmouth Square offal into food for the fishes.

On the other hand, Caleb didn't much fancy himself as a murderer.

Regretfully, he said, "You may be right. Our friend doesn't look like much of an actor."

Libby drew a breath to tell him in no uncertain terms what she'd really meant, but his next action forestalled her. Lifting the blackmailer as if he were no more than the bundle of rags he resembled, Caleb said, "You listening?"

The Hound wheezed his assent.

"The lady here thinks we ought to let you go. Now, I think that would be a downright foolish thing to do. But I always try to please a lady."

Libby choked slightly.

Caleb ignored her. "You going to make me sorry for a little Christian act?"

"No."

"Make me sorry, and I might have to hunt you down like a mad dog. Got that?"

"Yes."

"All right. The lady just saved your worthless hide. Show some gratitude."

Another shake reinforced the order.

"Thankee," mumbled the Hound.

"Good. Now, let's tidy you up a little." He set the fellow upright and distastefully brushed his hands over the damp clothing. "Fine. About the way you looked when you came in. Does this hombre"—Caleb jerked his chin toward the hostler, still making himself small in the straw—"have something for you?"

"Do you mean to tell me—" Libby began strongly.

"Quiet," Caleb told her. "You're interfering with local commerce. If he slinks back to his bosses without what he came for, they'll suspect something. We want to keep our ruckus nice and quiet. You may have noticed our friend never objected to paying, just to the amount. It's possible the extra was a little something the bosses didn't know about in the first place."

The Hound's throat worked, but no sound came out.

Scuttling into a stall, the stableman pawed a strongbox from a dark corner. With trembling fingers, he lifted the lid and removed a fat purse.

"Toss it," Caleb warned.

The bag landed in a pile of moist horse droppings.

The unsavory location didn't seem to bother the Hound. His wary gaze was directed at Caleb as he groped for the purse.

"That's fine," Caleb said. "There are a few other things you need to remember. This afternoon you came, you picked up what you came for, you left."

Nodding, the Hound edged toward the freedom of the outdoors. Caleb's gravelly voice stopped him. "Just keep in mind there are also a few things you need to remember to forget. The lady and I weren't here. You never saw us, wouldn't know us again from Adam and Eve. Make any attempt to follow us or find out who we are, and I'll take you apart and feed you to the sharks. Got that?"

The Hound hawked and spat. "Got it."

The gob of spittle landed too near Libby's skirts. She drew them back fastidiously and earned a feral stare that she returned with cool disinterest. This pitiful terrier couldn't frighten her, despite Caleb's story of a secret society holding the town to ransom. All it took to stand up to village bullies was a moderately strong backbone. She let her scornful gaze dwell upon the sorry-looking bully until he grunted and stomped out of the stable.

He turned and glared malevolently at Libby. "Bitch singer. I know where to find you," he said, and ran.

Face darkening, Caleb took a step, then stopped, breathing hard.

"Shoulda killed the son of a bitch," said the liveryman.

"He's right," Caleb confirmed. He pulled a handkerchief from his pocket and passed it to Libby. She bent to dab at the splotches marring her gown.

"It's practically ruined," she mourned.

"So are we unless we get out of town."

She lifted her head. At the moment, the condition of her good green wool seemed infinitely more important than the threat offered by a petty felon. "Really, Mr. Logan, aren't you overreacting? The whole thing was so—so *opera buffa.*"

"What's that mean?"

"Buffoonish. Idiotic."

"I wish I could agree. As it is," he added tightly, "I'm going to have to decide what to do with you."

Libby gave up her gown as a lost cause for the moment. "I assure you, I can take care of myself. I have for years."

He grabbed her elbow and pushed her up into the buggy with an exasperated air. "Under normal circumstances, I don't doubt you can." Flapping the reins, he clicked at the single horse, which heaved forward. "Will you kindly get it through your head that the circumstances aren't normal? The Hounds are nothing to laugh at. They kill people who object to their business methods."

"But he wasn't even armed."

"He might have figured he wouldn't need a gun to deal with our friend back there. That doesn't matter. Take it from me, even if the Hound you saw happens to be a buffoon, the rest of them are ruthless. They won't like being bested. Be scared, will you? Otherwise, you soon might be dead."

Libby regarded her escort. Caleb himself didn't look scared. His heavy brows were drawn together over his Roman nose, and his lips were pinched tight. He looked like a man thinking furiously.

"You jumped into the fray with a certain amount of enthusiasm, I thought," she remarked to the horse's swishing tail.

Acidly, he replied, "I didn't have much choice, if you'll recall. You were already trying to drown a total stranger. Next time find out who the enemy is before you join the war."

Libby shifted on the wooden seat. Its splintering surface seemed to chafe her in defiance of all her petticoats. Right was always right, and running away in the face of wrong was unforgivable. For some reason, it disappointed her to find out that Caleb Logan was just another pragmatic American without the imagination to understand honor. The double irritation made her waspish.

"I suppose you could have walked away and left that pathetic fellow to be beaten to a pulp."

He made a low, disgusted sound.

"Maybe not," he admitted. "A man can only stomach so much. But I'd feel better if that Hound hadn't seen me—or you. He knows where you're performing."

Her shrug was an elegant gesture borrowed from her mother. Its ostentatious indifference fanned his own ill temper. She said, "I'm not afraid."

"You should be! If you continue singing—"

"If I continue—"

"If you do," he went on, overriding her heated interruption, "he'll come after you. God, I should have known that saloon is just the sort of kennel to attract the Hounds. Girls and gambling are a surefire lure."

Libby hated the saloon, but it was one thing for her to criticize it and another to hear Caleb's contempt for the place. He presumed she belonged there, didn't he? That it was her natural milieu? His scalding condemnation was meant to apply to her, too.

"It's not where I would have chosen to give a concert—if I'd been given a choice," she repeated stubbornly. Caleb would never believe her, but pride demanded that she defend herself. "Is it worse than any other taproom?"

"It's a hellhole," he told her bluntly. "And there's something else you don't seem to have noticed.

"What's that?"

"You told him my name."

Chapter 4

"**M**r. Lo—" she stopped.

She *had* said his name. Not once, but twice. The memory rocked her. Libby considered the whole episode tawdry nonsense, but Caleb apparently didn't. He'd made it sufficiently clear he didn't want his identity, or hers, revealed to the Hound. She felt ridiculously guilty, as if she'd betrayed him. Which was nonsense, of course, but . . .

"I'm truly sorry," she said. Apologies had never been easy for her, and how long had it been since she'd allowed herself close enough to another human being to need to offer one? "I should have realized you were warning me not to mention names. It was very bad manners of me."

"Bad manners," he repeated incredulously. "I seem to have failed to explain the situation to you. There's more than one reason I'd rather not tangle with the Hounds. Manners good or bad aren't worth spit right now."

"They may not be an important consideration to you, but they are to me."

"For Chrissake. You sound more like a schoolmarm than a—"

"I thought about teaching," she interrupted to keep him from finishing the description. "It doesn't pay well enough."

"Well enough for what? Oh, never mind," he said

before she could answer. "The only important consideration right now is living till tomorrow at two
o'clock."

"Why two o'clock?" Libby asked patiently.

"Because that's when the *Red Jacket* sails for Sonoma County, and, God willing, we'll both be on her."

The day's series of events took new shape. She stared
at Caleb in disbelief.

"Do you mean you've been indulging in all this
twaddle about dogs and Portsmouth Square to drive me
into scurrying off with you to your ranch? I've already
told you, sir, I'm not interested in playing the part of
your wife." A desire to hurt him that sprang from her
confused emotions led her to add, "I wouldn't be interested under any conditions. Temporary or permanent."

He gave her a sidelong glance. "As a matter of fact,
I don't recall offering you that particular choice."

Heat flushed her cheeks, and Libby knew a bright
blush revealed her mortification, but she said, "I have
the choice of jumping out of this worm-eaten rig."

He looked at her again. She meant it. Her feet were
braced against the footboard and her arms were stiff,
palms flat on the seat, ready to push off.

"Don't do anything else foolish," he advised sourly.
"Broken bones aren't going to save you from the
Hounds."

"I don't believe in the Hounds. I think you made
them up," she told him contemptuously.

"Oh, for—are you plumb crazy, or do you just read
too many penny dreadfuls? If you think I could make
up the Hounds of Portsmouth Square to lure you to my
mud castle by the sea, you damned well deserve to find
out how real they are."

She simply put up her chin and stiffened her back.
Even after the ugly little fight this afternoon, he
saw, she managed to give an impression of regal elegance. Her skirt might be stained with mud, but the
golden twist of braids remained firmly in place, and so

did the floating scrap of lace she wore instead of a bonnet. No doubt about it, she counterfeited a lady to perfection. Queen Libby.

A sharp pang shot through him when he thought of what she'd look like when the Hounds got through with her. He'd be cursed before he'd steam comfortably away and leave her to be raped and cut up.

Julia filled his mind. God Almighty, he couldn't get himself killed while his sister lay at home waiting to see him again before she died. He knew of a loosely organized group of men that was forming to rid the city of the Hounds, but nobody took the group seriously. It wasn't yet powerful enough to protect citizens who stood up to the Hounds from reprisals.

Caleb tried to reason with Libby in a more conciliatory tone. "I can tell you think I'm shivering in my boots for no reason. Humor me, will you? Get your things, and I'll take you out of the kennel you're living in and put you up at a decent hotel. Under another name. Then tomorrow we'll get on the steamer, and we can work out the terms for your stay on the ranch."

Libby's chin jutted out in determination. "How many times do I have to tell you? Nobody keeps me."

Well, he'd never been any good at being conciliatory. "Tell me, how have you survived on your travels? Generally I endorse a spirit of independence, but yours must be damned inconvenient at times."

Libby regarded her hands. The immaculate white mittens had picked up a smudge; no wonder. She concentrated rather fiercely on the stain.

"I travel with my accompanist," she said. "We've never run into any trouble."

"Until now. God help that mimsy piano player trying to handle you."

He sounded curt, and Libby didn't try to fool herself into thinking it was because he didn't like to picture her with another man. More likely, he'd gotten tired of her unwillingness to yield to his wishes. The conversation was starting to wear on her, too. She didn't try to explain that it was she who usually handled Malloy, not the other way around.

She peered upside down at the watch pinned to her bodice. Nearly three. The day had begun so well, and now it was ruined.

Kennel was an all too accurate description of Malloy's choice of hotel, she thought. Kennels had fleas. And she had to exert herself not to scratch an itch as Caleb pulled up in front of the building. But at least it was her kennel, for the time being anyway, and she was making her own way in the world. She knew what Uncle Adelbert and Aunt Edith and all her cousins at the vicarage would say if she allowed a man to keep her in luxury.

Precisely what she'd say about herself.

Running to the horse's head to soothe the animal as it pawed the hollow-sounding planks of the pier, Caleb said, "Can you get down by yourself?"

She smiled, letting a very faint, ladylike snort escape her. "Yes, thank you." She climbed down, making a moue of distaste at the hotel-cum-saloon built over the water. "Perhaps London Bridge was like this once. Long, long ago."

They faced each other, Caleb absently stroking the animal's neck. For such an arrogant man—arrogant even in cowardice, she thought—he had very gentle hands.

She moistened her lips, seeking the right words. After uttering a few polite, hackneyed phrases, she would forget Caleb Logan, his invalid sister, and his harebrained proposal forever.

He didn't give her the chance to murmur them. The rickety pier, aquiver with moving men and carts, excited even their sad-looking nag. Libby wouldn't have thought the poor beast had any spirit in it, but horses didn't like wooden footing. The gelding tossed its head, jerking the reins Caleb held looped around one wrist, and neighed with equine unhappiness.

"I'm going to turn the buggy where there's more

room," Caleb said rapidly. "Don't do anything stupid."

"Stupid?" she protested furiously.

"Stupid. You pack. I'll be back for you as soon as I return this rig to the livery stable."

"For the last time, don't bother, Mr. Logan. Nothing will happen to me. And—you've got your sister to think about."

The horse was approaching a state of acute distress. The reins wrenched Caleb's arm up as the frightened animal tried to rear in the traces.

"Go on!" urged Libby, horrified. "The brute'll have the whole pier down in a minute."

Part of her wanted Caleb to waste time arguing with her, but he demonstrably couldn't. His attention was all on bringing the horse's head down. Once he had accomplished that, Caleb began the laborious process of coaxing the shuddering ton or so of horseflesh forward to a slightly wider section of the dock, where the rig could be turned in safety.

Libby admired his confident, firm way with the horse. It resembled the aplomb he'd originally shown dealing with the brawler. Perhaps, she thought doubtfully, he was one of those men who could deal with a simply physical situation as it came up, but afterward became overwhelmed with scruples, or nerves, or something.

Scruples she understood. And it wouldn't be too much longer, she thought with grit-toothed cheerfulness, before she'd reenter a life where she could afford nerves as well. One week. One more week to earn five hundred dollars.

Caleb spared her a last glance as he led the horse and buggy toward solid ground, after managing the complicated business of turning them around. The gelding had evidently decided to trust Caleb's rock-steady hands.

"I'll be back," he called.

Prudently not thinking about Caleb's hands or how

she would feel if he ever touched her, Libby straightened her mittens and walked into the hotel.

The place didn't look any different. It was still depressing. Libby frowned, comparing the stark and splintered lobby with the Georgius's plush elegance. Ah, well. She'd made her bed and she'd sleep in it.

And if she dreamed, it would not be about Caleb Logan. Not again. She couldn't figure him out. He didn't seem to be a coward, and yet he'd run away from the paltry threat offered by the cur of Portsmouth Square. The danger hadn't seemed so great to her. But Caleb had found it impractical to deal with the Hound—short of killing the man. Thank goodness she'd managed to keep him from doing that.

She sighed. How she hated having to be practical. Americans, so busily claiming the continent, never seemed to have time for the things that mattered to her. Music and gracious living . . . and the occasional risky venture that had spiced up the life she'd lived with her dear, foolish, flawed parents.

Should Caleb actually come back for her, Libby would just have to say no so loudly he would believe her. Her forehead creased. He hadn't shown any particular amenability to accepting her wishes so far.

She'd had to say no often enough. After her parents' deaths, she could have had her pick of hardy frontiersmen . . . if she'd wanted to live the rest of her life in barely settled Canada. Not one of her suitors had ever inspired the slightest tendency in her toward wanton thoughts. But the thoughts Caleb inspired were undoubtedly wanton. In fact, they were positively lustful.

Libby looked around the lobby. Privacy wasn't a commodity the rough accommodations of the road could always supply. She'd been an unwilling witness to intimacies between her fellow travelers without desiring to emulate them. And more than one of her admirers had tried to overcome her resistance with forcible kisses; kisses were as far as any of them had gotten. She was a *very* loud screamer.

Some time in the last few years, she'd simply decided her nature must be cold. But Caleb . . . Caleb made her feel warm and female. She winced with embarrassment that her blood tingled for a man who despised her even as he declared his intention to have her.

In any case, marriage and the acts that went with it were not for her. She had set out to fulfill her own destiny when she'd buried Maman and Papa fifteen hundred miles away. The caskets had been plain pine, unsealed against the damp forest ground. By now, moisture and earth and God's insect scavengers would have invaded the coffins and the shrouds, and reduced the occupants to the ivory of their bones.

So much for the flesh, she decided with a mixture of sadness and wistfulness. Nothing lasted. Desire—even the little she knew of it—formed a snare to distract her from her real goal. England.

Home.

She sighed. Her feet ached in their high-topped kid shoes. Her whole body ached. Thank God she wouldn't have to perform tonight.

The stairs had been badly set in a wobbly frame. She tripped slightly as she removed the key from her reticule. But a key turned out to be unnecessary; the door swung open at her touch.

Libby hesitated before stepping carefully inside. The room didn't appear to have been disturbed much. Only one object seemed to be out of place. A simple dress of faded calico. It lay crumpled on the floor, its hem shredded to tatters.

Pure fury made her scream. Malloy. It had to be Malloy. All her work. All her money. He'd stolen everything.

Her piercing shriek brought men crowding onto the balcony.

His belly heaving, the proprietor pushed through the crowd. "Here, here! What's goin' on? Who's been murdered?"

When he saw the dress, he looked annoyed. "What's all your screeching for?"

Libby tried to compose herself. Forcing her voice down to a normal tone, she said. "Someone has been in here. All my money is gone."

"Robbed, huh?" He didn't look surprised. And why should he be? Libby thought. His customary patrons no doubt existed from day to day by stealing from one another.

"Robbed, yes. I demand to know if anyone was seen entering. The clerk at the desk downstairs promised he would watch for intruders while I went out."

"Homer!" he yelled. The clerk shoved his way through the crowd.

"Seen somebody bust into Miss Owens's room?" the owner asked.

"Nobody! I swear." Then Homer blushed painfully. "Well, nobody 'cept that piano player feller."

"I believe I tipped you a very generous amount to keep anyone from coming in."

"Yeah, but we all know—I mean, I kinda figured he was the exception-like."

His employer began to smile. The expression struck Libby as no more appealing than a snarl.

"Break it up, boys. You want to gawk at Miss Owens, you'll have to wait till tomorrow when she'll be appearing exclusive on our own stage right next door. Tell your friends. Libby Owens, prettiest songbird in Frisco. And she can sing, too . . ."

With many backward glances, the onlookers gradually dispersed. "You, too, Homer," he added, and the desk clerk left, pulling the door gently shut behind him. Only the owner remained with Libby in the room.

Libby bent and picked up the ruined dress, hugging it tight. Two years. Two years she'd worked to keep her voice at its height, to preserve her looks against sun, drying wind, and a limited diet. Harder than any indentured washerwoman, she'd labored over the trunks full of expensive clothes that transformed her from another penniless orphan into a concert singer who was worth paying good money to see and hear. Malloy had stolen two years of her life, and for a few moments, she indulged herself in the luxury of hating him.

Hating felt good. It filled up the bleak empty corners of her heart that spending the day with Caleb had created.

"All rightie, now. We're going to have to decide what to do with you, ain't we, Libby?" the owner said, standing too close to her.

She stepped back quickly, but there was no space for retreat in the tiny room. "I'd prefer to maintain a business relationship, Mr.—" She didn't even know his name. "And I am Miss Owens," she reminded him, to establish social as well as physical distance.

"Well—Libby," he drawled, "a business relationship's just what I had in mind. Now your fancy man's took hisself off, seems to me you'll be needing a new— partner, let's say."

Don't lose control, she told herself sharply. Stare him down. You're taller than he is.

Shivers weakened her knees and numbed her wrists.

She said, "As a matter of fact, I will be needing a new accompanist. It shouldn't be too hard to find someone proficient on the piano in a town this size. I understand a number of the people coming West are quite accomplished. Of course, performing in public is a little different from parlor playing. If it's unavoidable, I can sing with fiddle or even guitar. And given the state of my finances"—she huddled the violated dress defensively to her breasts—"I think I might sing tonight after all."

She was willing to say anything to get him out of her room, so she added, "So you see, I'll have to start preparing now."

He shook his head. "I don't think so, missy. Not tonight. Your only performance tonight'll be private. For me."

Libby felt bile burn at the back of her throat at the

nearness of this awful man with his sour breath and avid stare and the shocking, soft press of his overfed belly against her thighs. Cringing away, she caught the backs of her knees on the side of the bed. Willy-nilly, she sat down, and he followed her, his hand touching her breast while the other clenched her braids to hold her head still for a kiss.

"Keep away from me!"

The man's skinny arms were stronger than they looked. She screamed, loudly and repeatedly, an ugly, hoarse-edged sound she couldn't believe came from her throat.

The screams opened her mouth to his first evil-tasting kiss. Dirty fingernails scrabbled at her bodice. Libby felt a pinprick. A long, burning scratch scored her skin through several layers of material.

Wildly, she brought both of her fists up, hitting him. His teeth clicked together, biting deeply into the tongue he'd thrust out for another assault. Blood reddened his bristly chin.

With a guttural cry, he lurched off the bed, his hands clapped to his face.

Libby was up and around him in an instant, flying through the door and across the balcony to the blessed, uneven stairs. At the bottom, she risked a glance over her shoulder.

He stumbled toward the rail. Heedless of anything except escape, she lifted her skirts and bolted for the safety of the public street.

Fleeing, Libby didn't look up until the boardwalk turned to dirt. Gradually, she slowed, then turned. Panting and holding on to the stitch in her side, she surveyed the pier and close-packed buildings.

Men sauntered in the Sabbath afternoon. The stares she attracted were curious rather than admiring; a few, perhaps kindly, strangers stopped, but when she shrank away, they exchanged shrugs and strolled on.

Libby caught sight of herself in the dim reflection of a shop window. Humiliation stabbed her. No wonder those men ogled. The girl in the glass looked like an object for charity. Plaits of hair hung around her ears. Her pretty piece of beige lace tangled in a mouse's tail past her shoulder blades. A strip of the beautiful green wool above her heart had been ripped beyond mending; bits of embroidered lawn tufted through the gaping hole.

Instinctively, she tried to pull the tear closed, and then she realized that her watch had disappeared, too. That seemed more of a catastrophe than the slick smear of her own blood that came away on her fingers. The catch must have scratched her when it came undone. Much worse, her worldly goods now consisted of the clothes she stood in, and they were in none too good repair.

Libby forced herself to think. Everything she'd done since she'd arrived in San Francisco struck her as being unforgivably naive, but she wasn't simpleminded enough to return without reinforcements to the hotel. Hotel? No, Caleb had been right. Waterfront brothel. Before she went back, she would seek out a constable or a sheriff, whatever the law called itself here. But it might take hours to find such a person, and in the meantime darkness would fall.

Wind curled around her calves, reminding her of another danger. She cast a suspicious glance at the clear, innocent blue sky. How long before the fog rolled in?

Her most urgent needs were shelter, something to eat by morning—in a word, money. The familiar problem.

She refused to panic. She'd been earning her own money for a long time now. And she was not going to run to Caleb Logan, bereft and bleeding and falling at his feet to beg for the crumbs of his generosity.

Or to discuss his *terms* . . .

As well as she could, using the murky reflection as a guide, Libby repinned her hair. Despite the trembling no amount of willpower could control, her fingers worked deftly enough to transform her back to respectability in a few minutes. A sense of haste forbade any further mourning over her gown; thanking Providence for small mercies, she shook out the lace and tied it around her shoulders, hoping it would pass as an unorthodox fichu. It covered the rip better than she had expected.

Satisfied that she'd done what she could, Libby walked steadily away from the shush of waves and bright glint of water at the end of the street. She'd trust none of the San Franciscans prowling disreputable districts on a Sunday afternoon. But shops were open here and there, manned by clerks who could presumably give directions when asked.

And surely somebody—somebody safe—would know the way to so notable a landmark as the Jenny Lind Theater.

Chapter 5

L ibby shifted from foot to foot in the unheated hall-
way and concentrated on her breathing exercises.
She'd already memorized the opulent decorations, re-
designed the gold medallions on the brown wallpaper,
and gone beyond desperation to fatalism about when
she'd next get a chance to visit a commode. If she were
ever in the position to furnish a home of her own, a
prospect that appeared remote, she wouldn't overlook
the necessity of placing something to sit on in the entry
hall. A plush wingchair, or a parson's bench, or even a
modest three-legged stool . . .

A harried waiter in a chophouse, so crowded she'd
felt reasonably secure walking into it, had given her
directions to the theater. Its locked doors had sent her
heart plummeting, but a playbill attached to the side of
the yellow sandstone structure advertised the fact that
"Tom McGuire, Impresario," lived nearby.

Intent on her purpose, Libby only smiled grimly as
she walked through the Sabbath day quiet of Portsmouth Square on her way to McGuire's. If there were
any desperadoes lurking in the shadowed alleys, they
stayed out of sight.

At least the well-appointed hall indicated that Tom
McGuire could afford an advance against her earnings.
Assuming he hired her, of course. Libby warned herself about overconfidence and began humming scales
at half voice, both to warm her throat and to take her

mind off her various physical discomforts. A day in the chill, fresh air wasn't the best preparation for an audition.

Toward the top of her range, a note rang technically on pitch but lacked the shimmer of vibrato she thought it should have. She stopped, began again at the bottom of the scale. Repeated the contrary note. Better.

"You've got the instrument," came a grudging comment.

As she knew well, *instrument* meant voice, raw talent. With a gleam of hope, she faced a man whose shrewd eyes assessed her white cheeks and the stains on her gown. Making a shaky decision to trust in her showmanship, she slipped into the concert singer's position, with her shoulders back, spine straight, and knees slightly flexed to keep from locking, and simply let poor, mad Lucia's lament of love and loss pour out.

Lucia di Lammermoor had been the first full-scale opera she'd ever heard. The remembered glamour of the Covent Garden opening was a far cry from Tom McGuire's front hall, and the Donizetti heroine's inability to control her own destiny had always struck Libby as feebleminded, but now she sang the aria with all the pathos the composer could have wanted. After today, she'd never criticize luckless, abandoned, unjustly accused Lucia again.

Servants gathered behind the impresario. Libby sang her way to the last tortured note, which echoed on and on in the frigid, stuffy hall until McGuire turned and called to those behind him, "All right. That's it. Show's over."

Whispering and scuffling, the servants returned to distant parts of the house. Libby could hear footfalls and occasional shouted comments; she waited until the noises died away and it became apparent that the impresario wouldn't be the first to speak. "Mr. McGuire? My name is Elizabeth Owens and—"

"And you can sing. Truly sing."

The remark startled her. Like Caleb, he didn't seem

to be a person who parted with compliments easily. Relief washed through her. He liked her voice. He liked the way she sang. He was going to give her work . . .

"So, Jehoshaphat, woman, what possessed you to appear down on the 'front last night?"

Her relief turned into anxiety. "It was a mistake," she said. "I allowed my accompanist to find a suitable location for our performance and that's what he chose. He's no longer with me."

"You're better off without him, I can tell you. He didn't do you any favor, booking you into that kind of place."

"No, I realize that," Libby agreed. "May I ask how you know where I appeared yesterday evening?"

"I know everything that goes on in Frisco—in a theatrical sense," he said with a simple pride that carried conviction. "The Jenny Lind's the finest stage in town, you know."

He looked her up and down, not lustfully, but as if assessing her value in hard cash. His small eyes seemed to count every mark on her gown and see straight through the scarf hiding the tear in her bodice. Libby couldn't keep nervous fingers from rearranging the disguising folds.

"I've been told the Jenny Lind is the best. That's why I'd like to appear there. My repertoire is extensive—besides opera, I can sing ballads and popular songs. I memorize very fast—"

"I can't afford you."

"I'm quite willing to work for whatever you pay principal singers." It would be bad business, she reminded herself nervously, to price herself too cheap.

"Not a matter of money. I can't afford to hire a woman from the saloons. Not and keep my good name. Tom McGuire offers quality. Exclusive acts only. No exceptions. Ever."

The staccato phrases pummeled her ears. McGuire receded swiftly, as if she were viewing him through the wrong end of a spyglass. Then he loomed close, the image in the glass reversed. Libby blinked, and he stopped moving. No food since the early lunch with Caleb, she thought vaguely. Too much had happened. Too long on her feet. The weighty crinoline dragged on her waist where the corset, even though it was loosely tied, pinched with cruel metal fetters after eight uninterrupted hours.

"I see," she managed. "Of course, you must stick to your business principles."

If only she'd stayed true to her own principles and refused to perform last night. But she'd already set foot on the stage before it dawned on her that the long counter backed by mirrors, with the brass rail stretching its width near the floor, must be a bar. A bar where men swilled raw spirits, a rail where they rested their boots, mirrors that magnified the merry flicker of candlelight and reflected the scarlet of that damnable, damnable red dress.

"I must beg your pardon for bothering you at home. Please forgive me for intruding."

"Not at all. Pleasure to hear you sing."

She found herself in the middle of an empty street. Pulling herself up to take stock of her situation, she saw that the area looked familiar. San Francisco, for all it was growing by leaps and bounds, wasn't the huge city its citizens liked to think it was. Surely—she shaded her eyes—surely the boxy shop over there was one she'd visited before.

"It is not that I would be less than honored to employ you in my store," Jacob Klein said gently. "It is that I cannot promise a woman like you would be unmolested."

"What kind of woman am I?" Libby's voice shook.

"An extraordinarily beautiful one. The kind men fight over and sometimes kill for."

Libby opened her mouth to speak, but instead moistened her lips and looked away. She knew her own face. Its precise oval happened to be the currently popular shape. Her short, thin nose and her white teeth were straight. Her figure, except for her unusual height, was good. More than good. Its excellent features had been catalogued by her mother so often that Libby had come to despise them. She had taught herself not to mind that smooth shoulders and firm breasts and a narrow waist brought in gawkers to fill her audiences. Her appearance formed part of the illusion she built to draw in customers. If they came to leer, they left with their money's worth in superb music.

Men used to faded women who grew wrinkled at thirty in their war against the wilderness might pay to stare at her, but she'd never believed herself the sort of legendary beauty to goad sane men to heart-thrilling exploits.

"I'm tall," she protested. "And my eyes aren't blue or brown or anything normal. They're *green*. I'm hardly Helen of Troy, Mr. Klein. My looks just aren't that—that refined."

His broad cheeks creased in a smile, his first since he'd found her on his stoop. "I am afraid men are so crude that refinement is not always what catches their attention, Miss Owens. Sometimes they see only the flesh, that is true, and then any passable body will satisfy the appetite. But once in a while the flesh reflects the spirit within, and that is what men see when they look at you. I do not mean to distress you, but you are a desirable woman. You would not be safe under my protection."

Libby had never had a reason to beg before. She hadn't guessed it would hurt so much. "My money has been stolen, Mr. Klein. I can't go back to that place— the place where I was staying. I—I haven't got anywhere to sleep tonight. Please."

They sat on wooden crates in the alcove that served as his living space. He pounded on his knee with a hamlike fist.

Libby said, "I'll do any sort of decent work."

"Be sensible now. Surely you know there are people who would take pleasure in harming you, just to prove that the protection of a Jew is worthless. Only Indians and Chinese rate lower than Hebrews.''

Nothing colored his tone but gentle matter-of-factness. Suddenly, Libby felt ashamed. Jacob Klein faced a world more threatening than hers every day of his life.

"I'm sorry," she said, rising. "I shouldn't have come. It was thoughtless of me. I don't seem to have counted the feelings of others in my calculations lately.''

Lumbering to his feet, he opened his mouth. He was such a nice man that Libby thought he probably intended to deny her statement. Suddenly she couldn't bear to get lost in a labyrinth of polite contradictions, so she rushed on, "Besides, I'm sure Miss Sarah would have some objections to my presence.''

The geniality she remembered from that morning reappeared. "It is possible. She is a tigress, my Sarah. But is she the only one who might take exception?'' At Libby's murmur of confusion, he said, "You have not mentioned Caleb Logan.''

"No.''

"Mmphf. Yet the friendship of such a man is not to be dismissed lightly. Simple logic—''

"No.''

Jacob pursed his lips. Plainly, he considered her desire to toil in a general store rather than to accept the patronage of a prosperous rancher equal to lunacy. Libby pushed away the memory of Caleb's proposal. The sting was too fresh to think of, let alone explain.

"There must be police of some description,'' she said. "I imagine the authorities will find me a place to stay for the night. If you could direct me—''

"The only place the alcalde could suggest is over the calaboose. Every inch of the city is rented. I could lease out the floor under our feet if I wanted to. Even the tents are full. And it is the same for the priest. You would need gold, a great deal of it, to obtain anything vacant and suitable.''

"Well. I shall just have to get along as best I can."

She imagined what sleeping in an alley would be like, and resolved to try the beach. There would be fewer human predators. At least she sincerely hoped so. And come dawn she'd consider what kind of work to seek next. Laundry or sewing, perhaps. Or cooking. A little warmth of optimism suffused her. Thanks to her mother, she did know how to cook—certainly well enough to please the typical maltreated American palate. After today, no honest employment seemed too menial.

One thing was sure. She'd never return to sing in a saloon again.

Perhaps the plans she wove showed in the expressions flitting across her face, because Jacob Klein said with sudden vigor, "No more foolishness. The fog is on its way. I will take you to Caleb now."

"No."

Without her bearlike guide, Libby knew she would have been lost in seconds. Abetted by spring's early dusk, the fog confined vision to the distance of her wide skirt, smothering all sense of direction.

Jacob hadn't wasted any more energy arguing with her. Shrugging on an overcoat, he'd simply clapped on a round-brimmed hat and waited by the open door until she slowly, stiffly followed him. Common sense forced her to admit the value of his reasoning.

Common sense was a vastly overrated quality.

But it was either Caleb or the beach.

Time evaporated in the eerie gloom. Sounds were distorted; their own footfalls barely carried to her ears, but the woodwind complaints of shorebirds pierced the moisture-laden air with nerve-wracking intensity. Only the shrill peeping of the sandpipers and the gulls' hoarser replies disturbed the unnatural quiet. Libby couldn't control the apprehension she felt that they weren't alone in the blank, deceptive mist. Walking cautiously through the fog-shrouded city, she knew it was best to stay small, invisible, and undetected.

The smell of the salty sea air alerted her to the district they were approaching.

"Mr. Klein!" she whispered. "What are we doing so close to the ocean?"

His answering mutter sounded almost as low. "Caleb keeps a room here. On Sansome Street. The pier is just beyond."

Libby had to choke back a strangled laugh at the irony of finding Caleb so near to her starting point. Jacob Klein came to a halt.

"Now we climb."

She balked at a steep ladder.

"What is this place?"

"The *Niantic*. Her crew abandoned her to search for gold and never came back. The bay got filled in around her. Poor old lady, she shall never sail again." He patted the curved wall as he stepped aside so Libby could ascend.

Holding her capacious skirts in one hand and clinging to the ladder with the other, Libby inched her way upward. At least the fog hid the no-doubt scandalous view she would otherwise have presented to anyone standing below. A boat. Caleb had left the sea for life as a rancher, but he rented a room on a huge, land-locked boat. She stifled her laughter.

Once on the deck, which seemed to form part of the roof, Mr. Klein led her swiftly into the interior of the ship. The low-ceilinged corridors couldn't have been much altered from the structure's sailing days. Used to the pitch and roll of ordinary vessels, Libby found the dead steadiness under her legs odd and rather sad. As if someone had plucked a mermaid from the water, dried it off, and preserved it out of its element, under glass. She understood why Mr. Klein called the *Niantic* a poor old lady.

He paused at a door. Light spilled through a crack at the bottom. Very quietly, he stated, "You will not want me here. Do not look so despairing. I saw how Caleb watched you this morning. He will take good care of you."

Libby's independence rebelled at the idea she needed taking care of. At the same time, she did feel the tiniest possible craving to be held, pampered, and assured that everything would be all right. Having met Caleb, she thought it likely he'd just invent some new way to insult her, but the craving didn't go away.

She began to whisper a word of thanks. Mr. Klein, demonstrating exquisite tact, had already retreated down the passageway. With every tired muscle in her body tightening in anticipation, she knocked on the door.

The silence from within made her realize she'd heard muffled sounds a moment earlier. Impatiently, she knocked again.

As the door creaked open, lamplight silhouetted a tall male shape, and Libby's shoulders slumped with relief. Before she could speak, she was yanked inside.

Whatever she'd expected from Caleb, it wasn't harsh handling. Then it occurred to her that perhaps this wasn't Caleb.

She darted backward, or tried to, but the man's grip on her wrist tightened and brought her up short. When she tried desperately to pull away, her arm was twisted painfully.

But Libby pulled harder.

A scream was building inside her and threatened to burst from her throat when Caleb's voice said sharply, "Give it up! You'll only hurt yourself."

Libby stilled instantly. The stranger didn't relax his hold, but the pressure on her shoulder eased as she obeyed.

Six men had tensed at her entrance. Now all but two lounged back against paneled walls. Her jailer continued to stand, his clamp on her wrist as impersonal and final as iron shackles. Caleb sat on a bunk thrust under the overhang of a built-in cupboard.

A gun was pointed at his head.

The six-inch barrel gleamed faintly blue, a long runnel of mellow lamplight flowing over its cylindrical surface as the hand holding the weapon wagged it.

"Cover her," said the man with the gun.

One of the lounging figures reached into a baggy pair of pants and produced a pistol, pointing it at Libby.

"Changed my mind," the first man said. "Cover Logan."

He ambled toward Libby, not allowing his body to intrude between Caleb and the henchmen. Using the muzzle of his gun, he lifted her chin. Grinning, the man who had been holding Libby's wrist dropped it.

"Not a good time to come calling," said the one who seemed to be in charge, his accent pure Botany Bay. Now Libby realized that Caleb had told her the unvarnished truth. The Hounds really did exist, and they were ready to kill. The Hound said, "What's your name, dearie?"

Her anger was futile, but it cleared her head. She whispered, "Elizabeth."

"Lovely name, eh, mates?" He rubbed the muzzle gently under her chin, then down her slender neck, caressing the slight hollow of her throat. "Lovely," he repeated. "Mine's Smitty."

She glanced at Caleb for guidance, but he was watching Smitty with an intensity that told her nothing. A rapidly purpling bruise showed under the lock of black hair that fell over his forehead.

Outnumbered five to one, he hadn't a chance. Libby recognized that, recognized as well that her arrival must have worsened an already hopeless situation. But . . . she was standing. Her hands remained free. And Smitty was smiling at her.

Her wits sharpened by a lifetime with people who loved to take risks, Libby tried to assess the possibilities open to her. Maman's down-to-earth advice for attracting beaux sounded in her ear. "Use your eyes. And your bosoms. Men are easily distracted."

Maman could not have foreseen her daughter with a smiling rogue who was pointing a gun at her.

Libby knew what he wanted. The same thing the saloon owner had wanted. What men always wanted, and what Caleb had assumed she was willing to sell without regard to her heart or her honor. She could tell from the way Smitty stood so close that his legs pushed her crinoline out in a circle behind her. From the glitter in his smile. Even from his scent, musky and pungent. The smell of danger, and lust.

The longer she kept him talking, the longer she stayed—whole. The longer Caleb lived.

"How do you do?" She cringed inwardly. You'll have to be livelier than that, Elizabeth, she thought.

"Better since you walked in. Much better."

There didn't seem to be an answer to that. Libby didn't dare another peek at Caleb, but a familiar sound, part *whir*, part *snap*, brought her head around in astonishment.

One of the loungers shuffled a deck of cards.

"You like card games?" Smitty asked. "We all have our little vices, eh? They're cutting cards, you see. Winner gets the pleasure of teaching Mr. Logan a lesson in manners. A permanent lesson, I guess, but—"

"That's 'er!" said the man who was shuffling the cards. Libby remembered his pinched face. "That's the bitch who threw water all over me!"

"So save your cackle in case you catch cold," Smitty advised. "I'm talking to the lady." His gaze shifted to the fluttering deck. Something about the blank rigidity underlying his grin jolted Libby into awareness. He had the look of a true gambler; she'd seen it too often to mistake the sickness it betokened. Furiously, she tried to invent a way Smitty's weakness could be used to benefit her and Caleb.

"Poor Tim doesn't like you much," Smitty continued, his concentration still fixed on the flashing cards. "He has this problem, see, with the ladies. Not that he's a nance, you understand. It's just that the ladies have never taken to him, somehow."

His inattention caused the muzzle to dig into her neck. She didn't have to pretend breathlessness. "Poor Tim," she said. "Ladies do take their fancies, don't they? Myself, I think a man should *be* a man."

Her tone was a masterpiece of vulgar, half-scared flippancy. Smitty's scrutiny turned back to her.

Forcing her lips to part alluringly, she quickly reviewed the mannerisms of every man-hungry female she'd ever observed in action. With deliberate archness, she tried lowering her face and then peeping back up sidelong through her lashes. Not too far up; Smitty wasn't tall. He had muddy-brown eyes and jug ears, and he soaked up the flattery like a sponge.

"Ain't never had no complaints . . ."

Caleb controlled himself with a strenuous effort. What in heaven or hell had brought Libby here?

He'd never met anyone before with such a genius for being in the wrong place at the most inopportune time. Why the hell couldn't she have been in her room when he'd gone back to the hotel for her? And whatever game she was playing, he hated it. Recalling her avowed distaste for amateur theatricals, he felt the cursed twitch that had bedeviled him lately start up in his cheek. Libby was too many women. First the enticing seductress on the stage, then the untouchable lady of quality in church, then a hoyden with a handbucket. And now a trollop, yielding to the man most likely to provide her with a profit. Even her accent had changed. That intriguing British edge had become sharper, the vowels broader and drawn from several steps down the social ladder. Which was the real Libby?

He didn't imagine he'd have much longer to mull over the question. At no time since the Hounds had stormed his door had a gun failed to be pointed squarely between his eyebrows. Caleb had outfaced death enough times at sea and on land to keep himself from flinching, and if he railed in his heart, it wasn't at the inevitability of dying, but because he'd been caught unprepared by jackals he despised. The Hounds had tracked him down quicker than he'd expected.

As for Libby, he didn't know if he wanted her to revert to the irritating, unflappable arrogance she'd displayed at the livery stable, or if the only important thing in this hellish coil was her life, however she could contrive to save it.

He couldn't help but admire the expertise with which she played the fish on her string. In some way she was less beautifully turned out than she had been this afternoon; the abundance of hair couldn't be called messy, but it sat looser, as if the arrangement might topple over any minute, and the sort-of-shawl thing tied around her shoulders didn't suit the rest of her outfit. However, the effect enhanced the impression created by her brash behavior. Details awry in her appearance didn't seem to put off Smitty. He withdrew the pistol from Libby's velvet collar and growled happily, like a dog being petted just right.

"Of course, the game falls flat if there isn't something at stake, doesn't it?" Libby murmured when Smitty's tales of his accomplishments with the female population for hire in San Francisco dwindled to an end.

Smitty squinted at Libby. "Game?"

Caleb thought Libby had never looked so angelic. "The game of life," she suggested softly. "And death."

A shark's grin spread across Smitty's face. "You like playing rough, do you?"

She squealed as he tickled her between her breasts with his gun. Caleb swallowed a lump of something and reminded himself that if he moved now, Libby and he would both die. Besides, she was smiling. "Smitty dear," she said, "what's the point of a game without a prize?"

"True enough," conceded Smitty. "So what's the pot?"

"I told you. Life or death."

Chapter 6

Smitty chewed on the idea for a while. Finally, he jerked his head toward Caleb. "What's he to you?"

"Just a friend." Her elaborate innocence left no doubt as to what kind of friend. "Mr. Logan's really generous to his particular friends."

Smitty frowned. She added hastily, "But he's so strait-laced. That gets, *you* know, boring sometimes. A girl likes a bit of excitement now and then." She fell smoothly back into the rhythm of speech she, as a schoolgirl, used to hear from housemaids flirting with baker's boys. "A real man isn't afraid of a teensy risk. And his word—a girl likes to think she can trust a man to keep his word. Else where would she be?"

"With a bastard in her belly and bootmarks on her bum!"

Smitty and the others hooted. Libby gave him a coy look, wondering how to keep this oaf on a single topic long enough to beguile him into a trap that seemed more likely to succeed every time his eyes glanced at the card's being shuffled.

Pouting shamelessly, she said, "Now, that's not the way to win a girl's trust. It's better when men talk nice."

"And then what?" Smitty asked.

Libby made her words as low and sweet and inviting as she knew how. "And then she talks nice back. Would you like that, Smitty?"

73

Suddenly Smitty had to use his unoccupied hand to adjust trousers that apparently had become too tight. The Hounds, all except Tim, who scowled, sniggered at their leader's plight. Keeping her eyes wide and fixed on Smitty, Libby noted at the edge of her vision that the other gun remained trained on Caleb.

"That's just about enough!" Caleb roared, half off the bunk before the butt of a pistol caught him full on the cheek. He crashed to the floor.

Smitty never moved. Neither did Libby, because the click of a hammer cocking was loud in the abrupt silence. A moment passed, then two. Libby drew a shaky breath. Why had Caleb turned into a knight errant at the worst possible moment? He lay motionless, but she could see he was still breathing.

Smitty eased his thumb off the hammer and remarked, "Partial to you, is he?"

Maybe she could turn Caleb's quixotic poor timing to good account. She preened. "I'm his favorite."

"I bet you are." Smitty's expression grew mean. "But how many tricks you can play in bed isn't exactly a matter of life and death."

"Smitty! The things you say! Of course not. It's the game that's worth life or death. The game that makes the difference."

"The difference in what?"

"In whether a girl is willing—or unwilling."

Coming to slowly, Caleb heard the Australian say, "Just what do you propose?"

And Libby, sounding businesslike, replied, "A simple cut of the deck. High card sets Mr. Logan free. Deuces and jacks wild."

"And I get the girl and the game," he said with satisfaction.

"Smitty." She made his name a caress. "Where's your sporting spirit? Sweeten the pot. Winner takes all. I've always wanted to be part of the stakes. It's . . . exciting."

Libby's voice was full of promise. Beyond the

pounding in his cheek—God, were some of his teeth loose?—Caleb felt tension curling around him.

Smitty gave a short bark of laughter. "Done! Pass those cards over here."

Caleb peered through slit eyelids. He saw Libby's skirts swing saucily as she reached out and impudently plucked the deck from Smitty's hand.

Wits fuzzy from the blow and fall, Caleb realized Libby had some female, and therefore incomprehensible, goal in mind. He couldn't believe she was so addlepated as to imagine the Hounds would release either of them voluntarily. But he'd let her play out this little scene before he made his next move. *Any* move would probably get them both killed pronto—but Libby'd be better off dead than dragged away to Portsmouth Square. And he'd rather die quick and on his feet than slowly and helplessly on the dusty floor.

Oh, God. Julia. I'm sorry, little sister . . .

"I'll cut," said Libby. "It makes me feel . . ." Since she didn't know what a sluttish, gambling-mad woman would feel under the circumstances, she let her voice trail off suggestively. In truth, her heart beat with sickening thuds and her undergarments clung to her sides, clammy from armholes to waist. If this was how Maman had felt at all those card parties, why had she gone back again and again?

Without giving Smitty a chance to reply, Libby fumbled with the cards, praying no one would notice how her slight awkwardness covered the scurry of her fingertips as they sought the obvious places for markings. Not the corners; they were unfrayed. No unobtrusive but oh-so-significant differences in the pattern that decorated the backs of the cards. Then the nap of her thumb caught on a tiny notch cut into the edge of an ace. There. And there. One of the simplest systems for fuzzing her mother had ever taught her.

Relief almost made her drop the deck, but it wouldn't do to appear quite that clumsy. Sashaying to the chair serving a small desk, she continued to smooth the edges with trembling delicacy. Ace, king, queen, jack . . .

Smitty laughed. "Think you can stop shaking long enough to cut?" he asked jeeringly.

Reminding herself of the disaster overconfidence could bring, she carefully kept triumph from coloring her reply. "So much excitement makes me giddy."

"Get on with it," said Tim sourly.

"Shut up," Smitty told him with insulting casualness.

He held his pose of indifference well, Libby observed, but it was only a pose. She could see a great swatch of sweat growing down the middle of his shirt.

"All right, Elizabeth. Your terms. But only jacks are wild. High card wins. Hurry up."

"First for you." Her gaze held Smitty's as she split the deck. Smirking, he took the card she offered, but as she verified with a quick glance that it was, in fact, a king, the flutter of lashes on Caleb's cheek distracted her. Willing him to stay safe and still, she found the card she wanted.

Jack of hearts.

Smitty's expression congealed.

"Don't mean nothing," one of his men grunted.

Libby hurried into speech. "Oh, but we know better, don't we, Smitty? The game is everything. Some people don't understand. But we—we do." Despite her most dulcet effort, Smitty's face lost none of its pinched and calculating virulence. Calculating whether it would be more amusing to have Caleb killed before or after Smitty raped her? She tried not to sound desperate. "Besides, we can always play again another time."

Miraculously, it was the right thing to say. Smitty's grating laugh rang out. "Damned straight. That's it, mates, get going."

Oaths and protests filled the air. Smitty said, "I told you, out!"

They filed out, grumbling. Smitty kicked the door shut after Tim, whose complaints sounded more heartfelt than those of the others. Shaking his head, Smitty said, "A bucket of water, eh?"

"I—I'm afraid so," answered Libby cautiously.

"Not the worst thing a woman's done to Tim." He grinned. "Me, I know how to appreciate a female with spirit. And I can be generous, too."

Libby made herself sigh with what she hoped he'd take for longing. Thank goodness, his vanity was so large that he preferred a semblance of cooperation from his bed partners. Otherwise, her bait would never have hooked him into the crowning stupidity of following her suggestions.

Now the problem was to get him to honor them.

The telltale muscle beside Caleb's mouth twitched again. With dreadful archness, she exclaimed, "Oooh, I just had a feeling what kind of man you were the minute I saw you." It was gratifying to be able to speak the literal truth. Could she be blamed if Smitty's interpretation of her comment happened to be more flattering than factual?

"Yeah, well—"

"And I could tell you'd never be one to—to welsh on a bet," she lied.

Caleb fought an insane desire to laugh. Libby may have maneuvered four of their enemies out of range of murdering her and him but if she thought this randy coyote would be content with a quick cut of the deck and a few fulsome compliments, she had to be innocent past recovery—and Caleb knew she was far from that.

He'd never witnessed a smoother fleecing. If they lived through this, he'd have to remind himself never to wager anything more valuable than a matchstick with her. He stifled another spasm of laughter. His blond enchantress was a cardsharp!

As Smitty continued to wheedle, Caleb began to second Libby's opinion of the Hounds' leader's general intelligence. The poor ass was wrapped so tight around her little finger, they'd need a crowbar to shuck him loose. Caleb wondered, too, if Libby had outsmarted herself. By flaunting her numerous attractions, she'd ensnared Smitty in the trap sprung by her clever handling of the cards—but by the same token, she'd made him reluctant to leave without a share of the stakes.

Without Libby.

The thought tensed his body, which was already aching from the necessity of lying prone and useless while Libby did her wayward best to save his skin for him.

Libby saw Caleb's shoulders hunch and wondered what he was waiting for. Surely if he'd overcome his reluctance to attack the Hounds before when there were five of them, he could do it again when only Smitty remained. Couldn't he? What kind of man was he? Suspense made it impossible for her to attend to whatever ribaldries Smitty was mouthing.

"Even if Logan's one of your regulars, you got no call to turn me down. Me and you could have a right good time before he wakes up. It's not like we'd be taking anything away from him. Once a cherry's popped, it's popped, and yours—"

Snarling with a rage that welled up from nowhere, Caleb lashed out an arm. It hooked Smitty's foot out from under him. The instant the smaller man fell, Caleb rolled to his knees and brought his fist arching down to land a punishing left against Smitty's unprotected jaw. The impact felt so good that Caleb smashed the jaw again.

Lifting his arm for yet another blow, he was startled back to the present by a persistent tug on his shirt-sleeve.

"Mr. Logan! You've got to stop! You'll kill him."

So he'd returned to *Mr. Logan*, had he, while filth like Smitty received sugary words and downright obscene promises? He tried to shake her off, but she clung fiercely. "Killing him is what I want to do," he informed her.

Her face was full of revulsion. "But—he's already unconscious. You can't just pummel defenseless people to death. It's dishonorable."

Raising Smitty by the lapels, Caleb felt reasonably satisfied with the way the bloodied head lolled backward, and dropped the Hound with a thud. Rather unsteadily, he got to his feet.

"And what do you imagine he was going to do to us, Miss Owens?" He gave her name sarcastic emphasis. "Don't fool yourself into thinking your playmate Smitty ever intended to let either of us live for long. Granted, he would have kept you around for a while to liven up his fun—"

"That's disgusting." She spoke with the meticulous accent he was used to hearing from her.

Caleb beat down his temper the way he wanted to beat in Smitty's face.

"Is that what it is? Frankly, I couldn't tell what your feelings on the matter might be. You had all the tricks to keep old Smitty slavering over you." His own ferocity shocked him silent. By God, he sounded jealous. Over a cardsharping saloon girl?

Libby clutched at the thin lace around her shoulders as if it would keep her warm. Reaction had set in, and she could barely keep from shaking in earnest.

"I needed to make the diversion intriguing enough. Otherwise he was going to let one of the others . . . one of the others shoot . . . You're bleeding."

Even if she was feigning her concern, playing another one of the roles she slipped into and out of with such ease, Caleb didn't care. She looked as if she were about to faint. With an oath, he pushed her almost gently onto the bunk, stepped over Smitty, and picked up a squat bottle.

"Here. No, don't spit it out, swallow. This brandy's from France. One more sip. There, that's better. Just one more . . ."

The foul, burning stuff nearly came up again, but Libby found that it did stop the room from spinning. She hugged herself. "There's nothing wrong with me. I never faint."

"It's allowed," Caleb said, beginning to feel more

amusement than anger. "Everybody expects females to faint now and then."

She changed the subject. Pointing to Smitty, she said, "We need to do something about him."

Caleb rubbed the back of his neck. "I'm glad you realize it. What's the fog like?"

"Thick. But—no. Mr. Logan, please. No killing." The Hound meant less than nothing to her, but somehow she couldn't bear to think of Caleb murdering an unprotected man in cold blood. She tried to come up with a way to convince him Smitty was of more value alive than dead. "If Smitty disappears, all those others will carry a grudge against you forever. You'll never have any peace. They'll know who did it."

"And you think they won't blame us for the condition he's in now?" he asked derisively. Then he sighed. "I suppose it doesn't matter much one way or the other. Whether he's dead or not, our goose is cooked. The Hounds aren't going to forget."

He looked at her. "I hope you're not going to argue with me anymore, because I'm no longer a patient man. We're both getting out of town tomorrow. And we're leaving the *Niantic* right now. I want to be somewhere else in case Smitty's friends come back to see if he's ready to share."

A hat pulled low was the best disguise he could contrive. The limited wardrobe he kept in the city contained a long, caped coat that he wrapped around Libby.

The rhythm of Smitty's snorts changed slightly as Caleb hoisted the fallen Hound over his shoulder. However, there was no response to Libby's tentative prod, so Caleb simply carried his limp victim out onto the deck. The sea breeze cut smoky patterns into the fog; visibility was limited to two feet one moment, ten the next. Despite Smitty's weight, Caleb swarmed down the ladder with a matter-of-fact grace that reminded Libby he'd said he had once been a sailor.

A few buildings away from the *Niantic*, Caleb climbed down one of the pilings supporting the pier and dumped Smitty in a sitting position on a relatively dry patch of mud. From above, Libby tipped the contents of Caleb's bottle over Smitty's clothes.

"Waste of good brandy," Caleb pointed out.

"You never know. Perhaps he'll wake up and forget that he hasn't shot you," Libby replied. "Then he might leave us alone."

"I've got a better idea," he said. He arranged the gun in Smitty's lap at a careful downward angle and pressed the flaccid index finger around the trigger. "With any luck, his finger will twitch."

Libby pretended she hadn't seen what he'd done. "Where shall we go?"

He scrambled back up onto the pier and pulled her into the concealing mist.

"There's Jacob." He sounded uncharacteristically hesitant.

"Oh, no. We can't bring the Hounds in on him."

"That's what I thought," Caleb agreed. "Let's try the Georgius. The man in charge'll look the other way. For a consideration."

Weariness dragged so hard at Libby that only Caleb's grasp kept her moving. When he stopped at a corner, she sagged. He picked her up and carried her. Not even the shock of light and heat roused her as he entered through the rear of the hostelry.

Caleb didn't anticipate running into trouble, and he had none. As far as the manager was concerned, Mr. Logan was paying for privacy for himself and the lady, and privacy he would get.

Libby's skirts billowed like a great bell resting on its side when Caleb got her settled on their room's only bed. He sat on the edge to pull his boots off. It took time without a jack, and the grunt that escaped him as the second boot released his foot resounded so loudly that Libby stirred.

"Wha—? Where are we?"

He slid closer to her and sank into the softness of the feather mattress. Hell. He'd turned over the idea of sharing a bed with her, and here they were, sharing a very nice bed. Unfortunately, Libby's exhaustion was too profound to make any of the good reasons for being here together practicable.

"Safe," he told her with rough comfort. "We're safe. You can sleep now."

She whimpered and curled into a ball, then straightened quickly, as if something had stabbed her. "I can't. It hurts."

Caleb had never heard her admit a frailty before. Patting her anxiously, he found only one wound, a scratch above one breast that had been hidden under her lacy shawl.

He stared mindlessly at the ragged, bloodstained tear in her gown.

"Who did this to you?" Libby tried to twist away from the pressure of his big hands on her upper arms. "Who did this?"

"Don't know," she mumbled. "Never knew name."

His hands tightened, wrenching her up, and her eyes opened, a dazed and frightened green. "Did he force you? Libby, wake up! Do you need a doctor?" *Who?* Not Smitty, and certainly not the piano player; of all names, she must know his . . .

His vehemence brought an almost coherent response. "Of course not, silly. No doctor. My stays hurt. Could you . . ."

Her eyes lost their near-focus, and she dropped her head trustfully onto his shoulder.

"God, Libby," he muttered.

At least what had happened to her fell short of rape, however she'd been handled while they'd been apart. Maybe, he thought viciously, she'd invited some other man's rough touch. Immediately, he rejected the ugly suspicion. Not Queen Libby.

The jealousy he wouldn't acknowledge faded, but an angry, pervasive awareness of Libby—warm, cuddlesome, and for once passive—lingered. She was lucky *he* scorned rape.

Fumbling with the knobby, cloth-covered buttons, he eased the dress down to her hips without removing it and, after studying the corset in some confusion, unwound the laces from their hooks completely so he could free her from the garment without lifting her inert arms. It took longer to identify which petticoat deserved the blame for thrusting up her skirts. After tugging experimentally at the knot of strings at her waist, he deduced which was the crinoline and how it had been tied, and pulled the horsehair contraption off over her legs.

With his handkerchief, Caleb washed Libby's scratch with water and the soap that rested next to the ewer. As an afterthought, he swiped at the dried blood on his own face. Throughout, he left her chemise in place and maintained rigid control over his natural tendency to investigate the satiny flesh so easily within reach. The dull ache gathering between his legs wouldn't require much encouragement to harden into a more painful condition. And Libby, the cause and the cure, was dead to the world.

Sleep changed and softened her beauty. She looked younger and very sweet. With her hair falling down and one slim hand tucked under her cheek, she was so endearing that Caleb forgot the annoying contradictions she posed. Wriggling the bedspread out from under her, he covered her to the chin. Then he removed his own pants and shirt, turned down the flame in the lamp, and slipped in beside her.

He expected to drop off at once. God knew his activities in the last thirty-six hours had been strenuous. But one minute slowly chased another until half the night had passed, and he remained tense and wakeful.

Libby's fault, of course. He lay next to her, listening to her quiet breathing and small stirrings. His companion through the crazy day. The heart of the madness. Leading him into wild fantasies and nearly calamitous adventures.

The midnight hush did nothing to soothe his urge to

reach for her in the darkness, and take a long, tantaliz-
ing time to remove all those finicky pieces of clothing
women found it necessary to bundle around themselves. But he couldn't. At least he shouldn't. Libby
might be in love with her piano player. It wouldn't be
right. Worse, it wouldn't be practical. A mettlesome
woman like Libby would never forgive him for seduc-
ing her into a betrayal of her lover. And he didn't want
her to hate him; he wanted her willing in his arms.

It occurred to him that he must not be quite awake.
He floated in a twilight where motion seemed too
damned hard and sensation crowded out every other
kind of reality. The part of him that ached felt huge,
engorged with something like honey heated to a sweet,
tormenting simmer. He couldn't remember ever feeling
so full of power and need, and he groaned aloud with
the pain and pleasure of it.

His guttural cry lifted Libby out of a deep sleep. She
struggled halfway to consciousness, instinctively turning toward the agonized noise. Darkness surrounded
her. Existence reduced itself to a black, smothering
softness.

Confused, Libby said drowsily, "What is it? Mr. Logan? Can I help?"

And then Caleb was calling her "dear heart" in an
urgent voice. One of his arms encountered hers, and by
the time her sluggish brain registered that the softness
was a down mattress she wasn't occupying alone, he'd
pulled her too close to think at all.

The only thing that seemed sure was her desire to
hold him, comfort him, keep him safe in his great need.
A coverlet made a barrier between them; she felt cotton
and little lumps of embroidery. His arm flailed it aside,
and it was replaced by the homely brush of flannel and
wool that rasped against her sensitive skin. She tried to
find a path through the thicket of fabrics, but her blind,
frenzied movements only bound her tighter in the wel-
ter of material. Trapped in a nightmare where Caleb

needed her help and she couldn't move her lower limbs at all, she sobbed in frustration.

The sound cleared Caleb's head. Damnation, between the two of them they'd gotten Libby wrapped chaste as an Egyptian mummy below the waist.

It would have been funny except that the heavy, honeyed pulse flooding his groin precluded humor. And if Libby's actions were any indication, she felt the same kind of distress as well. He'd have to think for both of them. Breeding a child on her when he didn't know the extent of her involvement with another man would be a real bastard's trick. But there were other ways to remedy the pangs of desire.

He was years away from being some kid unable to conceive of anything more carnal than a hand's embrace. It didn't matter. Not now. Pain throbbed for release, pleasure for stimulus. Anything Libby did would spur his excitement, because . . . because he could taste her hair where a tendril of it lay across his lips. Because even tied up in her clothes with her body lodged against his she teased him with the image of her bountiful ivory breasts imperfectly contained by her chemise. Because he'd been furious with her and jealous over her and scared to death for her. And the brief, unsatisfying spurts of violence that had punctuated the day hadn't really achieved anything but to add to this hot onrush of arousal.

Caleb could imagine her hand. Its palm would be slender and strong, the tapering fingers warm and welcoming. Another groan escaped him.

Libby whispered frantically, "What can I do? What do you want?"

"This."

Half awake, she felt his hand urge hers to stroke a shaft that strained upward. This must be the source of his agony. Obedient to his prompting, her fingers swept up and down. Springy hair tickled her palm, and a picture formed of softness below, hardness above.

The picture jarred Libby fully awake.

As she jerked away from Caleb's flesh, his fist closed gently to push her hand back into place.

"Don't stop," he said, his voice so slurred she barely recognized it. "I won't hurt you. I'd never hurt you. Things won't go too far, I promise. You don't have to be afraid. I need you. Just give me your touch, Libby. Beautiful, golden Libby."

Darkness closed in, absolute. It didn't judge.

Somehow the impossible seemed inevitable. Her throat tightened. The only light in the room was a glimmer from his eyes. She remembered the lonely years in which no one had needed her. She couldn't say no to his terrible need, or to the praise he continued to murmur in short, thick phrases.

Perhaps this was akin to what those other men wanted, but it felt different. Caleb didn't frighten her, although her heart thumped as if it would burst and odd little fires licked at her veins. Caleb persuaded, he never ordered. He never took. The touch he used to show her how to please him didn't insist. It seduced. When she lingered to learn the extent of the corded steel that underlay his smooth skin, he let her decide how long to explore.

The reluctant glimpses she'd caught of couples joined in passion had taught her that people and beasts mated in much the same way. But knowing in theory that human love followed the pattern of familiar creatures differed sharply from the actual experience of a man's body.

Caleb was a healthy male animal.

At the realization of what her role would be, female to his male, if he were to let things "go too far," the flames in her blood rushed together, setting loose a damp warmth in the juncture of her legs. Tentative delicacy changed to a firm, leisurely caress. The dance of her hand across his flesh developed a pleasurable meter. Surrendering to an almost musical delight, she stroked, cupped, stroked, cupped. Caleb gasped.

"Say my name."

"Caleb."

He helped her increase the rhythm.

"Say it again."

"Caleb."

"Again."

"Caleb."

His shudders shook them both. After the last convulsive ripple, he relaxed so completely that Libby felt jolted and bewildered. His transformation from anguished passion to a drained content she could feel through the acute conduit of her palm was so abrupt that all the fascinating, unsettling fire inside her died to embers, then to ashes. Obviously, he needed nothing more from her.

The darkness seemed very cold.

A minute passed. The fluffy down beneath them shifted as he leaned over her and began sifting through the intertwined layers of her clothing. Libby inched toward her side of the bed.

"You don't have to do that," she said, afraid the words would strike him as doltish, not knowing what else to say.

"I want to." His baritone sounded normal, even cheerful, and it made her want to cry. "You were so sweet, Libby. It's my turn to pleasure you."

Constricted jackknifing motions brought her to the edge of the mattress. Rather than fall helpless and bound to the floor, she halted and said, "We're both tired. I'd rather sleep, really."

"Dear heart, there's no reason for you to go without." The feathers bunched and cascaded as he slid closer.

Merciful God, if he persisted in making it sound so innocently natural, she might fall prey to insanity a second time and let him . . . let him . . . She didn't know precisely what he planned to do. The hot, liquid, wholly wonderful lust stirred within her to whisper that she ought to find out.

But that way lay the ruin of what little dignity she

had left. A surge of dismay stiffened her resolve. Caleb assumed that she was a whore. Now he knew her for a wanton as well.

And he was right, she thought. Her woman's body had reveled in the power to please him, gloried in the supple glide of skin against skin. He might have been guilty of overpersuasion, but no stretch of wishful thinking could accuse him of force. The responsibility for succumbing to the appeal of Caleb's sensuality was hers, and so was the result. She'd become the loose woman he thought her.

She gulped back tears. "Can't we sleep? Please?"

He spoke gently. "I meant what I said. I wouldn't hurt you or take any chances that might beget a child. It can be however you want."

"I want to sleep."

Despite the fact that the bedtick failed to shift and the frame didn't creak, he suddenly sounded very distant. "All right. Will you let me help you out of that infernal swaddling? You can't be comfortable. I won't do anything you wouldn't like."

The tears spilled. Farfetched notions that she wouldn't like Caleb's touch were the least of her worries. The treacherous glow in her deep, soft female places proved that she'd like it beyond honor or independence or disgrace. Even an impersonal contact might destroy her precarious self-discipline. She'd probably beg him to teach her another sensual lesson.

Grittily, she said, "Thank you, but no. I—good night."

With a formality as cold as if they weren't lying side by side with his seed spilled between them, he replied, "Good night—Miss Owens."

Time had no meaning in the utter blackness, but after a while, his breathing became deep and regular. Libby stared at the invisible ceiling, wrapped in pantalets, a chemise, three petticoats, a soiled and wildly itchy merino wool dress, and the remnants of her pride.

Chapter 7

L ibby watched Caleb sleep with hatred a hot, green spark in her eyes.

Dawn had long since brightened the window. Without a brush, there was little she could do to style her hair, but she fingercombed the worst knots from the four-foot-long mass and contrived a single crooked plait down her back. Every stitch she had to wear had been rendered laughable. The gown would have to be remade with a new bodice. Crushed and stained, its skirt bore eloquent testimony to yesterday's misadventures. Her crinoline she discovered on the floor; it had been mashed into uselessness. Laces as well as a number of hooks had disappeared from the corset lying beside it. Making the best of a galling situation, she'd donned the gown, which fit poorly without those essential undergarments. She felt sordid and miserable in consequence.

But Caleb's real sin lay in the shallowness with which he slept. He sighed, rolled from back to front, even growled something unintelligible from time to time. But he didn't wake.

And Libby couldn't convince herself that he wouldn't—at least for as long as it would take her to use the white enamel utensil sitting in its compartment in the commode.

The ewer was dry; some water sat in the bowl, but it had an unappetizing pinkish tinge and she couldn't bring herself to taste it. She'd had nothing to eat or drink since lunch the day before, a fact that brought her no comfort. Between hunger, thirst, and the pressure in her lower body, conflicting instincts were rapidly building into tangible pain.

Caleb yawned, flung out a wiry arm—and subsided back into sleep. Libby's ordinarily keen sense of humor gave no sign of functioning. With short, angry movements, she tied the now-tattered lace over her shoulders, made sure her surviving buttons were decently buttoned, and walked stiffly into the corridor.

A visit to the outhouse relieved one set of problems, but brought her no closer to solving others. For the time being, she couldn't escape dependence on Caleb Logan. San Francisco bristled with hazards. Libby was all too aware that she had no money, no clothes, no employment.

Shame scalded her. After ministering to Caleb's desires, she accepted that she deserved to have no reputation, either, except of the bad kind. Though her virginity remained intact, she now knew things—very nice things—a virgin wasn't supposed to know. A good part of the shame came from a single unavoidable fact: she felt deeply disappointed that she hadn't learned more. Thirty-six hours' acquaintance with Caleb Logan had left her vulnerable to him in a way she'd never experienced with any other man. To her mind, vulnerability amounted to a greater sin than her new, illicit knowledge.

In addition, justice demanded an apology to Caleb for landing him in such a pickle. Her careless use of his name had brought Smitty and the others down on him. How would he be feeling about her after such an eventful night? He'd called her Libby in his passion, but she absolutely refused to think about his passion.

The whole episode, she decided, ought to be ignored. Unfortunately, a vivid and accurate impression of Caleb seemed to be imprinted on the inside of her palm. Worst of all, she didn't want to lose the recollection. Curling her fingers into a tender first to preserve the memory of silk over steel, Libby forced herself to open the door, and met Caleb's black scowl as it rose from the wrinkled shirt he was pulling over his head.

"Where the hell have you been?" he asked angrily.

A tiny smile curved her lips. A more loverlike greeting might have overset her; his forthright, disagreeable attitude calmed the jittery consciousness of him that had stalked her all morning. Closing the door behind her, she said, "I went to the necessary."

He jumped up from the side of the bed to loom over her. "Of all the—what do you think the pot is for? Don't you have sense enough to stay put? We came here to keep from being seen!"

"I know that." Come what may, she had no intention of explaining her unwillingness to squat over the commode while they remained in the same room. "No one outside the building saw me. It was quite private."

"And is the hall private? Or the lobby? Or wherever else you've gone waltzing to today?"

"Honestly, Mr. Logan, I went only to the necessary. I'm sorry if I alarmed you. There wasn't any way to tell how long you would sleep. And I truly regret not listening to you when you told me what the Hounds are like. It's all my fault they found out who you are, and, well, obviously you just are not the man to deal with them. So if you think we should get away from them, I'll follow your instructions from now on. Anything you say."

It was her second apology to him in two days, and the handsomest she'd ever offered anyone; she felt rather proud of it. Remembering the chamber pot, she added, "Anything within reason."

Ignoring the deadly insult Libby had just delivered with limpid and innocent eyes—*not the man to deal with them*; was that her opinion of him?—Caleb expelled a hard sigh. "Don't you know what I thought when I woke up and you were gone?"

Slowly, she shook her head. Caleb stared at her in

frustration. Cold fear had gripped him when he arose to the realization that Libby had disappeared. His first anxiety was that she'd been so guilt-stricken over what had happened between them that she'd run off to confess to her piano player. Succeeding it was the gruesome possibility that Smitty had located them and kidnapped her from the bed without rousing him.

The miniscule chance that either could be true raised him to a towering rage just reaching its height when Libby coolly walked through the door.

His wrath fanned higher as he remembered that she'd blithely roamed the hotel and environs. "God knows," he said acidly, "you're more trouble than any female I've ever met before. But you were . . . good to me last night, and I can't just shrug you off. I'm going to protect you, Libby—whether you like it or not."

"I want to tell you to go to the devil." She faced him squarely. He wished he could trust the quiet, cultured voice and frank manner to be the real Libby, even if she did say the most shocking things for a female. "But I can't. If you're willing to take me out of San Francisco, then I'll go. You must understand, though, that last night must be forgotten. It will never happen again. If that's the kind of return you expect from your investment, then you're going to be cheated."

The defiant chin trembled. He wanted to put his arms around her until the trembling stopped. The force of his desire to comfort her, and seduce her, jolted him. It wasn't a sentiment a casual lover had ever inspired in him before.

Caleb considered himself fairly abstemious. That didn't mean he'd reached the age of twenty-nine untried. Women in port towns supplied a service he'd used between seafarings in exchange for a set price, and the occasional Indian or Mexican girl he visited nowadays always seemed grateful to be treated gently and rewarded with a trinket.

Sometimes the payment would be more substantial if he saw the girl's family in need. A vision of Libby's

reaction if he were to offer her a side of beef under-
mined his fury and tickled his sense of humor. Somehow, Libby was different from those other bed partners.
Certainly he'd never had the least bit of trouble dis-
missing any of them from his mind. A premonition that
Libby would be less easily forgotten shook him.

"Tell me something," he said abruptly. "Why didn't
you let me please you last night? I swear I'm not some
damned Lothario convinced no woman can resist me,
but I think—I'm sure—you felt something in that bed
with me."

In fact, she'd been a plush and intoxicating armful,
sweetly willing. Up to a point. And even then . . .
Maybe loyalty to her lover, the piano player, had gotten
in her way. In the way of both of them.

She clasped her hands and looked straight ahead,
right through him. "I'll accompany you to your ranch.
Naturally, I understand you merit some recompense for
your . . . protection. Therefore, I'll pretend to be
your—your betrothed, if that will make your sister
happy."

Caleb was flooded with satisfaction. "Wife," he said
softly. "I want you to act like a wife."

The fascinating green of her eyes was almost frightened, but her chin retained its determined angle. "A
betrothal should be enough to convince Miss Logan
you're in good hands."

Hands. Her willing, giving hands. Under the circumstances, it was a remarkably lewd thing to have said,
but her expression didn't reflect any knowledge of rib-
aldry. She simply stared at him, half anxious and half
defiant.

"There would be—compensations—for both of us if
you agreed to behave as my wife," he said, careful not
to spell out the monetary compensations in case she
decided to fly back into her impersonation of royalty
again. "I still owe you a hefty share of pleasure, remember?"

Her eyes widened and darkened, and her small, full

mouth opened to let her pink tongue lick it in quick, nervous flicks. Caleb found himself moving closer, his arms reaching for her as she swayed slightly toward him.

She gasped and turned away sharply. "I'm not going to discuss it, Mr. Logan. Ever. And if you persist, I'll walk out that door, come what may."

She would, too, he thought. Women.

The idiocy of seeking an outdoor facility when a perfectly good chamber pot sat not five feet from the bed must be some feminine quirk. Even Julia had exalted notions of the importance of privacy; she'd tried to talk him into planning a covered walkway from the new house they were building to the privy. He wondered briefly if that sort of genteel imbecility would appeal to Libby.

Caleb brooded over the revelation that Libby had accomplished one thing for him—well, two, counting her service last night. Not only had she brought him an intensity of sexual release startlingly out of proportion to the act they'd performed, but she'd pierced the shell of preoccupation that allowed him to think of almost nothing but losing his sister. He ought to be grateful, he thought, because thinking about Julia hurt.

He'd be able to see his sister tonight. Probably. Unless some accident delayed the riverboat, or the Hounds kept him and Libby from boarding at all.

A vague restlessness seized him. He abandoned the attempt to set things right with Libby. "Fine, an engagement it is. Now I'm ready for some food," he said.

Relieved that the frown had faded from his face, Libby replied warily, "Breakfast sounds wonderful."

"Don't go out while I'm gone. And for God's sake, don't open the door unless you're sure it's me."

Pulling his hat low over his distinctive nose, he slipped out.

When he returned, he called softly before Libby eased the door open. Turning swiftly, he grabbed a tray from someone still in the hall and backed into the room with his tall body guarding her from inquisitive eyes. Realizing his intention, she swayed behind the door during his maneuver. Then she swept the door closed.

"Take these, will you?" he grunted, moving his elbow slightly to indicate the newspapers folded under one arm.

He'd bought them to provide a neutral method of passing the time. Not all women, or men for that matter, could read. Despite his questions about her background, Caleb didn't doubt that Libby, with the cultured accent she could adopt at will and her fierce insistence on being treated like a reasoning being, had picked up an education somewhere in her checkered past.

"Newspapers?" she breathed, obeying with an eagerness that made him smile. "Recent ones?"

"All within the week," he vouched. "Are you going to read or eat?"

"Can't I do both?" she asked without looking up. "Oh—I beg your pardon. Did you want one? The *Pioneer*? The *Bulletin*?"

"No, no. I'm not stupid enough to get in the way of barefaced greed."

She laughed and accepted a plate of eggs and biscuits, both liberally moistened with gravy.

Disposing of his own breakfast, Caleb watched her as she balanced the plate on her lap and craned over the tiny lettering. Sometime between last night and this morning she'd lost another couple of years. The familiar green dress hung limply, no longer swelling into the fashionable bell shape. Libby still had breasts and hips, but with her hair cobbled into a schoolgirl tail and ink from the messy newsprint on her cheek, she could have passed for a well-developed seventeen.

Uneasiness prompted him to ask, "How old are you, anyway?"

Libby turned a page. "Four-and-twenty. How old are you?"

"Thirty next October."

"Mmm."

Obviously there was no competing with the news-papers, so Caleb paced until the restlessness impelled him to stronger measures. "I'm going out."

Her head came up. "You said it wasn't safe." She sounded surprised.

"It's not," he said hurriedly. The last thing they needed was for her to decide to take another little con-stitutional. It occurred to him she probably thought him too poor-spirited to poke his nose out the door in case a Hound lurked there. Jaw tightening, he added, "There are a couple of things I have to take care of before we go. For one, I presume you have clothes. They'll have to be fetched."

A slow, painful flush reached the roots of her hair. "All my trunks are at that place."

"Where you were singing?" At her nod, he took a breath and went on, "Are you going to tell me what happened after I dropped you off yesterday?"

"If I must."

She got up to return her empty plate and fork to the tray. A mirror hung over the washstand. At the sight of her face, she dipped a thumb into the much-used water to scrub the ink from her cheek.

"Libby."

When he said her name like that, she suffered from an unaccountable yearning to burst into tears. Instead, she fastened her gaze on the floor and haltingly told him about the theft of her savings and the saloon own-er's attack.

He swore, with soft, short, ugly words she'd never heard before. Caleb's anger felt like a balm to her hurt pride. Would he swear with such sincerity if he truly regarded her as a doxy?

"You—you believe me?"

"I believe you never looked twice at that scum who tried to—God, I should never have let you out of my sight. You're a walking temptation." Before she could protest, he added, "How much money did you lose?"

He successfully diverted her. "It's hard to say exactly. Not all of it was American. About three hundred fifty dollars. Half of it belonged to him—Aloysius Malloy. And I'm only assuming he stole it. Someone else could have broken in easily enough . . .''

She was going to say, ''But I doubt it.'' Caleb didn't give her the chance.

''Do me a favor, will you? Don't defend your—friend—to me. There's not much I can do to get your nest egg back, but I'll see if I can retrieve your gear. If I'm not here in, say, an hour, find the manager and ask him to get you down to Pacific Wharf by two.''

''What point would there be in leaving San Francisco without you?'' she asked, and stopped, shocked at her own words. Caleb Logan could not be important to her. She fumbled for logic. ''I don't have anyplace to go.''

''For once, just once, could you keep from arguing? The ship's captain is Floyd Zachary. Use my name. He'll give you passage to Newtown. Anybody there'll be able to tell you where I stable my horses, and you won't have trouble picking up a guide out to the ranch. My foreman's Juan Arrile. He's trustworthy. Tell Julia—''

He rubbed the back of his neck, a gesture she'd seen him use before. ''Jesus. You'll have to use your own judgment. I don't know what it would be best for you to say.''

''I doubt there is a best when one is explaining to a sister why her brother isn't ever coming home,'' Libby said tartly. ''Although why the decent men in this town haven't gotten together to rid themselves of Smitty and his ilk . . .''

Caleb had in fact been approached about joining just such a committee of vigilance. He'd turned the group down as being no bread and butter of his, but he had no intention of telling Libby about it. The existence of the band was a desperate secret, and she was too apt to reveal what she knew no matter what the situation. Part of her incongruously high-flown notions of honor.

The lady's proud indifference could get all the brave men in San Francisco killed.

"Never you mind. I don't intend to run any risks in the street. Even if the Hounds are on the watch for me, I'll be one of hundreds out on a Monday morning."

Libby's large eyes widened. For some reason, Caleb's skin seemed to be—not precious, but at least worth saving to her, and didn't he know how memorable his looks were? Unsure how to tell him without embarrassing herself by sounding as if she were impressed with him, she said, "But you won't just fit in. You're so tall and—and, Mr. Logan, it's not easy to overlook you."

In fact, today Caleb's dark eyes snapped with life. Despite the bruise on his forehead and the raw scab lying across one cheekbone, his skin flushed with healthy color. He radiated sinewy toughness. Libby's spirits sank another notch. Perhaps her scorn had prodded him into fulfilling the promise of his reckless eyes. Now he wanted to dash off to confront dangers that had already nearly destroyed him. She couldn't explain the inconsistency of her attitude; she only knew that when he talked about running away from the Hounds, disdain filled her, only to be swamped by terror at the thought of him outside on the street, hazarding peril.

Libby wondered what, besides the Hounds, he was willing to dare. So far he hadn't insisted that she accept a complete physical relationship, but . . . What if he wanted her again? Men's carnal appetites were insatiable, weren't they? Married women always talked as if their husbands' demands never ended. For the first time in her life, Libby didn't trust herself. Caleb's new tough attitude didn't at all detract from the attraction that had nibbled away at her defenses from the moment she'd seen him at the bottom of the brothel stairs. No—from the instant he'd jumped onto the stage, and held her eyes with his, and grinned as if he could read in them the most secret wish of her heart . . .

She didn't have to worry about him importuning her

this minute. Set as he was on going out, he was already fiddling with the doorknob. Besides, people didn't just toss decorum to the winds and throw each other into bed to indulge their lusts during the day. Surely. Otherwise, the business of living would never get done.

"Trust me," he said. "I won't go looking for trouble. Latch the door behind me."

Libby tried out the Americanism that she'd heard but never used before. "Okay."

He smiled at her suddenly, a warm, conspiratorial smile that alarmed her even more. "That's my girl," he said, and left.

Libby returned to the newspapers, disgruntled and on edge.

His girl? He seemed very casual about claiming possession. *His* girl? Staring unseeingly at an advertisement for patent medicines, she considered what it would be like to be Caleb's girl. Able to touch him whenever, wherever she wanted. Not feeling obliged to turn away when he wanted to touch her back. To be like Ruth in the Bible . . . "Whither thou goest . . ." To be yoked in tandem with a man in love with California.

Never to go home.

Just as well, she thought with a grain of bitterness, that he probably had meant nothing at all. His girl, indeed.

Determinedly, she applied herself to the *Bulletin*. The luxury of fresh news wasn't one that often came her way.

So absorbed was she that she didn't notice Caleb's return until he pounded on the panels and shouted her name. The trailing hem of her dress, hanging longer than usual without internal support, tripped her as she hurried to unbolt the lock. Caleb's yell descended to a bellow. "What's going on in there? Are you all right?"

"Be quiet," she screamed. "Do you want everyone in the city to hear you?"

Instant silence prevailed. Then, softly, but with a note

of irritation that carried plainly through the door, he said, "Let me in, woman."

She stepped back quickly as he marched in, carrying a trunk over each shoulder. Their round-topped shabbiness was familiar and beloved.

"My things! You've got my things! Thank you. Oh, I'm so glad."

Her sparkling relief affected him so much that he couldn't scold her for scaring him half to death—again. He grunted noncommittally as she flew from one to the other, checking the contents. "Nothing seems to be missing. How did you get them back?"

"All it took was a short talk with the owner. Seems he had some sort of accident, so he didn't say much. We came to a mutual understanding."

His tone sounded so mild that Libby frowned at him suspiciously. "What kind of understanding?"

He inspected a graze that looked newer than the others splitting the skin of his knuckles. "We agreed that if he ever lifted a hand to you again, or mentioned your name, or so much as thought about you, I'd come back and . . . have another talk with him."

She knew it. She knew he'd go looking for trouble. At least he'd been able to deal with the variety he'd sought this time. "Caleb Logan, that's very gallant, and of course I'm grateful, but—you're the one who insisted we avoid attention. Then you go out of your way to attract it."

Caleb shrugged. "The worst has already happened. Short of open warfare, the Hounds can't be broken. So the best we can do is hightail it out of here. They don't operate outside the city, so we should be safe once we're at my spread, the Manzanita."

In spite of his own explanation, he couldn't quite figure why it had seemed so important to get away from Libby this morning.

Maybe the restlessness that had driven him outside was connected to his discomfort at how young and innocent she appeared in her mussed gown. Guilt could play no part in his motives, he told himself firmly; why should it? They hadn't even done anything last night. Not much of anything, anyway. But he knew without figuring out why that he'd feel happier in Libby's presence once she found an outfit in one of her trunks that would make her look like the experienced woman he'd become used to.

"Now," he said brusquely, "you've got about an hour to change before the carriage I hired comes to the back entrance."

Shoving newspapers out of his way, he sprawled out on the coverlet and arranged his long legs for the most comfort. Ostentatiously, he closed his eyes.

Libby considered ordering him from the room and caught sight of her disheveled self in the mirror. Disgust at her hypocrisy almost choked her. She'd lost the right to insist on propriety when she'd let herself be a party to his passion.

Counting the minutes, Libby assembled the items she wanted. Facing the wall, which at least gave her the illusion of privacy, she unbuttoned her bodice to wash quickly, upset that she hadn't taken advantage of Caleb's earlier absence for a spit bath. Pulling her arms from the sleeves but still keeping the tattered gown around her, she laced herself into her second-best— now her best—corset and pulled on clean petticoats. As quickly as she could, she scrambled out of the old dress and into one of sturdy black serge. Then she exchanged her pantalets for a fresh pair, using her skirts for concealment. She turned to Caleb.

Whether or not he'd kept his eyes closed, the curve of his mouth revealed that he hadn't gone to sleep. Aware of what a waste of time it would be to agonize over how much he'd seen—after all, it was a trifle late to reestablish the proper distance between them, although she would have dearly loved to do so—she said, "If you wouldn't mind, could you please ask the kitchen to heat a flatiron for me?"

He sighed noisily, unwilling to budge. The afternoon

promised to be full of activity. Even an uneventful journey north would require hard, dirty, physical labor, and he would just as soon rest up for it. "You don't need to iron anything, do you? You look good to me."

Libby glanced down at herself. An expert packer out of necessity, she knew her appearance was as free of wrinkles as could be expected. Serge stood up fairly well to being folded. Nonetheless, if the possibility of presenting a tidier front to the world existed, she intended to take it. Nor did she relish the idea of showing herself in public with shapeless shirts, like any country woman. *No* woman, no matter what her circumstances, would have put on any of her bonnets in the condition they were in. Fashion was important. More than ever after her recent escapades, she wanted the armor of the right clothes, properly worn.

She owned a single crinoline, it needed a pressing, and it was going to get one.

"A flatiron, please, Mr. Logan."

Cursing under his breath, Caleb went out. He returned long before the implement could have been heated.

"If a simple flatiron is too much to ask—"

He cut in, "Give me what you want ironed. They'll take care of it down in the kitchen for you."

His curt kindliness warmed her. Hoping that the activity would make her quick blush seem natural, she stooped to retrieve the crinoline from under the bed, where she'd kicked it that morning. "Will there be time?"

"They swore they'd hurry. And they won't get paid if they don't. We're going to make that steamer if I have to tow you naked to the wharf."

Blush deepening, she passed him the crushed bonnet and mangled undergarment. Seconds ticked by slowly after he'd gone, or would have if she'd still owned a watch. The trinket had been important to her. Papa had given it to Maman as a birthing gift, his token to her for presenting him with a healthy daughter. Libby had

WILD CARD BRIDE   103

cherished it because it reminded her of the love that had sustained them all, even after the moneyed, care-free days were over and done with.

Tiredly, she scolded herself for repining when she'd already regained more of her possessions than she'd anticipated ever seeing again. Then she sought out her brush and began ordering her hair. Normally, that was a chore she'd perform before buttoning her dress, to avoid the necessity of lifting her arms over her head in the tight-fitting styles she'd brought from England. But dressing with dispatch had been more urgent today.

This time her senses remained astretch for his knock, and she let him in immediately. ''Three minutes,'' he told her, thrusting her property into her hands.

Within two, she was garbed and ready, the crinoline sandwiched between her petticoats to protect the un-weathered skin of her legs as well as the underside of her gown from the abrasive horsehair. Tying now neatly pressed satin ribbons under her chin, she lowered the bonnet's attached veil to its full length, hiding her face from any but the closest scrutiny. Black gloves completed her ensemble.

Treading in Caleb's wake, she nodded at the sight of the narrow-seated carriage he'd chosen, completely closed except in the front. The varnished sides curved to hide both of them as they seated themselves side by side.

Caleb snapped the reins and clucked. The carriage moved forward. Driving briskly—but not too briskly because he didn't want to advertise that they were in a hurry—he allowed himself to be distracted by her dole-ful appearance.

The traveling dress was simple and dark, and on the whole Caleb approved. They had a long, muddy way to go. But the black net seemed excessive; he liked looking at her. ''Do you have to wear that thing over your face?''

The veil made her mysterious. ''Isn't black becoming to a grass widow?''

"Don't talk about yourself like that."

He sounded stern. Libby's resolute breath pushed out, then drew back the gauzy material hanging down to the base of her throat. "Have no fear, Mr. Logan. I'll try to be a perfect little lady for you."

Her own sarcasm embarrassed her, it revealed the hurt she felt so clearly. Rapidly, she continued, "Although 'little' isn't the most apt description, is it?" With a gesture, she indicated her length of limb.

Caleb steered around a huddle of Chinese men, so numerous that they blocked the street despite their efforts to fold themselves out of the way of iron-shod hooves and tall carriage wheels. "That's ridiculous. You're just the right size."

Before she had time to absorb the compliment, he went on with more energy, "Those poor beggars. Just off the boat, from the look of them. I wonder how many will survive a year in the promised land."

Craning her neck for a last glimpse of the turret-shaped hats, Libby asked, "Is California unsalubrious for Chinese people?"

He laughed harshly. "You could say that. Haven't you heard? Chinese baiting—and sometimes killing—is a sport around here. Even Indians will kill a Chinese for no more than the hell of it."

She thought of Jacob Klein. Only Indians and Chinese, he'd said, counted for less than a Hebrew. "That—" She swallowed. "That really is hellish."

Light conversation seemed out of place after that, and Caleb grew increasingly morose. Libby's nose, even swathed as it was, caught the strengthening scent of salt and seaweed and rubbish. At last Caleb remarked, "Pacific Wharf. No turning back now."

The soft comment might not have been meant for her, but it sent a queasy, sinking sensation through her middle.

She reflected how lucky it was that the queasiness wasn't in response to her first sight of the *Red Jacket*. Travel by water always exhilarated her. The trim little stern-wheeler, deck piled high with boxes and crates, didn't trouble her midday meal in the least.

"You're not afraid to travel by steam, are you?" said Caleb, helping her onto the deck.

Boiler accidents were so common that they went unreported unless an explosion resulted in spectacular loss of life. "Thank you for asking," Libby answered politely. "What would you do if I said yes?"

"Tie you to the railing, I guess."

He spoke absentmindedly, his eyes on the work the sailors were doing, but for a moment Libby's lungs refused to draw in breath. Caleb was capable of doing precisely that.

"Anyhow, you don't have to worry about the engine. I always take a look in the boiler room before we set off. And the *Jacket*'s a dependable little thing."

The captain stopped swearing at deckhands straining to secure the cargo long enough to greet Caleb respectfully by name and stare curiously at Libby's shrouded form. When Caleb failed to introduce her, he raked his eyes more particularly over her figure.

"Lounge right that way, ma'am. Private for you and the lady, Mr. Logan. You're our only passengers this trip."

The words were inoffensive, but the man's manner was not; his faint grin showed what function he thought Libby filled in Caleb's life, and she longed to slap it from his face.

Instead, mindful that she owed it to Caleb to be as inconspicuous as possible, she stayed mute and, she hoped, dignified as she stepped carefully against the slight roll of the deck toward the cabin. Too late now for second thoughts. She allowed herself one wistful backward glance at the tall-masted ships clustered at the southeast end of the harbor.

Selecting a bench bolted to the wall, she watched Caleb through the open door. He disappeared down a hole in the deck, presumably to inspect the mechanical innards of the ship, and then reemerged and moved along the men, exchanging greetings and quite openly checking their work. No one seemed to object. The level of shouting rose. A shudder ran through the boat. The porthole behind her revealed the great wheel beginning to turn. They eased away from the wharf and out onto the bay.

Dreamily, Libby thought of nothing but the green water streaming off the wheel until Caleb put his head through the door to demand, "Are you all right? Do you need anything?"

"A bucket, do you mean?" she asked with more precision than delicacy. "No, I don't suffer that way. I never get seasick."

"Well, if you're not—" He glowered suddenly. "Could you unwrap yourself so I can see you? I'd rather not talk to a faceless head."

A tart note crept into Libby's reply. "It sounds perfectly hideous. However, I assumed you'd like me to be as anonymous as possible while we're traveling together."

"Not that anonymous. Anyway, the presence of a lady with me raises questions whether you show your face or not."

"Indeed? The captain doesn't seem to suffer from doubts about the meaning of my presence."

Surprisingly, Caleb reddened. "That needn't bother you. He won't look at you that way again."

Fiercely, Libby told herself not to take his championing of her seriously. His concern was probably for his own reputation, not hers. Still, she hadn't expected him to stand up for her at all, especially since the captain's opinion of her and Caleb was what Caleb himself believed of her and Malloy. "A captain on his own ship? Is he apt to mend his manners?"

"He'd better," said Caleb grimly. "I own an interest in the steamship company."

Libby couldn't repress a smile as she pushed the veil up and touched her hair to make sure it had stayed tidy inside her bonnet. A tiny, treacherous glow began to spread through her. Perhaps Caleb cared, just a little. It shouldn't affect her. It did.

"Come out on the deck," Caleb ordered. "You'll never see a finer afternoon on the bay."

She stepped into an invigorating breeze that plucked at her skirts and made everything smell deliciously clean. To her left, gossamer fog wreathed the open jaws of the Golden Gate, but the rest of the bay danced under a sun that picked out shining whitecaps twinkling like diamonds on seagreen silk. Libby pulled off her gloves and, shading her eyes with one hand, peered back at San Francisco. Even its jumble of mud-colored buildings was burnished to a glow by the cleansing sunlight.

Then they slid by a solid dark bulk that hid the familiar landmarks from sight.

"Angel Island." Caleb nodded at the forested hilltop bursting up from beneath the water. He tilted his chin forward, indicating a marsh alive with green, shifting reeds. "San Pablo Bay. We'll go through there and then enter an estuary."

Usually, she preferred nature to be nicely landscaped. But Caleb's enthusiasm infected her. The farther they steamed from the city, the higher her spirits flew. She stared around in fascination. Gulls swooped and egrets stalked away from the clanking paddle wheel on spindly, comical legs. The going here seemed smoother. Under her feet, the deck diminished its roll as the steamer plowed out of the grip of the Pacific's swells.

"It's not really level at all, is it?" she asked, rapt. "It looks so still, until you see how everything sways or bends. Like watching God breathe." She glanced over to see Caleb's face kindle at her eagerness, and added inadequately, "So eerie and beautiful."

"Not everyone sees the beauty."

"How could anyone miss it?" She held out her arms, ready to embrace the world. "The sun feels so good and the water's like silk and I didn't know there were so many shades of green! A day like this is such a gift. How can anybody remotely alive fail to appreciate it?''

His expression changed, and Libby cursed her heedless tongue. ''Mr. Logan, I'm so—truly, I didn't mean to remind you.''

He turned on his heel, but didn't walk away. Instead, he said slowly, ''I don't think about Julia every minute, especially since—never mind. But it's as if a knife's sticking in my ribs, and every once in a while I look down and remember the damned thing's still there. Why I let her talk me into leaving the ranch when she—''

He broke off. Libby exclaimed, ''But what—'' She stopped as the supreme tactlessness of the question hit her. If Caleb had jaunted off in search of amusement while his sister lay near death, it was simply none of Libby's business.

''What made me leave at all? You're right; I shouldn't have.'' Caleb snorted at her widening eyes. ''Don't look so surprised. What you're thinking is easier to follow than the pole star. For example, right now your eyes are big as saucers, your forehead's all puckered up, and your mouth is pursed into a kind of bow.''

''Please!'' she protested. ''You make me sound like a—a monkey.''

''Only if it's a beautiful monkey.'' As always, the compliment was delivered so offhandedly that Libby couldn't take it for anything but an empty demonstration of Caleb's intermittent charm. He pointed to the crates piled behind them. ''I came because of the wallpaper.''

''Wallpaper?''

''And china and chandeliers. We've even got a dining room suite and bedroom furniture, a piano and a new kitchen stove in those boxes. Julia ordered all of it from back East for our new house. She had a fit—that is, became agitated,'' he corrected himself, ''when I suggested sending Juan to nursemaid the stuff to the ranch. The doctor warned us specially about letting her get excited, so I gave in. She's not usually mifty. In fact, she's a hardheaded businesswoman in her own right.''

It was the first indication he'd given that Julia might be human after all, and Libby bit back a smile. "Ladies do tend to become—agitated—when their household goods are at stake.''

"I suppose,'' said Caleb, without conviction. "She's been looking forward to all that decorating nonsense so much, I wanted her to have a chance to unpack the boxes, at least. She'll like that. She'll like—'' He hesitated.

He wanted to say that Julia would like Libby. Caleb was sure his sister would take to his golden-haired "betrothed'' as long as Libby stayed the way she was now— recognizably ladylike. It bothered him that he didn't know whether the flashy tart she'd produced for Smitty came from a past she might revert to at inconvenient moments. Julia wouldn't like that at all.

No, he thought, he was wrong. She'd be highly amused, but not at the idea her brother had brought that kind of woman home with him. And Caleb found that he wanted to spare Libby both Julia's amusement and her scorn.

Sensing his mental withdrawal, Libby turned away her too-expressive face and saw firmer ground rising on the outskirts of the marsh, along with a crevice in the bank flooded by salt water. The *Red Jacket*, which had appeared so small and light out on the bay between the immensities of sea and sky, began a ponderous turn into the estuary.

"Slower going from now on,'' Caleb said. "The Petaluma's navigable, but only barely. It's going to be a long afternoon. I should have brought you something to read.''

"Thank you, I have my Bible,'' Libby answered promptly, feeling a slight twinge of guilt at using Holy Writ to buff up her good name. "This isn't my first voyage, you know. My family came over from England, in '48. I adore sailing, but it does sometimes leave hours to fill. What will you do?'' she asked with a touch of malice. He deserved to be paid back for his unwanted perceptiveness.

"I'll have more than enough to do, never fear." His black brows were raised. "What sorts of things do you read besides newspapers and your Bible?"

"Whatever I'm fortunate enough to find at hand. We left most of our library with my uncle in England, and I sold the few books we carried with us when my parents died."

After a skeptical moment, Caleb asked, "What brought your family over? Desire to go adventuring?"

"Desire to go on eating," Libby contradicted. She lifted her face to the sun. For once she wouldn't worry about freckles or sunburn. So early in the spring, surely the rays couldn't be too destructive. "My father had a great enthusiasm for speculating, especially if the business was ruled by a complete lack of practicality. If a theory was new and had no chance of success or useful application whatsoever, he invested in it."

"Any number of inventions sound unlikely at first."

"Delivering mail by hot-air balloon. A bridge across the English Channel. Perpetual motion. Poor Papa." She shook her head, half smiling. "His final inspiration was to take what was left of his inheritance after—after my mother ran through some funds he'd rather counted on—and buy land in North America. He'd heard about your John Sutter, you see, and the community on the Sacramento. And he'd read about Aaron Burr's attempt to carve an empire out of Mexico. Papa believed he could create a sort of fiefdom in western Canada."

"Burr failed pretty spectacularly," Caleb pointed out. "And even Colonel Sutter has his ups and downs."

"More ups than Papa ever had, I imagine," she said, and laughed suddenly. "I loved it, you know. The excitement of new investments, the breathless waiting to see if this scheme or that would bring him the success he longed for. None of them ever did, of course. He was quite mad, I think, and very lovable."

The water curved away ahead; their paddle wheel pushed them steadily along what was now no more than a saltwater creek. Caleb leaned sideways over the low rail. Libby realized he was estimating the angle of their approach as the *Red Jacket* neared a bend.

His glance flicked continually from the prow to the point where the little river began to snake over the floor of a shallow valley. She thought he'd forgotten her, but he said gruffly, "I've known men like that. Fine men. You can't judge people just by their knack for business."

"Papa did. He hated being a failure. The next venture was always going to repair our fortunes, but he never picked the right one, poor darling. Guessing wrong finally killed him. My mother, too."

Crewmen shouted at each other and stared tensely ahead. Caleb abandoned his sentry post to walk back to Libby. "What happened?" he asked.

Libby searched for words. "We weren't—weren't very well equipped for living in the wilderness. The mansion, the native servants, and the abundant crops that Papa envisioned never materialized. We barely got by. Then Papa met an inventor. The man said his machine would make impure water clean."

She curved her shoulders despite the bright sunshine. Caleb watched her, a frown gathering on his brow.

"Papa always had the strength of his convictions. I tried to tell him and Maman that the man was a crackpot, but they wanted so badly to believe they'd found a way to make a fortune and go home . . . Papa bought the rights to the invention and sent me off to a wedding. To get me out of the way, I think, so he could test it in peace. You know how people gather from miles around for weddings and funerals on the frontier. I stayed ten days. When I got back, my parents were both dead. Typhus."

Caleb choked back the remarks he wanted to make about an idiot who'd allow his wife to taste suspect water. After all, he couldn't tell Libby her father deserved to die. He thought over her story.

By God, he believed her. She had come down in the world.

"What then?"

"Then I made up my mind to go home. There wasn't any money left after I sold the land. We owed everybody, including the man who'd invented the water machine. The only method of earning my way back to England I was willing to consider—"

His narrow glance brought a flash from her green eyes. "I've been offered marriage by men who meant it," she said pointedly.

He grinned.

Libby pulled her gloves through her hands. Farmers looking for a wife with the same emotion they would use to choose a brood mare, men she didn't know and who didn't know her. "But to stay in Canada or the States—no. So I sang. I lived from what I made and saved every penny, hoping to find a ship in port once I reached San Francisco." She waved at their small craft. "This isn't exactly what I had in mind. And it's taking me in the wrong direction."

His attention once more locked on the fast-approaching bend, he asked, "Thought you said you don't gamble."

"I don't." The accusation amazed her.

"Lady, you gamble for higher stakes than any female I ever met before." He spoke before she could deny it again. "Who's waiting for you in England?"

"Family," she said simply. "I thought I told you. I have an uncle in orders. He and my aunt will take me in. There's always room at the rectory. And I miss the life. Cultivated fields, hedgerows buzzing with bees, clotted cream . . ."

His laugh cut off as the *Red Jacket*, with a groan and a lurch, scraped bottom and came to a full stop with its snub nose immersed in foaming brown mud.

"There, see, the captain's found some entertainment

for me already," he shouted over the curses of the crew. The sailors were grabbing poles and leaping into the shallows.

Libby's mouth fell open as Caleb knelt on one knee and tucked a pants leg neatly into one high boot.

"You did say this river—"

"Creek, estuary—slough, dear heart," he reproved, switching to his other leg.

"You said this slough is navigable, didn't you?" she demanded firmly, although her heart pounded at the unexpectedness of the endearment.

"I must have said 'barely navigable.' " He, too, wrenched a pole from its rack and swung his long legs over the rail.

Full voice, she shrieked, "Wait!"

The volume halted him half over the side. Startled faces lifted toward them from the water. Caleb clung to keep from falling headlong, and Libby asked, "What do you want me to do? Shall I get off the boat to lighten the load?"

"For God's sake, never scream like that again unless there's a reason for it!" he roared. Touched and exasperated by her offer, he added, "You don't have to trudge around in the muck with the rest of us. Be sensible, woman. We'd need a rope and pulley to hoist you back on board once those petticoats got wet. Besides, your few pounds aren't going to make a difference one way or the other. Sit tight and try not to trip anybody doing his work."

Unjust as she felt it was to stay aboard adding to the burden the men were laboring to shift, she had to admit the good sense of his commands. She saw him drop lithely into the creek. Cleaving through the calf-high water to the soggy bank, he joined the crewmen fitting poles under the prow. To Libby's amazement the combined leverage eased the stern-wheeler afloat fairly quickly.

As the afternoon wore on, she came to appreciate that the swift, competent maneuver was the result of frequent practice. The boat ran ashore again and again as the stream narrowed and twisted in its vaguely northward path. Finally, she pulled a box to a convenient section of the deck and sank down onto it, folding her arms on the rail to provide a cushion for her cheek. The vessel had run aground a fifth—or sixth, or seventh—time.

Caleb called, "Hey, there, lazybones, catch!"

Libby raised her head just in time to receive his jacket, followed by his fine-weaved shirt. Bay rum had been completely overwhelmed by the smell of two days' exertions. Smoothing the stained garments, she wrinkled her nose at the tang of sweat. But instead of dropping them to the deck, she folded the shirt and jacket carefully and laid them on her lap. Her fingers moved over the material in small circles. Pretending to be Caleb's affianced wife while keeping him from making her his mistress would call for an ingenuity she wasn't sure she possessed. Horrible to be glad the masquerade would only have to be endured as long as the rest of Julia's life . . .

A few of the crewmen shucked off their shirts in imitation of Caleb. Glad to abandon her unpleasant flow of ideas, Libby reflected that she'd never seen such a parade of bare male torsos before. Several handsome sets of muscles rippled. Caleb's were the nicest, she decided objectively, although he looked far too thin in comparison to the others.

It hadn't dawned on her how really dark his face and hands were until she saw the paler skin of his chest and back. Trim muscles rolled beneath the faded tan; had he been a uniform glossy brown all over during his seagoing days?

You're tipsy, Elizabeth, she thought. Tipsy on crystal air and yellow sunshine and lack of sleep.

Her thoughts drifted. How odd Americans were. Here stood Caleb Logan, shareholder in the steamship line, half naked and working hard as any navvy at the dirtiest job of the voyage. Her imagination boggled at the picture of an English gentleman under similar circumstances.

Caleb, on the other hand, seemed to be grunting and striving simply for the sake of pitting his strength against the massive, stubborn weight of the boat. His joy in physical labor gave her a peculiar sort of gladness that made her lips quiver up in a smile.

At the same time, her eyes clouded thoughtfully. How she wished he'd shown more of a sense of honor when faced with the Hounds. Then she recollected where she'd been and what she'd been doing the first time Caleb had seen her and grimaced at herself. Giving public concerts for money stretched the boundaries of ladylike behavior; by the most lax standard, singing in a saloon snapped them.

Sighing, Libby also noticed, even at this distance, that she could count his ribs. The unnatural thinness challenged her instincts as a cook. He needed a solid diet of bread and beefsteak, thick stews and egg custards to fill him out to his proper proportions. Who had taken charge of the kitchen on that ranch of his since his sister had fallen ill?

With a creak, the *Red Jacket* responded to the poles and slid back into deeper water. This time, the crew let out a cheer rich with obscenities and vaulted on board with an air of triumph.

"Is there cause for celebration?" Libby asked as Caleb pulled on his shirt.

"That was Cloudy Bend, last shoal in the creek till Newtown," he told her. "No more unscheduled stops."

"How much farther is it to your home?"

"A mile by river, then ten overland. My place is actually closer to the town of Petaluma, but Newtown's the end of the line. I haven't been able to convince the other directors to chance the *Red Jacket* all the way to my doorstep."

"Why not?" she asked. The trip so far hadn't inspired her with a particularly good opinion of the slough's ability to support water traffic. The part they'd just traversed had been crammed with obstacles to any-thing larger than a canoe.

"Oh, the creek gets narrow after Newtown," he said blithely, slinging his coat over his shoulder. He sniffed. "My clothes are getting pretty ripe. I shouldn't have thrown them at you like that."

"It didn't offend me. There are worse smells than honest sweat."

"Kind of you to say so. Have you started to think about your dinner?"

"Not yet, but I shall soon, I suppose. What time is it?"

He squinted at the sun. "Maybe four, four-thirty. A couple of hours till dusk. We should dock in about fif-teen minutes. If you want to refresh yourself, there's a, um, facility in the lounge."

Libby had seen the facility, a chamber pot big enough to be called a thunder mug, located modestly behind an Indian blanket strung on a rope across one corner of the cabin. It must be reserved for the use of the passengers, she thought. On several occasions, she'd had to avert her eyes when one of the crew relieved himself directly into the creek.

"Thank you," she said meekly.

After taking advantage of the opportunity provided by the facility, now that Caleb had reminded her of it, she returned to her box and sat, studying the whale-backed hills crowding in on the waterway. The tall grass that softened the hills' seamed surfaces shaded from green to amber to dun. Clusters of scrub oak grew stubby and arthritical under hammerblows from a per-petual sea wind that blundered inland in great puffs through crevices in the knolls. Except for the *plop-plop* of frogs diving for safety into the shallows and the high, thin cries of constantly wheeling birds, no sound rose over the clattering paddle wheel. Even the men had qui-eted down.

The vista couldn't have been more different from the symmetrical order of Little Paddocks, and yet it was very lovely. Perhaps because the softly mounded hills pressed reassuringly close, or because the grass grew high and the oaks low, Libby found herself drawn to the mild landscape.

Just as she was thinking there couldn't be any other souls for miles around, a settlement swelled up on the bank. It contained nothing more than a fragile-looking wharf and a few makeshift frame structures, but she took it for their destination because there obviously wasn't anything else. She stood up, pulling on her gloves.

Her ears echoed with the comparative silence when the wheel ground to a halt, dripping and gleaming. The crew resumed their obscenity-laced conversations as they bustled about the unloading. A feeling of journey's end, of slowing down and satisfaction came from the men, but Libby couldn't share in it. The hardest part of their travels had ended; hers had just begun.

Her heels wanted to dig into the deck of the little steamer. She felt her toes actually curl in an effort to grip the planks. Caleb, too, had a shadow across his face when he said, "Ready? I hope you can ride without a sidesaddle."

"I'd prefer one, naturally," she replied, with a trace of her old hauteur, "but if none's available, I can make do."

There really wasn't any reason, she decided, to tell him about the mule she'd ridden until Saturday.

"Good."

He escorted her across the gangway to the short dock, his clamp on her arm possessive. A few steps down the town's only street, he stopped at a hut made from undressed boards. Luscious smells poured out of the open door, along with a welcome gush of heat.

"Fresh bread," she said, cheered. "How lovely."

"If you're hungry now, Ma Pringle will oblige. Just go in and ask. Tell her I'll settle up later," Caleb told her.

He headed toward a building that had the look of a stable, and Libby peeked into the shanty.

A plump woman with flour dusting her iron-gray hair smiled at her. A decent, kindly body, Libby thought.

"What can I do for you?"

"Are you Mrs. Pringle? Mr. Caleb Logan suggested that you might be able to spare something for us to eat," Libby said, seeing a chance to put her campaign to fatten up Caleb into action.

The woman's face sharpened with curiosity. "Mr. Logan, huh?"

No explanation a decent body would be inclined to believe for a young woman's presence with Caleb occurred to Libby, so she ignored the question implicit in Ma Pringle's voice and continued, "A few sandwiches—anything that wouldn't put you to too much trouble which we could carry while we travel."

The cook reached for a cooling loaf and began slicing. However, the curious gaze never strayed from Libby.

"Won't take but a minute. Going on out to the ranch, are you? You a friend of the Logans? Known 'em a fair spell?"

"Not very long, no. If you don't have any meat at hand, cheese would be very nice. And whatever you could give us to drink, if you please, Mrs. Pringle."

"Call me Ma. Everybody else does." Assembling sandwiches with amazing speed, Ma surveyed the black gown, black bonnet, black gloves. "You a widow woman?"

Remembering Caleb's reaction when she'd called herself a grass widow, Libby forced her hands to stay half curled and serene at her sides. "No, I'm happy to say I've never suffered that kind of loss. Thank you, Mrs.—Ma," she said as the cook handed her the sandwiches wrapped in oilskin and a small brown jug. "Mr. Logan said to tell you he'll settle the bill with you later."

"No trouble," Ma called as Libby backed out of the shed. "He's always good for it."

Caleb had two shaggy-backed ponies waiting, one bearing a high-pommeled wooden saddle and the other a lady's plain leather saddle. "Turns out Julia left her extra tack out here," he explained. "The crates and trunks will be sent on tomorrow. What have you got there?"

"Provender," she answered with a mischievous glint. "Have you someplace to store it? I thought we might get hungry on the way, since it's—did you say ten miles?"

"About halfway between here and the sea," he murmured absently. Taking time out to eat appealed to him. Julia had been weak but sensible when he'd seen her last. He felt a twist of shame that he shrank from knowing if she'd gotten worse in the past week. A brother who loved her should be with her; because he was her brother and loved her, Caleb flinched from finding out if she had deteriorated.

He compromised. "Let me stow your stuff in my saddlebags. We can't picnic long, mind. I don't want you out of doors longer than need be after the light goes."

He tossed her onto her horse and then mounted his own pony, settling with apparent comfort into the carved seat and leading them away from the buildings and to the west.

"Why?" she asked after she'd arranged her skirts as well as she could. "Is this dangerous country?"

"Most of the bears have been run off," he answered literally. "And it's the wrong season for trouble with a resty elk. There are gopher and rabbit holes, of course. And snakes and poisonous spiders. But the real reason is, wherever two-legged predators go, it's better to be safe than sorry. I can't set guards on every foot of my land."

"Are we on your land?" She looked around with renewed interest. Caleb had said he'd bought up several

Spanish land grants, but she had no way of guessing how large such tracts might be.

"This is it."

The note of pride proved his claim to love his piece of California. Pulling up, he pointed back at the brown curlicues of the creek. "Water forms our eastern boundary. The Manzanita takes in everything to the ocean. We cover three hundred fifty thousand acres."

Libby stared at him. Caleb's holding made him a more extensive landowner than a duke.

Her hands fell slack, allowing the pony under her to curvet. Without needing to think, she shortened the reins and tightened her knees to bring the beast into control. Fist on hip, Caleb leaned back in his saddle.

"I'm glad you know how to ride. It'll come in useful. Life can be restricted out here if you're not at home on horseback. We don't have many roads yet."

"I'd noticed that," said Libby, understating considerably.

He turned so they could follow a thin ribbon trodden through the grass, which grew belly-high on the stocky ponies. Narrow pods with dual, prickly spurs nodded above bladelike leaves. They caught at her skirts as she passed. "What is this grain?"

"Wild oats. Good forage . . ."

Caleb described the plants and animals that made his country bountiful, while she encouraged the flow of information with a question or two. The shadow lifted from his face, and his eyes shot sparks. Libby listened, and looked, and felt herself begin to glow in reflection of his enthusiasm. At the top of a gentle swell, she exclaimed in pleasure. A valley lay beneath them. It resembled a teacup with its interior enameled the golden orange of poppies.

"*Copa de oro*," he said. "That's what the Mexicans call poppies. Cup of gold."

"Do we have to cross here?" she asked impulsively. "Couldn't we go around and not bruise them?"

"The plants are hardy. They're wildflowers."

"I know. I've seen them before. But something doesn't have to cost money to be precious. And this is a special place."

He'd never seen her all soft and glowing in appeal before. New, faintly purple shadows made smudges underneath her eyes, reminding him that she'd been worked hard yesterday, one way or the other. Measuring the distance of the sun from the horizon, he said, "Tell you what. We can stop here to eat."

He tied the horses to a stand of brush and stomped a circle in the grass so they could look over the rim of the valley. Libby removed her bonnet to feel the breeze play in her hair and laid out the sketchy meal. The sea air must have stimulated her appetite, for she made quick work of her share of the sandwiches, but when he fetched her the jug, she gave it back to him after one distasteful sip.

"What, pray tell, is that?"

Caleb took a swig, spluttered, and recorked the bottle. "Mission wine. I don't drink enough to remember how bad the stuff is. The good fathers planted the grapes, but they weren't great shakes as vintners. The general owns all the vineyards around here now; maybe he can scare up a reliable winemaker."

She wanted to hear more of the carefree note in his voice, so she said obligingly, "The general?"

"General Vallejo. He's my neighbor on the other side of the creek."

Even Libby had heard of the Californio leader. "He still lives here? After the Bear Flag party held him hostage? Doesn't he resent Americans?" Watching light move through Caleb's black hair, she wondered why she didn't resent one particular American at this moment.

"Hell, no, he loves us, God knows why. Grubstaked half the Yankees in northern California before the gold was found. Now there may be a few more settlers coming in than even he foresaw."

Caleb no longer sounded amused, just reflective. Libby asked, "Does the number of settlers upset you?"

He lay back in the grass, turning his head to look at her as she sat upright in her sober black, cushioned by wild oats.

"Not as long as they leave me, and mine, alone. I'm a peaceable man." The dark eyes held her. "For example, right now I find it difficult to believe that forty miles from this spot some crazy Australians want to kill us. If the world happened to be sane, the only problem facing me this very minute would be how to steal a kiss from the prettiest, pinkest mouth I've ever seen."

The world wasn't sane; Libby felt as shaken and disoriented as if one of the region's frequent small earthquakes had just rippled through the ground under them.

Her mind couldn't find any logic behind the private earthquake or the song in her blood that rose to match the suddenly faulty rhythm of her heart. Not classically handsome, obstinate, too thin, arrogantly sure she was no better than she should be. If he lived by a code of honor, it was far different from the one she'd been taught to revere. And yet he seduced her just by looking relaxed. She hated the careworn expression he wore when he spoke of his sister. If she could delay its onset, even by a little . . . Besides, the knowledge she'd gained last night of his man's body was so far outside the rest of her experience, it seemed unthinkable under the red sun burning its way toward the horizon. A kiss, though, something gentle and easily denied . . . a simple kiss . . .

The sensual song drowned out logic. Murmuring, "You don't have to steal anything," she leaned over him.

The instant the words *steal a kiss* escaped him, Caleb tried to think of a way to call them back. He'd said them because he'd gotten a little muzzy with food and twilight, at ease with only Libby for company. A kiss would be nice, but he didn't expect to get one. And even under other circumstances, he wouldn't have descended to wrangling over a contact that had no value if both parties weren't agreeable. Nothing Libby had done all day had indicated any intention on her part of continuing the explorations they'd begun in the feather bed.

But then she breathed his words back at him, and her face was close, so close. Her eyes appeared huge and unfocused, green with the clear crystalline purity of water over sand before the thick lashes swept down.

She pressed her lips to his briefly, sweetly—*too* sweetly. As Libby lifted her head, before she could take a breath, he pulled his arms out from behind his neck and pushed her, very gently, down into the grass.

He was so quick her mouth stayed pursed, like a moist pink berry. She'd kissed him with the innocence of a woman who'd never outgrown the uncomplicated smacks of childhood, like a girl with no practice at kissing at all. His brows came together in a heavy frown.

"Wait a minute," he muttered in confusion.

"Oh, God. I shouldn't have done that. Whenever I'm with you I do wretched, awful things. Pay me no mind. Forget I did it. Let me up, please."

Instead, Caleb rested his weight on one elbow and kept one arm, strong with muscle, across her waist to hold her still. He traced a tendril of fair hair straying across her forehead. "I purely don't understand you, Libby Owens."

A hiccup of laughter escaped her. "How could you? I don't understand myself."

"What kind of woman are you?"

"The ordinary kind."

"Hah. No, don't look away, Libby. Talk to me. The piano player—did he ever hurt you?"

"He stole my money!"

"I don't mean that. Did he ever—oh, hell, did he ever hurt you in bed?"

"Of course not! I'm not that sort—but I can't claim not to be that sort of female, can I? You have too much evidence to the contrary. What am I going to do?'' she whispered to herself.

"Right now? We have to ride." He wasted another moment frowning down at her. His opinion of the piano player had never been high; at the least the son of a bitch had to be a thief and a kept man. Never in his wildest dreams, though, would Caleb have expected Libby to choose a clod as a lover. He didn't see how he could be mistaken. Her hesitant cooperation last night suddenly appeared to him in a new light; not only lack of trust, but lack of skill. He had no doubt that ripe, enticing Libby had submitted to the act of love many times. But she was as untutored in its niceties as the rawest virgin.

She wriggled her shoulders against the cage formed by his arms. "Mr. Logan, I think you're right. We should go. The sun's almost gone."

"Why can't you call me Caleb?" he complained in a murmur.

"Very well. Caleb, let me up this instant!"

Protectiveness flooded him, vying with admiration for her spirit. "I'm glad you don't suffer from a weak character," he said seriously. "You don't like to be abused, do you? I can be patient and tender."

She moaned.

"Maybe you were with your piano player a long time. Loyalty's a fine quality, but you shouldn't stick by somebody who treats you like dirt. He won't change. That kind never does. Libby, I swear I'll be better for you than a bastard who'd hurt you and rob you blind and leave you to fend for yourself in a strange city."

Caleb suddenly remembered that the future wouldn't include Julia. His cheeks yellowed to a dull bronze. "We'll talk more later," he promised, hoisting her to her feet without ceremony. "How much time have we lost?"

Libby snatched up her bonnet as she pushed through the grass toward the ponies. "I can't tell what time it is," she answered crossly. "I don't have a watch anymore."

Caleb grabbed the oilskin and jug. With a wistful glance at the poppies, Libby thought that Caleb would be in too great a hurry to worry over the fate of some wildflowers. But once they mounted, he set a fast pace around the rim of the valley. Her last view as he straightened their course on the opposite side was of thousands of blooms in the act of closing themselves to the dark and cold of coming night.

As the sunset faded to pink, then deepening blue, they had no choice but to slow the ponies' canter to a walk. Caleb's terse comments dried up the farther they rode. Finally, Libby heard nothing but the creak of leather, noises made by their horses, and an occasional agitated *click* from a low-flying bat.

A quarter moon rocked in a sky strewn with stars. Its gleam wasn't enough to guide the animals' steps, adding the dangers of insecure footing. Libby's pony seemed tireless, but she was not.

Discomforts piled up. Arms and neck already stiffening from the effort of directing more horse than she'd ridden for years, she felt bands of tension tightening around her forehead. Caleb's silence developed a dreary quality. The taut feeling around her temples blossomed into a full-blown headache. Every bounce in her pony's gait woke another bright stab of pain in her aching head.

How he could endure that wooden saddle, she couldn't imagine. His posterior must be beaten out of iron.

A cluster of lights ahead hung lower than the stars. The featureless profile that was Caleb turned in the saddle. "That's the ranch house."

"Ah."

The pain in her head made it impossible for her to feel anything but gratitude for approaching deliverance. The Manzanita might be the gateway to hell; as long as the devil ahead of her gave her a bed to lie in, she'd enter eagerly.

Chapter 8

Recklessly, Caleb urged his pony to a fast trot as they neared the structure towering at the top of the hill. A contrary urgency to see Julia flooded him. He didn't know who Juan would have on duty at the gates tonight, so he called in his bad Spanish as well as English, "*Abruere la entrada!* Get that gate open *pronto, comprende?* It's Logan out here."

A smattering of Spanish answered him. One of the huge double gates groaned backward. He reined in long enough for Libby to catch up with him before he stampeded through. Flinging himself from the saddle, he covered the packed earth of the central courtyard with giant strides and hurtled up the stairs to the family quarters two at a time.

Emerging from the clean, cool emptiness of the out-of-doors into Caleb's "ranch house," Libby thought she really had been delivered into the chaos of hell. Lanterns and torches in brackets cast an orange glare over men and women streaming in seemingly aimless confusion as whiplash-lean dogs, the teeth in their grinning mouths gleaming, barked and leaped. Amazement shocked her headache into manageable proportions.

The dimensions of Caleb's home were undeniably grand. A two-story-high square rose around her, with rooms located in walls deeply recessed under massive overhanging roofs. More fort than house, its gray tinge betrayed the fact that the bricks of its construction had begun their existence as mud. A ripe stink of drying hides permeated the place, huge and open to the sky as it was.

Thank God, her pony wasn't moved by the confusion. The beast stood stock-still and produced a contented whicker for the lanky man who shouldered his way to her knee.

"*Hola!* That is—do you speak English? Welcome to the Manzanita. I'm Juan Arrile. Caleb—I guess Caleb was in a bit of a hurry. Let me give you a hand here . . ."

Gratefully, Libby accepted assistance dismounting. Juan shouted and received a flood of Spanish and a few giggles in reply. Nevertheless, a boy came running to lead both ponies away, and the crowd began to disappear into the shadows under the wide wooden balcony that circled the second floor.

"You'll have to forgive everybody for rushing out. We're all at sixes and sevens lately. There's sickness in the house."

"Yes, I understand Miss Logan is unwell. I hope she's mending?" Libby had to look down slightly into a bony but pleasant young face.

Its expression hardened. "No," he said shortly.

"I'm so sorry." Poor Caleb. Poor Juan, too. He looked as harrowed as Caleb did at the mention of Julia. A sweetheart? She wondered at the name and accent. His Spanish, as far as she could tell, sounded fluent, but his English was stolidly American. Conscious of her own brittle accent, she said, "This is an awkward time for me to have come. Matters just seem to have worked out so that I'm here."

"Oh, visitors are always welcome. One thing about an old adobe like this, there's lots of room. I'll have one of the women make up a trundle for you in the guest quarters. Up this way."

On the balcony the odor thinned, replaced by air fresh from the sea that felt balmy against her skin in the sheltered lee of the eaves. Windows, glazed behind their protective grillwork, ran in a long row along the inner wall. One of them blazed with light. As they passed it, Libby heard Caleb and could no more have kept herself from stopping than she could have voluntarily refrained from filling her lungs with the soft Pacific air. She didn't listen to what he said, just the even, too-controlled tone. Anguish seeped out with the quiet flow of words.

Juan also checked. From somewhere in the courtyard came the strumming of a guitar and laughter. The contrast between the cheerful human sounds below and the flat desolation clear in Caleb's voice made Libby bite the inside of her cheek, hard, in sympathy.

The window darkened momentarily. Caleb's stony gaze rested on her for an instant, before it shifted to her escort. He came around to the door. "Juan. For Chrissake, enforce some quiet, can't you? And find Teresa while you're at it. There wasn't a soul with Julia when I came up. I don't want her left alone again."

Softly, Libby said, "If Miss Logan requires nursing, perhaps there's something I could do."

Surprise flashed across his face. He nodded, once, and then stayed rooted by the door, forbidding and withdrawn. The lover in the wild oats was gone. She couldn't just forget that he was standing there and behave normally, because her preternatural awareness of him operated as strongly as ever, so she saw the girl on the bed through the focus of his grief.

Hair as coarse and black and abundant as Caleb's had been bunched into two stubby braids that barely brushed Julia's shoulders. It must have been cut to make sure it didn't drain her strength during her illness, Libby realized, trying not to be scandalized by the sight of the butchered hair. The doctor must have suggested shearing; it was a commonly tried remedy when nothing else served to bring down a fever.

Between the braids, Julia's chalky face was gaunt, just as Caleb's was, and the lack of padding over her fine, strong bones emphasized the resemblance of sister to brother. Even the high-bridged nose was Caleb's in miniature. Only Julia's eyes deviated from the family pattern—not in color, because they too were so dark a brown they were almost black, but in clarity. Caleb's eyes, even after a night of heavy drinking or waking from a blow hard enough to stun, never looked anything but clear and knowing and hard. Julia's blinked incessantly, as if the candles bothered her, and her pupils had shrunk to tiny points that made the irises look faded. The unvarying pinpoints gave her a rather blind look.

The invalid struggled against the exquisitely worked rose-wreath quilt that lay around her as if the light folds were a smothering mass of winter blankets. Bending, Libby boosted the dark-haired girl into a sitting position. She told herself that the shudder of distaste she felt quiver up her arms could only be due to the sensation of clutching a bundle of bird's bones. Julia was so thin. It would be foolish and unkind to give rein to the uneasy intuition that Julia's apathy and wandering gaze contained a whiff of something unclean.

Scolding herself for failing in charity, Libby removed her own bonnet and smoothed the quilt into crisp perfection. "How lovely to meet you, Miss Logan. Your brother speaks of you often."

The conventional phrases woke no glimmer of interest from Julia, whose silence was beginning to seem ominous. Those strange eyes wavered.

"But I can see you're tired right now," Libby went on, at a loss. "Is there anything I can do to make you more comfortable? Or would you rather just be private with Mr. Logan?"

A languid hand moved. "Cal's back. Did you know Cal's back?" The little voice was languid, too.

"Yes," said Libby. "He brought me to visit you. Do you want to rest now?"

"I never do anything but rest. Rest and rest. Teresa brings me my medicine and then I sleep. And I dream. The longest, loveliest dreams, full of soft lights and bright colors. I dreamed Cal came back."

A harsh sound broke the stillness by the door. Libby didn't turn her head because she couldn't bear to see what would be in Caleb's face.

"You're not dreaming, truly. I'm here. Mr. Logan is here. We want to help you. Tell us what you'd like us to do."

Disconcertingly, Julia giggled. What a pretty girl she must have been once, Libby thought.

"We could dance. I love to dance. Caleb dances like an angel. Not Juan, though. He stands by the punch bowl and glowers. Caleb dances with all the girls but he never marries one. He needs to be married." In another swift change of mood, Julia let tears trickle down her white cheeks, leaving two shining snail tracks in their wake. "He used to be a sea captain, you know. Captain at twenty. He likes taking care of people. It's in his blood. If he has no one to take care of, he'll die inside. Just like me. He'll die."

Caleb perched awkwardly on the feminine quilt and took one of the clawlike hands in his. "Julia, stop fretting yourself about me. All I want is for you to rest and build up your strength."

"Something to eat? A hot drink? Broth?" suggested Libby uncertainly. Julia's symptoms didn't fit what she knew of common illnesses. In fact, Julia's conversation resembled nothing so much as the ramblings Malloy was prone to in the initial rapturous stage of a drunken spree. Caleb's sister couldn't be drunk. There was her extreme thinness and the doctor's diagnosis. Could her heart be so damaged that it restricted the flow of blood to the brain? Libby couldn't think what other explanation there could be for a woman, described by her brother as energetic and business-minded, who spoke and acted like this one.

The mention of broth made Caleb nod approvingly. "Now there's a good idea. You could drink some nice soup, couldn't you, Julia?"

"No." It was the first uncompromising statement

Julia had made. "I'm not hungry. Why is everyone always trying to make me eat?"

"Some food might make you feel better," Caleb tried again.

"I'm never going to feel better."

The horrible thing was that the dull voice didn't rise. It remained languid and detached. Unanswerable. Libby shivered.

"It's not so bad to be dead, Cal. I don't mind for myself. It's just more sleeping and dreaming. But I mind for you. You need someone if you're going to be alive."

"Julia—"

The blue-veined lids dropped, but when Caleb tried to pull free of her grasp, it tightened. Julia murmured, "You don't know yourself. You'll hide all your feelings till they're buried so deep you won't be able to show them anymore. You need a wife, Cal. A wife. A wife."

Libby felt her heart turn over painfully at Caleb's quiet endurance. No wonder he'd been searching for something, anything, to put a stop to this unbearable soliloquy. No wonder he'd taken refuge in drink Saturday night.

Libby could have borrowed some fortitude from the wine she'd refused earlier as she sat gingerly next to Caleb and touched Julia's fingertips where they peeped out from Caleb's brown fist.

"Miss Logan. Julia. Please, don't worry so about Caleb. He took your advice. That's why I'm here. I'm Elizabeth, and Caleb and I are going to be married."

"Married?"

The exclamation didn't come from Julia. Juan, closely followed by a short, round-faced woman in a scoop-necked blouse and heavily embroidered skirt, strode toward them. Coming up behind was a smiling man whose brown, hooded robe revealed sandaled feet.

"You really did it?" Juan went on delightedly. "Brought home a bride? You could have let us know, Cal! Goddamn! Oh, *me pesa,* padre. Sorry." He spoke several sentences in quick Spanish.

Apparently he was explaining Libby's status, for the priest inclined his tonsured head. *"Felicitationes, señorita."*

Libby sat and stared at the rosary dangling from the rope around his waist. A priest. Now she had sunk to telling lies to a priest?

The conversation roared by her in an unintelligible flood. She looked from one participant to another, trying to follow it by inflection and expression. The priest pointed to Julia, speaking in an emphatic way that caused Caleb's sister to nod several times, although when she spoke it was still in that terrifying, uncaring tone. The brightly skirted woman who had come in with Juan plucked at the priest's sleeve, her words high-pitched and impassioned. The gold bracelets on her arms jangled. Caleb stood and said something sharp. Juan's confused scowl and frequent glances at Libby pricked her to alertness.

"May I ask what is going on?" She pitched her question to cut through the babble.

The priest was patting the short woman's braceleted arm, as if in agreement.

Julia said, "Teresa's right. It's for the best, Cal, you'll see. There's no use in waiting . . ."

Then the priest took Libby's hand, pulled her to her feet, and placed the hand in one of Caleb's. Pronouncing what Libby recognized as a Latin blessing, he ignored Caleb's strong "Hold your horses here—" and simply raised his voice until both of them were shouting.

Libby realized what the man was doing; he was trying his best to marry them. Gasping with shocked laughter, she dragged her hand from Caleb's clasp, but without faltering in a syllable of his singsong Latin, the priest grabbed it and folded her fingers back over Caleb's knuckles.

It was the most abbreviated marriage service Libby had ever heard. Within a minute, the priest stopped yelling and beamed at them with simple goodwill.

"There," said Julia, warming almost to satisfaction. "There. It's done." Her braids showed up black and bushy against the muslin pillowcase as her head lolled to one side.

Libby's laughter faded in the face of Caleb's tight-lipped fury. She whispered, "Really, if it makes your sister happy, where's the harm? This can't be legal. I'm not Roman Catholic; are you? And no one could accuse you of being a willing bridegroom!"

"Oh, it's legal all right," Juan assured her, coming forward to pound his employer on the back. Caleb wrenched away and backed the priest into a corner, talking urgently. "The civil authorities recognize the padres. As far as the sovereign state of California is concerned, you're Mrs. Caleb Logan."

"But we didn't make any responses. Caleb spent the whole . . . ceremony"—she didn't know what else to call the gabble of Latin—"telling him to stop!"

"Not the first time the padre's legshackled a reluctant groom," grinned Juan. His gaze turned admiring. "But why Cal should want to wait to marry you, ma'am, is beyond me."

Libby spared Julia a cautious glance, but the girl seemed to have succumbed to sleep. "Caleb, tell them! Tell them we can't be married!"

Caleb turned away from the priest, who was shaking his head in a kindly but final way. The lamplight drew harsh lines down his cheeks and put a dangerous glitter in his eyes. "The padre's very positive about it. Sorry, Libby. Seems you're my wife, after all."

Chapter 9

Libby sank down on the edge of Julia's quilt. Quite of their own accord, her hands started to shake. The rest of her body felt numb, as if all the shock of suddenly finding herself a married woman—wed to an American—was accumulating in her hands and they were trying to shake it out.

With a muffled oath, Caleb crossed the room and covered her fingers with his own. Their warmth halted the mortifying quiver, but she snatched her hand away and glared at him in accusation. "Aren't you going to do something?" she hissed.

"I am doing something," he growled back. "I'm making the best of a bad situation." He looked down at her bare fingers, his grin bleak. "I'll get Pablo to start beating out a ring for you tomorrow. A married lady deserves a ring." His gaze continued to dwell on her, unreadable. "Pablo's our blacksmith—also our goldsmith. He'll make you something pretty."

Juan, the priest, and the Spanish woman listened with unconcealed interest. Their presence kept her refusal quiet and polite. "No, really, Caleb. I don't want a wedding ring. I didn't want a *wedding*."

"See how well I chose?" he said lightly to Juan. "A frugal wife. Libby, Pablo will make you a suitable ring. No more and no less. You don't want to shame me, do you?" Leaning forward, he whispered in a kind of controlled snarl, "We're just pretending a little harder than

134

we meant to, that's all. I don't want to be married any more than you do. Play along, and we'll treat ourselves to a nice annulment as soon as may be." Aloud, he continued, "Now, that's enough talk. Julia's asleep, and you should be, too."

If sleeping meant inhabiting Caleb's bed, Libby decided she'd never close her eyes again. "I mean to stay with Miss—with Julia if I can be useful."

Excited sentences poured from the woman, making Libby suspect that she commanded some knowledge of English, whether or not she chose to speak it.

Caleb listened, then nodded.

"Teresa—oh, this is Teresa, our housekeeper—says she can manage on her own. Besides," he added, his grin becoming savage, "she thinks a new-made wife belongs with her husband on their wedding night."

Libby persevered, leaning toward him to mute what she had to say. "That's not too wise. You found your sister alone a while ago. I can stay with her."

He caught her meaning immediately. "Teresa's trustworthy." His undertone carried to her ear on the warmth of his breath. Undercurrents of anger over this trick of fate, which she knew he must feel as bitterly as she, couldn't keep the soft, moist puffs of air from feeling intimate against the unguarded skin of her ear and throat. "Been the housekeeper for donkey's years. She thought Julia was sleeping and went to talk to the padre."

"But I—"

Unexpectedly, he took her face in his hands. "Libby. You've been performing or conniving or hiding—raising Cain generally—for two days. And don't tell me how well you slept last night, because those circles under your eyes will make you out to be a liar. If you want to lend a hand tomorrow, you can." He glanced toward Julia, brows twitching together, before adding to Juan, "Have Libby shown to a room, will you?"

The bemused expression on Juan's angular face might

have struck Libby as amusing under less charged circumstances.

"Well, uh, sure, Cal, whatever you say, but where—I mean, which—" He coughed delicately. "That is, does Mrs. Logan have a preference for what room she's put in?"

Juan's astonishment shook Caleb out of his frowning contemplation of his sister's sodden sleep. Libby, her green gaze fierce, hadn't budged from Julia's feet. Caleb woke to the possibilities this disastrous turn of events created. Maybe something could be salvaged.

Libby opened her perfectly shaped lips and said with determination, "Yes, I do have a preference."

Smoothly, Caleb interrupted, "Why don't you find a trundle to move into the office off my bedroom, Juan? That'll make a suite for the two of us, and Libby can decide how she wants the furniture arranged later. Clear?"

Juan obviously didn't find it clear at all, but he lifted his shoulders. "If that's what you want, boss."

He ushered Libby onto the balcony and to another door. "This is your—Cal's—oh, hell. I mean, horse shit—I mean . . ." Shadows clustered too deep for her to see if he flushed, but his light young voice sounded horrified. "I beg your pardon, ma'am. We sort of got out of the habit of watching our language since Julia's took so sick."

"That's understandable, although profanity isn't my favorite mode of expression."

As she said it, Libby thought what a prude she sounded. Mrs. Caleb Logan, married by mistake. Unwanted wife of a man who'd almost succeeded in making her his mistress only the night before.

"I'll try to watch it," Juan promised.

Libby tried to make her smile friendly. She could feel it waver around the edges. "Just carry on the way you would if I weren't here. Please."

Propping open the door, he disappeared inside. The distinctive scrape of flint against steel heralded the budding of flame in a lamp with a handsome nacre shade. Rather cautiously, Libby stepped into what was plainly a man's bedroom.

The bedstead had no headboard and only short posts, but it was built long, to accommodate Caleb's inches, and wide—Libby resisted thinking about why it might be wide. An oak wardrobe dominated one corner, a matching side table supported basin and ewer, and that was all. There weren't even curtains covering the tall window to mar the room's spartan simplicity, though shutters would provide privacy when Caleb thought it necessary.

Libby couldn't help speculating how often, and with whom, the master of the Manzanita required privacy.

Chin going up, she asked, "Where is this office I heard about?"

Juan showed her an arch half hidden by the bulk of the wardrobe. "This is a—well, the Mexicans built these little rooms off the parents' bedrooms for their daughters, see? No outside entrances, so the girls couldn't, uh . . ."

"Couldn't get themselves compromised. Quite. The English built those little rooms, too."

His sigh was grateful. "I guess parents are the same just about everyplace."

So are their daughters, she thought, breath coming fast at the thought that Caleb planned to sleep in one of these rooms. And so are the men who plan to seduce them.

"Will it take long to bring up another bed?" she asked.

"No, as long as that's what you and Cal want . . ."

"That's what I want."

She didn't try to excuse herself or explain why so newly married a couple preferred to sleep apart, but merely looked at him expectantly. The tactic worked.

"Yes, ma'am," said Juan. "I'll see to it right away."

"Thank you. And—shall I call you Mr. Arrile or Juan?"

His grin almost split his face. "I don't know that anybody's ever asked me that before. Make it Juan."

She smiled back. "Thank you, Juan. My name is Elizabeth, but my family used to call me Libby."

"Welcome, Libby. Sure am glad you're here. I'll see about the trundle for you."

She passed the time until the bed arrived investigating the alcove through the arch. Its furnishings appeared as functional, and as suited to Caleb, as those in the bedroom. A kneehole desk, built tall to accommodate his long legs, with a multiplicity of drawers. A chair. A businesslike cast-iron safe. The only frivolous object on display stood in the place of honor atop the desk: an intricately detailed ship's model, complete to muslin sails and a toy sailor clinging to the eagle's nest.

The ship's figurehead was dressed, or undressed, much as Libby herself had been at the saloon. Libby looked at the carved breasts, round and shiny and hard as apples, and read the nameplate. MARY ROSE. BOSTON.

"Who are you, Mary Rose?" she said softly aloud. "And why does that strange man who is my husband keep a ship named after you?"

A perfunctory knock brought her back to the bedroom, where she found men fitting together the pieces of the extra bed and a young girl clutching a pile of linens.

Her "Hello" prompted a chorus of "*Hola*, senora" in reply. Like Teresa, if any of them spoke English, none was going to admit it. Once the bed had been installed next to the desk in the office and the men had left, the girl gently shooed Libby out of the way and tucked in the bedclothes with neat-fingered efficiency. Libby wondered if the servants were always so industrious, or if news of the wedding had already circulated.

She didn't care one way or the other. It was bliss to have someone else deal with clean sheets, kindly and impersonally strip off her travel-stained clothes, throw an unfamiliar nightgown that smelled of lemon verbena over her head. Tension drained from stiff muscles at the nape of her neck as the maid brushed her long, fine hair until it stood out in a pale cloud around her face and shoulders and past her waist.

"Nice," said Caleb from the doorway.

The maid effaced herself. Libby waited until the re-verberations of footsteps across the balcony faded away and the stillness in the room became weighted with meaning before she said at random, "The house servants seem very well trained."

"They know their jobs. Teresa takes care of all that," he said indifferently.

"About Julia—I'm sorry she's so ill. Caleb, what are we going to do?"

"Nothing."

"But, good God, Caleb, we can't stay married to each other." She heard the thread of uncertainty in her voice and looked away. She didn't want to stay married to Caleb. She didn't!

Caleb saw the strain in her eyes before she averted them. All his questions about her past and her connection with the piano player boiled together with his knowledge that she found him, Caleb Logan, wanting in some way. The mixture produced a froth of anger and . . . lust.

"Neither of us intends to be tied forever. But there's not a thing we can do about it right now. For tonight, Mrs. Logan, we're man and wife."

Libby gulped as he laid his hand against the side of her slender neck. His flesh was warmer than hers, his hand big and hard with calluses, so she felt fragile and even a little dizzy. He rubbed a strand of her hair between his fingers as if assaying the texture.

"To think some idiots look for gold under the ground. Your hair is so beautiful, Libby."

"People will gossip. They'll know we spent the night together. If we're going to seek an annulment, we can't let it seem we've c-consummated the marriage."

"Is it the piano player?" he asked abruptly.

Her whole being had been concentrated on getting the scandalous word out in the open between them; for a moment his change of subject left her gaping. "Malloy? What's he got to do with us?"

"Very little, I hope."

She finally comprehended what he was driving at. "Aloysius Malloy has never been my lover. Oh, what's the point of repeating it? You're not going to believe me."

"I'm glad you realize it." He pulled her to her feet, his hands unbearably gentle. "We'll get along much better if you don't try to lie to me."

She set her jaw. "I won't sleep in this room with you, Caleb."

He stretched his neck and eased his shoulders without removing the mild hold on Libby. "Why not?"

She couldn't work up the will to pull away from his demoralizing touch. The window stood uncurtained and accusing. She could hear hushed voices, the bark of a dog, and someone singing, quietly now, in tune with a single guitar. Steps rang out here and there. It frightened Libby that even though she knew anyone passing by could see her in a nightgown, almost in Caleb's embrace, her body stayed quiescent and content under his hand.

The realization helped her to move. She would not submit to Caleb and become exactly what he thought her.

Twisting out of his grasp, she said, "There's no answer to a question like that. When you ask *why not,* it means you've already decided my reasons don't have any value."

"I would never say a thing like that."

"No, but you'd think it," she retorted shrewdly. "Julia is right. You—"

The explosion when it came was quiet and furious.

"Don't tell me about Julia. I don't want to hear about Julia! I came to you to forget for a while—"

Even now he didn't force her. The naked pain broke against her like a wave, but his hands made a tender frame for her face and he grated, "Libby," giving her time to draw away before he kissed her.

Hot, angry compassion rose in a flood inside her, bringing her arms up tight around his neck as her lips pressed back hard in an attempt to convey the fierce comfort she wanted to give him. They clung to each other, not moving, hardly breathing.

Slowly, a different kind of heat trickled into the kiss. Caleb murmured something deep in his throat. Libby felt his hands shift; he seemed to like handling the soft mass of her hair because there was a small tug on her head when he flexed his fingers on her back, gathering her to him more closely.

"Dear heart, open your mouth."

"What?"

"Open your mouth when I kiss you." He put a finger to her lips. "Like this."

More in surprise than anything else, her lips parted and then closed over his finger. It tasted faintly of salt and entirely of Caleb. In a gesture that went back to the strong instincts of babyhood, she licked it with her tongue and sucked gently.

The pleasure it gave her made her eyelids flutter briefly. When she opened them, Caleb was smiling down at her. His finger came away with a little pop that wasn't ridiculous but intimate, and he replaced it with his mouth.

"Just . . . like . . . that."

With aching slowness, he ran his tongue over her lips. His mouth seemed to steal her breath. She couldn't get any air, couldn't think, didn't want to think. His hands continued to stroke, to warm, to soothe. His tongue finished its deliberate circuit and pressed forward.

The invasion felt like the fulfillment of wishes so secret she'd never even guessed them. Without shame, abandoning thought, Libby courted this strange kind of kiss. Her head fell back. She went on tiptoe. Her arms unlocked from his neck so she could clutch his hair. She tried to surround his tongue with her own, sucking lightly to encourage him to delve deeper.

A strangled noise burst from him. Rearing back, he stared at her incredulously before a rueful smile narrowed his eyes. "Lady, you are full of surprises."

She came to earth with a thump.

"Did—did I hurt you?"

"No, of course not."

"Did I do it incorrectly?"

"Well, hell, Libby, one way isn't exactly more correct than another. Different people enjoy different ways."

"You didn't find that way—enjoyable?"

His arms were still around her. They tightened. "I'm not made out of wood, you know. I enjoyed it. If I didn't like that sort of kiss, I wouldn't have started one."

"Then why did you stop?"

Frustration bubbled in Libby's veins, making her voice subdued and resentful. She ought to be feeling glad, she told herself. She'd come perilously close to chancing her virginity. No matter that submission to Caleb felt more like victory than surrender. It would be defeat. Under no circumstances could she risk letting Caleb consummate this fantastical marriage.

Her internal conversation left her so depressed that she jumped when Caleb chuckled.

"I wouldn't have stopped but you startled me. It was pretty easy to tell you'd never been kissed that way before. I didn't expect you to get so good at it so fast. You're very sweet, Libby."

"You keep saying that." Standing in the circle of his arms, she looked up at him steadily. "Sweet. But you mean easy."

Their kiss seemed to have blunted the edge of Caleb's desire, at least temporarily. The little muscle at the side of his mouth pulled his smile awry. "No, dear heart. No man would ever call you easy."

She caught both his meanings. There wasn't any use pointing out to him that she'd never had to be this difficult with a man before. All her defenses were tottering under the onslaught of his touch, and here she was, wearing nothing more than a scanty nightdress which revealed not only ankles but calves. It scarcely provided a barrier to sight, let alone the insidious warmth of his arms and the lean, supple feeling of his chest and thighs against hers. Flushing, she pulled away.

Her eyes fell. She saw that the tips of her breasts had formed aggressive little peaks, showing pink through the white cotton.

"Look at you," said Caleb huskily. "Look at me."

His pants buttoned over a wider expanse than usual. Libby's palm, then her whole body tingled.

"We're going to be sleeping in mighty close quarters. What do you think is going to happen if I kiss you again?"

With ragged determination, she answered, "You can't kiss me again. There must be some other room where I can sleep."

"Any number of them, but frankly I don't relish being branded a steer on my wedding night."

"It wasn't a typical wedding. And there's not going to be any wedding night."

His dark gaze measured her, the lovely body tense in the too-short nightgown, the cornsilk hair loose and drifting. A sparkle of unshed tears brightened her eyes to a green like jeweled glass.

"We could make a bet on that if you like, Libby."

"I've told you before, I don't gamble!" How could he possibly believe her? Even she could see how events had contrived to paint her. A scarlet woman. Desperately, she continued, "I've said no. I'll scream!"

The reckless gleam in his eyes grew brighter. "Scream away," he advised.

Libby drew a deep breath. Caleb dropped his attitude

of conspiratorial amusement and clapped his hand over her mouth.

She bit him.

"Ow! No, stop fighting me, it's all right, Libby! I want you, and I think you want me, too. But I won't use force, and I'm certainly not going to beg. Besides," he added tightly, "I know how loud you scream, and I don't want you waking up Julia. Where's the trundle?"

She pointed. He stalked into the office, picked up the light bed under one arm, and headed out the door with it.

Pillows and a blanket littered the floorboards behind him. Libby paused to gather them up, wrapping the cover around her shoulders as she traced Caleb by his trail of bumps and thuds into a chamber on the other side of the quadrangle.

Empty in the elusive moonlight, it smelled of earthen walls. She guessed that it wasn't regularly occupied.

He brushed past her, returning with a candle, which he kindled and set on the floor.

The flame illuminated her bare feet. "Get into bed," he said briefly. "You'll catch your death."

She winced. Julia had caught her death. Warily, she slid between sheets agreeably stiff with clean-scented starch, arranging the blanket over the uppermost sheet as she did so.

The small pool of radiance didn't extend to Caleb's face. Libby waited.

Finally, the scratch of his soles faded toward the veranda.

"Caleb."

His silhouette wavered in the doorway as he turned. "What is it?"

"Who was Mary Rose?"

There was silence, then a short laugh. "I don't think I'll tell you."

Chapter 10

Despite her odd surroundings, Libby slept well, and if dreams enlivened her slumber, she didn't remember them when she woke. Soft morning light poured through the grillwork, painting elaborate shadows on the gray clay walls. She decided to ask for curtain material as soon as possible.

Would she be here long enough to make them up? It seemed she was committed to playing out this charade until Julia's death released both her and Caleb. Perhaps, after the annulment, he'd organize her passage. She'd just have to borrow the five hundred dollars fare from her erstwhile husband and pay him back from London. She could give voice lessons. If she lived with Adelbert and Edith and sent Caleb every penny she ever earned, it shouldn't take longer than the rest of her life to balance the debt.

She made a wistful sound. Her truncated saloon career may have produced dire consequences, but singing in the taproom had been extremely profitable for the one performance it had lasted. Quick money, Malloy had said.

Not easy money, though. She wondered if Malloy had spent it all already.

The same maid appeared, apparently drawn by the tiny noise. Libby wanted to ask her if she'd been waiting outside for a long time, but didn't know how.

Behind the maid trooped a line of menservants, bearing a chamber pot, a real bathtub, and cans of steaming water, as well as Libby's trunks. Libby pulled the blanket to her chin. The men dropped their burdens after inspecting her thoroughly out of the corners of their eyes, and bowed themselves out.

Thrusting back the covers, Libby ran over to touch her trunks, thinking that Caleb must have specially ordered someone to start out with them from the dock before dawn. Then she sighed.

"Don't be a ninny," she said out loud. "A carrier brought them with Julia's boxes, that's all."

"Senora?" asked the maid, busy with the tub.

"Nothing." She searched her sparse Spanish vocabulary. Few operas were sung in Spanish. "*Nada.* What is your name?" Pointing to herself, she said, "Senora Logan." Then Libby pointed at the maid.

The girl laughed. "Ascensión, senora."

The bath was Libby's first in two weeks, and she gave herself up to it with hedonistic pleasure, splashing and soaking, using all the soft, yellow soap and a liberal amount of a light floral perfume the maid offered. When she finished, her hair hung in great ropes down her back. Although fine, the profusion of hair grew too thick to dry quickly; taking the comb from Ascensión's hand, she tugged at tangles and threaded a pink ribbon through to hold the wet strands off her face. The ribbon matched a pink-checked dimity the maid unearthed from one of the trunks and seemed to approve of, from the way she held it up and smiled. Wondering a little what Caleb would make of pink dimity and damp ringlets bouncing almost to her knees, Libby let Ascensión lead her to a large, airy dining room. The wide refectory table held only one place setting. If this was where the family customarily ate, Caleb had already breakfasted and departed.

As Libby entered, nine rhythmical bongs rang from an eight-day clock that sat on an oak sideboard. Nine o'clock was far into the working day for a rancher.

Telling herself it was silly to be miffed by his absence, she chose from an incongruous array of food-stuffs, including gelid porridge, fried mush, flat corn cakes that she recognized as tortillas, and withered winter apples. The table provided enough to still the embarrassing growls from her stomach, but nothing that would have tempted a less sharp appetite. Caleb and Julia couldn't be blamed for their thinness.

A chat with the cook would be an enjoyable duty for a new-made wife . . .

Giving up on the pulpy apple, she wandered around the central veranda until she came to Julia's room. Caleb's sister looked very small, lying unnaturally straight as she slept under the pretty quilt. Teresa rocked in a corner, a wad of tatting rolling from her lap.

"How lovely," Libby said, fingering the yards of handmade lace. "Being able to create something like this must be a joy."

She met Teresa's wary gaze with a limpid one of her own.

"Languages are so interesting, are they not? I don't know any Spanish, really, but I'm hoping you'll help me learn. I admire the way you understand English."

Grudgingly, Teresa admitted, "I understand—a little. I speak—not so much."

"Oh, you do wonderfully. I wish I spoke Spanish half as well. My mother was from Calais, so I know French. And I've picked up some Italian and German. But your language is new to me."

Teresa thawed slightly. "It is filled with color and beauty. But most Yanquis appreciate nothing that is not Yanqui."

"I'm not a Yankee, Teresa. May I call you that?"

"You are duenna here, senora. Senor Cal brings you home. It is your choice what to call a servant."

"Senor Cal," she said, trying out the name cautiously, "tells me that you've been the housekeeper here a long time. He says you're an excellent housekeeper."

"The senor is kind." Was there accusation in Teresa's tone? The separate beds, then the separate rooms, must be common knowledge.

"Yes." The sad assent sounded too self-pitying for Libby's taste; she smiled brightly. "Now, tell me what I can do to help you with Miss Julia."

Teresa denied that she needed or wanted help. Libby insisted. The polite wrangle lasted until Libby said, "Senor Cal said I could assist you in the sickroom."

Senor Cal worked. Teresa threw up her hands and began to describe Julia's routine.

Libby listened and asked few questions. Nursing Caleb's sister appeared pathetically straightforward. The senorita slept almost constantly. When she woke, she was to be dosed with a medicine the Yanqui doctor had left. She did not want to eat. She seemed to be too constipated even to put an attendant to the trouble of helping her use the pot. Soon she fell asleep again.

Libby nodded soberly. "When may I take my turn? You must have other duties around the house."

"The maids to watch, the looms to inspect, the cook—"

"Ah." Libby's smile made Teresa suspend her litany and sit up in alarm, her tatting abandoned. "The cook. I would like to have a word with the cook."

"Since the senorita is sick, Senor Cal leaves the kitchen to me."

"Yes, but while your time is taken up with more important matters, I can make sure your orders are being carried out. Besides," she added with perfect sincerity, "I have some recipes I want prepared for Senor Cal. He needs fattening."

Caleb seemed to be the surest way past the housekeeper's guard. The rocker swayed, and Teresa's olive hands began to pick amid the scattered threads. "He does not eat when his heart is grieved. He would not stop for food this morning."

The remark stung. Libby told herself she would get over her absurd feeling of guilt at Teresa's evident scorn for the new Senora Logan, who so signally failed to perform her obligations as a wife.

"He is upset over his sister's health," she answered evasively. "Why did you talk the priest into performing the wedding last night? You did, I could tell."

"My senorita, she send Senor Cal away to San Francisco and then she get worse and worse and worse," Teresa burst out. "The only wish of her heart is for him to find a wife who will cherish him. He brings you, the priest is visiting—why delay?"

"But a marriage requires consent. There must be forms to sign—"

"You have already said you will marry Senor Cal; that is consent, *sí*?" she asked unanswerably. "The good padre, he allows that the respected Senor Cal and his wife sign the parish book a little late, as a favor. This is your fear? That all is not legal?"

The sudden note of cautious approval set a bell ringing in Libby's head. Teresa must have concluded that her new duenna was skittish of the master's bed because the ceremony hadn't been sufficiently orthodox. "Yes," she said in relief. It would be nice not to have Teresa glaring at her for her entire tenure as Caleb's wife.

"But, senora, this is a false scruple," the housekeeper said earnestly. "Not even the Holy Virgin herself would want you to cheat Senor Cal of the comfort to be found only in—"

"You haven't told me when I might sit with Miss Julia," interrupted Libby quickly.

Lips compressing once more in censure, Teresa assigned her part of the night watch. Libby agreed without complaint. It wasn't until she was in the courtyard, peering through doorways in search of the kitchen, that she understood how the housekeeper had meant to insult her. A woman too scrupulous or too proud or too cold to fill her proper place in her husband's bed would have no one to inconvenience if she stayed up with an invalid through the darkest part of the night.

A clatter of crockery warned her that the kitchen must be near. She found it as much by scent as sound, a dim room dominated by a huge hearth, where beans simmered in a large kettle. Ghosts of old meals hung almost tangibly in the air. The most forceful smell was a strong odor of olive oil. Children wearing nothing but long, once-white shirts chopped and pounded vegetables and chased dogs through the gloom. Their soprano chatter vied with the yelping of the dogs to create a cheerful cacophony. For a moment, Libby grinned in appreciation at a scene Brueghel could have drawn. Then, as she counted how many young children with knives worked unsupervised, she called out sharply, "Who is in charge here?"

Instant silence prevailed, broken only by a puppy's yip. The animal was quickly scooped up and petted into quiet by a child who scuttled back into the safety of anonymity among his fellows.

Their reaction startled her into realizing how alien she must appear to them: taller than most women, blond, speaking a gabble of English in an angry-sounding voice capable of carrying over the entire compound. She thought of a class called to order by a strict schoolteacher and almost grinned again. But the stricken faces reminded her that as far as these children knew, they had just met the ranch's new mistress, a personage of great potential power in their lives. They had every reason to fear, and she had none to laugh.

The same unwanted worm of sympathy that afflicted her around Caleb squirmed through her vitals as she softened her voice. "Hello. *Hola.* Do any of you speak English? I'm looking for the cook. Can you tell me where he is?"

No one answered directly, but several fell back from a short figure whose white hair was bound at the nape of his neck in a long queue. Expecting another child, Libby felt a frisson along her back when she looked down into a wizened countenance like those she'd seen under conical hats in San Francisco.

A Chinese man. And from the thousands of wrinkles that crisscrossed his ochre skin, pulling his eyelids and the flesh under his jaw into wattles, a very old man at the end of a long, hard life.

"Oh, dear," she said faintly. Spanish she was ready to tackle. Surely it would share some of the characteristics of friendly, familiar French and Italian. But so different a language as Chinese seemed a challenge beyond her capabilities.

One of the children, a boy with a bowl-shaped haircut, stepped forward. Libby sank into a crouch and smiled to encourage his bravery. Button eyes regarded her without blinking.

"Senora? This is Wang. He speak some Spanish, no English. *I* speak English."

"I see. And you would be willing to tell Wang what I say, and then repeat to me what Wang answers?"

"*Sí*, senora."

"That would be a very great help. What's your name?"

"Manuel."

"Well, Manuel, please tell Wang that I thank him for breakfast this morning."

Manuel proceeded with a torrent of Spanish, far longer than Libby judged he needed to transmit her opening gambit. Whatever he said caused the diminutive cook to bow deeply in her direction as he responded.

"Wang says he is honored to please the first wife of Senor Cal. What does that mean, first wife?"

"Heavens. Er—something unChristian. You don't need to know right now. Tell Wang that excellent as breakfast was, there are dishes I am used to from my home in England that I would like him to serve in the future."

By the time Libby finished, Wang had reluctantly agreed to her presence in the kitchen to show him and his legion of assistants how to make her mother's savory ragout. She thought that was all he could stand to start with; his wattles were quivering violently.

It was too late to nudge Wang into embellishing the beans and tortillas he had planned for the coming midday meal, so Libby contented herself by listing the ingredients she would require for the next day. When she mentioned how much beef would be needed, Manuel's black eyes gleamed.

"So much? That would take a whole cow!"

"You mean there's no meat hanging? I thought this was a cattle ranch."

Manuel wisely refrained from replying to her querulous mutter. With both hands, Libby pushed her hair, which was dry now and drifting in irritating waves, away from her hot cheeks. Improperly aged beef would be tough and tasteless. She increased her mental estimate of the quantity of herbs that would be necessary.

"Tell Wang to have a steer slaughtered. I'll want the forequarter and hindquarter cut up small and stewed overnight. Save the organs and heart; they can be put into side dishes tomorrow. The rest should be hung until it's fit for roasts and steaks."

"But—but, senora, Wang cannot order a whole cow to be killed."

"Whose permission is needful?" Manuel's brow furrowed. More slowly, Libby asked him, "Who can order a cow to be killed?"

"Senorita Julia. But she is sick. Since the fever, Teresa, she is in charge. We used to eat meat and eggs every day, but Teresa does not like waste."

"Indeed."

Libby didn't miss the point in Manuel's artlessly offered information, or the especially cherubic expression that accompanied it. She appreciated the hint. Teresa was due for a surprise.

Others might be willing to subsist on flat corn cakes and legumes, but she was not. In fact, none of the ranch's population could go on indefintely without some variety in the diet, Caleb especially if he needed to be tempted to the table. Hiding a short-lived quiver of misgiving—they *had* to eat, whether she possessed any actual authority in Caleb's house or not—she told Manuel to inform anyone who asked that she was responsible for the cow's doom and retreated to do something about her hair before lunch. No, dinner, she thought. She'd have to remember that the ranch operated on farmer's time. The major meal of the day was at noon.

Entering her room, she stopped, sure that she'd mistaken the entrance. The she saw her own brush and comb, a dainty set of horn with her initials inset in silver, laid out on a dressing table.

Someone had certainly been busy. The room was unrecognizable. Over newly polished floorboards lay an Indian rug pattered with red lozenges. Cardinal-red calico covered the window. More of the red appeared in sections of the sunburst quilt decorating a tall bed with a fashionable rosewood headboard that must have come from a furniture maker in one of the eastern states. No sign lingered of the humble trundle. Above the dressing table had been bolted an impressively large looking glass. Next to her brush and comb stood a pewter vase foaming with wildflowers. Investigating the rosewood wardrobe, she found her own clothes neatly hung or folded. Among the familiar fabrics glimmered a sheen of scarlet.

"Oh, dear God in heaven, no."

The decadent dress must have been packed with her things before it could be claimed by its owner. Quickly, Libby pushed it to the back of the wardrobe and slammed the door.

Forehead wrinkled in thought, Libby brushed and braided her long mane, having considerable trouble because the homemade soap had stripped all its oils, leaving it full of energy and continually lifting off her head in response to the currents of air flowing through the room. Even when she'd tamed it into a tight coronet, tendrils wisped enticingly about her forehead and cheeks and refused to be contained.

"Oh, bother!" The effect could be interpreted as flirtatious.

It left her feeling ill at ease to realize that she had no way of guessing who had plundered Julia's crates for the new furniture that surrounded her. She presumed someone must have, since she'd observed no comparable furnishings in the rest of the adobe, but whether Caleb or Juan or Teresa had been responsible for the transformation, the room gave no clue.

And she emphatically didn't want any of the three of them to take the tender little curls clustering about her face as a sign that she wanted to catch Caleb's eye.

Hooves stamped and harnesses jingled in the courtyard, while the basso roar of many voices made it clear that the men had come in from the fields and pastures for their meal. Feeling rather shy, Libby went out onto the balcony and saw them flooding into the section of the ground story directly beneath her. That must be the common eating area.

After her years in the womanless West, she ought to be used to causing a sensation, she thought with an inward grimace, but when the hands' conversation stilled and all eyes swung to her dimity-clad figure, it took an effort of will not to bolt out of the big, dark dining hall and back into the sunshine.

Hopping backward over a bench, Juan rapidly zigzagged around tables until he reached her. "Were you looking for the family dining room, Libby? It's—"

"No, in fact I was looking for you." At his quick upward stare, she added, "Or anyone who can authorize the slaughter of some beef. I'm afraid I overstepped my bounds and told the kitchen people for heaven's sake to use meat in tomorrow's dinner."

"You can tell anyone to do anything you want," he said in surprise. "That is—Cal didn't say you couldn't."

Each looked away awkwardly. A wife's orders were subject to her husband's will. Libby fought distaste. Juan considered her as much one of Caleb's possessions as the cow whose fate they were discussing, whether she had proved to be a satisfactory acquisition or not.

Juan licked his lips. "As far as I'm concerned, some meat on the table sounds good. Come to think of it, pickings have been purty lean around here lately. I'll okay you a steer if you want one. Teresa's been taking care of that kind of thing."

The unstated warning was clear. "I've already had a talk with her," she said firmly.

"Well, then." Juan looked relieved, but his gaze roamed the tables, where the hubbub had gradually expanded once more. Her visit must be causing quite a strain, Libby thought. Perhaps the ladies of the house were supposed to avoid this area. "Can I walk you to the family quarters?" he offered.

"No, thank you. I know the way. You eat your meal."

"Yes, ma'am. And I'll surely be looking forward to tomorrow's dinner."

Smiling to acknowledge the hopeful compliment, she picked up her skirts and made her way to the other dining room. The same unoccupied seats and single place setting greeted her. The only difference she could see in the food since breakfast was the addition of a bowl of beans.

Trying not to notice the taste while she chewed, Libby contemplated her morning's work. She was clean and prettily dressed. A light, flowery smell still clung to her wrists, although she suspected the scent of olive oil hung about her as strongly as that of perfume. Juan would support her about the beef, and tomorrow's dinner might be edible. She'd made the first advance in a working relationship with Teresa. Not a friendship, it was true, but at least a mutually understood and respected drawing of battle lines.

Besides, what did she want with friendship? The difficult, happy-and-unhappy link she had forged with Caleb confused her enough. Even while adding up the list of her accomplishments, she felt a gnawing discontent. Abandoning the food as a lost cause, she wandered to the window and watched as the ranch hands remounted and rode their stocky ponies out the gates of the courtyard. Caleb's lean, distinctive form wasn't among them.

Just as well, since her imbecile emotions had reduced her to spying out windows to catch a glimpse of him. Obviously Caleb Logan didn't find the sight of her necessary to complete his day. She was just lucky he hadn't been downstairs eating when she'd pushed her pink-checked dimity and unruly curls where they weren't wanted.

"A covered walkway to the privy?" The carpenter fingered his many-pocketed leather apron. "If you say so, Mr. Logan."

"I say so."

"Be a sight to see, that's for sure. Not even the general has a thing like that."

Caleb appraised the work already completed while the carpenter talked. A fine, large house, its planks primed and ready for the white paint Julia had chosen.

"Any trouble out here in the last week?" he asked when the other man paused for breath.

"Nah. Coupla drifters broke from digging for gold where there weren't any, got riled there weren't no work for 'em, either." The carpenter flexed bulky shoulders. "Didn't take much to convince 'em to move on. Hear the general's got some squatters won't get when they're told. He's too soft."

"General Vallejo doesn't like killing people," Caleb agreed. He scratched his chin. He should have hit Smitty harder. Hell, he should have gotten rid of Tim when he'd had the chance and avoided the whole stinking mess with the Hounds. Funny how Libby's crusading spirit had made it hard to see things straight.

"How long before the house is ready to occupy?" he asked.

" 'Nother three weeks or so to paper and paint and set out all them doodads delivered this morning. A covered walkway, huh?"

Caleb left him ruminating and remounted. Passing the little valley full of poppies, he noticed that broken grass still formed a cushion where he and Libby had lain and kissed.

No doubt it had been a mistake to have brought her to his home. Married, by God, at least for now. Plain bad luck, the padre being at the ranch. But even if they hadn't gotten trapped in their plot to fool Julia, where was he supposed to have taken her instead? A line shack? Or to a rooming house in Petaluma or Sonoma to be exposed to the untender mercies of the local bravos and gossips?

Besides, the plain fact of the matter was that he'd wanted her with him. He still did.

The simple truth of that statement kept him thoughtful all the way into the courtyard. Tossing his reins to one of the waiting pairs of hands, he made his way to the forge. A middle-aged man greeted him.

"Senor Cal! I have finished. A beautiful ring!"

Caleb rolled the wide, smooth band between thumb and forefinger. "A fine job, Pablo. But will it fit?"

"Ascensión, she bring me a glove of the senora's to make sure. It will fit, Senor Cal, I promise. Is it true what they say, hair of gold and eyes like spring leaves?"

Caleb stiffened slightly as jealousy bit deep. Pablo, too? "It's true."

A light of artistic enthusiasm shone from Pablo's eyes. "You will want more jewelry for the senora, yes? There are many stones to marry with such beauty. I could use the turquoises in the strongbox, and the emeralds from Brazil."

Relaxing, Caleb nodded. Emeralds did sound more likely to appeal to Libby than a side of beef. "Draw some designs. Something for around her neck, maybe. I'll have to think on it. See what you can come up with."

"With pleasure, Senor Cal."

The spurs on Caleb's boots jingled as he trod heavily up the steps. The jaunty sound mocked him. His grief over Julia didn't go away just because he was thinking of Libby. His unwilling bride provided a—a counter-irritant, that was it, like a fomentation applied to the feet to relieve an aching head. Whether she provoked him to passion or laughter, or even rage, her presence constantly reminded him that he couldn't escape being alive.

Still, it was past time he spent an afternoon with his sister.

Chapter 11

❦

"**C**aleb Logan, I vow this is the last solitary, unappetizing meal I intend to sit through if I have to slaughter beef myself and eat it in the kitchen with the children."

The quiet dining room didn't answer. Libby threw her napkin next to her scarcely touched plate and stalked out, crinoline swaying.

Although daylight had just begun to fade, a lamp had already been lit in her room, its glow warmly welcoming. The bedclothes had been turned down. Libby sank into their scented softness and hugged herself. She could hardly complain about the quality of personal service, however matters stood in the kitchen. It must be her own perversity that made Caleb's hospitality seem like an insult without Caleb. She closed her eyes against the pretty furniture.

When she opened them, full dark made a black line out of the crevice between the curtains. It seemed very late. Pulling a shawl over her shoulders, she tiptoed across the deserted balcony to Julia's room.

"Caleb. I didn't expect you to be here."

"Get me that bottle of medicine, will you? She slept through her last dose and now she's restless."

Libby stood silently as Caleb measured out a spoonful and coaxed a fretful Julia into swallowing it. Almost immediately, the pale girl subsided into sleep.

"Where's Teresa?"

"Sent her to bed," he answered. "Hours ago. Why aren't you sleeping?"

"It's my turn to stay up."

He stretched long arms over his head. "What time is it?"

"I'm afraid I don't know. No watch." She caught him looking at the spot over her breast where the silver watch had hung. Hastily, she added, "I just assumed it must be after midnight. Everything's so quiet."

"Quiet as the grave." Gently, he straightened one of Julia's braids.

Libby put the backs of her fingers to her mouth to press back words of sympathy she didn't think Caleb wanted from her. Finally, she said, "I've been waiting to speak to you about—about the children."

"What about them?" he asked blankly.

"There seem to be at least a dozen. How are they being educated?"

"The priest comes from Sonoma now and then and leads them through their catechism. That's what he was doing yesterday. Everybody seems to think his being here was—fortuitous."

She refused to be distracted by his oblique reference to their wedding. "Catechism's very valuable, but they should also be learning their alphabet. And ciphering."

"There's been some talk about starting a school in Petaluma. That's all it is so far, talk."

"Surely a man with three hundred fifty thousand acres can spare the pittance required to hire a school-master," Libby said.

Caleb snorted softly. "Now there's a wifely comment."

"Can't you?" she asked, aware of a flush burning her skin.

"Yes, Libby, I can afford it. All right, but I'll have to ask their parents. Some may say no. Most of the children are working to stretch the family earnings."

She hadn't expected such an easy victory. "Thank you."

"It's a good idea. Having his letters gives a boy self-respect."

"Girls benefit from education, too," she flared.

"It may be harder to sell parents on sending the daughters. I'll try. Now come here."

"Why?"

"You're a suspicious thing, aren't you? Because I want to see how wifely you're ready to be."

Her startled green gaze met Caleb's grin. He reached out and took her left hand, his grip warm and hard as he slipped a broad gold band over the third finger. "It looks good there. You have pretty hands."

She tugged free. The ring felt cold, slow to draw heat from her body. "I'll make sure you get it back when—when all this is over."

His grin faded. "Why won't you accept anything from me?"

"I don't have a choice, do I?"

"That's not what I asked," he told her. "Is my gold worth so much less than other men's?"

"You think I'm a whore," she whispered.

"No! I said that wrong. I can tell there haven't been that many others. Maybe no more than one. I wouldn't care what's in your past if I thought you—" He stopped.

She twisted the ring around her finger. "If I what?"

"If I thought you understood you belong with me. Belong to me."

Holding up her hand, she said, "I see. Another heifer for your herd, bought with a gold ring for my nose."

"That's twisting my words and you know it." He pulled her away from Julia's bed, into the shadows. "You're mine, Libby."

She could feel the strength of his body and smell the clean, heady scent of him. He, too, must have had a bath. Libby had to order herself to step away. "Indeed. Has this been declared a slave state? I'm not up on all the political news. You don't just want a mistress, you want a concubine! When are you going to listen to me?

I am not a piece of merchandise you can pick up off
the counter and take home with you!''

"You are home with me,'' Caleb pointed out. "And
it's not a crime to want to sleep with my wife. Not
mistress, Libby. Wife.''

She held her breath. "You said you never used
force.''

"And I won't,'' he said irritably. "Would you stop
looking at me as if I'm a fate worse than death?'' Tiredness cut grooves in his thin cheeks.

Drawing a long, shaken breath, she remarked, "You
need some rest. Best get it while you can.'' Following
his glance toward the bed, she gave him a hesitant
smile. "Teresa told me what to do. If there's any
change, I'll run outside and cry for help. I really can
make myself heard when the occasion demands.''

A huge yawn caught him unawares, and he barely
covered it with his hand. "All right. Libby—''

"Caleb, don't make me argue with you any more
tonight.''

He shrugged, then said, "Good night,'' and turned
to the door. At the entrance he paused briefly. "Julia
keeps her magazines and such in that cupboard over
there.''

She glared in frustration at the empty doorway. "Oh,
would you stop being so confoundedly generous!'' she
muttered.

The only motion under the quilt was the slight rise
and fall of Julia's chest. Libby sighed and investigated
the contents of the cupboard.

Novels by Dickens and Scott stood next to better-
thumbed volumes of gothic fiction. A tall pile of *Godey's* drew her. Their newness impressed her; the date
of the most recent marked it as only eight months old.

Not even the colored fashion plates could hold her
interest. Julia lay perfectly still, her mute torpor somehow accusing. Libby drifted to the bedside. Caleb
hadn't replaced the stopper of the little medicine bottle
quite straight, and she lifted it out. Before she could

push it back in, the sweet odor of cloves tickled her nose.

Laudanum. Many ladies physicked themselves with drops of the opium and alcohol blend for everything from toothache to their monthlies. Never before, though, had Libby seen anyone swallow the potent elixir by the whopping great spoonful as Julia did.

Maman had once given Libby a minute dose of the stuff for a sprained ankle; she remembered a black cloud of sleep interrupted by vivid dreams, and feeling groggy when she finally woke up.

Laudanum.

Reluctantly, because it seemed like a violation of the still form, Libby rolled a *Godey's* into a cylinder and, pushing the quilt aside, bent to place one end of it among the eyelet lace that covered the bodice of Julia's nightgown, and listened through it.

"What are you doing?"

The sharp question made her jump. "Oh, Teresa. Please never lurk like that again. You startled me. Come and let me listen to your heart with this." The older woman backed away from the makeshift tube as if it were a snake. "I know it must seem odd. Just do it, please. I cannot be sure without a comparison."

Teresa bridled but remained obediently motionless as Libby put the tube to her chest. "What is this?"

"A test," Libby murmured. "Shhh."

A solid *thump-thump* rewarded Libby's effort to hear. She straightened, carefully unrolled the magazine, and returned it to the stack in the cupboard.

Teresa's eyes flickered uneasily from Julia to Libby. "The senora is satisfied?"

"Oh, yes," Libby said. "At least, I think so. What was the doctor like, the one who examined the senorita when she had the fever?"

Teresa turned her head and spat.

Blinking, Libby absorbed the answer. "How may I send a message to San Francisco if I do not wish to trouble Senor Cal with it?"

It took patience to convince the housekeeper that the senora's motives in going behind the senor's back were pure. Libby yawned with more than lack of sleep by the time dawn began to overtake the lamplight.

"Thank you, Teresa. Have someone bring paper, pen, and ink to my room. I will have a letter ready for the courier before he leaves."

After leaving Julia's bedroom, Libby checked the breakfast and dinner preparations in the kitchen. The writing necessities she had requested awaited her when she returned to her room. She allowed Ascensión to plump the pillow and pour water for washing, but smiled a refusal at the girl's motion to help her out of the crumpled dress. "No, *gracias*. Go along now."

Ascensión left, trailing a doubtful look. The first letter Libby wrote, handwriting cramped because she had to bend over the dressing table, came swiftly. She read it over and signed it *Elizabeth Logan* without a pause. Then she stared at the signature for a long moment, the pen shaking in her hand. Only one day had passed since her farcical wedding, and already some part of her thought of herself as a new, different person. Caleb's bride.

Controlling herself with an effort, she addressed the outside flap to Caleb's agent in the city. The second letter took longer, although its contents were shorter. Explaining the present situation to her aunt and uncle was out of the question. After nibbling on the end of her pen, at last she scribbled that she was safe not far from San Francisco, the guest of a ranching family. "I plan to take ship for home as soon as may be. I remain your loving niece, Elizabeth."

All would depend on what sort of answer she received to her first letter, but with any luck, the unsatisfactory note would precede her by no more than a few weeks.

Depending, of course, on how often vessels left for the foreign waters outside the Golden Gate.

Holding the papers concealed in the folds of her skirt,

Libby stepped onto the balcony and peered down at the workers filling the courtyard. Teresa had described the courier as a very young man with mustaches of which he was inordinately proud. Catching sight of a youngster whose sparse, heavily oiled facial adornment seemed to fit the bill, Libby ran down the stairs to give him her letters.

Caleb noticed the pink and white skirts swirling across the courtyard. Libby seemed in quite a hurry this morning. He'd sat alone at the breakfast table, wishing she would join him and not sending for her because she must either be with Julia or asleep at this hour. The unexpectedness of seeing her as he stepped out of the dining room brought a sudden spurt of pleasure. Then the unreasoning lightening of his spirits died a rapid death as he watched her approach Luis and speak to him with animation.

The vise that had closed on Caleb's gut released its grip. Impossible. Seven years separated Luis's age from Libby's; the boy still suffered from a cracking voice and prominent Adam's apple. However much the youngling might be attracted to a beautiful older woman—and he was staring at Libby as if she'd miraculously descended from heaven—she would regard him as hardly more than a child.

Fine, thought Caleb. You've found one male on the ranch you don't have to be pea-green jealous of.

He was turning away in disgust at himself when a movement from Libby stopped him. The blond head dipped close to the dark one, and her hand emerged from her skirt to pass over something white and folded small.

A letter? But Libby claimed not to know anyone in this part of the country except . . .

The piano player.

Mouth tight and brows a single line, Caleb met Libby as she came back up the stairs.

"Good morning," Libby offered tentatively, noting the signs of temper. "Did you get any rest?"

"Enough." He brushed by her.

Libby screwed up her courage. "Caleb, wait." Impatience clear in every line of his lean body, he jerked to a stop one step below her. "Will—will you be home for dinner? I've got something special planned."

"What game are you playing at, Libby?"

"I don't know what you mean."

"Then let me spell it out for you. You can send messages to anybody you like—don't bother to deny it, I saw you. Despite what you said, this is a free state. You're a free woman. But for you to go from hiding secret letters to wifely solicitude in less than five minutes puts a strain on me. A big strain."

"And you think there's none on me? Everything about our situation is unnatural."

Their faces were on a level. Caleb looked straight into her eyes. "I'm glad you realize it. Libby—damn it to hell and back, I'm acting like a fool. The situation *is* unnatural. You won't come to me and it makes me loco with jealousy to see you with another man. Any other man."

"You can't think—not that boy—"

"No." Relief that he could say it with sincerity made his deep voice warm. "I've got that much sense." He took her hands in his and ran a blunt fingertip over the gold band. "Don't let yourself be tied to the piano player. He's not worth one of your smiles."

Below, dogs yelped and children chased them. Men cursed good-naturedly in English and Spanish as they tried to avoid the small, rushing figures. A pungent smell of horse and hides, only partly thinned by the freshness of early morning, rose in the air. But Libby's world narrowed to Caleb's scent, Caleb's touch, as he traced the exact dimensions of his ring on her finger.

"Aloysius Malloy has never been anything to me. How many ways do you want me to swear it?"

He dropped her hands. "We'll get along better if you give up all this prevaricating. Just don't write to him, okay? After a while you won't hanker after him anymore.''

"Oh, Caleb. Sometimes you're so kind. And so wrong. I haven't sent Malloy any messages. You can call the courier . . .'' She looked over his shoulder, but Luis had disappeared. "Oh. He's gone. Well, someone can go after him and bring him back. Read the letters if you want to—'' Recalling the contents of the first letter, she broke off.

"Will I like what I read?'' he asked grimly.

"I would prefer that you didn't see one of them,'' she admitted. "I can't explain without—'' Without raising possibly false expectations, she thought. A rolled-up copy of *Godey's* wasn't much to hang a life on. Miserably, she added, "I can't explain at all.''

To her surprise, he didn't rail at her. "And the other letter?''

"To my family. To tell them where I am and that I hope to come home to England soon.''

The hard dark eyes grew harder. "I see.''

"If we pretend with each other, we'll both go insane. You know you want this travesty of a marriage ended as soon as I do.''

"I said I see.''

"Will you be at dinner?'' she asked hesitantly.

"Lady, don't push me.'' He was down the stairs, ahorse, and through the gates before she could react. Sighing, she considered her self-imposed tasks for the morning. It was a long list.

Libby toured the common dining room at noon to make sure the meal being set in front of the men did her justice—and also, she knew, in the hope of hearing an appreciative word or two. After all, the diva in her had gotten used to applause. The Libby who was an uneasy houseguest was finding it hard to rise above a hunger for approval. Even if it was for nothing more than her mother's ragout.

Certainly the workers seemed to find the meal an event worth comment. Or, rather, an encouraging lack of comment. After the first few noisy bites, they settled down to serious eating, awarding her stew the accolade of blissful silence. Smiling, Libby sought the family dining room.

"I'd about decided you weren't coming," Caleb said.

She forced herself to walk calmly to the table and take her place across from him. "Why should you think that? I'm very attached to the idea of regular meals. Overgrown as I am—"

"You've said that before. Don't be foolish. You're the perfect size."

For once the compliment came with no overtone of mockery or blighting lack of interest. His blunt statement was more believable than any amount of flowery commonplace, and her fingers tightened on the ladle. "I—I didn't look for you to be here, either."

"Why not?" He gave her a tiny grin. "I'm attached to regular meals, too."

"Then I expect you to eat hearty, sir. Wang has suffered to bring you something edible." She set a brimming bowl in front of him.

He chewed and raised an eyebrow. "You got Wang to produce this? How? It's good!"

"Through an interpreter. And I have a confession to make." She savored a ladylike bite of meat and vegetables. "There wasn't any beef hanging, so I ordered a cow to be slaughtered." His expression changed, and Libby put down her fork. She'd enjoyed her forays into the kitchen, but Caleb might well regard them as meddling, plain and simple. "Juan thought you wouldn't object. Not that he's to blame in any way—I did the ordering. But, Caleb, really, all these people who work for you need meat occasionally to stay healthy. It's false thrift to scrimp on food. If you're angry—"

"I'm not angry," he said in a strange voice. "Except that you think I'd starve my workers."

"Not starve, precisely. I got the impression that certain economies have been going forward since . . . since Julia has been ill."

He pushed his bowl away. "Not on my say-so. No meat hanging at all? Out with it. What's been going on?"

Libby repeated Manuel's story, deleting his artless comments about the housekeeper. Her careful consideration did no good; Caleb listened with set lips and then said, "Teresa."

"She seems so completely devoted to you," Libby interjected. His grim taciturnity frightened her a little. She'd wanted to curtail Teresa's excessively saving disposition, not to cause the poor woman to be dismissed from the Logan's service. "I'm sure Teresa was only trying to do her best. She's trained the maids beautifully. It's just in the kitchen that things need some supervision."

"And you figure to supervise."

She bent over her bowl to hide her face. "I know what you think about me. Let me assure you, my presence won't defile the food. Or the children."

"I'm pretty sure you don't know what I'm thinking," Caleb said. When her eyes lifted to his, he said, "If you want to add taking over the kitchen to your wifely duties, far be it from me to stop you. I can't complain about the dinner."

A smile flickered across her face. "You could take a few more bites before it gets cold."

He loaded his fork. Eating her own portion with an inner satisfaction that had less to do with the ragout than with Caleb's returning appetite, she started when he laughed.

"Is something amusing?"

"You could say so. Just yesterday I was thinking it would take more than a side of beef to win your heart."

"Considerably more," she retorted hotly, and then blushed. "I didn't mean that the way it sounded. My heart isn't for sale."

He smiled and used a piece of bread to sop up the gravy. "That's a pretty dress you have on, Libby. I liked that pink one better, though." He stood and headed for the door, running the side of his hand lightly over her cheek in passing. "It matched the roses in your cheeks."

Her skin seemed to retain the memory of his touch. "There's not a thing wrong with this dress!" She held a protective hand over the high neck of her sober gray gown. It was well-cut half mourning, left over from the death of a distant cousin years ago, and worn now in penance for trying to take Caleb's fancy with the pink dimity. If anything, she'd reasoned as she'd changed into it this morning, she should be laboring to avoid inciting his lust.

"That's what I said," he said, lips quirking, and left before she could retort.

"You're as irritating as any husband, and that's no lie," Libby called after him, and burst into giggles as his laughter boomed in the contained space between the balcony roof and balcony floor.

She slept away the afternoon, and again found Caleb attending Julia when she crept into the sickroom to begin her watch. The next day followed the same routine, as regular as a monastic rule, and the separation forced by their different schedules began to lull Libby into a feeling of safety from Caleb's desires—and her own. She couldn't quite ignore the hot tremors that weakened her legs when he paused while saying good night, but she took comfort in the fact that there was literally no time or place for him to teach her what the promise implicit in the heat and the tremors meant. Julia's illness was the overriding concern of them both.

On her seventh day at the ranch, the doctor came.

Libby had lain down to rest in preparation for another night of sickroom duty but ran to the courtyard as soon as Manuel pounded on her door to tell her that a Yanqui had arrived. She'd been suffering increasing disquiet at administering the laudanum, but every time she skimped on the amount, Julia became agitated, and the next person to sit with her tipped a generous slug of the stuff down the sick girl's throat. Fearful of raising

Caleb's hopes for his sister only to have them dashed again, Libby had waited in silence for a response from his agent. Her request had been simple. Send the best doctor in San Francisco to the Manzanita at once.

Leather satchel sagging into the dust of the courtyard at his feet, the man was rubbing his skinny hindquarters with both hands. In shape he resembled a crane, with a thin, curved body and an enormous aquiline nose. By torchlight she couldn't read his eyes, but they squinted shrewdly as he limped forward to take Libby's hand.

She smiled. "Welcome. I'm Elizabeth Logan. Did you have a good trip?"

"Sam Simons. Dr. Simons. No, I did not. Bilious by boat and martyred on that damned wooden saddle. What kind of tomfool contraption is that for a Christian to sit on, anyway?"

Libby tried to bring her mouth under control. "I've noticed the Californios use them without discomfort. As well as Ca— Mr. Logan, my husband, of course. Thank you for coming such a long way. Your patient is up here."

Leading the way up the stairs, Libby told him as much as she knew about Julia's condition. He grunted when she mentioned rheumatic fever.

Caleb was spooning beef broth into Julia as they entered. He looked up in surprise, allowing his sister to turn her head away from the clear liquid in weary repulsion.

"Dr. Simons is here to examine Julia, Caleb."

Brows drawing together, he made room for the doctor, who immediately bent over the bed, saying gruffly, "Are you the young lady who doesn't like to eat?"

"I sent for him to come," Libby said quickly. "I know it wasn't my place, but it seemed to me that Julia ought to be seen by another physician. I hope you don't mind."

"Of course I don't mind," Caleb told her. "I was going to do it myself except . . . she's been so bad since we got home. It seemed so hopeless when from day to day I've expected . . .''

He'd been waiting for her to die. Taking his inert arm, Libby settled it around her waist and wrapped both of her arms around him securely.

Simons prodded Julia here and there, asked her questions, and studied her through every rambling answer. He stared into the pinpricks of her pupils and, as Libby had, produced a funnel to listen to her heart.

Finally, he nodded as if he'd reached a conclusion and ushered Caleb and Libby out the door. ''Can anyone else stay with her? I want to talk to you.''

Caleb called down for Teresa, who panted up the stairs in alarm. Juan came pelting after her. After calming the housekeeper, Caleb led the way into the sitting room, another big rectangular space with whitewashed walls and massive furniture. Without comment, he waved Juan and Simons toward the settle. Libby stood next to him tensely.

The doctor sat, hands bunched on his knees and large nose quivering with outrage. ''The only thing wrong with Miss Logan is the poison you've been feeding her.''

Chapter 12

"**J**esus, Mary and Joseph," Juan whispered, and bolted from the room.

"Excitable young man," said Dr. Simons without approval.

Caleb was staring in astonishment at the space where Juan had been. "I knew he was fond of Julia, but I didn't realize . . . There's nothing wrong with her heart?"

"Sound as a bell."

"But—she won't eat. Her body isn't functioning, and her mind . . ."

"Laudanum," Libby said into the silence after his voice trailed off. "When I found out what the other doctor had left for you to physic her with, I wondered. If you've never met ladies who depend on their 'drops,' you wouldn't have any way of knowing it's a powerful opiate."

Juan charged in, dragging Teresa behind him. Her round face creased in bewilderment. "Juan is gone loco," she wailed. "He say I poison my senorita—"

Without rising from his seat, Simons gave the impression of pouncing. "You're the one who started dosing Miss Logan with laudanum?"

"The medicine the doctor leave, *sí*," admitted Teresa, looking fearful. "He say, make her take it when she is restless. Senor Cal, he go to San Francisco and say, keep her quiet, make her rest. So I give."

"How had she been before that?" asked Simons.

Caleb didn't speak. After a quick glance at his employer, Juan said, "Skin and bones, tired easily. Fractious, which isn't like her. Complained at having to take naps. She came through the fever in February and never seemed well after that."

"If you'd had rheumatic fever, you'd be a while recovering, too," Simons grunted.

"It was a violent taking." Juan spoke tightly. "We didn't think she'd live." He paced to the door and back again.

Caleb's eyes reflected the lamplight. "All right. Her heart's not damaged. But you can't call her well the way she is now."

"How long has she been dosed steadily? Two weeks? And she hasn't been taking it of her own free will." Simons tapped his fingers on his thigh. "What kind of woman is she? No chivalrous lies, if you please. The bare truth. Is Miss Logan the easy, persuadable kind? Bends with every wind, does she? Not much backbone?"

Juan laughed, great, gusty guffaws that bent his lean frame in two. Caleb grinned. "My sister's even-tempered normally, but . . . no. She's strong as a pony and stubborn as a mule, even if she is prettier."

Simons lifted his nose. "Good. A steadfast disposition is what she'll need, the more obstinate the better. Mrs. Logan, who'll be undertaking the nursing after this?" He ignored Teresa, who began to weep into her hands.

"I will," Libby said. She looked at Caleb. "That is, if it's acceptable to Mr. Logan. Caleb?"

He didn't answer directly; instead, he picked her up off her feet and crushed her to him. The air came out of her in a startled peep, and her fingers dug into his forearms in a reaction against falling. She had time only to register that despite the way her ribs creaked under the pressure of his arms around her, her body obeyed instinct and tried to crowd closer. Then his mouth dove down onto hers.

The kiss was so hard and jubilant her lips felt the imprint of his teeth. Then he dropped her, sparing a moment precious to Libby to steady her on her feet before he headed out of the room. Juan followed, still laughing, his bony face almost handsome with the joy of relief. When they'd left, and their footsteps diminished in the direction of Julia's bedroom, the only sound in the sitting room was Teresa's quiet sobbing.

The knowledge that the housekeeper probably wouldn't thank her for sympathy couldn't staunch the wellspring of feeling inside Libby. So many people she was becoming fond of: Julia, Juan, Teresa . . . Caleb, first and foremost and most terrifyingly.

Unable to stop herself, Libby put her arm around Teresa's heaving shoulders and led her to the settle.

"Hush, now. No harm done. It was a mistake, a grievous error, yes, but all will be well now. The doctor will tell us how to make Julia better."

He cleared his throat, and his Adam's apple bobbed up and down. "Only two weeks using the laudanum, and her constitution and character are strong . . . hmpph. In my opinion, unless the facts are other than you have stated, there is no reason to suspect this episode will lead to a permanent craving. Once you begin to withhold the medicine from the young lady, she should be back to normal in a week or so." His prim mouth pursed further. "It may be a bad week."

"What should we expect?" Libby asked.

"Hard to say," Simons answered frankly. "I've seen opium eaters in the dens of San Francisco . . . well. Delirium and convulsions would follow taking the stuff away from a confirmed addict, but Miss Logan is hardly that. It is a case of wait and see."

"But she will get well?"

"Oh, not a doubt of it."

"Do you hear that, Teresa?" Libby hugged her gently. The housekeeper continued to weep. The almost silent tears drove Libby to a flurry of comforting old adages. "All's well that ends well. What's done is done; at least there shall be no lasting harm. No use crying over spilled milk—"

Teresa lifted a blotched face. "It is not milk that got spilled, it is Senorita Julia!"

"Yes, but she's not permanently spilled—that is, affected. We're going to make her better, you and I."

"Senor Cal, he not even look at me! He treat me as if I am dead!"

"He was in a hurry, that's all. When he stops to think, he'll know it was just your affection for Miss Julia that led you to—to follow the other doctor's orders too well."

Tears began to seep from beneath Teresa's eyelids again.

Libby had an inspiration. "Dr. Simons will need a bed made up for him, Teresa. I don't know how to ask any of the maids. Really, you're the only one who can handle the details. I can't imagine what all of us would do if you make yourself ill."

"I am never ill. I have not the time for sickness." Teresa's back straightened.

Libby's flexible voice altered to tones of the most abject humility. "I know. You do so much. Please, Teresa, could you see to a room for Dr. Simons? And I'm sure he'll have further instructions for us, so after that, come to Miss Julia's room and we'll discuss what's to be done."

Simons waited until Teresa left with a subdued bustle before he remarked in congratulation, "You are accustomed to handling a large household, Mrs. Logan."

"No," Libby said. At the surprised cant of his nose, she added, "My—my marriage is of very recent date. But I grew up in a house with a complete staff, and I suppose I learned a great deal about holding house from my mother. She was French and had a very firm way with servants."

He allowed his stiff mouth to smile. "I wouldn't call

it firm, but your way seems to work as well. In fact, I'd say you handled that *mestiza* a fair treat.''

A small, hot core of protective anger burned in Libby. Poor Teresa; dignity and pride both had received a terrible buffet tonight. *Mestiza* wasn't a word that was familiar to Libby, but it didn't sound very complimentary. She wanted to squash the doctor's pretensions by referring to Teresa formally by her last name, but she didn't know it. Coolly, she said, ''As it happens, I was able to reassure Teresa with the truth. While I haven't been here at the Manzanita long, it took little time for me to discover how invaluable she is to the smooth running of the household. Now, if you could tell me what to do for Miss Logan's well-being . . .''

His crane's face sharpened at the implied reprimand. Somewhat to her surprise, he seemed to accept it. Caleb's reputation—or Caleb's wealth—strangled whatever affront the doctor felt. ''Certainly,'' he said dryly. ''That's what you brought me out here to do. But first let me put something on that cut.''

''What—'' Libby forced herself not to jump as he touched her bottom lip with a cloth soaked in tincture. It stung.

''Your husband has a forceful way of expressing his affections, I gather.''

The kiss. Thinking of Caleb's exultant mouth against hers, she couldn't even rouse indignation that his teeth had grazed her hard enough to draw blood.

I'm becoming a different person, she realized. Oh, God. Who will I be before I escape? Sometimes silken, frequently harsh bonds were tying her ever closer to Caleb Logan.

Fog lay in thick streamers on the ground when Libby stepped out of Julia's room and paused to watch the morning chaos in the courtyard. She was coming to appreciate the order that underlay the seeming Bedlam. Cowboys, a rich mixture of races and languages, were calling for horses or raiding the kitchen for a bite before chores. Children ran errands and shouted, chasing the dogs, some of whom were hunting dogs and others scavengers kept to reduce the amount of garbage and number of vermin in the adobe fortress. Women swayed to and from storage sheds or joined Wang and more children preparing the mountain of food needed for breakfast.

A yawn caught her unawares. Barely able to lift a hand to stifle it, she decided she was too tired to worry about the coming meal. Caleb, Juan, and Teresa, and sometimes all three, had dropped by Julia's room all through the night. Relief had made Juan voluble. Teresa had been the most irritating kind of penitent, silent in Caleb's presence and filled with guilt and self-justification the rest of the time. Pity holding asperity in check, Libby had finally insisted that the other woman retire. Caleb had been quiet but constantly in motion, stalking the corners of the room.

His eyes had glittered as he helped her tend his sister, whose increasing restlessness Libby took as a good sign. The last time he'd visited the sickroom, he'd been with Juan, and the flicker in his eyes every time he'd looked at Libby had increased to a steady flame. Juan had been waving around a flask of brownish liquid, and Libby judged that both of them had been celebrating to perhaps the mid-point of the bottle.

Smiling through another yawn, she wended her way to her own room. Her tolerance for Caleb's method of commemorating his sister's return from the dead abruptly evaporated at the sight of his formidable length stretched out over the quilt.

"Caleb! What are you doing in here?"

His hat was cocked low over his face, and his black boots had left marks on one of the rust-red sunbursts. Libby put her hands on her hips.

"Trying out my bed," he said, teeth flashing in a slow, satisfied grin in the shadow of the hat brim. "Special ordered all the way from New York State.

Nice and long. Plenty of room. Comfortable, don't you think?''

"You're drunk."

"Yeah, I am, a little. Not so's it'll make any difference.''

"I don't know what you're talking about."

"No," he said thoughtfully, "I don't suppose you do. Damnation, Libby, how you ever hooked up with a belly-dragging varmint like your piano player—''

Tiredness washed over Libby in waves. "We cannot, cannot, cannot have this discussion again. I need to lie down. Please, Caleb.''

He didn't move. "Of course you can lie down. Come here, dear heart.''

"Go away, Caleb.''

"Don't you like the bed? I had it set up for you. Thought you'd take a fancy to real boughten furniture.''

"Are you the one who did that for me?" Relenting, Libby came closer. With as hearty a shove as she could muster, she pushed his boots until they hung slightly over the side of the bed, and sat gingerly in their place. "Thank you. It's a lovely suite.''

"You're too far away.'' His voice softened and darkened to a murmur like molasses.

"I'm fine where I am." Her head felt light and as if it weren't quite attached. She made her voice cutting to keep herself from giving up, giving in and curling next to his big, sprawling body. A fleeting image, almost a dream in miniature, passed in the blink of an eye; a doomed bee spiraling close to something irresistibly sweet but fatal.

"I owe you, Libby. Beautiful, clever Libby. Lonely, lost, little one.''

"Cal—''

"My debt hasn't been paid from our night in San Francisco. Remember?''

Libby licked her lips and looked away.

"And now I owe you more than ever. You've saved my sister's life. The rest of us would have let her die, and we would have been the ones killing her. I would have been her murderer, and never known.''

"Don't think that way. It wasn't anybody's fault, not yours, not even Teresa's—oh, Caleb, she's in despair, believing you blame her. Can't you speak to her?''

"Later,'' he promised, and reached out so fast her exhausted eyes saw the motion only as a blur. "This minute I have another wrong to right.''

His quick action pulled her up and over him in an instant. Libby landed with a thump, but the jolt didn't surprise as much as a grunt out of Caleb. He wound his fingers into her coronet of braids. "I know how to be gentle, dear heart. You deserve pleasure when you're being loved.''

His kiss was soft but firm; his hands held her head so she couldn't have evaded the warm, nibbling caress if she'd wanted to. She couldn't summon even a token reluctance. Their lips met and parted and met again with tiny, intimate sounds that began to form a rhythm with the shallow gulps of air that were all Libby could manage.

He kissed her until she was almost fainting from a combination of weariness and dizziness that gradually merged into passion. He tasted of brandy. Libby had never understood the savor of its astringent tang before; on Caleb's lips, however, the flavor was tart and alluring, with a lingering heat that worked its way into her veins and set them on fire.

Caleb felt the rigidity seep out of her body and eased her onto her side. Her hand wavered up to touch his cheek. It urged his mouth to seek hers again, but instead he turned his head and teased the center of her palm with his tongue before biting gently along the base of her thumb. She moaned, not in protest.

"Ah, Libby, yes,'' Caleb murmured. "I think of your hand on me when I lay down to sleep. And when I rise in the morning. And out on the graze land, and during the night watch when the rest of the place is cold and silent and we're the only two awake. Don't you remember?''

She placed little kisses up and down his neck. Her lashes tickled the sensitive skin behind his ear. "I can't forget. I've tried to—I ought to.''

"Don't talk like that. What we feel together is good. It's natural. You're a warm, generous woman. But you shouldn't have to be the one who gives all the time. Let me give to you.''

A strong current of pleasure filled Caleb when her hand remained unresisting as he lowered it slowly and folded it over his hardened manhood. At her touch, the shaft strained upward, mindlessly seeking release; half the pleasure for its master was the knowledge that this once Libby was willing.

Eager, even. The hand on his manhood rubbed it lightly but deliberately, while the one trapped between them clutched at his shirt, and she kept running her mouth, and sometimes just her tongue, over his lips, jaw, throat. Caleb wanted to rip his way through the barricade of her clothing and plunge into the golden port he knew awaited him. Mindful of his promise, he held back, damning the brandy that was robbing him of some of his control. He must flood Libby with such a torrent of satisfaction that she'd never look at the piano player again.

His fingers found the buttons at the front of her dress, shaking slightly as he pulled open each loop. When the last one came free, he slipped the detachable bodice from her shoulders to reveal the bands that covered her breasts.

"Caleb, kiss me. Kiss me the way you did before.'' Something akin to panic reduced her voice to a whisper.

Not until Caleb removed her polonaise did Libby realize the full extent of what was happening. She wanted to stop it; she wanted it to never end. She needed the kiss to muffle the frightened part of her brain that was still capable of thought.

He made a noise deep in his throat, part laugh, part growl. Then his tongue invaded her mouth, filling, withdrawing, filling again. She murmured her pleasure and wriggled her hands free to roam his face, his ears, the thick, alive hair cropped short at his nape, the bunched muscles of his shoulders.

He lifted his head to pull the pins from her braids and untie the ribbons that secured them. With aching slowness, he unknotted the ropes of hair and spread the rippling tresses fan-shape across the pillow. They had the subdued golden glow of cornsilk in the gray light insinuating itself through the curtains.

"This is all the fortune a man could ever want," he told her softly.

Heavy lids gave his eyes a sleepy, knowing look. Libby could tell his desire burned unabated, and that the sight of her hair unbound continued to inflame him . . . but passion gripped her, too, and demanded more immediate stoking.

Lifting a strand of her hair, she drew it across his mouth and followed it with her tongue.

"I know a deeper kiss that will please you," he said hoarsely when her tongue withdrew from a thorough exploration. "Here, we must rid you of all these petticoats."

As he sorted through the knots and bows at her waist, a dim sense of survival led her to say, "Caleb, you won't—that is, we shan't—before, when we were at the hotel, you said you wouldn't—that it's possible to exchange pleasure without—"

His fingers stilled for a moment, then he said quietly, "You are still afraid of consummating the marriage."

"Yes," she whispered, relieved that he, at least, hadn't boggled at plain speaking.

He wrenched the last tie open. "I would take care of you, Libby, if there was a child. You wouldn't have to fear."

"You don't understand!" A sob hiccupped into laughter. "No, of course you don't. You're a man. How could you know what it's like to be abandoned in a hateful place, destitute, with your only sensible course to sell yourself for the right to a place at some hard-scrabble farmer's table? I didn't bargain myself away so cheaply two years ago, and I won't today, either. I will not become a—a nothing! No one has to take care of me!"

Caleb left her skirts where they were and pulled her into his arms, holding her until her choked laughter ceased. Tenderness sprang up within him and fed the heavy, pulsing ache in his loins. "All right, dear heart, all right. I promise. Just touching."

"When you kiss me, I . . . How do you make me feel this way, Caleb?" He felt her eyes on him as he pulled her skirts over her feet in one large heap. With what sounded like simple, innocent amazement, she said, "Look, you're rumpling all my things again, and it doesn't even put me in a passion. And I'm letting you steal away my shoes and—and do that—" She sighed at the caress his hands gave her calves in the process of removing her lisle stockings. "I feel no shame."

Caleb had told the truth when he'd said he wasn't too drunk; the toasts he and Juan had drunk to Libby, then Julia, then Libby again had only freed the reckless streak from his native hardheadedness.

The liquor had pushed him to try his luck in his—Libby's—bed, a notion a cardsharp like Libby ought to appreciate. But his pleasantly muzzy state was receding, and he knew he shouldn't remind her of how she'd revealed what she was, or encourage her to talk about shame. "There's more than one kind of passion."

"Is there?" She didn't take the statement the way he meant it. Her green eyes, wide with fascination, followed the motion of his fingers, busy with his own buttons. "Are you going to teach them to me?"

Congratulating himself for negotiating successfully around one possible lover's reef, Caleb promptly ran aground on another. "There was a girl at this house in Marseilles; I learned a lot there that can pleasure us both." He pulled experimentally on the satin ribbon nestling in the valley between her breasts.

She scooted back against the pillows with so much speed the ribbon whipped out of its holes. "What girl? What kind of house?"

The strip of blue dangled from his hand. "Just—a girl. You know. You're a woman of experience."

"Not that kind of experience."

The celebratory drinks were wearing off. Caleb rubbed the tight-feeling skin of his face. "If you insist on me spelling it out, she worked in the kind of house a man visits when he's not partial to the arses of other sailors and his ship's been two months at sea."

"What was her name?" Libby's little pink mouth, so full and inviting a minute ago, had firmed into an uncompromisingly straight line.

"How the hell should I know?"

"Was it Marie-Rose? Mary Rose?"

"Libby, you take the strangest notions. The young lady and I didn't enjoy that kind of acquaintance. If we were introduced, it's a social nicety I don't remember," he said with the sarcasm of an incipient hangover. "I was too busy keeping a weather eye peeled to make sure none of her associates coldcocked me for my bankroll to do more than get value for my money."

"Which she obviously provided." Her normally warm voice could have frozen ticks in a grizzly's coat on the Fourth of July.

"That she did." All white and gold pressed up against the dark cherrywood headboard, Libby was lovely even with a schoolmarm's scowl contradicting the effect of lace and whalebone. "And we will benefit." Ignoring the first pounding in his skull, he tried to gentle her again with teasing. "If it brings you pleasure, it'll be the best money I ever spent in my life."

She responded with a wild swing that fended off his reaching hands but failed to budge the rest of his big-boned body an inch. "Money! Is that all Americans think about? Besides fornication and—oh, yes—the absolute moral imperative to stamp your big, dirty boots all over every godforsaken mile of the New World."

"The land is here, and people are filling it," Caleb said reasonably. "Can't blame them for that, as long as they're not trying to take my land away from me. And I never heard that Britishers have anything against making money—or fornicating, for that matter. They just don't talk about it. Bad taste. But, believe me, that doesn't stop them from doing both."

"Indeed? What a perceptive reading of the English character. You've left out a few things. Such as the Crusades and Shakespeare and Trafalgar. Frankly, if you intend to while away the morning with edifying tales of the education in harlotry you purchased in the stews of Marseilles, you must excuse me. I need some sleep. I'll be nursing your sister tonight."

Caleb swore. Libby's sudden, inexplicably cantankerous mood finished what the brandy's dissipation had begun; while his arousal throbbed as potent as ever, he was too thoroughly exasperated for the patient lovemaking he was determined to lavish on her prickly hide. And he couldn't let himself take what she so stubbornly refused to offer. It would be rape. She looked too much like a doe, tawny and huge-eyed and cornered against a tree. He stood, grabbing for his shirt, and demanded, "What is it you think Britishers have that Americans don't, anyway?"

Libby hugged her pantalet-clad knees to her chest. Her breasts and the soft, secret places between her legs ached with disappointment. She would have surrendered everything except the asset of her virginity, the only part of her old self the last week had left intact . . . if only he hadn't made it so clear that he considered her merely another whore. "Honor," she answered.

His harsh laugh bit. He leaned over her, caging her against the headboard with his long arms. His veins and muscles stood out in sharply sculpted relief. "Lady, leaving you alone in this bed is about as close to your idea of honor as I'm ever going to get. And don't expect me to be this buffleheaded and noble the next time."

He cut off her breath with a quick kiss that managed to be dismissive and possessive at the same time. Bunching the shirt in his hands, he kicked her skirts out of his way across the rug as he strode out onto the balcony.

His impatient stride almost carried him into Sam Simons's spindle-legged form. The doctor looked askance at Caleb's bare chest and the prominent and well-defined state of rut Libby had condemned him to, which his half-undone trouser buttons left unconcealed. Barking a "Good morning!" Caleb brushed by Simons. When he reached his own room, he slammed the door.

Simons continued on to his patient's bedside with an unremitting air of disapproval. An irregular household. He'd heard enough of the argument between husband and wife to know that Mrs. Logan had refused to submit to the intimacies enjoined on her by God and nature. Beautiful women traded on their beauty to shirk their obligations, even when those duties were easy, he thought dispassionately. After all, what need she do but open her legs and pretend not to be repulsed for a minute or two to fulfill her function as a vessel for her husband's seed?

Against his will, he'd been rather impressed with her statuesque blondness last night. That was before she'd snapped at him so rudely, of course. And over a half-breed maid!

No surprise in her not wanting the attentions of that husband of hers. Inhospitable, surly brute. Spent the night drinking, too, from the looks of him. An uncaring brother. As for his indecency, erupting into daylight near to buck naked and aroused like a stag in season, it was all of a piece. The man hadn't even thanked Simons for traveling forty miles under impossible conditions. A boor. However, the unsatisfactory nature of the patient's family made no difference in Simons's treatment of the drugged girl; his oath bound him to do his best, and he would. He owed it to himself. But Simons intended to prepare a very large bill.

Logan didn't even give him the satisfaction of paling at the sight of that bill. When he confronted the rancher with a neatly itemized account at the dinner table, the first time his host had appeared after their initial meeting that day, Logan simply nodded and tucked into his food. The doctor remembered that he was rumored to be a man of awe-inspiring substance. Simons wasn't, and he resented Logan's moneyed indifference.

As Simons was pushed by an amused cowhand into another penitential saddle in preparation for the ride to meet the riverboat, a servant delivered a wallet filled with cash as well as a sound slap on the pony's rump that started the animal with a jolt. A number of people in the courtyard laughed. Simons didn't appreciate the humor in the situation; as he bounced helplessly up and down, his teeth clattering together with bone-jarring force, he didn't appreciate it at all.

The trip to the city by water was miserable beyond belief. The crew actually expected him to jump overboard and help pole the steamer off the innumerable sandbars the pilot's incompetence caused it to strike. They said some very vulgar things when he refused, and not behind his back.

All in all, it wasn't unpleasant to confine his conversation to the other passenger on the small boat, a man named Malloy. Despite a dreadfully common Irish accent, he displayed a flattering curiosity in Simons's visit to the Manzanita, and an interesting limp.

Chapter 13

"**W**ho are you?"

Libby set a plate on Julia's bedside table and sent the maid who'd been rocking quietly to find Caleb. "I'm Libby. Don't you recognize me at all?"

A thin hand tugged at the end of one short braid, while its owner continued to study Libby with confused concentration. "No," Julia said slowly. "That is—this is going to sound crazy, but—have I dreamed about you? I mean, is there any reason why I should have? I—I think there's been something wrong with me."

"Yes," agreed Libby gently. "But you're getting better now. Almost well."

"I am? That's a relief. I feel weak as water. Did I take the fever again?"

"Not exactly." Libby wished with all her might that Caleb would hurry. It was his place to explain to his sister how she'd almost been killed with kindness. "It was a sort of complication from the fever, you might say."

"Oh. The doctor warned us there might be effects. Cal went into a tizzy, took it more seriously than I did. I guess my brother was right and I was wrong. Is there food in that dish? I'm starving."

Libby lifted Julia, who exclaimed at her own feebleness again, and held the dish under the other girl's chin. "Wild strawberries and cream. I though you might like a change from broth." And a mild kick to get her system working.

"All I've been eating is clear soup? No wonder I can't sit up by myself." Faint color lingered in her cheeks.

Noting the mark of embarrassment, Libby handed Julia the spoon and refrained from commenting on the flush, the first change she'd ever seen in the blanched lifelessness of Julia's complexion. "Some of the children went out to the beach to collect these for you. They assure me the strawberries are ripe, although I've never heard of white ones before."

"The sand covers them so they don't get red," Julia answered, and then swallowed a mouthful of berries and thick cream. "These are so good!" She took another large bite.

Her attack on the fruit made Libby look down to hide her relief. Surely so much barely controlled ferociousness must be a sign of returning health. After a minute, Julia said, "I seem to be full. But I ate hardly half a dish. I don't understand."

Libby pushed the plate aside. "It will take some time before you enjoy your normal appetite again, I imagine. You haven't eaten a full meal in a fortnight."

"Fourteen days?" asked Julia, fright entering dark eyes whose pupils expanded briefly with emotion. Libby wanted to cheer at this additional sign that the drug's hold had been broken.

"That's what I was told. I came to your ranch eight days ago."

Gold flashed on her finger as the curve of Caleb's ring caught the lamplight.

Julia whispered, "I can't remember two weeks?" Almost at once she shook her head and directed a troubled look at Libby. "It's kind of you to take so much time from your family to look after a stranger." She nodded at the ring. "Your husband must be a patient man."

It was Libby's turn to flush. "Indeed, you would know that better than I."

For a moment, the temptation to confess the imposture and accidental wedding was overwhelming. The words crowded into her throat, ready to spill off her tongue. She took a breath and became aware of something—not a sound, or a change in the air—a simple, sure knowledge that they were no longer alone. A shiver licked at the base of her spine; the tips of her fingers tingled. Without turning, she knew who stood behind her.

"Julia?" Libby had heard Caleb's voice hard with anger and light with amusement, and burred with a passion that threatened to melt her bones, but she'd never heard that particular note in it before—tentative and cracked. If hope could be pure sound, barely stirring the air, this would be it. The sound of love.

"Oh, Cal!" Julia endured his rib-cracking hug happily, emerging from it with a rueful grimace. "What's been going on? Did I sicken again? This very agreeable lady's been taking care of me—I guess. I—I can't seem to recall much. So mortifying."

"Don't you fret about that. You're on the mend now. That's all that matters."

Julia frowned at Libby over Caleb's shoulder. "My brother suffers from very few male idiocies, but once in a while he likes to protect me from things for my own good. Would you please and kindly tell me what's wrong with me?"

"I think in this case Mr. Logan must be the judge of what I say."

Julia sank back down into her pillow. "Got you buffaloed, has he? You don't want to pay too much attention to that ship's captain manner of his. He whips out orders that way because I haven't found him the proper wife yet. When I do, she'll be the kind of woman to make sure he toes the mark, never fear."

Shifting slightly, Caleb brought Libby into his field of vision. Her hands bunched into resolute little fists, and her lips parted. Without a doubt, she looked like a female about to set off some emotional cannonade. Perversely, little as he intended her to be his legal wife, he was damned if he'd let her deny that her fate was to belong to him.

His sister spoke first. "You don't need to look so scared. Cal's really just about housebroken. Say what you want to him. I do, Mrs. . . . I'm sorry, if we've been introduced in the last week, I just plain can't call it to mind."

"Logan," Caleb said softly. "Her name is Elizabeth Owens Logan. Libby's my—she's mine."

"Married?" The news dragged Julia onto one elbow. "Are you cracking a joke? It's not funny, big brother." Sotto voce, she hissed, "See what you've done, you oaf. She's all upset. What's the matter with you? There's no call to torment the woman. The poor thing probably doesn't understand your tomfoolery."

Libby damned the Logans, brother and sister, for perceiving altogether too much. She summoned a cool smile. "Caleb is telling the tr—" Pausing for a long, insulting moment, she corrected herself. "We went through a wedding ceremony one week ago. Everyone here knows me as Senora Logan."

"You're supposed to be thrilled, Julia," Caleb pointed out. "You've told me often enough to get married."

"Well, but I never expected you to do it. The Almighty will bear me witness you've turned up that prow of yours at every female I've ever put in your way. Any one of the general's daughters—"

"—will never grow a furlong of bright yellow hair," Caleb interrupted. His gaze, running slowly over the crown of braids on Libby's head, reminded her of the way he'd spilled them across the bed. "Libby's is like a river of gold."

The glowing spark in his eyes made Libby forget the angry pledge she'd made that morning to avoid his strumpet-taught touch at all costs. Obedient to his outstretched hand, she crossed the room and placed her palm against his, staring back at him helplessly. His large, warm fingers closed over hers, encompassing them completely.

"Oh!" The exclamation broke the gaze spinning some sort of spell between her and Caleb. Julia's startled expression brought Libby back to her senses. "Things really are that way with the two of you?"

Libby didn't know what the other woman meant, but had no chance to ask for a clarification, because Julia continued, "And you're married already? When did you meet? Have you been keeping secrets, Cal? Did you know Li—Mrs.—Oh, I'll just call you Libby, if I may— have you been acquainted a long time and never told me?"

Interposing her body so Julia couldn't see, Libby tried to wrench her hand from Caleb's grip. The attempt was useless; Caleb's strength must have been threefold that of the Hound who'd held her hand captive on the *Niantic*. Before the memory had time to feed her outrage, Caleb grinned at her with all his infuriating charm and lifted her fingers to his lips for a light kiss.

While she was trying to recover from the feel of his mouth, warm and moist against her fingertips, he tugged, and she tumbled willy-nilly onto his lap.

American manners might be different from British, but they couldn't possibly be this different. Properly modest married ladies didn't sit plump on their husband's knees in the company of others on either side of the Atlantic. Scrambling from his lap, Libby stuttered, "Caleb, behave yourself, if you please! Your sister will think I'm a—a—"

His grin turned unrepentant, and Julia was laughing, a rusty caw that shook her whole frail body.

"Jerusalem crickets, you two *are* married. Only married people act like that. Welcome to the family, Libby."

"Say 'Thank you very kindly,' wife. She'd never forgive me if I didn't give her a hint when she's failing in

her manners; a great one for the properties is Libby,"
Caleb added to Julia. Libby sincerely hoped that Julia,
whose dark eyes were beginning to dim a bit, missed
the dryness underlying his light words.

"You've been lucky, brother," said Julia, sighing and
plucking at the covers. "A real lady, and a beauty to
boot. I hope you appreciate your good fortune."

"Oh, I have no intention of letting Libby get away,"
murmured Caleb. "Going to sleep on us, are you?"

"Mmm? No," Julia said uncertainly. "But I surely
do feel peculiar. Not feverish, exactly. Kind of all
atwitter and tuckered out at the same time. Everything
hurts, only it's not really pain. I want something but I
don't know what it is. You say I'm getting better?"

Her tone made it clear she couldn't imagine worse.
At least, Libby thought, it wasn't the languid, uncaring
drone induced by the laudanum. Caleb shook his head
slightly, and Libby nodded just as unobtrusively to show
that she understood and agreed. At this point Julia's
health would be best served if she didn't discover that
what she unknowingly craved could be found in a bottle
now locked in Caleb's desk.

"Truly, you are much improved," Libby stated
firmly.

"If you say so." Julia didn't sound convinced.
"Well, tell me how you met Caleb, Libby. I never heard
of any tall golden goddesses in this country, so are you
newly come to Sonoma County?"

Hesitating, Libby glanced for help to Caleb. Devils
gleaming in his eyes, he wrapped an arm around one
of the bed's bottom posts and lengthened his face until
it attained a blandness as complete as such distinctive
features could achieve. "Well, Libby?" Amusement,
and some emotion a little more pointed than amusement, put a drawl in his deep voice. No, he hadn't
forgotten—or forgiven—the argument that had drawn
their idyll in the cherrywood bed to a premature close.

Her chin jutted. If Caleb wanted to throw down a
gauntlet, she would be happy to pick it up. "Your

brother attended a concert I was giving in San Francisco. I must presume he was ravished by my way with a ballad, because he introduced himself afterward. We . . . became engaged to be married the next day.''

"Cal likes a singalong as much as the next person, but if he moved that fast I doubt it was the music he couldn't resist. You weren't giving this lady any time to change her mind, were you, Cal?''

"I generally know what will suit me as soon as I see it,'' he remarked casually.

Not one surface in the room held a speck of dust; nothing needed to be straightened away except the dish of strawberries. Libby snatched it up. "I'll take this back to the kitchen.''

Julia spoke hurriedly. "You know, I might be able to manage another bite. Please don't run away, Libby.''

"Of course not, if you don't wish it.'' Her escape blocked, Libby edged next to Caleb on the side of Julia's bed and held the bowl while Julia took the spoon.

This time she ate much more slowly. "Don't mind our teasing, Libby. It's just our way, and I'm always tetchy when I'm taken by surprise. The honest truth is I'm very glad to have a sister. In fact . . .'' She put the spoon down. "I do believe one of those odd dreams really was about you. You were wearing widow's weeds—very fetching you looked, too. Not every woman can support so much black. Cal, if you ever take one chance too many, you'll have the consolation of knowing your funeral will be graced by the most ornamental widow in California.''

"Doesn't seem to me that'll be consolation enough,'' Caleb said.

"No?'' A grin eerily like Caleb's own flitted across Julia's thin face. She'd been right, Libby decided. A Julia with animation lighting her from within was a very pretty Julia indeed. "Well, you're safe from evil omens—as if you'd care!—because the dream wasn't about a funeral, anyway. It was a wedding.'' She stopped and tilted her head. "At least, that's what I keep thinking, but it wasn't like any wedding I've ever heard of before. People were hollering and bellowing. One of the padres from Sonoma was here, and Juan and Teresa and . . . Was it your wedding?''

Libby bit her lip in defeat. "The service took place here in your room, yes.''

"Glory." Dark lashes spread like fans across Julia's cheeks. "Was the whole thing as downright pixilated as I remember?''

"Oh, yes," Libby said simply. For the first time since the night she became Caleb's temporary wife, the memory of her wedding struck her as comical. "The priest couldn't understand us, and we couldn't understand him, and Caleb was shouting in—what did you call it?—his best sea captain's manner. But no one would listen. And you're right. We'd just arrived here from the city, and I was wearing black serge. Not the most propitious color for a bride.''

Julia gave that rusty laugh again. "Thank goodness! For a few minutes, I was afraid Cal had gone and married a humorless woman. But I should have known better. He'd never make that kind of mistake. I must say, he's shown good taste in picking out a wife. How did he happen onto you? Was it a subscription concert for charity?''

Caleb answered Libby's swift glance with a reassuring touch on her shoulder. "It was a public concert, Julia. Libby got stranded in San Francisco. She's an orphan, and when her parents died and their homestead up north failed, she took up singing as an occupation.''

"You're a real concert singer?" Julia sounded awed. "Like the Swedish Nightingale?''

"Not precisely. Miss Lind makes rather a better living out on her performances than I ever did." Libby smiled, relieved that Caleb's sister wasn't shocked or disgusted, and tried to point the conversation in a different direction. "I heard her several times in London. The clarity of her high notes is astonishing. If you were to close your eyes, you wouldn't believe those pure, clear sounds could come from a human throat.''

Caleb's hand kneaded the taut muscles over her shoulder blades. "I like your singing. It's warm and sweet. It draws a man.''

As always, his touch made her want to forget why it would be a good idea to avoid such demoralizing proximity. "Thank you. But it hardly bears comparison with the most famous voice of the age."

"Oh, I don't know." The words rumbled softly in her ear. "I think I'd rather hear a real live woman singing love songs to me than some bird's chirp any day."

Libby couldn't help it; she chuckled at the absurdity of anyone holding her talent in more regard than Jenny Lind's. The hand on her back took advantage of her softened mood to slip around her waist.

The solid feeling of it made her want to relax back into the cradle of his chest, and with a start she realized that in a minute she'd be perched on his lap again.

Caleb felt her belated stiffening and wondered how long Libby was going to be able to fight her instincts as well as his. The last bit of resentment over her high-handed eviction of him from what was, in fact, his own bed dwindled into a sort of left-handed sympathy for her plight.

She wanted him. He was sure of it now, and had no intention of letting her forget it. The memory of his pig-stupid blunder in telling her about his adventures in Marseilles made him wince. If he hadn't let the brandy do his talking this morning, they might at least have found some comfort in each other's arms. As it was, he was going to have to tame her skittishness all over again.

"We have a piano coming," Julia said wistfully. "I haven't played in years, not since Cal sent for me from Boston when he bought this place. That was five years ago. I was sixteen. I probably won't recognize any of the notes when I see the sheet music."

"Did you sail around the Horn?" Libby asked. Caleb

ignored her discreet efforts to free herself, and tightened his grip, placing a kiss in the feathery curls that had come loose at her nape. He heard her soft sigh, and smiled.

Julia nodded. "It was a wild ride, but I made it! The minute the ship set anchor and Cal rowed out to meet me, he started apologizing for this big mud castle he was bringing me to keep house in, and saying how he'd build a proper frame house someday and fill it with pretty things."

"Almost ready," Caleb said. "In two, three weeks, we'll take you for the grand tour."

She made a face. "With me bundled in the back of a farm wagon, no doubt, and you lifting me over every second step once we get there? Cal hasn't let me breathe deep, let alone ride a horse or run up the stairs since I had the fever," she complained to Libby.

A querulous edge that hadn't been there before sharpened her voice. Caleb reached his other arm around Libby and patted his sister's hand. "That's over, now, Julia. Once you're up and around, you can do all things you used to do. Do you remember the doctor who came to examine you yesterday?"

"No," she said bluntly, and her face crumpled. "Oh, dear God. Cal, I can't remember!"

"It's all right, Julia. Listen. The doctor says you're going to be well, very soon. There's nothing to make you worry. Caleb, tell her," begged Libby.

Although not a strand strayed from the stubby braids, Caleb smoothed the black hair back from Julia's forehead. "All true, little sister. You'll be better tomorrow, and better still the day after."

"Then why do I feel like this?" Julia demanded, twisting away from his hand fretfully.

"A little too much bedrest," said Libby. "But, you know, it might be advisable to try to sleep now, so you can wake up tomorrow to sunshine."

Julia's unpracticed laugh was tearful. "The sun never

shines in the mornings here. The sea's such a jealous neighbor, it sends the fog so we can't forget it's there."

"Nevertheless." In Libby's brisk English accent, the quibble was an order. "Come, now. I'll sing you a lullaby, shall I? And you can hear how little I am, compared to a nightingale."

Without waiting for agreement, Libby began to sing. Caleb felt her ribs expand under his arm. The ballad sang of false love and a sea that couldn't be crossed.

The melody had a soothing cadence, and Libby's way with it reminded Caleb of a fiddle's achingly sweet lament. She sang all the old, sad verses simply. At first he just listened, watching Julia's eyelids grow heavier, and then, as Libby repeated the song more softly, he began to pay attention to the lyrics. The ocean between Libby and England could be crossed, but only with difficulty and at great expense. And if she had come to understand that the piano player had played her false, then that was one stumbling stone removed from his path in bringing her to an understanding.

Finally, Julia lay breathing deeply, and Libby's song murmured to a halt. She sighed, her blond head resting back against Caleb's shoulder.

"Never heard a nightingale I liked better," he told her quietly.

"How do I always end up in your arms?"

"Because that's where you belong."

Her green eyes were shadowed as she turned to face him. "No." She lifted her palm to his cheek. "I cannot be the woman you expect me to be. Not that I blame you for what you think I am; after all, how can you not believe the evidence I've handed you? The pity is one of us couldn't be more foolish."

"And then what?" he asked, mildly curious.

"Then you might be gullible enough to accept the truth." Rueful self-knowledge curved her lips. "Or I could learn to live with the lie. At least the two of us might be happy for a space. Unfortunately, we've both seen too much of the world to fall prey to that kind of folly.''

"Riddles?''

She shook her head. "Fact. Unpleasant things, facts. Let me go, Caleb.''

Even as he loosened his grip, he said, "Never.''

She stood up. "You'll have to eventually. Nothing can stop me from going back to the life I was meant to live. My homecoming will be a nine-days' wonder, and then to Little Paddocks I shall be Libby Owens, who went to the New World and found it not to her taste. I shan't be Elizabeth Logan anymore.''

"There's a big ocean between you and London, Libby,'' he reminded her. "You can't get over it without my help.''

"You said you'd put me on a ship,'' she whispered furiously. "You gave me your word! I should have known. An American's word—''

"Oh, my word is good,'' he said, showing his teeth. "But I'll honor it in my own good time, wife, and in my own way.''

The waxing moon and the stars had lost their nightly battle with the fog hours before and the only illumination in the anonymous little room in a building on Portsmouth Square came from a lantern turned down low. Its light was barely enough to create a dim glow in the amber liquid swimming in a glass set on the table.

Aloysius Malloy's eyes dwelt on the oily shimmer of the whiskey with sick yearning. Smitty smiled. Observing the other man closely, he picked up the shot glass, fondled it, and then tossed off the draught with a smack of the lips. Malloy's Adam's apple bobbed in sympathy.

"Too bad you won't be having a drink for a spell yet,'' Smitty said.

With an effort, Malloy wrenched his gaze away from the drop pooling in the bottom of the glass. "Indeed, it's all one to me," he replied with an imitation of indifference.

"Glad to hear it." Smitty slapped the glass back onto the table. The crack of glass meeting oak made Malloy jump nervously. "When you've finished doing your bit to help us even the score with Logan and his piece of skirt, you can treat yourself to a grand drunk, courtesy of the Hounds. Until then it's Adam's ale for you."

"You know everything I know about Libby. I went up to Sonoma County to pick up the gossip about them, as you ordered me. I drew you plans of his steamboat. Their sawbones spilled his guts, and I told you everything he said," Malloy protested. "There's not another thing I could be doing for you. Libby's not likely to let me within five miles of her husband's ranch without raising a hue and cry—for my head, I wouldn't doubt. We didn't exactly part friends. And now she's a rich man's wife. She'll be listened to; trust Libby for that."

"Wants your head, does she?" asked Smitty thoughtfully. "What would she do with it, pretty as it is, parted from the rest of you?"

Caution belatedly smoothed the sullen lines from Malloy's features. Since the Hounds had beaten him sober and forced him to shave regularly, the almost feminine lines of his mouth and chin, coupled with a thin-chested frame, had attracted a great deal of attention from certain of his new masters. He'd learned to endure their crude and pleasureless perversions, but he certainly didn't want to add Smitty to their number. Smitty scared him. Sometimes when the Hound talked about Libby and this Logan, who had actually gotten Libby to marry him from what Dr. Simons had let drop, Malloy saw spittle gather at the corner of Smitty's mouth and a rapt, rabid gleam in his eye.

"She might be imagining she has cause for a grudge or two," Malloy said, picking his words carefully. "You know what females are."

Smitty's lips lifted from his teeth. "I know what Elizabeth is, all right." He followed with a stream of language so foul that Malloy goggled. Not at the obscenities, but that anyone would apply them in a literal sense to Libby.

"—lying, whoring calico queen!"

"Is it Libby Owens you'd be talking about?" Malloy asked incredulously. "A woman so straitlaced she wouldn't recognize a man between her legs if there were one alive dauntless enough to part them? The vicar's niece?"

"If that piece harks from a vicarage, it must be a parish worth visiting."

"And so it is, for all I'd be knowing about it, but—"

Smitty's laugh grated. "Whatever she pretended while she was traveling with a muff like you, the jade's nothing but a nickel whore."

Reflecting that there was no such thing in San Francisco these days, Malloy kept his mouth shut. At least Smitty's tastes appeared to lean away from other men.

"Her goods were on the block right enough the night I ran into her. And she knew better than to playact the nun with me. She's a whore—a cheating one at that. Elizabeth owes me, and so does Logan. Make no mistake about it, Miss Nancy, that's a debt I mean to collect."

Chapter 14

"**I**s there a problem between you and Cal?" Julia asked.

Libby leaned against the rough boards of the corral. It seemed to her that nothing but problems tied her to Caleb. He was patient, she granted him that. There was something terrifying about his certainty that he had only to wait for time to ripen her desire. At the right moment he'd be able to shake the tree of her stubbornness and have her fall into his arms like a harvest peach.

The attraction that flared higher every time he slipped inside her defenses to touch her—and he'd managed to do so with maddening frequency during the last few days—had reached a fevered pitch. If he set his arm around her again, or placed one more surreptitious kiss at the nape of her neck, or looked at her just so as he smoothed another tendril of hair away from her fore-head, she was afraid she'd scream from the harsh, biting frustration. Or—or bite him. Or throw herself into his arms and beg him to recommence the interrupted initiation into love she hadn't let him finish twice before.

The register in Sonoma remained unsigned. Their strange, limited marriage existed in a limbo whose walls tightened around her day by day. Caleb wanted the kind of relations with her normally enjoyed by couples whose vows to each other were in earnest, despite the fact he intended to annul their own farce of a wedding out of existence. Once he did that, it would be as if they had never been married at all, a state more final than divorce, which would drag scandal after their names for the rest of their lives. The law would simply forget that Libby Owens had been Caleb Logan's wife in any sense whatsoever.

But not if the marriage were consummated.

Caleb wasn't thinking straight about that, she thought, and touched a splinter lightly with her fingertip. The point gave her a very salutary prick, puncturing her flesh as if to tell her, *Touch me and I will make you bleed. Embrace Caleb and he will make your heart bleed.* Fishing a handkerchief out of her apron pocket to blot the red bead that gathered on her finger, she knit her brows. It was obvious what part of his body Caleb was thinking with, and she had to protect him—both of them—from the consequences.

The problem, she wanted to explain to Julia, was that while circumstance had tricked her into becoming Caleb's bride, she couldn't allow herself to be his wife.

"Caleb is all that is kind," she said. "He has advertised for a schoolmaster to teach the children. He supports me when I speak to the servants—and so do you," she added with more warmth. "How could there be a problem?"

Julia waved away Libby's attempt at drawing red herrings across the trail. "Of course he sees the sense of your suggestions. Why shouldn't life be more civilized and pleasant for all of us? He's not a barbarian, after all."

Libby hid her face behind a hand she raised as if to shield her eyes from the sun. She was learning not to give either of the Logans the opportunity to read her expression when she disagreed with them.

"I've never known Cal to spend so much time close to home before. I declare, he must think the mill and the far range are running themselves." When Libby failed to respond to this hint, Julia added with a stiltedness that was completely unlike her, "Sometimes when two people haven't been acquainted very long, little difficulties can loom larger than they really are. Love can't always guard against misunderstanding.''

Slouch-hatted wranglers opened a gate, and a small herd of tall, deep-chested horses thundered into the corral. Libby inspected them with every appearance of interest. "Is this the stock Juan wants to break to riding?"

Julia accorded the horses barely a glance. ''Yes. A tinhorn looking to do some prospecting traded them for mules and a grubstake. Men blinded by their dream of gold will do any fool thing. Juan thinks the animals have been mistreated, but if anyone can gentle them, Juan can. He's a wonder with horses. With everything he tries. Libby, please talk to me. I feel we can be friends, you and I, and I'm worried for you.''

The blunt attack left Libby without defenses. "Of course I wish to be friends.''

''Sisters, too.'' Julia frowned. ''The new house will be ready in a few days. Would it be better if I stayed on here? In the adobe?''

''Give up the house?'' Libby didn't have to feign shock. ''That's *your* house. You planned every board and nail in it. Caleb built it for you!''

''Yes, well, it's Cal's, after all, his and yours, and I thought perhaps you and he needed some time alone together to—to get used to being married.''

''Oh, Julia.'' Privacy wouldn't cure what was wrong between her and Caleb; it would only allow it to come to destructive fruition. ''Thank you, but I know Caleb wouldn't hear of it. And neither would I. I'm the interloper, not you.''

''You keep saying things like that. Don't be ridiculous. You're family now.'' Julia hesitated. ''There aren't as many rooms in the new house, you know. I can't say why Cal's being so mysterious and won't let us go take a peek, but, anyway, we'd only planned two big bedrooms. Your current arrangements . . .'' Her brisk little voice, which always bubbled along like a mountain stream, dwindled away.

Much as Julia resembled Caleb in coloring, the differences between their voices never ceased to astonish Libby. Caleb's was rich and deep, its tone a reliable weathervane of his changing moods. Julia's was like Julia herself, small and quick. Anyone less like the drugged, languishing creature Libby had first encountered would be hard to imagine. Her animated movements and now-bright eyes reminded Libby of a busy brown sparrow. Plainspoken common sense colored her speech.

"Most folks who come out West don't concern themselves so much with what's fashionable."

She meant married people usually slept in the same bed, Libby thought. "It's what I'm accustomed to," she offered weakly. "A gentleman and a lady maintain separate chambers."

"I'm surprised you can bring yourself to call him by name. Lots of wives prefer the formality of 'mister.' "

"He asked me to call him Caleb," admitted Libby.

"And you have a terrible time denying him anything, don't you?" Julia cocked a brow at Libby's helpless wave of the hands. "Oh, I've seen you, tempting him with second helpings and those little cakes you've been making, and pretending as hard as you can that you don't like it when he sneaks up on you with a kiss. You watch him, too, when you think he isn't noticing."

Libby put her hands to her cheeks. They were burning hot under her palms. "Julia, there are some things friends, or even sisters, shouldn't say to each other."

"Don't you think I know that?" Julia burst out. "But I see you two so unhappy and—and I want to clunk your heads together!"

Libby laughed to reassure her sister-in-law. "Thank you. But Caleb and I butt heads often enough without any help. It is kind of you to offer."

"Oh, Libby, I'm sorry. I shouldn't have said that, but—well, never mind. My original idea is the best one. I'll stay in the adobe, and you and Cal take the house. Maybe without an audience you'll feel less—less constrained.''

Without stopping to reflect, Libby said, ''It's not your presence that—'' She stopped. Ultimately, it might be to Libby's benefit for Julia to know, or at least strongly suspect, that Caleb had yet to make her his wife. Until annulment proceedings had been instituted, however, the incompleteness of the marriage would result in countless embarrassing moments like this one.

A week of steady eating had put enough flesh on Julia's bones to soften the stark Logan features, but she'd gone pale again in her concern. Libby hated causing that worn look. Softly, to distract her, Libby said, ''Oh my, they're saddling that splendid bay. Do you think Juan will be working him this afternoon?''

A tinge of pink relieved the whiteness of Julia's complexion. ''He said he might,'' she responded nonchalantly. Keeping her gaze on the horse as it wheeled, trying to rid itself of the saddle, she added, ''He's going to mate that one with some of the Californio ponies, and see what results. God made all creatures to go two by two, Libby. That's in the Bible. Are marital relations so frightening to you?''

''We shouldn't be talking like this,'' said Libby despairingly. ''You're not even a married woman. It's hideously improper.''

Julia's eyes shone with an earnest light. ''You worry too much about propriety. It isn't seemly for a wife to refuse her husband, either. I may be a spinster yet, and for sure no man's ever done to me what men do to women to make babies, but I'm looking forward to finding out what it's like. You're not—it's not *Cal* you're scared of, is it? I know he bellows and swaggers a bit, but really he's considerate as can be. Reasonable, even, for a man.'' Her similarity to a small, businesslike bird increased as she cocked her head at a considering angle. ''Usually.''

Libby repressed the desire to stamp her feet amid large, satisfying clouds of dust, like the horses. ''I can assure you, my feelings for Caleb are just the same as the day I married him. If anything," she muttered to herself, "they've grown."

Julia brightened. "Then you and Cal can get to work making me an aunt."

Several of the wranglers had strolled near, and they nudged each other.

"For heaven's sake, the men can hear us!" Libby tried to glare, but her eyes met Julia's and both young women choked on laughter, Julia's delighted and Libby's rueful.

More quietly, Libby continued, "I can't promise you a nephew or a niece. Please, Julia, as—as my sister, just let it be. And you mustn't even think of not moving into the new house. Caleb would be so hurt, and I'll be quite content in one of the smaller rooms. I couldn't reconcile it with my conscience to put you out, and I'd miss you terribly. Who'd defend me from Teresa?"

"She likes you well enough. She's a prickly creature."

Libby saw a chance for enlightenment. "That doctor who was here—he called her a *mestiza*. It didn't sound very nice."

"You've never heard the word before?" Julia looked no more than mildly surprised. "It just means part Indian and part Mexican. He was wrong, though. Teresa's a full-blooded Pomo."

It made Teresa seem more exotic. "She's such a homebody."

"Women are the world over. Tied to the teepee or the lodge or the house," said Julia without resentment.

Libby thought of all the roaming she had done. "Not always."

"Teresa was brought up by the padres. After the Mexican government took the missions away from the Church, the general controlled them, and was pretty good to the Indians, I guess—except that they couldn't leave. Then there was a horrible smallpox epidemic, and almost all the local Indians died. It was lucky Teresa was here instead of in Sonoma or at the Petaluma rancho. Afterward the general brought other tribes to work his lands. When Captain Fremont commandeered all the Vallejo cattle to feed the army—it was barefaced robbery, really—"

Libby noted that Julia and Caleb shared the same strong feelings about property.

"Anyhow, those Indians ran away. He's still one of the richest men in California and pleasant to talk to, but . . ."

"You don't like him?" Libby asked.

Quickly, Julia replied, "I do, really. Only he has a reputation," she added, making an eloquent face. "With women."

"General Vallejo?"

Julia sighed. "Yes. You have to know sometime, because you're sure to meet him and the senora, and however many children they have now. Eight or nine, it seems to me. I've gathered Teresa got sent to this rancho way back when because the general's eye fell on her."

"Oh."

"If there was a baby, she must have miscarried. Any road, she never bore a child. And it was ages ago. I hope you don't think less of Teresa—"

"Of course not. I've learned a woman doesn't always have a choice." The looks they exchanged were warm and unhappy at the same time. "Poor Teresa. No wonder she's so fond and fierce about you and Caleb. She has no one else."

"Yes. She told me about the medicine."

Juan came out of the barn, his wiry energy all concentrated on the bay. He approached the horse slowly and steadily, his chaps and spurs dragging in the dust, and the women could hear his soft croon as he talked to the stallion.

"We thought it would be easier for you not to know until you'd had a chance to recover," Libby said finally.

"In case I drank off the whole bottle at once?" Julia laughed.

Libby remembered the cracked wisp of sound that had been the best her sister-in-law could produce a week before; now her rich chuckle, so unexpected from such a lively but trenchant young lady, drew appreciative narrow-eyed glances from the wranglers.

"Perhaps we were worrying about nothing. The doctor said being strong-minded would help you get better."

Gaze fixed on Juan as he grabbed the bay's mane to hold its great head steady and breathe into its flaring nostrils, Julia murmured, "Oh, I'm that, all right. Self-willed and always sure of what I want. Only sometimes I'm not wanted back."

Juan leaped into the saddle, and gave the horse its head. The animal careered around the corral, and men and horses scattered out of its way. The face Juan bent over the mane while he whispered into a flattened ear was a mask of tense excitement.

Julia gripped the splintery surface of the fence with white-knuckled fingers. "Don't concern yourself over the laudanum anymore. No more dreams, no more fidgets. My life is exactly what it was before Teresa began giving it to me. In fact, it's better, since the fear of heart failure is gone. I'm cured, thanks to you."

Libby murmured a disclaimer.

"I thank God on my knees every night that you were nosy," said Julia seriously.

Caleb's promise to teach her more things she shouldn't know flashed through Libby's mind. "Curiosity isn't always a virtue. But I'm glad I was nosy, too."

The bay trumpeted one last defiant protest, then stood still, long neck hanging and sides pumping in and out. Juan sat easily, then clucked and directed the mount in an amble around the enclosure.

"I'm going to find some way to reward you, Libby.

If you won't let me stay away from the new house, I'll think of something else.''

Strain made Libby's smile thin. "Forcing opportunities to—to further a longer acquaintanceship won't necessarily lead to the end you desire.''

Juan approached the spot where they leaned against the fence, and Julia replaced the momentary look of longing on her face with a bright smile. "I know. Sometimes auld acquaintance doesn't accomplish horse-feathers.''

Pausing only to compliment Juan on his horsemanship, Libby slipped back into the courtyard and made her rounds. With the air of one disposing of a distasteful chore, Julia had abdicated responsibility for the kitchen after her first taste of a pudding Libby had coerced Wang into making by the gallon. In addition, on the slim basis of her diagnosis about Julia's condition, Libby had been elevated to the status of ranch physician. So far, all she'd been called upon to do was bind a sprain, but conscientiously she checked with Teresa to see if anyone had complained of feeling ill, and sighed with relief that no one had.

"What have you to show me today?'' she asked, smiling.

Teresa might have misapplied the unfamiliar draught left by a Yanqui doctor; her knowledge of the remedies to be compounded from native sources, however, was wide-ranging. Libby sniffed minty yerba buena, "for when the stomach rebels, and for breeding women,'' said Teresa, pointedly not staring at Libby's tiny waist. Ignoring the reminder that the Manzanita's mistress was known to have failed to cooperate in any activity that would result in needing a palliative for nausea, Libby stuck her finger in a jar of ooze. "Aloe,'' Teresa identified the substance for her. "For burns and sunburns. You will need it soon if you do not guard your face. It is May and the sun strengthens.''

Guiltily, Libby touched her nose. It wasn't peeling, but the precious mirror bolted to her wall had already told her several freckles marred its short length. The bother it would have been to blinker herself inside a cottage bonnet every time she moved through the sunny courtyard from one part of the cool, shadowy building to another, as she needed to continually throughout the lengthening days, had induced her to leave her bonnets hanging from their hooks in the wardrobe. Were her standards slipping so noticeably?

Slapping at the gray film of dust clinging to her skirt despite the apron, she skipped up the stairs to change for supper. Julia's coming back to life had returned the household to normal hours. Caleb appeared like clockwork for meals, no matter how hard he had to ride in from the range or the fields. Briefly, Libby pondered the significance of Julia's intimation that he hadn't stayed at home so much during other springs, but the matter wasn't, after all, her affair. Nothing that happened at the Manzanita or to its master was her business, she told herself brutally. Soon enough she'd be packed away onto a Britain-bound ship, and Caleb would be free to look for a wife he wanted to keep.

Ascensión was waiting with a smile and the dove-gray gown clean and neatly pressed. Catching a glimpse of herself in the mirror, Libby faced what it showed unswervingly.

Freckles spilled across her nose and her cheeks. Unlimited sunlight had painted streaks in her hair and lightened the curls at her nape from old gold to white gold. The apron she wore wasn't the frothy scrap of black silk a lady would don to protect her clothes from illusory dirt as she tripped after the servants in a conventional house. It was a sturdy, enveloping garment meant for a woman whose work required real effort and contact with food and soil.

The result wasn't unattractive, she thought with clear-sighted detachment. Or wouldn't have been, had she aspired to life as a milkmaid. Or as the wife of a frontiersman.

It bore little resemblance to the milk-white gentility required of a gentlewoman.

Stripping off the apron, Libby presented her back to Ascensión for help undressing. There was nothing she could do about the signs of the sun's invasive finger on her person. She owned no pearl powder or paint, and wouldn't have used them if she had; cosmetics were unnatural contrivances, sure proof that a woman was fallen. Caleb believed her fallen enough already. Libby compressed her lips. She wasn't about to offer him additional evidence about her virtue, or lack of it.

"Pardon, senora, have I pinched you?" Ascensión asked anxiously in Spanish.

Libby answered carefully. She was learning to distinguish meanings in the swift torrent of the language, and speaking was following slowly. "No, *gracias*. I will have the pink dress. The one you like."

Whether or not Caleb's mouth quirked knowingly when he saw her in a gown they both knew he fancied on her, she needed to demonstrate to herself that there was still a London lady inside her, ready to come out and sail away at a moment's notice.

Ascensión beamed and opened the wardrobe. When the time came to leave California, Libby thought, she really ought to leave the pink for this willing and efficient helper. She was suddenly positive she'd never wear it again after she left. It would remind her too much of her helpless rush of happiness at Caleb's approval.

Watching the maid lift the dimity folds high to keep them from brushing the floor, she decided the dress would have to be taken in and up for the slim, short Ascensión. In fact, there would probably be material left over to construct another dress. The pastel prettiness would become the girl's apricot skin and blue-black hair. Would Caleb admire it as much on her as he did on Libby? And would Ascensión be as eager to please and skillful in tending to the senor's needs as she was to the senora's?

Abruptly, Libby rejected the idea of making a gift of

the dimity. She'd find something else to give Ascensión.

In the dining room, Julia nodded approvingly at the sight Libby made sweeping through the door. "Now, that's a style that suits you. Cal, Libby's really in looks tonight."

Libby tried not to flush as Caleb's appraisal moved down, and then up, her entire body, ending with her hair. "Mighty fine," he said, with just the faint, conspiratorial smile she'd expected. Not only expected but hoped for, she realized.

Uncertainly, she touched one of the ringlets she'd arranged to escape from the soft chignon anchored at the back of her head. It was a new fashion with curls tumbling down behind instead of bunched at the sides, as she was used to for evening wear. "I saw it in one of Julia's magazines," she said.

Julia's gaze moved from her to Caleb. "By the by," she told her brother when neither spoke again, "I'm going to provide my illness with a silver lining. Every stitch I own hangs on me. Libby could use refurbishing, too. All her things are lovely, of course, but a bride ought to have a trousseau."

"I don't need any clothes. I have more than enough already," Libby interjected.

"Libby." Caleb didn't embellish it; the way he said her name was a gentle rebuke. He nodded to his sister. "Make a list of what you'd both like. I'll have the agent round up all the fol-lols and deliver them on the *Red Jacket*."

"Don't men just stupefy you with their dear, simple ways?" asked Julia of the ceiling. "Cal, no doubt this will seem amazing and frivolous to you, but Libby and I would prefer to choose our own dress materials and such. As a matter of fact, we insist on it."

"Not I," objected Libby. "Please, I don't need any new clothes."

"Well, I do," Julia said. "And what would people

say if I got all rigged out and you didn't? We'll go to San Francisco and visit the importers' warehouses—''

"No!" said Caleb and Libby at once.

"It's not as if I were ever seen, really. People shan't say anything," Libby hurried on. "Shall we eat? The poulet en casserole has probably cooled long enough."

Julia seated herself with a dark look at her companions. "Which poulet is this?" she asked, handing her plate to Libby to be filled.

"Jesus, Manuel said." Libby wrinkled her nose. "It seemed rather blasphemous to dump the poor bird in a stewpot once he told me."

"It's a common name hereabouts," said Caleb indulgently.

Libby gave her attention to her own portion. "So I've found."

"Has she spoken her Spanish for you yet?" Julia demanded. "I never heard anybody pick it up so fast."

Libby swallowed and laughed. *"Gracias, mi hermana.* You're mistaken, though. I'm still woefully backward."

Inspecting a piece of chicken speared on the tines of his fork, Caleb said, "Who's teaching you?"

"Manuel. And Teresa, of course. I find I learn faster from the words of songs."

"Why don't you sing and play the guitar for us tonight, Libby?" Julia suggested.

Libby demurred; Julia persisted and finally sent the serving girl who entered with fresh biscuits to fetch the instrument. Caleb listened to the courteous nonsense—why should Libby pretend modest doubts about her performance when they all knew she excelled at it?—and interrupted. "Have you always played the guitar?"

"No, that's what I've been trying to explain," said Libby, cheeks pinker than her gown. "Diego only began showing me the chords a few days ago. I'm not very accomplished."

"Oh, Libby, how you fib! Your practicing is as good as most folks' parlor playing."

Caleb pushed his plate away. Diego matched a fine singing voice with liquid eyes and a muscular physique. "You won't need to bother learning the guitar. There'll be a piano at the new house. You'd rather play that, wouldn't you? More a lady's instrument."

At that moment, Diego entered, carrying a guitar tenderly in both arms. At his employer's words, he stopped. "Senor Cal does not wish the senora to—"

"Just leave the guitar, please, Diego," said Libby quietly, not looking at Caleb.

Handsome features impassive, the man deposited the instrument on the credenza. As he left, his gaze met Caleb's for a telling moment. Chagrin bit Caleb. Sympathy, not hurt pride, put constraint in Diego's dark eyes. Damnation, did the whole ranch sense the jealousy that wracked him every time he thought of Libby sharing time or a smile with someone else?

The vivacity in Julia's voice had iced over. "There's nothing unladylike about a guitar, Cal. John Fremont's wife plays one, and she's a Missouri senator's daughter."

"I wasn't aware Missouri had become the last word in what's genteel hereabouts," Caleb snapped.

"Jessie Benton Fremont is a celebrated beauty. She's been the toast of Washington city. If she plays the guitar, I suppose Libby can," said Julia in a withering tone. Thoughtfully, she added, "The woman's married to a lout, of course, but that can happen to anybody. What's gotten into you, Cal? Poor Diego must have thought you didn't want your wife contaminated by anything so *mejicano*."

"He knows better."

"How you can—"

Caleb shoved his chair away from the table. "Let it be, Julia."

"If that's how you want it. Let's talk about the trip Libby and I are going to take to San Francisco."

"I'm sorry, Julia, but we can't go to the city," Libby said. "The Hounds are after us."

Chapter 15

Candles guttered in their sockets by the time the story of Libby and Caleb's adventure with the Hounds had been told to Julia's satisfaction. Mercifully, she neither exclaimed nor clutched at her brother with fear, but at the end said only, "Pity. They're not good enemies to have. Has there been any sign they've been busy among our accounts in the city?"

"Our agent hasn't reported anything. Jacob's keeping an ear to the ground with the other shopkeepers."

Libby opened her eyes wide. "Do you really consider them intelligent enough to realize that your business associates might provide a—an avenue of attack?"

"They don't have to be smart," Julia explained calmly. "They only have to be killers. At least, like all wild dogs, they stick together in one place. We won't have to look for them on the Manzanita." She sighed. "I certainly understand why none of us will be traipsing off to San Francisco soon. I guess I'll go to my room and start on my list. Would you like to join me, Libby?"

"My wife and I have matters to discuss." Caleb's deep, soft rumble set Libby's breath fluttering in her chest.

"Good night, then." Julia patted Libby's arm as she passed. She turned in the doorway. "It looks to be a pretty sky out there. No clouds yet, for a wonder. Why don't you show Libby our stars, Cal?"

The twist of his lips held a distinct challenge. "Well, wife? We can study up on the constellations."

"I imagine you can reel them off by heart, captain," Libby answered, but she put her hand in his and let him lead her across the veranda, down the stairs, and out through a gap in the double gates. Once they were outside the square fortress, sounds from inside cut off with startling absoluteness. Avoiding the stables, they strolled in silence until they reached a grove of oak trees, their crippled forms black in a silver wash of moonlight.

Something brushed her cheek, and she reached up and touched pale velvet petals with leaves like silk. "What is this?"

"Virgin's bower," Caleb answered absently. "It's a parasite."

"Oh." The darkness concealed her bitter smile. He couldn't have made the opinion of every person on the Manzanita clearer if he'd deliberately tried to insult her.

He seemed in no hurry to begin a conversation. Struggling for a topic that wouldn't fan their differences into an argument, she said, "Tell me, why did you stop being a sea captain? Was it only because you felt the call of the land?"

"Partly. Mostly. But I'd been on the lookout for someplace to light and settle and make a home for Julia. Our grandparents brought us up. Godly people. Grandfather had a heavier hand with a lash than any bosun's mate I ever ran afoul of. Our family has some shipping interests, and I was twelve when I talked Grandfather into letting me sign on as a cabin boy. Julia was just a little thing then. I swore that someday I'd rescue her from baked beans every Friday and Grandmother reading out loud from the Bible during meals."

"And you did."

"So I did." With no change in his reflective tone, he continued, "She's not the only one who's stumped as to why we don't act more like man and wife."

"We aren't man and wife."

"Close as makes no difference."

She picked a long spray of the virgin's bower and held it to her lips. "If that were true, we wouldn't be talking about it. Married is married, and not married is—nothing. This middle ground we've stumbled onto is too shaky to be the foundation for any kind of relations."

"Dear heart." Caleb's rough fingers rivaled the caress of the flowers against her skin in gentleness. "What do you want to hear? That I think about you constantly? It's true. That other women can't fire my blood because they aren't tall and golden and shaped like a goddess—because they aren't you? That's true, too. That I came near to smashing Diego's teeth down his throat at the thought you two had spent time together? Those are all the truth."

She tried to look away from his face, where a faint sheen reflected from his eyes. "What do you expect of me? Never to grow old? I won't always be—what it is you think I am." She couldn't say beautiful. Anyway, Caleb wouldn't care how she'd look in twenty years. He had made it clear she wouldn't be necessary to him that long. "My looks are changing already. Freckled and faded—"

"I like seeing the sun in your hair. And your skin is like buttermilk. Luscious."

"What is it you think I could give you that you couldn't have from a hundred—a thousand—other women?"

"None of them is you," he said. "Don't you know men will want you when you're eighty?" He was all too aware he had no business implying forever. This was a strictly limited arrangement. He swore softly. Libby had always been a creature of the sun to Caleb, but tonight she could have been Diana, lovely and lonely under the moon's fitful gleam. Why did they both have to be lonely? Forever was very far away. The importance of *now* overpowered him. "I want you, Libby

Logan. I have since I saw you on that stage. I've chased after you drunk and sober. You live in my house, but it's not enough. I want you in my bed. While we're married, I want you to act like my wife.''

His finger progressed to tracing the curve of her jaw. Libby had to clench her muscles to keep her head from rolling from side to side to help the exploring fingertip. ''You haven't asked me what I want,'' she said. She hated herself because the whisper sounded weak.

He pushed the stem of flowers out of his way and brought his lips a hairbreadth from hers. ''What's that?''

''To go home. Home to England.''

He kissed her, feather-light caresses that moved from her lips to her chin, from her chin to her suddenly heavy eyelids, and back to her lips again. ''But that's not all you want, is it, Libby?''

She tried to will her arms to fall by her sides, her feet to retreat at least a few steps out of danger's way. Instead, her hands dropped the stem and locked behind his neck, the palms kneading slightly to feel the short hair at his nape, the underlying skin and muscle and tendons. She buried her face in his shoulder, shaking her head in surrender.

''Tell me,'' he urged.

''I want—to touch you,'' she whispered in jerky phrases. ''I want to—to feel things, all the things you've promised to teach me.''

Just one more hour with Caleb, whispered the yearning that raced from palms to suddenly heavy breasts and through her lower body. Even her scalp tingled. One more hour needn't destroy their plans, she thought with desperation of her longing. As long as he didn't tamper with the physical proof of her virginity, an annulment would be safeguarded. Not even the prospect of enduring doctors and depositions could extinguish the force of her need to be with this man, to feel important to him in the way she had during their night together in the city.

Her fingers pulled apart to curve into claws whose nails dug possessively into his neck. As soon as she realized what she was doing, Libby released him, but he laughed, low and soft, and tightened his own grip around her waist. "I'm sorry," she gasped.

"Nothing's wrong," he assured her. "You don't have to scratch me to ribbons, but I like it when you forget all the prunes and proverbs. You're very sw—" He remembered how she'd objected to that description. "You were made for loving."

"I become wanton when you look at me," she said soberly. "How does that happen?"

He laughed out loud. "Just the way things are between us. I've got no complaint—as long as you save all that wildness and willingness for me. Promise. Promise me, Libby."

"You don't need a promise. No one else has ever made me feel so many impossibilities at once. I guessed why you bristled so at Diego. You needn't be concerned about how I look at other men. I don't. Shall I tell you the truth? No matter who else is in a room, I only ever see you."

Caleb wanted to believe her with an urgency that left him raw and aching. He slid his fingers inside the row of ruffles that began a demure several inches below her throat. The skin there was very warm and smooth. Meeting the barrier of her chemise, he played with the narrow lace that bordered it long enough to hear her impatient sigh before slipping lower to find the pliant flesh of her breasts.

A little whimper broke from her throat, and she dropped her forehead against his chest. Caleb rested his cheek in her hair, letting the herbal smells that clung to her wrap him in a sense of peace. Reaching an understanding with Libby brought him a bone-deep happiness he found he had no desire to question. Maybe he wasn't the first man to discover these two ripe breasts, or the sweet, tight furrow between them; it would have to be enough that he was the first to waken her to her passionate nature. Below the happiness lurked an impulse to tear and thrust his way into physical union *now,* while she cuddled so trustingly close, stretching up against him as if that would allow his roving hand more freedom within the confines of her bodice.

The emotions teetered like ore balanced on an internal scale, unlike any conflict he'd ever felt about a woman before. His manhood made itself felt, growing rigid—uncomfortably so—while the lazy confidence of well-being Libby gave him kept his hand and voice relaxed. "Time to go to bed. No point in shifting the new furniture around until it's moved to the house."

"Of course it—" She went very still. "You mean that the furniture stays but I move? Into your rooms? Caleb, don't shame me like that."

He liked the pink dress, but it was too restricting. Retrieving his hand, he used it to cup the fullness of one breast. "Where's the shame? You're a married woman." Other people's opinions never affected him much, but if they influenced Libby, he'd use them without a twinge of conscience. "A man could get damned tired of the pitying glances that have been coming my way. Everyone acts like I'm a bull that came under the knife. Not to mention my sister's tactful questions about my health and what have I done to that poor girl to scare her out of my bed?" He plied the breast with gentle squeezes and tried to read her expression. Her eyes had no color in the half darkness. "When you're in my arms and I'm inside you, I won't let you be scared. I swear, Libby."

She beat at his chest and shoulders at that, flailing blows that must have hurt her worse than him, but when he released her, she threw herself against him in a hard embrace. Not knowing what else to do, he rubbed her back until her panting slowed to more normal breathing. "You're not giving me a choice about sleeping in your rooms, are you?" she asked finally.

"No."

"How could you make me?"

The storm over, she sounded as innocently curious as a child. Coolly, he reminded her, "I own the Manzanita. We were married in front of witnesses, so most people would say I own you. Do I have to threaten you with bars on the windows?"

He felt her sigh. It lifted her breasts so they pressed more firmly against his chest, and his manhood stirred. "Don't. If—if I agree to come to you and we do the things you talked about before—not risking the annulment, you must see we can't go that far—but just . . . touching, will you object if I keep my own room?"

"Dear heart, separate rooms make us both ridiculous. We would have been lovers already except that I showed up drunk. That's a mistake I'll never make again with you. You can count on it."

"Well, I am glad of that, but we were not going to be lovers. We were just going to—to be—"

"Particular friends?"

Libby moved restlessly in his arms. Her foot slithered a few inches as the heel fell on the virgin's bower. How odd; it had no scent. In Caleb's mind, she knew, being able to recite prostitutes' cant as she had to Smitty made her close to a prostitute.

With a sharp stab of self-knowledge, she remembered her vow never to go begging to this man. "Caleb, please." It was barely a whisper. "Leave me something."

As coldly as his condition allowed him, he toted up the odds. With her peculiar ideas of honor, Libby would never renege on a bargain, once it was struck. Well, he wouldn't himself. He'd just make damned sure he had stated the contract in such a manner that it gave him room to interpret the terms a little differently from what the other party might have intended. That wasn't double dealing but plain New England common sense.

Libby was staggeringly beautiful, seemed well read, had her fair share of female accomplishments mentionable and unorthodox, could even be called clever in her own lack-ballast way. If she possessed the faintest life-saving trace of common sense, he'd never caught a whiff of it.

"I'll stand by what I said about the furniture," he said. "And if you haven't figured out yet I want you willing or not at all, I plumb can't think of a way to convince you. Come to me tonight. Every night. I'll love you as fully as you'll let me."

The resistance drained out of her on a long exhalation. Her breath cooled, then warmed his cheek as she nestled closer, and her body softened and molded itself to his as well as it could in its prison of corset and crinoline.

"Yes, Caleb, please."

He scooped her up cradle-fashion, his action so quick it surprised a trill of laughter from her. Retracing their steps, he shouldered his way through the gates.

"Let me down! People will see! It's not decent."

"Maybe I want them to see."

In the orange torchlight, strain stole the merry look from around her eyes. "Is that your real object? Showing everyone the stallion has brought the filly with the odd kick in her gallop into the herd?"

His kiss burned on her lips before she could duck her head. "There is no herd," he said. "Only you. And I'm not a stallion, though by God you make me frenzied as one, only a man with a powerful need for his woman." In the act of setting her down, he held her upper body clamped to his so they'd both feel the gentle abrasion as he revolved her until her feet touched the ground. "Go upstairs, then, to my room. I'll be there in a minute."

She went with only one backward glance. Shy, he thought with pleasure. Not calculating as he'd once assumed, but shy as a woman unused to passion was of a man who startled her by taking her fancy.

The common room had its complement of wranglers and craftsmen drinking as they gambled for small stakes and swapped grandiose lies. Pausing in an unlit corner to keep his state of arousal hidden, Caleb spotted Diego plunking on his guitar. The sad little tune cut off, and Diego materialized by his side, saying in an undertone, "Senor?"

"I have a job for a couple of the men. There's some carpentry work involved, but mainly it needs to be done without a lot of noise . . ."

When he'd outlined what he required, Diego nodded in comprehension, studied his employer for a moment, and murmured, "We have wondered when Senor Cal would make his move. *Muy bueno*. A prize worth winning."

Since the prize was so nearly within his grasp, and his need has eased while he explained his plan, Caleb grinned. "A treasure." Nevertheless, a fundamental dislike of any other male's frankly stated admiration for Libby caused him to provide a distraction, even though it embarrassed him. "About the guitar. It's a fine instrument—"

The understanding in Diego's answering smile halted him. "The senor's concern was clear. It makes no difference." Outrageously, he added, "I am at the senora's service. Who would not be? But she cares for the music, that is all. The fires burning in her leap only when the senor is near. We have all remarked it."

Caleb measured the other man. Slowly his fists uncurled. "Libby may decide to go on with the lessons." With a chaperone in attendance, he stipulated to himself. Not that he distrusted Libby, exactly. Not after the sincerity of her declaration. *I only ever see you.* But Caleb sure as hell wasn't going to parade her in front of claim jumpers, either. After all, wasn't he supplanting the piano player? A man had to be careful of his valuables, and Libby had become very, very valuable.

That line of reasoning made him impatient for the reassurance of her ardent body pressed to his. "Use as many men as it takes," he said curtly. "Just get the job done before dawn."

The soft stamp of his boots on the wooden stairs brought Libby's head up to listen. Odd; all the men and many of the women wore boots, but her ear never failed to pick out Caleb's tread. Pulse clammering, she cast a look at her nightgown, laid neatly on the sunburst quilt, blew out the lamp, and stepped onto the balcony.

"I thought you were going to wait across the way," Caleb said. Faint suspicion threaded through his voice.

"There was something I had to get."

For a wild moment, Caleb wondered whether he could have misunderstood her, now and since their first kiss. Were all her protestations coy nonsense? Had she changed her mind about the nature their intimacies would take and gone to her own room to collect a condom? Would the piano player have even shown her what one was? The lover's glove wasn't a garment Caleb favored, although he'd resorted to the device in the past to protect himself when frequenting brothels. He had a shrewd inkling that, worn more than once by different customers as was apt to happen in such locales, the device would spread the diseases it had been invented to contain.

Of course, Dr. Conton's sheath had the side benefit of preventing seed from planting itself in a woman's womb. Libby'd made it clear she didn't intend to breed by him . . .

"What did you have to get?" The question was so harsh she shied away.

"Your—your hat. You left it behind the last time you were in my room, and I haven't known what to do with it." The shadow she held out to him bore the unmistakable shape of one of the white felt sombreros he wore for outdoors work.

Caleb closed his eyes, then opened them. "Forgive me, dear heart."

"Willingly. What have I forgiven?"

"Phantasms. Maggots burrowing through my brain. Come to bed with me. I need to feel that you're real."

In his room, with the shutters closed and the door locked, he made sure the lamp was full of oil and set it in the alcove so an erotic twilight reached the bed.

Libby stood quiet and still under his hands as he rid her of the skirts that wrapped her in petallike layers, moving only when he assaulted the hooks of her front-closing corset. "I had better deal with this," she said with an uncertain smile. "I've but the one left to me."

Beginning on his own buttons, Caleb watched her unwind the long laces. "Why do females squeeze themselves into those things, anyway?"

"So our frocks will fit." He could see the tide of color that ran all the way from the top of her chemise to her forehead when she slid the corset off over her arms and placed it on the pile he'd made of her other belongings. "Thank you for folding my things so nicely."

"I thought you'd like that better than me just throwing them around again. I *am* making a study of how to please you, Libby."

The flush washed and ebbed, and her eyes darkened to a more vivid green. Caleb's gaze wandered from her eyes to the flesh swelling over the crocheted lace that edged the neckline of her chemise. With a gasp, she turned toward the wall and fumbled at the closures.

Shucking off shirt and trousers, Caleb reached her before she could do more than tug open a single bow. "Let me. I've dreamed it so many times . . ." The way she stiffened and a good look at her expression changed his mind. It had been a warm day, and he hadn't worn undergarments. She acted as if she'd never seen a naked man before.

Well, it was possible she hadn't. Lots of people preferred a smothering cloak of darkness for their more interesting activities. Caleb didn't happen to be one of them.

"Does having light worry you?" he asked tenderly.

As if she couldn't help herself, she placed a palm flat against his chest. The tentative touch barely disturbed the black hair clustering there. "It was dark before," she said, the explanation incoherent until he remembered their night in San Francisco.

At the memory, his shaft, already aroused again by the act of undressing her, strained higher. Her eyes grew round as saucers.

"Light will increase your pleasure. And you'll be able to see that you can trust me," he said coaxingly, pulling out the pins that held her chignon in place. As the heavy weight fell across his hands, he added, "If you can't bear it, little one, I'll go blow the flame out."

"No, let it stay. I'm being silly. The fact is that I've never—I know it sounds unbelievable to you, but I've never taken all my clothes off in front of a man before."

"I believe you've never been treated the way you ought to be treated," he said. "Is anything else wrong? Tell me."

"I don't mean to offend you, but . . . you're so big."

His hands luxuriated in the wealth of her hair, and he laughed very softly. "Libby, you won't find many men who consider a comment like that to be an insult."

"Oh." She looked down again, and from her expression was absorbing the implications. Her fascinated gaze seemed to indicate that he compared favorably to the piano player in this area. Caleb hoped so, not because his virility needed that kind of reassurance, but because he wanted Libby to prefer him to anyone else.

Irregular breathing made her breasts rise and fall. The thin material of her undergarments formed the flimsiest of barriers. Although the pantalets that encased her lower limbs unfortunately weren't the abbreviated sort that ended just above the knees, and instead climbed to a tie at her waist, he could tell they did have the customary slit between the legs. "Would you feel better keeping what you've got on?" he asked.

Her beaming smile thanked him. "Yes, if it doesn't displease you. I—I do desire for you to be pleased, Caleb."

"I will be," he said with confidence, watching the rosy shadows of her nipples push against the soft muslin. "We've finally got you down to a sensible number of clothes. These won't get in my way as long as they're what you want.''

Libby heard the unstated corollary; he expected to seduce her past the few considerations of modesty that consorting with him had left her. And she had no doubt he could. Already the sight of his body, sinewy, lean with muscle, and very plainly aroused, had become less strange and more natural. He still drew her stare, but now she darted quick looks because his nakedness was so beautiful and so male. A trembling started low in her abdomen. With the unaccustomed, pleasurable weakness grew a soft, hot ache that she thought might consume her if she let it.

''Is it wrong to want to feel close to you?'' she whispered.

Exuberantly, he lifted her off the floor, his forearms crossed under her seat to bring her legs around his waist. Her arms clenched around his neck. At the same time the opening in her pantalets parted and left the flesh protected by her triangle of curls vulnerable to the feeling of his hard belly. Something velvety and blunt-tipped brushed her inner thigh, and in a sudden spasm of panic, she moaned his name.

Before she could blurt out her terror of learning too much, of changing into a Libby she wouldn't recognize, he swung her around, and around, in dizzying circles that made her cling tighter. When he stopped, they were next to the bed. Then she couldn't tell him her fear, because his face filled her vision, and his eyes were bright and intent, and the ceiling tilted as he laid her gently on the mattress, his own body following so there was never a moment to catch a proper breath.

It seemed he'd been right when he'd said that her pitiful shield of underclothing wouldn't get in his way. His hands moved over her, warm and firm through the muslin. Her breasts tried to rise to fill his palms when he cupped them. The gentle kneading was pleasant, as were the patient, lingering kisses he pressed on her lips and throat. The sweet ache diminished, and so did her fear.

"Libby." His face was rigid with control, but tenderness rumbled through his deep voice. "My golden girl. Touch me."

"Where?"

"Everywhere."

She brought her hands up from where they had been curling and uncurling on the pillow and ran them over his shoulders, down the hard slab of his back to his smooth, small buttocks. As she did, Caleb ran the tips of his thumbs over her nipples. The muslin dragged, its weave caught between the calluses on his fingers and the beading flesh underneath.

The ache came back in a rush, ebbing and flowing from the little, hard points of flesh he teased without mercy. This time it was fierce and hungry, and she made a small, demanding sound that brought an understanding, breathless laugh from Caleb. "Made for loving . . ."

Bending his head, he kissed first one angry red peak, then the other. Through the material, his lips and tongue soothed the throbbing into a slow, delicious rhythm that gave desire a melody, coursing louder and louder through her veins. When she let her hands stop so she could give herself over to the insistent singing in her blood, he lifted his head and murmured, "Learn me. There's no part of me I don't want you to know . . ."

So Libby stroked the coarse, strong hair back from his forehead, and traced the curve of his flat ears and the tense column of his neck. One muscle-covered shoulder blade winged under her hand as he pushed himself into a half-reclining position without faltering in the delicate lashing his tongue was giving her nipple. He was never less than gentle although tension quivered through his body just as glissandos vibrated from the strings of a harp, and the combination of the two extremes drove her into a frenzy. His movement had brought his ear close enough to nip, and she did. Even through her rage of passion, the worry that she might hurt him made her alternate her teeth with quick, healing forays of her tongue.

As if the biting and laving formed a signal, Caleb groaned, suckling hard and running a hand between her thighs inside the slit in her pantalets. The first probing touch startled Libby so much that she cried out, a note like music. The circular designs his finger drew in the slick, increasingly damp folds fed the ache and the frenzy, until she squirmed, clutching at his hand and trying to lift herself closer to the source of so much sensation.

Finally Caleb released her breast, pushing her knees up and apart and mounting her. His weight and the sculpted shape of his hips felt so good lodged against her body that they drove out any thought of annulment or honor or . . . They drove out any thought at all. He shifted, and dimly she realized that he was parting the swollen lips between her legs and guiding his bar of flesh into them.

Conscience and prudence fought a brief, violent war with desire, and produced a faint "Caleb, no—"

"I'm not breaking my word," he said thickly. "I won't enter. Just feel, dear heart, feel how good, how right . . ."

The round tip slid through the wetness and up through her tangled damp hair to rest firmly against her midsection. The long, hard shaft still pressed against whorls singing with a tension that must, it occurred to her now as she saw the shine of perspiration in the hollow of his throat, be akin to his.

Pleasure, he had said. This was the pleasure he had promised. It *was* pleasure, but so intense it was also pain, and she writhed, tiny cries escaping her that somehow increased it.

The deep, slurred voice he used to encourage her to temper her frantic bucking into easy thrusts that matched his filled her ears, overriding the pounding of her heart. Caleb rubbed his chest against her breasts, and the cotton stretched and bunched over aroused nipples, making her twist her head back and forth.

His elbows rested between strands of her hair. He caught her face in his big hands and held it still for an almost savage kiss, his tongue plunging into her mouth as if he owned it and it was his to take and fill. The solid, slim male hips rode her softness. His shaft, slick with the moisture her body produced, slid in ever harder thrusts over flesh that began to contract in helpless flashes of ecstasy. Tiny muscles deep inside her tried to grip something that wasn't there. Then the pleasure peaked and shattered and Libby sang out, "Caleb!"

Another groan wrenched from his chest. Rolling to one side, he pulled her hand to his body. Still gasping from her own release, she helped him to his, which spilled in three shuddering convulsions.

Warm tremors shook her arms and legs as Libby sank back on the pillow.

"Caleb," she whispered, awestruck, "Is it supposed to be like this between a man and a woman whenever they—we—?"

He collapsed next to her, and his chuckle sounded in her ear. "Better. No, don't turn away from me." A gentle finger insisted under her chin, bringing her face to face with him. "Oh, Libby. Tears? Why?"

"I don't know." But she did know. Anguish pierced her. He meant their loving would have been better for him if she had welcomed him inside her body. And there had been a moment for her, too, just at the end, when disappointment had mingled with the bursts of rapture that had gone on to overwhelm her. But she couldn't tell him, or he'd press for the virginity he didn't believe she possessed.

The frustration of a man whose not inconsiderable efforts to delight his woman have been rewarded with weeping eroded some of Caleb's satisfaction. An unpalatable thought crossed his mind. The fat drops leaking from between closed lids to meander down Libby's temples and soak into her hair might be for the piano player. Brows lowering, he hauled her a little too firmly back into his arms and settled her head in the crook of his shoulder. "Don't think you can get away with lying to me. It's too late for that."

"I don't mean to lie to you." Opening her eyes, she blinked to rid them of the last of the tears. "Sometimes it's safer to rely on, well, evasions. Are you angry?"

He stared at the ceiling. He knew what Libby was. How could he expect a woman who'd dragged herself along with an abusive lover over a quarter of a continent to depend on him enough to share her emotions? But that was what he wanted. Not just her body, lush and appealing as it was under its veiling of now-crumpled undergarments. Not just her company, either, although he never ceased to be amazed as well as stimulated by the quaint way in which her mind worked.

Caleb wanted *her*, her body, her heart, all of her smiles. He wasn't sure how long it would take to quench this thirst for her that afflicted him, but it would be a while. A considerable while.

"I'm not angry," he answered, instead feeling sad and impatient with himself for it. "I'd hoped to please you so well you wouldn't need to cry."

"You did." The smile Libby came up with was a poor thing, quivering around the edges. "I'm afraid of so much pleasure. It will make me weak, and I have to be strong." Sitting up, she turned as if she intended to leave the bed.

With a smooth motion, Caleb sat up behind her, fitting his arms around her ribs. The undersides of her breasts molded against his forearms.

"Where are you going?"

"To my room." She went rigid, even her breasts. "You promised—"

He recalled every precisely chosen word he'd given her. "It's early yet. Stay."

"Caleb, please. I—I'm tired. It's time to sleep."

"Are you?" He let one hand wander down, while the other slid up. "Is it?"

Her hair swayed against his face, throat, and chest as she shook her head slowly. For long minutes they sat quietly, his hands moving with painstaking care to refine each caress until her breath came in pants and he could feel her heart knock under the thumb charting the circumference of one white breast.

"How can I feel like this again so soon?" she asked as he gently turned her to face him.

He grinned. "The same way I can." Despite its earlier service, his shaft was standing to attention, eager to do duty once more.

Libby's lovely mouth fell open into a pretty pink O. At Caleb's mental image of what the shape would be perfect for, his manhood stood even taller.

"It hurts me to fail to make you happy," said Libby, her tongue flicking over her lips. His rod stirred the air. "Even though we can't do everything you would like, would you enjoy it if I—I took off the rest of my clothes?"

She looked at him with grave curiosity, as if she really believed he might say no. "You do make me happy," he told her, just as gravely, "and I'm mortal sure I'd enjoy that very much."

Her smile trembling uncertainly, she loosened the laces and uncoupled hooks so he could pull the rumpled chemise over her head. Then she crawled out of her pantalets. The actions were without artifice; Caleb couldn't understand how their innocence inflamed him more than any whore's practiced stripping could have done.

"The more I have of you, the more I need you. By the Horn Spoon, I knew you would be beautiful," he said at last. "But I couldn't guess how beautiful."

The pale froth of hair cascaded over her face like one of the waterfalls east in the mountains. She pushed it aside, crouching on her long, shapely legs, nipples visible through silky strands whose ends were long enough to refuse to obey her hand. Some of them met and mingled with the golden curls that peeked up from below the slight, womanly curve of her belly.

"The kiss," she said, "the special, deep kiss you talked about before. Would it answer your need?"

His gaze drifted over her. "Yes, ma'am, I believe it would. I can give it to you, and then you can return it to me, or—if we both deliver our kisses at the same time, our pleasure would be twofold."

Mutely, she nodded, gasping as he tumbled her lightly onto her side and began to ply her throat, then her breasts, then her belly and below with his open mouth.

Chapter 16

Libby dreamed that Caleb was still doing that aston-ishing thing to her, loving her most secret flesh with his mouth while she pressed shy, then fervent kisses where he told her. Ordered waves of pleasure burst through her, each one impossibly intense and yet succeeded by one even stronger.

They didn't fade away; instead the last one broke off with cruel abruptness when she woke in the middle of a drawn-out moan that turned horrified as she took in her surroundings.

Outside it must be so disastrously past dawn that the sun had risen high enough to burn away the fog and slant yellow rays into the courtyard. Inquisitive beams laid a pattern of widening ribbons across the foot of the bed. Caleb's simple, wide bed.

Covers tumbled to the floor. The oak doors of the wardrobe hung open, propped outward by the force of a number of her clothes which someone—she sincerely hoped it had been Caleb—had stuffed in next to its own-er's. The things she'd worn yesterday had disappeared.

It was humiliating to have slept so soundly that so much could be accomplished without waking her.

Most of the night had been consumed as dark half moons had gradually waxed under Caleb's eyes. His mouth had grown paler and more determined as he'd teased and suckled and lightly bitten her, yet he would give her no rest until she convulsed delicately in his

235

arms. When he'd finally allowed sleep to claim her, she had plunged into a well of unconsciousness so deep bugles wouldn't have wakened her.

The household was too well regulated for her to be left to her own devices indefinitely, no matter how much she would have preferred it. Leather thongs supporting the mattress creaked when she swung her legs over the side. Ascensión entered after a tactful rap.

Libby's limbs froze. Through a haze of embarrassment, she made herself speak calmly. "I shan't need you this morning, Ascensión."

The maid giggled. "It is afternoon, senora. Shall I not at least pour out water for washing?"

"Thank you, no." A dignified posture to enforce her commands had been pounded into Libby in childhood. She straightened before she had time to recall that she had no clothes on. Then it was too late. Ascensión's eyes widened and glazed.

"*Madre de Dios!*" she breathed. "The senor, he is a lusty lover, yes?"

Looking down, Libby inhaled to see conglomerations of tiny red dots clustering around and over her nipples. Here and there a very faint bruise showed blue under her fair skin.

She knew perfectly well that Caleb had never hurt her in any way. It must have been his weight and the occasional pleasurable graze of his teeth that had done the damage. And—of course. The pull of muslin between their bodies before the desire to please him had led her to give him the gift of her nakedness.

Though there was no point in evicting Ascensión now that the maid had witnessed Caleb's marks on her, Libby firmly repeated the request. With another doubtful as well as admiring glance, Ascensión went.

She had closed the door securely before Libby thought to ask why so many of her clothes had been brought to Caleb's room. To provide a choice, she decided carelessly, selecting a dress at random. Surely Caleb had done it, or ordered it. Unlikely for anyone trained by Teresa to initiate such a mistake; it would make double work when the small mountain of garments had to be carried back to the room across the way.

Handling Caleb's possessions, using his basin and washcloth and pulling his comb through her hair, gave her an odd feeling of intimacy. Her skin tingled, and even after she dressed herself, echoes of illicit sensation made the tips of her breasts thrust against all her proper layers of clothing.

As Libby girded herself with a deep breath to step outside, another knock brought Teresa bustling in. The current of fresh air that accompanied her caused the musky odor hanging heavy within the four walls to be all too obvious.

The scent of pleasure, Libby thought. The scent she and Caleb had made together.

The bed remained unmade; Libby hadn't seen much point to it, since this morning—afternoon, she reminded herself—the sheets were definitely in need of a change. Teresa inspected them with a professional eye.

"No blood?" she exclaimed.

Libby gulped. "Blood?" she asked faintly.

"Ah, well," said Teresa kindly. "The wound of love does not always leave a trace. It has happened so before. Do not fear, senora. No one will think the less of you."

"Th-thank you." Heavens, thought Libby. Recovering, she pointed to the wardrobe. "I'm afraid you'll be put to extra trouble taking all these clothes back. I cannot imagine why so many were brought in here, but please see that they are returned before—"

Teresa's round, pretty face went blank. "Pardon, senora?"

Libby started again. "My clothes belong in my room. I—"

"But no, senora. This is your room now."

The sincere certainty in Teresa's voice rang so true

that for an insane moment Libby almost apologized for the misunderstanding.

She rallied. "Nonsense. You mustn't think that because—that the living arrangement between Senor Cal and myself has changed. He himself said last night that my room would remain the same until the furniture is moved to the new house." By which time *surely* they could begin to unsnarl the legal ball of string they'd created for themselves and a ship setting sail for England could be found. "Senor Cal promised."

"Ah." Without a muscle twitching, Teresa managed to give the impression of vast amusement.

The rest of the day presented a full platter of activities. There was no excuse, Libby scolded herself, for the way she sometimes simply stopped in the midst of an absorbing occupation and stared about her, expecting Caleb to be near. As if, she thought uneasily, he had so successfully inserted himself into her life that when he was gone, half of her was, too.

"Libby, for heaven's sake, pay attention! What do you think about this new canezou, as they call it?" Julia held out an illustration. "It's such a soft, flattering style. I want you to get some."

Dragging her wandering attention back to the picture of the filmy underblouse, Libby picked the pencil out of her sister-in-law's hand and scribbled on Julia's side of the list they were compiling. "What I think is that the style would be lovely on you. Those tucks and billowing sleeves would—that is, they would—"

Julia chuckled. "Dress the scarecrow in some curves? Don't waste all that well-bred ingenuity trying not to offend me. It's hardly news to me I'm skinny."

"A slender form can be very elegant. Now that your health is back, you look very well indeed," objected Libby.

"I'm never going to look as well as you," Julia said philosophically. "Who knows, maybe I should order one of those bust improvers."

"No! Truly, Julia. They aren't convincing. What if

you get the kind made of wax and stray too near a stove? You could melt.''

"Oh, dear. But I have to do something to beautify myself or else . . . I have to do something.'' She flipped through the hand-tinted pages of the fashion magazine disconsolately. "I never know what to have made up. The dresses all look becoming on the ladies in the pictures, but the ladies all look like you! So I settle for copying the clothes my grandmother used to choose for me.''

Wisely, Libby refrained from asking what the *else* would have been and studied Julia as her mother would have—rigorously, for assets and flaws. "Your grandmother was right in one thing. A simple fashion suits you. Too many frills and bows would cheapen the lines of your figure. This dress, though''—she waved at the dead-leaf-brown alpaca—"is far too severe. It smothers you. Some tucks and shaping and an *occasional* ruffle . . .''

And then, in the middle of an animated discussion of primary colors which the magazine claimed were coming into vogue, Libby found herself staring out the window and listening for Caleb's step.

In the kitchen, Manuel had to recall her attention no less than three times and remind her what she had approved for supper. Wang singsonged scornful-sounding incomprehensibilities.

And while Julia hacked out to oversee the harvest and storing of the early vegetables, Libby lost track of counting linens being packed for the household's move so many times that Teresa lost her temper.

In the late afternoon, a field hand was carried in with a broken leg. The simple break had been rough-set by his comrades, and with Teresa she carefully checked their work and bound the injured limb to a straighter splint. With no time to change for dinner, she stripped off her apron and ran directly from the section of the workers' quarters partitioned off as a hospital area to the dining room.

Caleb joined her and Julia, still in his denim trousers and work shirt, although he'd taken the time to remove his chaps. His eyes met hers just once, and lit; then he concentrated on his food. Never a talkative man, he was so quiet during the meal that Julia ignored him and took up the conversation where they'd left it by asking what Libby would recommend the younger girl do about her hair.

Libby's glance at Caleb showed him withdrawn, the dark circles under his eyes prominent. His preoccupation didn't matter. He was here, even if his manner was uncharacteristically aloof. It assuaged the need to be with him she'd had since waking. Soon his mere physical presence wouldn't be enough and she'd want him to notice her, but for now she ate, and smiled, and contented herself with long, unhidden looks at his lips and his jaw as he chewed, at his shoulders where the muscle rolled as he moved his arms, and at his tanned fingers maneuvering his knife and fork.

Turning to Julia, Libby *tsk*ed as she contemplated the miniature bun her sister-in-law had contrived by slicking the short tresses away from her face. "Did they save your hair when it was cut off?"

"Scads of it."

"A switch," Libby said positively. "The only alternative is curl papers or tongs."

Julia sighed. "At least it'll be my own hair, and I won't have to buy any. Cal and—Cal would laugh himself sick if I tried to pass myself off in someone else's hair." The snap of her brother's teeth over a yawn interrupted her. She added, "You ought to be in your bed. You look like a two-day-old corpse."

"Thank you." A ghost of Caleb's infectious grin pulled at Libby's heart. "It happens I didn't get much sleep last night."

"So I heard," Julia patted her lips with a napkin. The linen didn't quite screen her echoing grin. It was a twin to his, and it was definitely approving.

Feeling scarlet burn in her cheeks, Libby kicked in

Caleb's direction under the table. Her soft-soled shoe connected with something solid. Caleb jumped but said smoothly enough, "Rode out past Two Rock today. Funny thing. The old Indian trail looked like it's been seeing some use. No sign of who it might have been, though."

"Travelers passing through," Libby suggested, regaining her composure.

"No doubt about it. Thing is, people usually go from one place to somewhere else. There's nothing out there."

"At least, nothing we don't own." Julia stirred her coffee. "Squatters?"

Caleb shrugged. "Could be."

Americans, thought Libby. A doubt put to rest weeks before woke and made her stomach roll like a hoop. Was Caleb a coward or merely so pragmatic she couldn't distinguish between the two unattractive qualities? She pushed away the rest of her supper. "Aren't you going to do something about them?"

Both Logans looked at her inquiringly.

"Even if you don't want to fight, wouldn't it be better tactics to encourage them to leave your property now rather than later when they're entrenched?"

The spoon slipped in Julia's hand, and brown liquid splattered. "Who doesn't like fighting?"

"Quiet, little sister." The telltale muscle beside Caleb's mouth twitched his lips into a half smile. "I can't fight people I can't find, Libby. This is a big spread. Where do you suggest I start looking?"

"Couldn't they be tracked?"

"A sensible idea," Caleb said with ostentatious patience. "Except that three well-traveled paths cross the Indian trail farther on, and I wouldn't be able to tell which one they'd taken."

Aware of Julia's openmouthed stare, Libby said only, "I see."

"If uninvited visitors are squatting on Logan land,

they'll make themselves heard or seen eventually. Then I'll deal with them.''

The rest of the meal passed in uncomfortable silence, the Logans eating while Libby pleated her napkin into intricate fan shapes. Finally, Caleb stood and stretched. ''Well, Julia, I'll take your advice. Coming to bed, Libby?'' he added casually.

The offhandedness of the question stung. So did his apparent assumption that she'd be joining him in bed from now on. Libby spat, ''No.''

''Suit yourself,'' he replied in an equable voice only slightly contradicted by the tilt of an eyebrow.

Misery compounded her anger. Now that his curiosity had been satisfied by a night in her arms, had the urgency of his interest slackened? Libby assured herself furiously that she didn't care, but as the thought ran through her mind, so did the realization that even his original, unsettling mockery had been better than indifference.

As he examined her set face, his softened. ''Oh, if I wasn't nearly forgetting.'' Patting his shirt pocket, Caleb withdrew a lady's watch on a long golden chain. Stepping behind Libby, he lowered the chain over her head.

''Right pretty,'' Julia approved.

''Libby lost her watch in San Francisco,'' explained Caleb. ''Do you like it, dear heart?''

So many emotions flooded Libby that she couldn't speak. The casing was chased gold, the back enameled in a delicate floral design.

''You sew a little pocket for it in your waistband, the storekeeper in Sonoma told me,'' he added helpfully.

''Yes, I've seen the style before,'' Libby managed.

Julia's forehead wrinkled. ''Of course you have, being from England and all. Are you all right? Forgive me, Libby, but you're acting downright peculiar. First you talk about Cal as if he's a rabbit, and now . . . if you dislike the trinket so much you can't bring yourself to say thank you, just tell the man and he'll buy you a different one.''

"The watch is exquisite." Libby pulled the chain off over her head, and it fell into her lap in a costly heap. Her fingertip barely touched the dusty blue of the miniature flowers. "I couldn't ask for a kinder or more considerate present. You shouldn't have ridden all the way to Sonoma today in addition to your other chores. Not for me. Excuse me.''

Caleb caught at her shoulder as she tried to brush past. "If you'd rather have something else—"

Something inside Libby broke. "I told you, the watch is perfect. A token of your affection—is that the right word, Caleb? A tasteful memento to mark a change in our—status. I gave you something and so you give me what you think I expect in return. Could you get one thing through that impenetrable American skull of yours? Some gifts don't require recompense. And some women don't, either.''

Wrenching away, she thrust his present into his hand and walked blindly out the door.

Julia let out her breath. "Something's very wrong with that woman. Cal, how much do you know about Libby?''

"Enough," he answered curtly.

"I've never met—never even heard of a female who reacts to generosity from her husband the way she does. You would think she was being tied to the foot of your bed and forced to be your mistress or some such.''

That struck too close to home. "Thanks. To make the matter clear, I've never forced her.''

"I know that, stupid. In fact, it's taken you so long I was afraid—well. Still—does she have religious scruples? The—the intimate side of married life can come as quite a shock to a sheltered girl.''

Dryly, Caleb said, "That's not the problem in this case.''

"Are you sure? What else could it be?" asked Julia.

"She loves you, Cal. I spent most of the afternoon with Libby. If ever a woman looked lovelorn, she did."

Exhaustion battled incredulity, and the tiniest fountaining of hope. "I haven't been able to figure out how her mind works, let alone her heart."

"Cal!" his sister exploded. "What's the matter with you two? I can understand why you married her. All it takes is one look. But why would she have married you if she didn't intend to be your wife? You're rich—"

"Thanks again."

"Okay, it's not your only attraction, or so I've heard. Don't get your precious male feelings all in a hoodoo. But think about it. San Francisco is stuffed with well-to-do men. A beauty like Libby could have had her pick. Why take you if she didn't want you?"

Because between the Hounds, the padre, and me, she didn't have much choice. Caleb pushed the thought away and ran a palm over his lower face wearily. "I'm not unhappy with Libby, Julia."

"That's a fine commendation after two weeks of marriage!"

"I'm too tired to prettify my speech to your standards. Don't bother your head about it." He kissed her cheek. "I know what I'm doing. Good night."

"I wish ladies used swearwords. Good night."

Caleb searched the courtyard in vain for a glimpse of Libby. Trudging toward his quarters, he felt a pang of conscience. He should have paid her more attention at supper. One part of his mind had been aware of her every moment, noting her easy conversation with his sister, grateful for their soothing women's talk that flowed around him without calling for a contribution from a mere male. It was restful. The other part had wearily turned over the puzzle of fresh horse signs and the debris left from the camps of careless men in places no one had any reason to go.

It wasn't easy thinking when his brain was benumbed in the euphoric aftermath of bedding Libby, getting so close to real lovemaking with her at last. She couldn't hold out long now. His peaceful exhaustion was so complete, it had blasted whatever sense he had where Libby was concerned. No doubt he could have been slicker presenting his gift. He should have recalled how touchy her pride could be. The watch was just a little something; it would take Pablo a while to create settings for the emeralds Caleb had already decided on for her. He would have to be more careful handling Libby when he gave her those.

Right now, after a rewarding but sleepless night and a full day in the saddle, he was tired . . . caught in the same trap he'd laid for his fractious light of love, he thought with a reminiscent grin that was an effort to produce.

Not much hope she'd be in his bed when he got there.

Surprise had rippled through him when she hadn't included a complaint about his little stratagem in her speech tonight. But she'd show up. After all, he'd made it impossible for her to sleep anywhere else. And it wasn't as if she had any real aversion to his company. That had gotten itself proven for damned sure. Impossibly, desire stirred and his body tried sluggishly to respond. Cursing himself with his last reserve of humor, Caleb stumbled into his room.

Using her arms to compress her skirts into a size that would fit in the gap between the gates, Libby saw a glow bloom between the shutters over Caleb's windows. She'd taken a walk in the clean outer air, but it had only served to bring the memory of last night closer. The immense black solitude was a pointed reminder of how rarely she'd been by herself these past weeks. Either she was with Julia or Teresa, or in the kitchen or . . . with Caleb.

Idiotic to feel lonely when she'd been alone for years now. Not just for years—forever. Her beloved, madbrained parents had preferred their own pursuits, and she'd had her music. For the first time, she wondered if little Libby would have poured all that dedication into practicing if there had been anyone in her world who'd wanted to spend time with her.

The cool breeze, the calm and faraway stars and drunken moon leaning to one side remained impersonal and serene, so she sighed and turned back. And discovered she'd fallen so far from sanity that the first thing she looked for upon reentering the courtyard was a sign that Caleb was still awake.

The shoot of loneliness grew with each step, until it was a towering, monstrous growth by the time she reached her doorway. Ascensión would come to help her undress, she thought. Someone would come . . . but the assurance brought no comfort because she didn't want Ascensión.

God help her. She wanted Caleb. And he'd tried to pay her off as if she were a whore.

For a moment, an emotion perilously close to grief blinded her to the fact that the room was dark. So unusual was it for the staff to forget to light her lamp that Libby stopped dead in her tracks. Dim moonlight seeped in and revealed something else.

The room was empty. *Empty.* No bed, no wardrobe, no pretty little dressing table. Drawn forward, hands outstretched as if she were sleepwalking, Libby ran her fingers over the bricks and found holes that marked where the mirror had been unbolted from the wall. Except for the gritty depressions in the clay, the room was exactly as it had been the first night she'd inhabited it. Even the musty, earthy smell was reclaiming it.

"You lied," she said aloud. Slowly, she sank to the floor. "I trusted you against my own better judgment, and you lied to me."

Wrapping her arms around herself for comfort, she rocked on her heels. Her thoughts circled endlessly and uselessly, like the skirts that billowed and subsided around her. The primary and most painful reflection drew a small sob from her every time it came to the forefront again. Caleb couldn't be trusted. He was dead to honor—if he'd ever possessed any in the first place.

He hadn't raped her last night, it was true, or even seduced her, and here in the dark and loneliness Libby chewed on the unpalatable fact that no man and few women would have blamed him if he had. She'd gone with him like the loosest lightskirt, and he'd given her only what she'd asked for. He had been honest in bed.

But outside of it . . . everything she despised in Americans, he possessed in overflowing measure. The cockiness of a new race, the deceitful practices of a people bent on consuming a continent. His imagination was limited by the boundaries of his land, and evidently he wouldn't even fight for the Manzanita unless winning benefited him directly. With an ache that burned deep down, somewhere in the region where he could make her feel the hot coals of desire, she wished he would fight for something besides himself.

Of course, he'd hit the saloon owner and Smitty, and she'd seen him hold himself back from attacking Diego. But that was jealousy springing from his possessive nature. Starkly she faced the fact that she wanted him to fight for her, not just what he perceived to be his property rights in her.

And somehow, sometime between their walk under the stars and this moment, he had contrived to make a hefty suite of furniture disappear without noise from a building put together so that every sound would echo through the courtyard like a rifle shot. She already knew why—to give her no place to sleep except by his side. But how? And when?

The plundered room held no answers for her. Libby got stiffly to her feet. All the answers were located in the last place she ought to endanger herself by exploring. The inside of Caleb Logan's head . . .

Chapter 17

Caleb emitted a heartrending groan when Libby shook his arm. She tripped over his boots as she took a step backward, but they were the only articles of apparel he'd removed before falling sideways onto his bed. So soundly asleep was he that her quick, sharp "Oh, the devil!" failed to elicit another groan, or even a murmur. The watch and chain lay in a shining puddle next to one lax hand.

"I am angry with you, Caleb Logan. Do you hear me? Nonsensical question," she added querulously. He stirred, beginning to turn onto his side. Libby snatched the watch by its chain out of his way just before he rolled over. It would have been a shame to allow the insensate oaf to crush the delicate links, she thought defensively. Libby didn't even try to explain to herself why she rubbed the enamel side against her cheek before going into the alcove to drop the watch and chain in a careful pile on the desk.

She had turned back to blow out the lamp when she paused, thinking it high time she began to exercise a little caution around the owner of this part of the county. Her life had been arranged on his terms long enough. Share his bed again?

He would have a long, lonely wait.

With a wary eye on the still form on the bed, Libby slipped out of her bodice and removed the most bothersome of her underclothes. Then she pulled the bodice back on without hooking it.

Several blankets were folded at the end of the bed, security against northern California nights that inevitably turned chilly. Without compunction, she left Caleb on top of his covers and stole the extra bedding, as well as the pillow his head didn't touch. Wrapping them around her, she discovered they weren't much protection against the alcove's hard floorboards. Stubbornly telling herself that she was comfortable, Libby composed herself for sleep.

Instead of slumber, unwanted memories and echoes of sensation came. If she kept her eyes open, the temptation to peek through the arch and study the fluid, relaxed lines of his sleeping figure proved too great to resist; if she closed them, images—tender, bawdy, stinging in their ability to make her smart with a lust she didn't want to feel—paraded across the insides of her eyelids. His hands, his mouth showing her secrets about her woman's body she had never even suspected. The glaze of excitement in his dark eyes. The sleepy, sated look of satisfaction . . . and then renewed absorption focused completely on her.

How lowering it was to contemplate the fact that if he'd only expended some of that flattering concentration on her tonight, she might be lying beside him this instant. She sighed, burying her head in the pilfered pillow. Knowing herself this well was turning out to be a very unpleasant experience. She wondered if she'd have a scrap of pride left by the time her half marriage to Caleb was annulled.

An acrid taint in the air made Caleb's before-dawn dreams hideous until he struggled awake out of a nightmare in which the ranch house burned and he couldn't locate Libby. He found the wick burned out in his lamp. Must not have remembered to snuff it, he thought groggily, so the oil had all been consumed. On his way to the pot, his toes got entangled with the corner of an inexpert bedroll poking out from the alcove.

"Oh, dear heart," he muttered.

Squatting, he got his arms under Libby's neck and knees and lifted her, blankets, pillow, and all. At the bed, he set her gently down. "You do get yourself into predicaments, don't you?" he asked softly.

Without opening her eyes, she murmured back, "You helped me into this one."

He rubbed his bristly chin. "Made you mad, did I? So mad you'd rather sleep on the floor?"

"Yes." She snuggled into the mattress. "No more procrastinating, Caleb. You have to contact an attorney and begin the proceedings to free us from each other. If you don't, I will."

"How?" he asked. "Just as a matter of curiosity, you understand."

"I could steal a horse from your stables and ride to Sonoma. Julia tells me there's a lawyer's office there. Or I could take the steamer to San Francisco."

"The Hounds?" he mentioned thoughtfully.

"At this point, it's worth risking them. I cannot endure any more." She said it calmly, but with conviction.

Feeling briefly for the men who'd have to work within sniffing distance of him today, Caleb pulled on his boots. Best not to try Libby's temper this morning by taking the time to wash and change. "Got money to pay your passage on the steamer?"

"I'm Mrs. Caleb Logan," she said ironically. "I don't need anything as vulgar as money. Your name is credit enough."

"Not if I advertise that I refuse to cover my wife's expenses," pointed out Caleb. "It's been done."

"You would do that to me? Yes, I suppose you would," she answered herself. Propping her chin on her folded hands, she regarded him. "What do you expect to gain from all this? The longer we engage in your charade, the more difficult an annulment will be.

I have no fancy to be notorious as a divorced woman, Caleb.''

''Worried it'll ruin your chances to make a better marriage?'' he gibed.

''I never intended to be married. Did you?''

''No. Well, someday.''

''But not to me.'' Libby's eyes darkened to the green that sometimes preceded storms at sea. ''Is that it?''

That was precisely it, although Caleb hadn't thought of the matter in those terms before. Ever since the padre had gabbled those unfortunate wedding vows over them, he'd kept Libby adrift in their leaky legal situation in order to give her time to get accustomed to his bed. Once she stopped struggling against their mutual attraction, he intended to abandon the ship of their marriage and set her up in her own establishment. It would be a second home for him, one he had every intention of visiting often. A common enough arrangement. Then, when he was ready to breed sons to help him run the Manzanita, a biddable virgin would present herself, and he'd marry her.

He shifted uncomfortably. If a man besides himself had been planning this future for Libby, he would have called him a bastard.

Still . . . she wanted to stay in their marriage as little as he. Less, maybe, from the look of the icy glare being directed at him from behind her mussed hair. He had to order his hands not to tangle themselves in the shining blond locks. ''A man wants children. You've made it very plain you don't. At least not mine.''

She sat up, winding her arms around her waist defensively. ''You don't understand!''

''No, I guess neither one of us understands the other.'' Surrendering to the persistent impulse, he touched her hair, then her cheek, then the smooth flesh imperfectly concealed by her open dress. ''But I have feelings for you, Libby. And I'm not giving you up.''

The breakfast bell clanged. They both started.

"Missed morning chores, I see." He bent and kissed her lightly. She didn't try to duck, but her body stayed tense, shaking a little, so he kissed her more thoroughly until the little tremors stopped and her arms crept around his neck.

"Caleb, if we don't part soon, I'll come to hate you." Her eyes searched his. "That would be so sad."

"Love or hate, we're bound together. Face it," he advised. "And—about the watch. I got it for you because it was pretty and I hoped you'd like it. That's all. No other reason," he lied.

"Do you know what the design on the back of it is?"

"Flowers," he said promptly.

"Forget-me-nots."

Surprise flashed across his eyes, and Libby felt a grim sort of satisfaction that her guess had been correct. Caleb hadn't meant his gift to be quite so sentimental. But he looked pleased rather than dismayed and kissed her again, soundly. "Good. I won't let you forget me, Libby."

She pushed him away. "Am I apt to under the circumstances? Go away, Caleb. Have your breakfast."

Lying abed until she was sure Caleb must have ridden out, Libby rose very late and began dressing slowly. A commotion in the courtyard failed to interest her, but Ascensión burst through the door to announce breathlessly that guests had arrived and Senorita Julia needed her at once.

Allowing the maid to pin to her hair the wispy cap required of a young matron, Libby left her work apron on its peg and rustled to the parlor. Julia patted the place next to her on the settee. "Come sit with us, Libby. Senora, may I present my new sister, Elizabeth? Libby, you've heard me speak of our neighbors, Senora Benicia Vallejo and her fine children."

Concentrating on the social task, Libby smiled into the handsome, square faces. "Yes, indeed. I am honored, senora."

A sturdy boy of perhaps one and a half started to climb her skirt. "Pretty," he said, grabbing for the trailing ribbons of her cap.

"Napoleon!" his mother said sternly. "Here, Adela, you take him."

"Oh, senora, may I not hold him?" Libby and Napoleon smiled conspiratorially at each other. Caleb's statement this morning had reminded her, in a way she'd never felt before, that she would die childless. It was a hurt that lingered. The plush baby flesh of Napoleon's arm brushed her cheek as he pulled on a ribbon again. "Forgive me for making a personal observation, but your children are so beautiful."

Senora Vallejo laughed. "Such a delightful compliment hardly stands in need of apology."

The parlor was large but there weren't enough chairs, and the younger children had arranged themselves on the floor. Libby glanced at Julia. "You will have to forgive me again. I'm not familiar with the customs in this part of the world. Would the children enjoy playing outside?"

The elder girls remained behind, but the smaller ones and all the boys dashed out at an indulgent nod from their mother, Napoleon sliding from Libby's lap and staggering determinedly along in the rear.

"I can see you will be an excellent mother," Benicia Vallejo said. Julia pursed her lips, and a flush burned to the roots of Libby's hair.

Not noticing the signs of discomfiture in her hostesses with superb aplomb, the senora murmured something graceful about Caleb's unexpected wedding and produced a box of Russian silver "as a remembrance," she said, handing it to Libby.

It had been etched with the initial "L" for Logan, and inside were a dozen tiny silver goblets. Feeling more like a fraud than ever, Libby gently closed the box. Her throat clogged with words she couldn't say.

"Libby tends to be struck dumb by presents," Julia rushed in. "How truly kind you are, Senora Vallejo. I know Cal will want to keep these in a place of honor in the new house . . ."

Benicia responded, her girls chimed in, and the conversation tinkled along merrily enough around Libby, who sat tracing the initial. The gold ring on her finger flashed against the cooler silver.

Finally, a warm, dry hand covered her restless fingers, and the senora said in her ear, "The first year of marriage is always very wonderful, and very terrifying. Do not let the strangeness blind you to the joys."

Libby couldn't help a small, rueful moue. "I shall try not to. I must seem horribly ungrateful. Your gift—"

"Not ungrateful," she was cut off. "Young. Not yet seasoned."

Libby protested, "Why, thank you, but I'm four-and-twenty, you know. Advancing age is rapidly overtaking me."

"So young," repeated the senora with a sigh.

Perhaps their guest saw her as immature because she fit into the same generation as the children of the large Vallejo family, Libby thought. Although she was already married, Epifania looked not a day over seventeen, and Adela and Josepha several years younger. Their scant years didn't keep either of the younger girls from making reproachful cow eyes at Caleb when he entered, accompanied by a robust man with side whiskers who walked immediately to Libby, taking her hand and kissing it.

"General," she said without prompting, standing to drop into the curtsy his gesture seemed to demand.

He held her hand perhaps a moment too long, but released it as soon as she hinted she wanted it back by rising to her full height. It topped his by several inches. Easily, he remarked, "You have brought a Juno among us, Caleb."

Raffish in his day's growth of beard, Caleb neatly cut between Libby and his guest. "She's Diana to me."

A flight of poetry was so unlike Caleb that Libby

just stared. Julia wrinkled her nose. "Not Diana. Too cold. Nor Venus, either. She's so fickle and flibbertigibbet, wandering off with this god and that. Minerva."

Libby backed away toward the door. "I'll see to lunch. Excuse me, please."

Caleb caught up with her halfway around the balcony. "I'd better shave and wash up before I sit down with polite company. Are you all right?"

"They brought us a wedding present." Her voice was stifled.

He reached out and stroked the back of her neck. Libby stepped away from the soothing hand. Frowning, he said, "I expect we'll be getting a few. It bothers your conscience, right?" He grunted. "This is getting complicated."

From her seat at Caleb's right at the refectory table, full for once even though the youngest children were being served a picnic meal in a shady corner of the courtyard, Benicia proceeded to make it even more complicated. "We must hold a fiesta to introduce Mrs. Logan to our friends."

Libby's gaze drifted helplessly over the circle of brightening faces around the table. "You are too kind," she said hollowly. "But we shall be moving our household during the next few weeks, and I think perhaps . . . later . . ."

"Sister, sometimes you carry your shyness too far," Julia interjected sternly. Caleb coughed into his napkin. Ignoring her brother, she continued, "Certainly, a fiesta! I don't know why we didn't think of one ourselves."

She and the senora plunged into plans, while Caleb controlled his coughing fit and Libby stared blankly at the tablecloth. She would have to run. Money or no money, she had to get away before the entire state had been hoodwinked into bringing gifts and good wishes. Before her soul was no longer her own.

Only—where could she go?

South were the Hounds. North was the sparsely populated nothing she'd come from.

Avoid San Francisco, she thought. That meant circling the bay. The little town of Los Angeles was also a port. But how to work her way six hundred miles south and not leave a trail Caleb could follow?

He might not want to follow. Perhaps, once she had disappeared, he'd be more than happy to let the memory of her recede until it was safely forgotten. The marriage could be set aside on grounds of desertion, and that would be the end of it.

Somehow that idea caused her heart to constrict in a knot even more painful than the pang she felt at the realization that she would have to go without saying goodbye.

"Squatters have been sighted?" Caleb's sharp tone recalled her to the conversation.

The general's full-blooded face was clouded. "A large party, well armed. In Newtown, they let fall that they have been prospecting without luck and they purchased supplies, but not many. They must be planning to live off the land—"

"Off our cattle, you mean," put in Julia, tight-lipped.

He shrugged expressive shoulders. "At any rate, they had no baggage train. Just fast, strong horses. Heading toward Mendocino."

Caleb's knife tapped the edge of his plate. The *chink-chink* grated on Libby's nerves. "Passing through, you think? Or making for the lumber mill? We've never kept a big payroll at the mill, but they might not know that."

"About time you took a little look-see out there," observed Julia.

Caleb's eyes, hard as flint, rested on Libby. She couldn't read their expression. "I do believe you're right."

He should have ridden out to the mill long since, he knew. Businesses didn't run themselves; property didn't maintain or increase its value without careful tending. Besides, he loved the land, all of it, and normally made a complete circuit every month, like a lover visiting his beloved. That he hadn't recently was due first to Julia's illness and then to Libby's presence. Even now, with an enemy pinpointed, he didn't want to let her out of his sight. That jolted him. When had Libby become more important to him than the Manzanita?

Throughout lunch she had sat looking lovely, a little remote, allowing Julia to carry the burden of hostessing. Not from shyness—damn, that had been funny; there was only one thing in the world that could make his Libby act shy, otherwise she was a lioness—but from simple embarrassment. These pleasant, dignified people believed he and Libby were married, and they weren't.

His restless fingers set his knife tapping against his plate again. The solution was clear. Regularize their situation by filing for annulment. Even if he wanted to stay married to Libby, and he didn't—did he?—she'd told him plainly and sometimes quite loudly that she didn't want to be married to him. Didn't want to bear his children. Didn't want him inside her in the most intimate kind of embrace . . .

He thrust back his chair violently. The startled expressions around him reminded him of the value of diplomacy. "Being a military man, you will understand, I know," Caleb said to Vallejo, who nodded gravely. "Now that I know where to find the squatters—or reavers—on the Manzanita, I have to take care of them as quickly as possible. Senora, senoritas, forgive me."

"Not at all." Benicia waved a hand in benediction. "But it is your bride to whom you should make your excuses."

"Oh, Libby's been prodding me to be out and doing. She admires men of action." Not quite sure why he'd added the last biting sentence, except to punish Libby a little, and also as an oblique warning to Vallejo that Libby was not available for casual preying, he bowed and left, yelling for Juan the moment he reached the balcony.

Chapter 18

That joyful bellow haunted Libby. Julia, too, had heard and recognized the reckless note. "I hope you're happy," she said as they sorted through the consignment of taffetas and brocades and tarlatans sent for their approval by steamer several days later.

"Lovely cloth is one of my weaknesses," Libby admitted, touching a green shot silk with wistful fingers.

"I don't mean the dress makings," responded Julia. "I mean Cal."

Libby rewound the bolt and set it aside. "It wasn't by my choice that he left. And it doesn't make me happy that he's gone. I wish he were back." It was the reason she'd hadn't run yet. Stupid, weak, maudlin—she called herself all sorts of names, but simply couldn't go without making sure he was safe.

Sleeping in his bed, since he was absent from it, and handling his things gave her a constant feeling of his presence. So strong was the sense that he was standing just behind her, she often opened her mouth to speak to him, only to realize he was off somewhere on the far-ranging ranch, possibly shooting or being shot at. It was very lonely. Caleb might be overbearing and untrustworthy and irritatingly enigmatic, but he was also the only person in all of California, or anywhere, to whom she could talk about their uncommon predicament.

Cold trickled down her spine. Right now—*right*

259

now—he could be pushing his commanding nose into a situation where he could get it shot off. A brave man? Or a dishonest and despicably pragmatic one? She pushed the questions away. They didn't seem as immediate as her fear of the reckless fits that overtook him and led him into danger.

Julia studied her face and relented. "Don't take on so. Nothing you said would get him to jump into any tussles he wouldn't have rushed to join no matter what. Loves a good fight, does Cal. Whatever made you think he was a milksop?"

"I never thought that, not really." Libby unfolded a packet of lace without looking at the rose-point pattern. "In fact, the first time I met him, he threw himself into a bout of fisticuffs—no, he started it. And then he called it rescuing me! I was so angry."

"But you forgave him."

"It wasn't a matter of forgiving. Actually, I don't believe he ever asked my pardon. He's very different from the kind of man I've always regarded as the ideal." Actually, Caleb was as rash as Papa in seeking out risk. Only the nature of the risks differed, and the degree of pragmatism or quixotry that surrounded them. And the kind of luck Caleb enjoyed. Papa had been attracted to glamorous failures like a moth sucked into the sun. Had he been more devoted to protecting his family's means of support, as Caleb was . . . but at least his folly had a kind of honor to it. Caleb had no honor.

"Libby, there's no such thing as a model man. Think how boring. There's only love, to make the ones we've got worth keeping. If we've got one at all."

Juan had ridden out with the other men. But Julia never spoke of the feelings Libby was sure the younger girl harbored for the foreman, and Libby respected her reticence. Holding up the lace, Libby said, "This would be pretty bordering flounces on that wine-colored velvet. We shall make it up for you."

"For me?" Julia's hand strayed to the rich material. "I thought you—"

"You'll look like a dark-haired Christmas angel in it. The blue silk is perfect for you, too," Libby told her. "The gentlemen shall fall to your feet in droves."

"I don't hanker after a whole troop." Julia visibly came to a decision. "The man I dream about would tell you he's not a gentleman at all. But he is. Oh, Libby, Juan's so kind and good. And he's good at things, too. There's nothing he doesn't know about horses and running a ranch. He's strong inside, too, where it counts."

"I could tell he was affected when you were ill," Libby offered.

"Oh, he worries about me, and coddles me, and sometimes he even looks at me as if—as if he thought I was pretty. I do so want to be pretty for him. But he won't ever say anything. The loony believes he's unworthy of me."

"Men do suffer from fixed ideas."

Julia gave a strangled laugh. "That's the awful part of it. Juan's the least notional person I've ever met. There is something—a reason for him to feel the way he does—but it doesn't matter to me. Only how can I convince him of that when he won't bring up the subject?"

"This problem," probed Libby with wincing care, "it isn't one a lady could insert into normal conversation?"

"His parents weren't married."

"Oh. Well—well, is illegitimacy such a bar in America? I know people will say cruel things, but your Alexander Hamilton was born out-of-wedlock—"

"Being Alexander Hamilton is different from being the natural son of a Sacramento dry goods store owner and a Spanish woman of—of easy virtue. The father did his duty by him, more or less; he took Juan away from his mother and boarded him out to be schooled. Only if they saw each other on the street, his father would walk right past. Couldn't stand for respectable folks to know he had a bastard half-breed son."

"Don't."

Julia tilted her head at Libby's gesture of rejection. "I know; ugly words, aren't they? That's what I heard a couple of the hands call him once when he had to fire somebody, and I asked Cal what they meant. He told me so I wouldn't say something to hurt Juan. As if I would! He's better than any of them!"

Libby thought of him as a nice boy, but she said, "A fine man."

"Now if only I could get him to look at me the way Cal looks at you . . .''

"Does Caleb look at me in any particular way?" she couldn't help asking.

"Like there's no one else in the room. Or maybe in the state." Julia's brown eyes began to sparkle again. "Like he's crazy-mad with jealousy and can't wait to cut you out of the herd and put his brand on you. Poor General Vallejo. I was scared Cal was going to string him up for a rustler just for kissing your hand."

"Jealousy isn't easy to live with," warned Libby. Nor was it pleasant to experience; she'd stuck out her tongue at the figurehead of Mary Rose that morning. It had given her a childish satisfaction.

"N-no," agreed Julia uncertainly. "But it might be nice as a change from being completely unsought."

The little *Red Jacket* rocked gently at its moorings. Caleb stretched out full-length on the bench in the passenger lounge. A slight scratching sound, different enough from the creak of ropes and shush of waves to penetrate his uneasy doze, brought him upright, thumb against the hammer and index finger steady on the trigger of the six-shooter that had been resting on his stomach. A gull roamed the lounge's deck with its short-legged, drunken-sailor walk, seeking scraps. At Caleb's movement, it cawed derisively and scuttled out.

Caleb growled—at himself more than the bird—and released the cock. A glance out a porthole verified the time; full night not yet shrouded by fog. Say eight-thirty. Stretching, he rose, called a quiet good evening to the guard who sat smoking a pipe in the boat's prow, and crossed the wharf.

Leaving the raucous fleshpots of the waterfront behind, he traveled silent streets until he came to J. Klein's New York Store. Identifying himself to the curt voice within, he slipped inside the narrowly opened door.

Grinning crookedly at Jacob, he said, "Glad you sent word you'd decided to go hunting."

"Yes." Jacob grinned back. "But we hunt the Hounds, we do not go hunting with them. My friend. It is good you could make it tonight. We need your hot head to inspire us."

"Your message caught me at the right time. Just finished chasing some squatters off my land."

"Without loss, I hope."

"Strangest thing." Caleb scratched his chin. "Damned stackwads set fire to my mill. Lost some lumber, but the equipment is undamaged. They ran clear off the property as soon as we got anywhere near them."

"It is a common tactic, burning someone out," said Jacob. "I speak from experience."

Caleb put a hand on the other man's shoulder briefly. "Who'd think they could drive me away? I own good title to the land, and if it comes to a shooting war, the government would be on my side. No, must have been somebody unhinged. Gone now, anyway." He dismissed the topic. "What made you decide to join this little necktie party?"

Leading the way up the stairs, Jacob shrugged. "Meeting your beautiful Libby, I think. It was not a surprise to hear you had married her." He ruminated. "She reminded me how a decent woman sees the world. I want my Sarah. I wrote her months ago, and perhaps, perhaps she will come, but she would not be happy in a San Francisco overrun with Hounds."

"So you're going to clear the streets of animal life."

"Just so. And you?"

"Yeah. Libby."

Jacob turned his bulk on the steep stairs to peer at him. "She pushes you to fight?" The question sounded disapproving.

"Not exactly. In fact, she's scolded me a couple of times for taking unnecessary risks. But whenever somebody mentions the Hounds, she looks at me with those green eyes like she doesn't know what I am. And the more I thought about it, the more I wasn't sure, either. There have to be some things worth fighting for, besides just what's one's own."

Smiling faintly, Jacob continued up the stairs. "I do not believe I have ever heard you say such a thing before. My congratulations on your marriage."

He said the last as they entered the upstairs room. Men who had had their heads together turned, their hard faces relaxing into good-natured leers.

"Cal! Caught at last, huh?"

"Heard the lady's some looker!"

"When are we going to meet her, boy?"

If any of them knew of Libby's appearance in the taproom, none admitted it. Countering the boisterous comments, Caleb waited for the frustration and wry amusement that a reminder of his wedding always roused to surface. Instead, all he felt was a vast yearning to be with Libby. To smell her light, flowery perfume rather than male sweat, to enjoy the caress of her eyes running over his body, and to hear the husky, inviting note in her voice . . . to talk. Just to talk about the small doings of every day.

Could he ever feel for some unknown, probably uninteresting virgin what he felt for Libby?

An odd stirring of pride—she was a looker, and a lady, generally speaking—made him flush; a vaguely familiar man in severe black seemed to take pity on him and intoned, "Let us ask God's blessing on this holy enterprise . . ."

It was the minister who'd led a service in this very room. Caleb's lips quirked. No one could claim the vigilance committee wasn't a respectable bunch, even if the alcalde was notable by his absence.

Ways and means were discussed and tasks handed out. One loud faction spoke up in favor of grabbing guns and storming Portsmouth Square that night.

"Good way to produce a lot of martyrs to the cause," Caleb said with mock enthusiasm. "If that's the point of this little exercise."

"What's that supposed to mean?" asked another man aggressively.

He stood and bunched his fists on his hips. "It means some forethought could keep the men in this room from being killed. Do we know that all the Hounds are in the square tonight? You think they're politely waiting for us to stroll in and escort them to the calaboose?"

"Getting hitched got you preaching caution, Logan?" came a scornful voice.

"I pick my fights," answered Caleb coolly. "And I fight to win. You want to enter an armed camp with no preparation, go ahead. The parson here's a fine speaker; I've heard him. He can throw you a dandy funeral."

After the grumbling died down, a few young men without wives or families volunteered to strike up acquaintances with known Hounds in order to seek information. The preacher administered an oath of secrecy.

"I just hope they're all as closed-mouthed as they swear they are," Caleb confided to Jacob after the others had left in trickles of two and three.

"I, too." The big man stroked his long beard. "And now what?"

"Home."

And Libby. Home. Libby. The steady chug of the *Red Jacket*'s engine and swipe of its paddle wheel repeated the two words until they became one image. Libby. Home.

Pablo ran out to draw him into the forge as soon as he dismounted in the courtyard. "Senor Cal, what you want, it is done!"

Simple square settings surrounded small, richly colored emeralds, dozens of them, all linked to create an intricately designed chain culminating in a pendant emerald as large as the first joint of Caleb's thumb. Earrings to match dangled from Pablo's stained fingers.

"You are pleased?"

"Pretty, Pablo. Very pretty. There'll be a bonus for you next payday."

Hell, *would* Libby accept jewels from him? The memory of her negative response to the watch, which had been trumpery by comparison, cooled his praise, and Pablo looked anxious. "If something is wrong, I can fix—"

"They're fit for a queen," Caleb roused himself to assure the goldsmith. "An empress. Libby will have to like them." And therefore the man who gave them to her.

But Libby was a damned unaccountable female.

He heard her voice when he reached the top of the stairs and followed it around a corner to the west balcony, which looked outward toward the sun falling into the ocean lying beyond the softly mounded hills. From somewhere a chair had been dragged to the spot, and she sat in it, leaning over a guitar, strumming a chord now and then and singing without words. Scales, he supposed. They formed a curious up-and-down melody like waves, and he thought, She's singing to the sea. She wants it to take her home. But she was home. Home with him.

Her slender hands stilled the strings, and her face, a pale oval in the gathering dusk, turned at his approach. "Every time I've looked up in the last week," she said simply, as if they were continuing a conversation that had been broken off a moment before, "I've felt that you would be standing there. And then I'd remember that you were gone and I didn't know if you were alive or d-dead . . ."

He came at her in a rush, pushing the guitar aside. It twanged as it hit the planks. Caleb fell to his knees, his arms going around her waist and his head resting on her breasts. She sighed and gathered him close, her cheek against the coarseness of his hair.

"You missed me?" he asked after a while.

"Yes."

"I wanted to be here sooner."

"All the other men came back two days ago . . ."

"Some business kept me longer."

Banners of fiery cloud faded to floating gray strips. Caleb sat back on his haunches. "I have something for you." Before she could protest, he added quickly, "Not for any ulterior motive. Not for any motive at all, except—hell, Libby, it would pleasure me to see you wearing something I gave you. You can allow me a little selfish pleasure, can't you?"

A smile trembled in her voice. "I have on your watch. Didn't you feel the chain?" She pulled the bauble from her waistband and swung it for him to see in the dim light.

"That was for day. These are for night," he said, pulling the watch over her head. He drew out the slim box Pablo had made for the emeralds. Opening it, he set the necklace around her neck and held the earrings up to her ears.

"Why do I have the feeling these don't suit an old calico apron very well?" she asked.

"They suit you. That's all that matters. Take them, dear heart. Please."

She couldn't keep the jewelry, that was certain. It was too close to nightfall to tell what the gemstones were, except beautiful and dark and obviously worth a great deal. But it was the almost humble note in Caleb's voice that Libby found irresistible. She could accept his gift for now and leave it behind when she left.

"Thank you, Caleb, for thinking of me." Taking the earrings from his hands, her fingers brushed his. Breathlessly, she said, "Has Julia been told you're back?"

"Not yet, far as I know."

Sliding a firm arm around her waist, he drew her to the interior of the ranch house. Below, in the courtyard, torchlight bathed the slight figures of Julia and Juan. Even from a distance, Julia's animated gestures and frequent laugh spoke of happiness.

"How's that progressing?"

Libby didn't pretend to misunderstand. "They are fond of each other. Julia mentioned . . . impediments."

"What . . . you mean his birth? I can't believe she'd let that—"

"Not her. Him. Pride can be a very inconvenient quality."

Caleb's soft snort stirred her hair, but if he was amused, he didn't refer directly to her comment. "Isn't it bedtime?"

"No. Not again. There's been time to think while you've been gone. We can't play at lovemaking and assume there won't be any consequences."

"I took damned good care consequences were one thing you don't have to worry about," he said tightly.

"I realize that. I do know that much about men and women. But—what we did—wasn't the same as real love, was it? It's not natural for you to have to deny yourself like that."

"Then let me . . ."

"And what will happen if I do? What if there should be a child? Will you keep me for your wife, wondering all the time how far I had fallen before you found me? Or would you annul our marriage anyway, and just keep me someplace well appointed and discreet? Good God, Caleb, what might I teach your child? I sing in taprooms and cheat at cards and heaven knows what other dubious accomplishments I can produce."

"Stop it, Libby."

"Let me go." His hard grip on her arm hurt. He released it instantly, but she repeated, "Let me go. Help me get away."

Caleb raised his face and seemed to be studying the first stars to make pinpricks in the sky. It wasn't possible to tell what he was thinking, or even if he was thinking of her. At last he said, "You win." He turned away from her, leaning against the rail. "I'll write the agent tomorrow and get a schedule for outgoing ships. They're few and far between, but there are some."

"And a lawyer."

"And a lawyer. You'll have to sign papers. I presume you can bear to stay until the legal formalities are taken care of?"

She wouldn't have to run after all. Relief made her voice soft. "Yes." Her hands went to the clasp of the necklace. "I think you should take this back. And the earrings."

He didn't move, nor did the tone of his voice change, but Libby stepped back a pace. "They're yours. Wear them, toss them in a trunk, throw them down the well—they belong to you."

"Under the circumstances—"

"Go to bed, Libby. I won't trouble you. But—go to bed now."

Libby hesitated, meaning to ask one more question. As soon as the first phrases of it formed at the tip of her tongue, she gasped, swiveled abruptly, and walked swiftly toward the refuge of Caleb's room, where he had promised not to "trouble" her. She was giving him up, and the last thing she had the right to ask was whether he intended to find another, saner woman who wouldn't withhold a welcome from the master.

Somehow she knew, despite his not quite honest dealings with her in the past, that he wouldn't come to his own bed tonight. Ascensión helped her into one of the new nightgowns, long enough to cover her ankles but cut low across the bosom, and smilingly refused to plait her hair. "Senor Cal," the maid said, brushing it loose over Libby's shoulders, "he likes it this way, *sí?*"

"Good night, Ascensión."

After the maid left, Libby went into the alcove to put the emeralds and the watch into a drawer in Caleb's desk. "Well, Mary Rose," she told the figurehead, "neither of us has him tonight.

Chapter 19

"**C**al, it's wonderful, but you didn't have to spend the night here going over every peg and nail."

Caleb shrugged off Julia's excited exclamation. The reason she had come up with for his staying in the new house might be what she really believed or it might be an attempt to put the best face on this latest rift with Libby; he was beyond caring what even his sister surmised about his relationship with his "wife." Yesterday he'd been ready to—to what? Throw away common sense, make Libby his wife in truth, forget revoking their marriage?

"Oh, Libby," Julia continued, "aren't you glad you decided not to sit in the old adobe and write a letter to your relatives? Just look at it!"

By Western standards, the Logans' frame structure was a mansion. Three narrow stories, painted a crisp white, reared against the cloud-dotted blue of the sky. Five years ago, it would have looked like a quarter of a proper house to Libby, but now she could agree sincerely, "It's very fine."

"But the curtains are at the wrong windows, Cal," Julia said, frowning. "The lace ones go upstairs, the silk-lined brocade belong in the library."

"You can fiddle all you want putting things right," Caleb told her soothingly. "Come around back now."

The kitchen and pantry stood in their own separate

building, about half the size of the huge kitchen in the adobe. Both women admired the spanking new stove, with its shining nickel fixtures and pristine coat of blacking. Libby studied the strange-looking wing that extended across what Julia assured her would be a garden. "What is that?"

A flush stained Caleb's harsh cheekbones. "Something I thought you—Julia would like. A surprise."

Exchanging mystified glances, Julia and Libby crossed the trampled dust that surrounded the house. Julia peeked inside the rear door and threw her arms around her brother. "A walkway to the outhouse! No tramping through the rain and dark!"

Her bonnet fell back, and the two dark heads inclined toward each other. Libby retreated, step by step, until she'd gone farther than she'd intended. The gables of the house had disappeared behind a rise in the ground, and ahead lay the valley of poppies. The intermittent rainfall of spring had kept the blossoms renewing themselves, and they bent under a steady, soft breeze.

Sensing someone behind her, she turned, half hoping it would be Caleb. But the tingling awareness his presence always aroused was missing, so she neither felt nor showed surprise when Julia looked past her. "Pleasant out here, isn't it? Cal calls this his valley of gold. Says he wouldn't want the other kind, not on our property."

"Neither would I," said Libby. "Not here. Of course, a delightful little gold mine in another location—"

Julia shook her head. "Gold attracts thieves and squatters. The ore gets dug up and carted off, but the land is eternal, or near enough that it makes no difference. The land matters." She poked at a rock with the toe of her shoe. "What kind of place do your folks have back in England?"

"A parsonage. Very large, very cold in the winter." To herself, she added, "I'm not sure how I would fit into it anymore. I'm not who I used to be."

"Did you grow up there?"

"No, my father inherited a house—a manor, really. He sold the home farm, and all we had was the building itself and a little park."

"How big?"

"Why, I couldn't say. Not a palace by any means."

Julia untied the bonnet hanging down her back and swung it by its ribbons. "How many bedrooms?"

"Eighteen," Libby admitted. It seemed in poor taste to compare the size of her former home with the one Caleb and Julia had just built. "It was very old— Tudor—and falling to bits. Once I put my foot up to the ankle through a floor. Deathwatch beetle. The drains were a menace. Caleb's walkway makes much better sense."

"Would you tell him so, then?" Julia sounded like an exasperated sparrow. "He's sitting in the parlor, glaring at the wallpaper. He thinks you hate the house."

Surely Caleb wouldn't care whether she admired it or not. Biting back a rejoinder, Libby followed the other girl, lifting her skirts away from the clinging spurs of the wild oats. Inside the house, Julia insisted that Caleb join them as she went room by room, pointing out the many excellences. Libby went red when she saw the cherrywood furniture crammed into a tiny room connected to an obviously masculine bedroom by a door with no lock.

Battling low spirits—it was only natural to be depressed, she assured herself, going through this house she wasn't going to live in for long—Libby made enough quietly admiring comments to satisfy Julia. Caleb's brows remained a thick, level line.

Circling the bed to reach the door again, Libby tripped over an article of furniture she hadn't seen in her first circuit, because it was one she had never expected to find. Caleb reached out a quick hand to steady her, and without thinking, she clung to him, staring down.

A cradle.

The workmanship was lovely, redwood varnished to a high gloss. For one lunatic instant, she could see Caleb's baby, black-haired, scowling adorably, rocking in the cradle's sturdy embrace. He wouldn't put her aside if there were a baby, she thought suddenly. He might think he could—he'd as good as said he would—but she knew him better. No man as deeply, instinctively possessive as Caleb would risk losing his child or the woman who bore it. He'd keep her fast in wedlock.

Some of the hard, withdrawn lines carved into Caleb's cheeks softened. "Libby?"

Horrible. Horrible even to think of trapping a man like that—especially Caleb, whom she loved.

Whom she loved.

Putting a name to the wild beat of her heart, the constant sense of his presence, the waves of pleasure she found in his arms, gave form to the confusion of feelings that had bombarded her for weeks. She looked from the piece of miniature furniture to Caleb's face. The harsh planes of cheek and jaw, knife-blade of a nose, and stern mouth seemed illuminated by her knowledge into a new and singular beauty. The red-brown sparks in his dark eyes burned right through her. Caleb, whom she loved.

Caleb stared back at Libby, torn between impatience and concern. She'd gone white as milk, and the source of her distress was obviously the cradle. What fool had put the damned thing in here, anyway?

He'd taken a private oath to wean himself from her. When it came right down to it, he couldn't do anything else in the face of her refusal to let relations between them become normal. The Manzanita had been home before she came, and it would be again after she left.

Maybe. Someday. About the time Gabriel's trumpet sounded.

When had her hurts begun to make him bleed? He reached out in an attempt to comfort. Where his fingers brushed her cheek, color rose under the perfect skin with its gloss of freckles.

"Senor—"

"What is it?" Libby and Julia both jumped at his snarl.

One of the wranglers twisted his hat in his hands. "Juan send me. He waits for you in the south field, senor, the one in garden greens—it is trampled. The signs are many horses, many men, much damage—"

Cursing, Caleb turned toward the door, then spun around to catch Julia in a great hug. She pounded him on the back bracingly and stepped back. Libby looked at him from across the chasm of the empty cradle. Leaning forward, she put her hands on his shoulders and pressed a soft kiss on his mouth.

"Don't get yourself killed, Caleb."

He grinned briefly.

The women stood still as waxworks as the *clip-clop* of hooves died away. Julia moved first, plumping a pillow, twitching a tassel into place.

"It's not fair that he has to ride out again already. He hasn't had any rest from the last time," said Libby.

Julia straightened a ruffle with a vicious tweak. "If you want to keep what's yours out here, you have to protect it."

"He didn't want to fight the Hounds," Libby ventured.

"Well, I should think not! He's got enough to do on our own land!"

Libby didn't answer. *Caleb, whom she . . .* Taking a china shepherdess away from Julia before her sister-in-law's unquiet hands could break it, she said sturdily, "What is there for us to do until they get back?"

"Curtains," replied Julia, blinking away tears. "And—I think the piano sets in the wrong corner in the parlor. Wouldn't you rather have it where the window can light your music? And—I don't know. There must be an almighty lot of boxes to unpack."

Pretending to feel brisk, Libby said, "Then we'd best get to them."

For some reason, a premonition of approaching doom

weighed Libby down. She'd never been given to psychic crotchets before, so the foundationless anxiety annoyed as much as it frightened her. Moving into the new house helped keep some of the creeping fear at bay. There were indeed a good many boxes to unpack. Days later, Libby was polishing utensils and setting them in neat rows for Wang to distribute around his domain as he chose when the open doorway to the kitchen suddenly darkened.

"You're surely a fine lady. Got anything to spare for a hungry man to eat?"

Instead of setting down the meat fork she held, Libby grasped it tighter. The unfamiliar, unshaven face thrusting through the door was preceded by a rank odor. She tried not to breathe. "Certainly, sir. We're happy to share. If you would wait outside, I can bring you some—some coffee and a piece of pie, yesterday's baking."

To her relief, he stepped backward. Quickly assembling the food, Libby set a tin cup on the plate with the pie and carried it in one hand. In the other she kept the long, sharp knife she'd exchanged for the meat fork hidden in the folds of her apron. The fellow might be harmless, a prospector down on his luck. Then again, she hadn't liked the way his close-set eyes catalogued the kitchen furnishings and lingered on her neatly fitting bodice and the bare skin of her arms where she'd rolled up her sleeves.

There had been a workman there earlier in the day, touching up a portion of the wainscoting that hadn't been finished to Julia's satisfaction, but he had had to return to Sonoma for a tool he'd forgotten. Julia was somewhere in the house with Teresa and a few of the maids.

Not smiling as she laid the plate in front of the man so he wouldn't have an excuse to mistake courtesy for invitation, Libby prayed he'd eat and drink and leave without making any trouble. She'd never had to stick a knife into anyone, and was fairly certain she wouldn't enjoy the experience.

He was stuffing the last bit of crust into his mouth when a second forlorn figure joined him. This one looked no more familiar than the first until he polished off his piece of pie and leaned against the outside kitchen wall, crossing his ankles and pulling a deck of cards from a sagging pocket. He leered at Libby, shuffling the cards in midair.

A Hound, she thought. It must be. Yet . . . he said nothing, just stacked the cards together with his clever fingers and tucked them away in his pocket. Then he and his companion walked away with loping strides toward the slough.

Everyone had promised Hounds never left the stronghold of San Francisco. She must have been mistaken. Muscles slowly unclenching, Libby replaced the knife and went to tell Julia.

"Tramps," said Julia. "We'll get a few of the men to sleep out here. And you'd better start carrying a gun."

"Surely—"

Reaching inside a slit in her skirt, Julia pulled out a small derringer. "It's more practical than a knife, Libby. Or a rifle. I'll show you how to fire." She admired the mother-of-pearl handle before slipping the lovely, deadly thing into her hidden pocket again. "In fact, if we make ourselves conspicuous enough about it, we may scare away anybody else who decides this is a good time to come calling. Though I suppose—"

"What?" Libby prompted her.

"Oh, I didn't mean to tell you, but you'd better know. Juan told me when he stopped by yesterday. Some of the hands caught a few of the reavers rustling a cow or two. Our men got a mite enthusiastic before Cal could arrive."

"Hanged?" Libby didn't feel any surprise; the penalty for major theft had been almost that severe not long ago in England. But a nearly forgotten distaste flooded her. No civilizing gloss of a process of law? This was a barbaric land.

"Of course, hanged. That's what a judge and jury would have done with them, too. Cal's law-abiding. He had them cut down and delivered to the county seat, with his apologies."

More tramps drifted through as the week wore on. Julia had posted a target on a column of the porch, and Libby had learned to hit it with fair accuracy.

Manuel had insisted on coming to the new house with Wang, whose Chinese accent still defeated Libby's English accent when they both tried to speak Spanish. The boy dashed in while Libby was plunking dispirit- edly on the piano. "Senora! A rider! Very Yanqui, very rich. He will have news of Senor Cal, *sí*?"

"Alas, not very rich," lilted an all-too-familiar brogue, "but I do have some news to relate. You're not quite blooming, Libby my love."

"Go help Wang," Libby said steadily to Manuel. After he had trailed out, she told Malloy, "You're not welcome here."

"No? And here I'd heard hospitality was a byword at these old ranchos. Looks like you're the new brush that sweeps clean."

The open mockery was counteracted by envy as his agate-colored eyes noted the wall covering of watered silk, and the Persian carpets overlapping each other in fashionable profusion.

"Have it as you please. Just leave before I have to summon someone to assist your departure."

"You wouldn't be throwing an old friend out into the elements without a bite to sup or a sip to lay the dust in his dry, dry throat, now, would you, acushla?"

"I doubt there are enough ardent spirits on the place to quench your thirst, Mr. Malloy," she said through stiff lips.

"Ah, but I'm that reformed," he assured her, show- ing her all his teeth. "Sober and seeking honest work. Your husband advertised for a schoolteacher, I believe.

Now there's a post I could relish. An austere school-room, full of quiet and industry, me passing on the knowledge of the ages . . .''

Libby laughed out loud.

"It hurts me," he said. "Yes, it positively hurts me to see you grown so cold and cynical. What happened to the innocent lass I used to know?''

"She spent two years with you. Get out, Mr. Malloy, or I promise I won't even call one of the men. I've got a gun, and it would give me great pleasure to shoot you where you stand. The pattern on that rug is practically manic with red splotches already. A little blood won't show.'' Frontier justice, she thought.

"And don't you even want to be knowing why I've come looking up a dear old acquaintance?''

"It doesn't take much imagination. I won't be black-mailed. My husband is well aware of the locale in which you left me.'' That didn't mean Caleb would want everybody else in the state to find out, and Libby hoped if she could frighten Malloy away now, that delicious tidbit of gossip would remain decently buried.

"Just one of the mistakes littering my misspent past,'' admitted Malloy glibly. "It's terrible what a man will do when the fit is on him. And here I've brought you news as a small token of my regret—''

"News?'' Julia paused on the threshold. "Can you tell us what's happening to my brother, Mr.—''

"Malloy, ma'am.'' He bowed almost with the court-liness of Vallejo. "Aloysius Malloy, Esquire.''

Without artifice, Julia inspected Malloy, and her quick step into the parlor and outstretched hand indicated that she liked what she saw. Libby's jaw fell slightly with disbelief. Taking another look at her former partner, however, she had to admit that Julia had reason to be impressed. Clean-shaven, his skin clear instead of gray, clothed in a decent coat, dashing waistcoat, and good boots, Malloy could pass for handsome. Compared to Caleb's rugged looks, Malloy's were perhaps a trifle girlish; still, no woman would have needed an excuse to claim to be attracted to them.

"I was visiting in Petaluma," he was saying, "and saw the hotel burn to the ground with my own eyes. The building belonged to your fine family, did it not? It's no wish of mine to be the bearer of bad news, but with knowing Libby so well and all, I decided it would be a betrayal of our past friendship—"

Before she could stop it, a derisive noise escaped Libby's throat.

"A betrayal, I say, to be traveling by without passing on the sad information."

"The hotel?" Julia sat down on the settee rather abruptly. "No, of course we're grateful you took the time . . ."

Libby waited impatiently through the laborious conversation that followed, finally breaking in to say she'd organize something for Mr. Malloy to take with him on the road. "Such a pity; he can't stay. Come along," she said, her sharp glance daring him to contradict her.

He rose gracefully. "Indeed, I must be on my way. But my heart'll be lightened by the memory of such kindness—and such flashing brown eyes."

"Miss Logan's brown eyes are spoken for," Libby stated, not quite truthfully, leading Malloy around to the kitchen. "And your heart was pickled long since."

"You wound me, Libby, you really do. I haven't touched a drop in more than a month."

With the flesh firm around his eyes and an air of sincerity hanging about him almost as tangibly as the odor of pomade, he did appear perfectly and charmingly sober. Libby trusted him less than ever. "I would like my money now, please."

"Ah, I feared you'd be holding a grudge over those few coins."

"You admit you stole the kitty!"

"Would denying it do me any good?" He caught the packet of food she threw at him. "Temper, now, me darlin'. Or does the master of the place like a little roughhouse in the bedroom now and then?''

"You are despicable."

"Alack, it is entirely possible I am. Also indigent, I'm afraid. With the best goodwill in the world, I haven't the funds to be reimbursing you just at the moment. You won't hold it against me, now, will you?''

"Despicable, a liar, a cheat—"

"Now, now. A fine flush it gives you to be calling me names, but your new family's fancy friends might have a time of it, deciding which of us is the liar if a story—the merest whisper—of how we were lovers were to waft about. The Vallejos are giving a party, you know. Well, of course you know; you're the guest of honor, aren't you, darlin'? I'll be there. They've engaged me to play. The story I could be telling—"

Libby didn't waste time reminding him of the truth. She said, "Caleb will kill you. Slowly."

He smiled unpleasantly, jiggling the packet. "Perhaps. Perhaps not. Husbands have been known to turn on the wives they expect to be models of fidelity once a small indiscretion comes to light."

Lifting her brows disdainfully, she said, "In your case, I have no doubt it would be small." Her mood was so savage that the extreme vulgarity of the remark pleased her.

Reddening, Malloy retorted, "And to think you used to pride yourself on being a lady!"

"I have so far remembered I am a lady that I have yet to put a bullet in you. Don't tempt me past the limits of my patience."

He laughed, but uneasily, and kept his gaze on her hands. Libby let her right hand drift toward her apron pocket.

"I'll just be taking my leave now," Malloy blurted.

Libby didn't bother to answer, but watched as he mounted and rode out of sight.

Turning on her heel, she came face to face with Wang. The withered skin of his lids drooped over eyes as old and unreadable and black as onyx.

Thank God he couldn't understand English.

Chapter 20

You used to pride yourself on being a lady.

Idiotic to tear herself to bits over words spoken by Aloysius Malloy, of all people, Libby told herself. But they repeated themselves to her late at night, when she lay in the little, close room next to Caleb's, driving away sleep. No doubt the fragile polish of her refinement was being worn away by the life she was living—had lived, for more than two years. The nature underneath, stripped bare in Caleb's bed, was hardier, more sensual, more alive than she had ever expected. Perhaps she was coarser, too, by genteel standards. Her mother's daughter. But she wouldn't trade what she'd learned from Caleb for anything. Anything. Oh, God, she loved him.

Her own reputation was hardly worth worrying about. Caleb's, though . . . There would be gossip enough when their marriage was dissolved. Could even his cast-iron pride bear the humiliation of being named a cuckold? And to so poor a specimen as Malloy? He'd come to hate the mention of her name, if he didn't already . . . Only the lowest kind of woman would let the possibility of trapping a man by conceiving his child even cross her mind . . .

You used to pride yourself on being a lady.

It was too bad, she thought clearly, that she hadn't managed to extort some of her money from Malloy. Then she could hire a lawyer to begin the annulment proceedings, and save herself the seductive agony of this temptation.

Getting out of bed, she went to the window. The sash was up, and she leaned out. No moon tonight, no stars. Just clouds making everything dark and mysterious. The wind keened as it poured over and around the hills on its nightly journey east.

The freshness barely seemed to penetrate the collected heat in her room. Libby rested her cheek on the sill.

A quick, jarring rhythm shook the boards of the house. Hoofbeats? Lifting her head, Libby strained her eyes, trying to make out a shadow flying through the darkness. Then spurs jangled and dragged across the porch, and a loud knocking overrode the whistling of the wind.

"Senora! Senorita!"

At the bottom of the stairs, Julia shook her head at the gun cocked in Libby's hand. "Diego," she said briefly.

The two husky field hands who'd been sleeping at the back of the house appeared, bristly and blear-eyed, but grim-mouthed, ready. One dodged the women to take the horse, whose coat showed wavelets of lather in the rectangle of light from the door. The other supported Diego up the steps into the hall.

Libby might not have recognized him. Soot made his face a blackened mask in which the whites of his eyes showed bloodshot, and his hair had been singed into corkscrew wisps that broke off when he pushed his helper away.

Reeling only slightly, he stood without assistance. "I am sorry, senora, senorita. The big barn in the west field, it is gone. And Senor Cal—he went in after men who did not come out. He—he did not come out, either." Tears made runnels in the soot.

Almost inaudibly, Julia muttered, "Cal. Cal. Dead?"

In a voice that seemed to come from a long way off, Libby asked, "Are there wounded?"

"*Sí*, senora. Many. They are being taken to the adobe."

"That is good; Teresa's there. Julia." Louder. "*Julia*. We have to gather medicines, linens, rags, anything, for the adobe. Get dressed. Hurry."

"Why? Cal is dead." Julia sounded as disinterested as she had when stuffed full of laudanum.

Caleb—not quite handsome, always infuriating, sometimes charming Caleb . . . gone forever? Never to be her lover, never to hear how much she loved him . . . "Other people are alive. But they're hurt. We have to help the living."

How odd, that the dead should assist the living. For a cocoon of numbness wrapped Libby with such thoroughness that she was sure she must be dead, too. She had never given him the one gift he'd asked of her . . . herself. It would be easier, better, more just, to be dead than to bear the clawing and biting of grief that pressed against her soft, insulating barrier of shock.

Julia shook herself. "Yes," she said obediently, and turned vaguely in the direction of the linen closet.

Heaving a crate full of pots and canisters into the hall, Libby caught sight of her reflection in the mirror that hung there. Her face did look dead, leeched of color, the muscles under the skin incapable of movement. Only her eyes were alive, pale and green and fixed. Crazy eyes, full of pain.

Diego took the crate from her arms and led her to the farm wagon outside. His hands lingered on her waist a moment too long when he lifted her into the back. She looked at him. The soot was still smudged where he'd wiped his tears, but there was an ardency to the angle of his body as he leaned over her, a calculation in the quick glance he flicked over her, that indicated his awareness of her new status.

Rich widow.

Diego ran around to the front of the wagon, leaped into the seat, and took up the reins. Closing her lips against an impulse to vomit, Libby reached out and folded Julia's lax fingers in hers. After her first, instinctive revulsion passed, she had to repress an impulse to laugh. If anything, she was the opposite of rich, barely a bride, and not really a widow. Dear God, she couldn't even be Caleb's widow.

"Don't cry, Libby." Until Julia spoke, it didn't occur to Libby that the noises escaping her tight throat and chest didn't sound very much like laughter. Julia's fist gave hers a weak squeeze. Both women remained silent as the wagon jolted over the nonexistent road to the adobe ranch house.

Eager hands pulled Libby to the ground of the courtyard and pushed her toward the ranch's makeshift infirmary. Dimly, she heard many voices saying, "Go. Go. Stop him. Make him take care of himself."

Too numb to wonder who was making trouble, she grabbed a bundle of clean rags and made her way to the low-ceilinged room. The flames of torch and candle, flickering orange and blue, seemed more real than the collection of damaged humanity they illuminated. Teresa's firm mouth and rounded chin swam across her vision. "He gets in my way. He will not let me bandage his arm," she said with asperity. "Take him away."

Cutting through the hazy light and bobbing figures like a single-masted craft through a river filled with buoys, Caleb's broad-shouldered, trim-hipped form stood tall. Behind her, Julia gulped. "Oh, God, thank you, thank you, thank you—"

"My love," Libby whispered.

The groans and curses of the injured covered her self-betrayal; of the few who could possibly have heard it, Teresa gave a short nod of approval and Julia said in a sudden return of her brisk manner, "I see Juan by the wall. Teresa and I can handle everything here. None of the burns looks too bad. You take Cal back to the house, Libby. He could probably use some cosseting. And so could you."

Caleb saw them and veered in their direction. Julia gave him a swift pat on the arm, which made him wince, and went straight to Juan. Libby peeled back scorched cloth to examine his left forearm. "He said you had died."

Caleb let her look, but said, "There's nothing wrong with me. Who told you I was dead?"

"Diego."

"Oh? That's right, he wasn't there when I got out. Must have left to tell you before we could push out the rear wall. When it came down, we had time to make it out through the hole before the roof collapsed." He coughed hoarsely. "You can stop poking. I've had worse burns picking a piece of fried rabbit out of a hot pan."

By this time Libby had taken in his hollow cheeks and the purplish bruises under his eyes. He smelled of burning. "We've got our orders. I'm to bring you up to the house and cosset you until you can't stand it."

He grunted. "That would be a powerful lot of cosseting."

Retrieving a pot of Teresa's aloe ointment from the miscellany of remedies, Libby just smiled. She couldn't seem to control that radiant curve of her lips. Caleb was alive. She wasn't a lady anymore. Perhaps she could be a woman, at least once, for Caleb. For them both.

Of the horses in the stables, Juan's newly broken stock was the most rested. Caleb saddled a pinto, favoring his left arm. He reached for another horse blanket.

"Do we need two horses?" Libby asked. "Can't I ride in front of you? It's not a long distance. This big fellow can carry us."

Surprise battled weariness in his expression. "You're talking mighty close quarters, Libby."

She took the blanket from his hands, folded it, and laid it on a rail.

Catching her by the arms, he frowned down into her eyes. "Fair warning. I'm not dead yet. If you sit on my lap for three miles, I'm not going to shake hands with you when we get there and bid you a gentlemanly good evening.''

''I wouldn't expect you to.''

''What game are you playing at, Libby?''

She rubbed soot from one of his buttons. ''I'm throwing myself at you, Caleb. With—with no conditions this time. Please take me home and make love to me.'' Her eyes met his.

Tired as he was, Caleb leaped into the saddle and pulled her up in front of him astride. The trip was short, the darkness around them so complete it reminded Libby of the first time Caleb had seduced her into touching him. How he kept the horse from stumbling or going fetlock-deep into an animal burrow she had no idea; she let her mind drift and her senses concentrate on the feeling of his big, warm body behind her, encompassing her. Every once in a while she twisted in his arms to place a kiss on his jaw or his throat. Outside, the scorched smell wasn't so noticeable, but she murmured, ''I'm going to give you a bath.''

''It's not Saturday.''

His teasing tone, and the brush of his thumb over her breast, made her melt further. ''We shall defy tradition.''

The clouds held no threat of rain, so Caleb relieved the pinto of everything except the bridle and staked him out to graze on the ripening oats. Inside, Libby brought the pitcher from her room to his and poured water into his washbowl as he undressed. She pushed him gently into a plain wooden chair to wash and rinse his hair. Leaning back with his eyes closed, he would have looked lazy and somnolent except that at the leisurely movement of her fingers across his scalp and the flat tracery of his ears, his man's body instantly began to swell with excitement.

The homemade yellow soap was almost a jelly, very slippery on his skin, and her hands slid over him slowly, intimately. Face and neck, shoulders that went taut when she touched them. Broad, muscular back and chest. Pausing to anoint the welt left by the fire with aloe, she bathed his arms. The hard, shapely thighs and legs. Feet. Then over the same masculine ground again, with a clean washcloth to rinse and a towel to dry. There was only one place on his body she hadn't attended to yet, and it stood tall and thick in silent demand.

"You could get into bed now," she suggested softly, "and I could wash . . . the rest of you." She ought to be nervous—she ought to be terrified, but she felt strong and clearheaded and right. Her love was alive, and tonight she would be alive with him.

Caleb chose the cherrywood bed, the one he'd ordered and never slept in. The only light came from the open door into the other room. The prospect of pitch blackness bothered him. He started to swing his legs out of the bed again, to kindle Libby's lamp, but the memory of fire all around, horses and men screaming, sparks shooting like fountains into the air as portions of the wall fell, stopped him. Tonight, darkness was a friend.

He didn't realize he'd spoken the thought aloud until Libby whispered in answer, "Yes." She stood naked and framed by the doorway, her hair a shining aureole around her.

"My golden girl," said Caleb.

She disappeared back into his room and doused the light. Then the bed creaked, and her hand found him. The soapy ooze slicked a slow, deliberate pumping that made his eyes roll back in his head. "Are you trying to kill me?" he gasped.

"No, oh, no. I'm so glad you're alive, Caleb." It was her turn to gasp when his mouth fastened, hot and fierce, on a nipple. Her fingers tightened in response. Groaning, Caleb gently pushed her hand away before his seed burst forth out of season. "I'm sorry. I thought you liked that," she murmured.

"I like it," he said thickly, lifting himself above her. "But I like this better. And so shall you. I promise, Libby. Open to me."

She moaned, a small musical sound, but her legs remained stubbornly closed. The moan ended his restraint. This glorious, golden creature was meant to be his; she had admitted it by offering herself to him; she had said she didn't expect him to wait. Using the leverage of his own legs, he parted her knees.

Caleb drew a long breath when she opened to him simply, naturally, without the resurgence of resistance he half expected. "I want you willing," he told her roughly.

"I am." Tendrils of her hair whipped him. She was twisting her head from side to side as he probed for entrance. Although the soap had dried, her own abundant dampness promised an entry that would be easy for her. But she was so tight. And innocent in this final culmination. She writhed, not seeming to know how to position her hips to help him.

The wetness, the tightness, the innocence drove him to surge forward, clenching her buttocks to hold her still for his quick, hard thrust. Above her, below her, inside her, he couldn't mistake the tearing of a thin piece of flesh that shouldn't have been there, or how her whole body stiffened in pain.

With a muffled oath, he withdrew.

Rolling way from her and sitting up, he demanded, "Why didn't you tell me? Why did you let me—"

"I can't even count how many times I told you. There aren't that many ways for a woman to convince a man of her virtue when he doesn't want to believe!"

"This is a damned fool way to try!"

"That wasn't my object," she said with so much bitterness that Caleb stopped running his hands along her night table searching for her lamp, and thought. Even leaving out the physical pain he was sure she had felt—God, he'd had at her with the force of a man wielding a hammer against rock he suspected of containing ore—it must hurt her to feel her sacrifice rejected.

"I shouldn't have said what I did," he grated out.

His seeking fingers found the lamp and kindling box. "Where the hell is that ointment?"

"In your room. Which particular remark among hundreds has animated your conscience?"

He came back with the salve and the lamp. The sight of her huddled big-eyed with the blanket clutched up to her chin reawakened his frustrated fury. He couldn't blame her for hiding herself from him, but he hated it, and even the realization that it was his own fault couldn't keep him from yanking the cover clean off the bed and throwing it onto the floor. "No more barriers between us, Libby. I shouldn't have sworn when—when I found out the truth. You deserved better. Here. Some of this will soothe the pain."

Libby slowly uncurled from the defensive position she'd assumed. She sat up. Looking down at herself, she sobbed once and tried to shield the area between her legs with her hands. "I forgot there would be blood . . . If I were really your wife, you wouldn't care if I heard you cursing or not. You'd think it was my duty to listen."

All Caleb registered was the horror that made her face blank and young when she saw that he'd made her bleed. Going back for the washcloth, he wiped the red stains from her thighs carefully, and then cleaned his loins so the sight of her blood on him wouldn't remind her. "I meant to go so gentle with you, to make everything so good for you . . . Damn it, Libby!"

The contrast between Caleb's consideration and his anger squeezed a shaky laugh from Libby. Her breasts swayed, and Caleb's jaw tightened. The muscle beside his mouth twitched, and so did his manhood, whose rigid length had subsided but now began to revive.

"I understand why you kept putting me off," he continued. "But, my God, you'd won. Why ask for this when I was ready to give you your precious annulment and let you go?"

The anguish that had clamped down on Libby's chest at Caleb's abrupt withdrawal didn't ease, but her heart

picked up a new rhythm. Love, sharp-toothed and unpredictable as a wild animal, clawed through her veins
like the blood he'd been so gentle wiping away. "It was
all I had to give you. It made me feel close to you."
And important to him. One flesh. The words of the
marriage service she hadn't understood mocked her
briefly.

"You were a goddamned *virgin*."

"Thank you, I am aware of that." If she was
damned, she'd go to the devil willingly before she'd
admit her love after a statement like that. Not sure if
she should laugh or cry, she said, "The strictures of
my ladylike upbringing forbid me to explain my exact
motives."

He used a phrase so loaded with indecencies she
couldn't guess who was doing what to whom, but it
must have been a potent obscenity because he looked
a little more cheerful.

"Here," he said again. "You'll be sore tomorrow,
but this stuff should help some. It's made my burn feel
better." When Libby regarded the ointment blankly, he
set his lips in a wry line and dipped his fingers into the
aloe.

At the first intrusion, her eyes opened wide and
green, and she whimpered. His fingers moved delicately, spreading the cool salve over flesh that first
shuddered from further hurt and then hummed with remembered pleasure. When a middle finger entered her
to anoint the wound his shaft had dealt her while plunging through her maidenhead, strong waves of sensation
rippled through her loins and down her legs. *"Caleb."*

"Did I hurt you again?" he asked through clenched
teeth.

"Oh, no. Not hurt." It was hard to speak through
such hot, all-consuming pangs. Much easier to lean into
his chest, to brush her breasts against bands of muscle
that jumped at the touch and let her hardened nipples
tangle in the black hair arrowing downward.

"I'm damned if I understand you, woman." From

his slurred tone, Caleb was finding it as difficult to concentrate on anything but passion as she was.

Libby tried. "I may be a mystery to you. You are certainly one to me." His finger began to stroke, in and out and in, and his palm kneaded, stimulating the tiny organ hidden in the swelling lips at the juncture of her legs. Her breath came out in a sob. "I never know what you're going to do. The simplest things about you change from day to day. I know you're not a coward, but you ran away from San Francisco and—"

Deliberately, Caleb tumbled her onto her back and, with his finger still stroking a slow rhythm, put his tongue to her damp curls. She tasted of soap and aloe and, very faintly, of metallic blood and the fresh moisture from her reawakened longing. He wanted to erase that moment of pain from her memory of this experience, and he wanted to keep himself from gabbing his participation in the planned attack on the Hounds. With her inconvenient honor and transparent face, the knowledge would be dangerous for all involved. This activity kept his mouth busy—very busy—and dulled everything but the honeyed waves of desire surging through his loins, swelling his shaft until he felt drunk with the sweet pressure.

The instant ecstasy began to wring a series of small, rhythmic thrusts from the hips his hands were holding as still as possible, he lifted himself up, murmuring reassuringly at her soft cry of disappointment. He fitted his body over hers. Filling her with aching slowness this time, he paused when he was firmly lodged to wipe his lips with her hair before he bent his head to kiss her.

Too far gone in passion to notice anything but their fullness and warmth, Libby opened her mouth at the coaxing nibble. His tongue, sleek and insistent, probed the tender undersides of her lips and started a counterpoint to the leisurely thrust and parry his hips were enforcing on hers. There was a pain that was separate from the stinging torment of desire, but it seemed to exist outside her somewhere, in some other woman, and it didn't interfere with the hot, whirling pleasure centered in the port Caleb found, visited, slid so teasingly away from, and found again. Each slow, slow visit deep within her made the pleasure sing hotter in her veins.

Time measured itself in the exquisitely slow impalements, the gathering moisture of exertion between their two bodies that made every movement an undulation, the deepening urgency of Libby's pants for breath.

"Gently, little one. Softly."

Surfeited with slow and gentle, Libby wrapped her legs around Caleb, instinctively hooking her feet over his buttocks and lifting her hips in invitation. "More, Caleb. Faster. Please."

His pleased chuckle sounded hoarsely in her ear. "So much passion. For me. Say it."

"Only for you. Only ever for you. Oh, please, I shall die from this."

"This?"

The smooth motion stopped with Caleb almost completely withdrawn. Libby opened glazed eyes to see his triumphant grin.

"I hate you!"

"Do you, dear heart?" He possessed her with a deep thrust. Another. Another.

"Yes!" Pain and pleasure built to a peak so high she sang out with it, a high, wild note, and then everything was pleasure, great sobbing chords that ebbed into the groans torn from Caleb's chest as he released his iron control.

The intimate muscles gripping him with all their tiny strength brought Caleb a burning release so draining that for a long minute it was all he could do to catch his breath without crushing the limp, sated body beneath him. Finally, he started to rise, but Libby clutched him and whispered, "Stay. It will be so lonely when you aren't in me anymore."

He kissed her nose. "I'm not going anywhere. But

you won't be able to walk if I don't give you a chance to heal. Here," he said, lifting away from her but sliding a long-muscled leg comfortingly between her sore thighs. "See? You're safe. I'm with you."

How odd. She did feel safe with Caleb. He might not be honorable, or even completely honest, but wrapped in his damp embrace, his limbs tangled with hers, and a yawn stretching his jaws so his strong teeth snapped next to her ear, her soul shuddered away from the thought that this paradise would melt into air like the thin layer of dew in tomorrow's sun.

The big hand rubbing circles over her back gradually slowed to a stop. His warm breath on her cheek deepened.

"No, I don't hate you, my darling love." She was careful to say it only when she was sure he'd fallen too deeply asleep to hear her.

Chapter 21

Harness jingled, voices floated nearby. All of the tones were male, but none was Caleb's, so Libby ignored them and reached out to feel the reassurance of his warm body beside hers.

Cool linen met her hand. Opening her eyes, she saw the jar of aloe jelly on her night table, and her clothes strewn any which way with Caleb's across the floor of his room. Consulting her conscience, she found she didn't feel any less for giving herself to Caleb and taking him in return. She felt . . . more. More knowledgeable about how to live life. Even more in touch with God, who had invented this marvelous way of expressing love. More the woman she had been meant to be.

Being a lady didn't mean much next to that—unless Caleb thought it did. Her movements slowed, brush in one hand and clean pantalets in the other.

Distinct among the other sounds, his low voice rumbled through the window. Without stopping to consider, Libby dropped the daytime things from her hands and threw on a wrapper. Flying down the stairs and onto the porch, she picked out Caleb's lean form with barely a glance and ran straight for his arms.

Out of the corner of his eye, Caleb caught the flutter of muslin and lace, a flash of white feet, slender ankles and shapely calves, the tumble of untamed hair. All the motion around him stopped as men fell into bemused silence. Drawing her protectively away from curious stares, Caleb inspected his treasure. Her mouth looked soft and defenseless this morning, still slightly swollen. Well kissed. Heavy lids brushed with bluish shadows gave her eyes a sensuality they hadn't had yesterday. Her unbound hair flowing down her breast fanned shining strands over his shirtfront and sleeves. She smelled of their loving. That lacy thing she clasped to her throat, while it covered her from neck to toe, hinted at the fact that the beautiful body underneath was bare and rosy with sleep.

She looked like what she was, a woman fresh from the bed of her lover.

"You should have stayed inside." Despite himself, Caleb's fingers lingered as he tried to detach her hair. Damn the interested audience watching their every move, anyway. Once Libby began to think, she'd suffer agonies of mortification at letting the wranglers see her like this. He shifted his weight to block their view.

Sweet little love, she'd needed her sleep, so he hadn't woken her to wish her goodbye. Besides, he had a job to do. Now he'd have to explain too many things.

The long strands had a life of their own this morning, clinging like silken cobwebs.

"Are you riding out?" she asked.

"I didn't tell you last night. We caught one of the reavers at the barn. He was, uh, persuaded to tell us where their camp is. You don't need to worry."

Her strong, tall lover, stupidly brave at all the wrong moments. He would learn to place care before defending his property about five minutes after his own last breath. Trying to compose her face to calm acceptance, Libby dipped her chin in a nod.

He bent his head to study her expression. "I mean it, Libby. I'll make a side trip to Sonoma and handle everything. The only trouble is—damn! Both of us should sign that register, but I don't want you gallivanting off in that direction with a roving gang still on the loose."

"What register?"

"The parish book." He frowned, but Libby didn't think he really saw her. "I'll go ahead and sign. You'll have to wait till we can get you the chance. The important thing is the will, and I can have that amended today. It's not a complicated document. You don't mind sharing with Julia, do you? She was sole heir before, but she'll understand. Half to her, that's only fair, half to you with the capital from a quarter of it in trust for our child—if there is one."

Her eyes got bigger and greener. "No—"

Maybe she was denying the possibility of his seed bearing fruit in her womb. The idea made his grip tighten, but her mouth was so vulnerable it begged for a kiss, so he gave her one. "Women have conceived their first time, like it or not."

The prospect filled Libby with anxiety as well as trembling joy; she rested her forehead against his chest where his heart beat fast and strong. "Keep your money and your property—and your name. I'm not prepared for you to die just so I can inherit a large piece of a country I detest." Did she? Ribbons of fog wreathed the morning in pink gauze. Milk-white sky had yet to paint itself blue. Dewdrops glistened on every available surface like diamonds scattered by a lavish hand.

The fingers bruising her upper arms became tender. "There's no time right now for your scruples, dear heart." He kissed her again, lips warm and masterful, and his palms slipped down over the thin muslin to knead the soft fullness of her buttocks before they pulled her close to the bone and muscle of his hips. "God, I hope you're breeding. If you're not, we'll have to see to it as soon as I can give the matter the attention it deserves."

A friendly pat on her haunch—as if she were a mare he expected to get a likely foal out of, she thought—and he walked her back to the door, keeping his body angled between her and the small crowd. Her resentment grew. He was ashamed of her for not being a lady anymore, for showing herself in her nightclothes in front of his men. He was prepared to make her his legal wife and keep her for breeding stock.

"I haven't stopped hating you," she said clearly.

Two dozen sets of bulging eyes turned to Caleb to judge his reaction. His hands easily spanned her waist; picking her up without even a grunt of effort, he carried her over the threshold and kicked the door shut behind them. Ignoring her thrashing arms and legs, he bent her backward and kissed her full on the mouth, hard, until her body went limp and pliant in his arms. "You disappointed your audience," she said when the demanding caress finally released her, furious that her taunt came out weak and breathless.

"I don't perform for an audience," he told her, setting her back on her feet with a thump. She welcomed the little jolt. It cleared her head. "And neither do you anymore. You're my wife now."

Libby was behaving badly and knew it. She was also angry enough to enjoy it. "You can own your house and your cattle and the sun rising and setting for all I care. You can't own me."

He jerked on the doorknob and looked over his shoulder at her. The movement pulled burned skin; his arm retracted to ease the pain. Concern flared in her eyes. Caleb's mouth widened in satisfaction. "Find something to do sitting down today. You must be— saddle sore."

Had there been anything to throw, she would have thrown it.

Julia returned a few hours later. Libby checked her full skirts to make sure they hid the pillow she was sitting on. Devil take Caleb for being right. She hadn't noticed so much as a twinge until he'd mentioned it.

Discords crashed from the piano as Julia slammed her hands over the black keys. "Are you going to practice?" Libby asked.

"What else is there to do?" replied Julia, moderating the noise into something that resembled a waltz.

"Did Juan go with Caleb?"

"He did." After faltering a few times, Julia marked the beat with violent downstrokes of her wrists. *Pompom-pom*.

Libby winced. "I'm going to take a walk."

"You can't. The reavers—"

"Caleb said not to wander toward Sonoma. I'll go toward the sea instead. Not far."

"But—"

"I have to get out. Just for a while."

"Oh, suit yourself." Julia switched to Beethoven with no better results, her manner suddenly elaborately casual. "Your Mr. Malloy is certainly charming, isn't he?"

"Malloy? I've never thought so."

"And handsome. And cultured. Do you think he liked me?"

There was a fine line to tread here. Libby couldn't praise Malloy without choking over the falseness, and yet a wholesale condemnation might drive her sister-in-law into defending him. Julia's feelings appeared to be in an uncertain state. "Of course he liked you. Anyone would. He's not the sort of person a young lady would want to encourage, though. Malloy's a trifle disreputable."

"Disreputable sounds just fine," answered Julia rebelliously. "I believe I'm in the mood for a disreputable man."

"What in heaven's name did Juan do?"

"Mr. Arrile has nothing to do with it." She ended the sonata on a hideously wrong note. "He left without saying goodbye."

Wandering vaguely westward, Libby felt as yielding as the grasses that flattened before the rigid bell of her skirt. Caleb was the most impossible man she'd ever met, but she knew with despairing certainty that if he rose out of the oats in front of her, she'd let him have his way with her. "In point of fact," she muttered, "you've become so besotted with him you'd insist on it." Sinking down, she stared unseeingly at the curtain of grass around her.

For a long time, nothing disturbed the underbreath of wind or the rustle and chirp of birds seeking a late breakfast. Demure brown sparrows hopped, and jays with feathers too vividly blue to seem real scolded near her still figure. The shadow of a hawk flitted across her face, making her blink.

As she watched the predator ride the air high above, its great wings outstretched, a man cleared phlegm from his throat and spat.

Libby froze.

"Good a place as any," someone said. The flat vowels of Australia twanged. "Logan'll show up eventually."

Hounds? She'd last heard that nasal speech on the *Niantic*. Hounds!

Sounds approached and receded. Libby waited until all around her was quiet again before she parted a section of grass and peered through the resulting arch.

She hadn't realized she was so close to the edge of the poppy valley. The angle was different from her previous view into its teacup perfection; she could see a silvery twinkle of water surrounded by lush, feathery cresses.

And Wang, bending to gather the greens. Another, shorter shadow was there, then not there.

Hoots carried from below when the gang sighted the elderly Chinese man. Biting her lip helplessly, Libby added up the time it would take her to run for reinforcements and knew it wouldn't be enough.

Pressing herself further into the cushion of stems, she pitched her voice deep and loud. "Leave him alone!" A burst from her pistol emphasized the order.

Men hit the ground, hugged it. The meadow offered little cover. One of them scuttled forward and grabbed Wang around the waist. Libby moaned. The cook looked brittle enough to break in two.

"You want the Chinee, you pay for him!" he shouted. "Show yourself!"

Not knowing what else to do, she fired again. By chance, the bullet must have hit a target; someone screamed.

Tears blinded her as if her own flesh had been ripped by lead. Holding the gun in two shaking hands, she called, "Let him go. I'll shoot to kill next time."

"No, you won't," said a voice directly above her, and a boot smashed down in front of her face. The spurs on the heads of the oats bonded with the horsehair of her exposed crinoline for a crucial instant. She was trapped.

Libby barely snatched her hands back in time. The gun disappeared under a dirty heel. "Well, lookee here. It's our Elizabeth."

Not Smitty. One of the others from that night in Caleb's room. Libby scrambled up, scrubbing the back of her hand across her cheeks.

"Everybody'll be happy to see you," he said, running his hand down over her breasts, then suddenly yanking at her bodice so hooks popped. "Mighty happy."

Controlling her sobbing breath, she stumbled after him, unable to break his grip on her wrists. Next to the spring, he released her with a shove that drove her into Wang. They teetered at the edge of the water. Libby flung herself to one side; clinging to Wang to keep him from going into the pool, she fell heavily into the greenery, carrying him with her.

"Look at that! She'll take a tumble with anything, eh, boys?"

"You pilgrims just don't know how to talk in front of a lady, do you?" The terse rumble came from outside the circle of leering faces.

Hands flashed toward guns; the simultaneous click of more than twenty hammers being cocked stopped the quick draws in midair.

"Maybe you better apologize."

Caleb prodded until the ragged chorus of "Sorry," became "Sorry, ma'am." Libby barely noticed. Once Wang wriggled enough to show he hadn't been hurt, she let him go and pushed herself into a sitting position. Caleb filled her vision. He sat tall and easy in his high-pommeled saddle, a rifle propped against his shoulder while he leaned over and held out his unoccupied hand in an imperative gesture.

"That's your hurt arm," she said, balking.

"I know that. It'll hurt less when I don't have to stretch it. Get up here."

He wasn't even looking at her, but at the captives as they were disarmed and tied together with stout rope. Quietly, Libby did as she was told, linking hands with Caleb and placing her foot on the toe of his boot to give herself a boost.

The muscles of the arm holding her uncoiled slightly when the last knot was tied and the prisoners began a slovenly march. "They're Hounds," Libby said.

Still frowning ferociously, Caleb settled her more comfortably in front of his saddle. The affection clear in the way he pulled her head to snuggle in the crook of his shoulder and arranged her legs so they would rest against the horse's neck, instead of dangling and bruising each other at each trot, made her heart break. She could be so content with this man under other circumstances. He couldn't help but be kindly, even when he was in a rage with her. As he was now. His anger was a physical thing; she could feel it rolling off him in waves. It kept the muscles of his arms contracting under her hands and made his breath harsh on her cheek.

"You're sure? Hounds?"

She nodded into his shoulder. "The accent. And one of them knew me."

"Christ. All the more reason you shouldn't be strolling around the countryside. I told you—"

"You said to stay away from the east."

"I meant east, west, north, and south!" he roared. "Don't you have any sense, woman?"

"Apparently not," she replied with spirit. "Is anyone taking care of Wang? He's too old for these alarums."

The old man rode by, his skirt up to his knobby knees, mounted on what must have been a reaver pony with the boy Manuel bouncing behind him. "You brought a child with you?" Libby gasped.

"Manuel brought us. He was out helping Wang find dinner—he said he heard you tell Julia it was safe—"

"That boy!"

"—and ran to fetch us about the time we heard shots." Grudging approval softened his growl. "Pretty shooting. You clipped one of 'em."

"I was aiming over their heads," Libby admitted, and was rewarded for her truthfulness with a quick laugh. But the anger still crackled around him.

The ragged column stopped at the frame house for supplies and then continued on toward Sonoma. Libby covered her face at the sight of her reflection in the hall mirror and ran up the stairs before Caleb.

"Thank goodness you're back!" exclaimed Julia, blocking her way. "Did you remember today's the Vallejo party?"

Libby dropped her hands. "Oh, no."

Caleb just cursed.

"Neither did I," said Julia. "Senora Vallejo sent a messenger to remind us. Both of you, hurry, wash up. Libby, what have you been doing to yourself? Rolling in the weeds? Don't bother to change; Teresa packed our best clothes and took them on. She should be waiting for us with them when we get there."

Late afternoon sun bronzed the hillsides on the other side of the creek as they rode into an adobe quadrangle much like the Manzanita's. People were sweeping the courtyard and hanging bunting and bunches of flowers, but the place had an abandoned air. "Sad, isn't it?" asked Julia quietly, when she and Libby had followed a smiling Vallejo daughter to a room set aside for the ladies to dress. "I heard he's put the building up for sale. Not worth the effort to keep up. It could be our ranch house, couldn't it, all bare and lifeless?''

"I grew up in this hacienda," Teresa put in unexpectedly. "It is accursed. Let it melt in the rain. It can return to the earth.''

Her hands twisted in Libby's hair, tugging painfully, but Libby's eyes met Julia's in the mirror they shared, and neither girl said anything.

Teresa, too, lapsed into silence, until she murmured a thanks to the maid who brought the party dresses, pressed to crisp perfection, while Libby pinned Julia's switch firmly into place and nestled a rose of kingfisher blue silk next to the resulting chignon.

"Is it all right, do you think?" Julia asked anxiously, turning her head this way and that.

"Perfect," said Libby. Still smiling, she glanced at Teresa for verification. The housekeeper was fussing quietly as she lowered the matching blue gown over Julia's hair, and Libby's eyes slid to the dress laid out for her.

The satin mellowed to a dull cranberry in the dim room. By sunlight, or candlelight, it would blaze flame-red, unmistakable.

"Not that one!"

Julia's head emerged. "What's wrong? Have you tired of it? I told Teresa to grab the fanciest thing she could find in your wardrobe. I knew anything you owned would be in excellent taste, so . . ." Her explanation dwindled away unhappily. "Oh, dear, I never should have agreed to having something made up for me first. Here, you wear the blue and I'll—"

"You'd disappear into that red thing. And I'd look as if I'd been stuffed into short skirts. I'll wear the dress I rode over in—"

"It is soiled. It is not grand. You would shame Senor Cal." To Teresa, the last was the clinching argument.

Libby tried to laugh. "The red then. It's no great tragedy. Only—I suspect Caleb would rather see me in rags.''

"Senor Cal is not so loco," said Teresa stoutly.

Resigned, Libby dragged her laces tighter to enable her to fit into the prostitute's gown. When she'd been tugged and pulled and pushed into the shape required by the decolletage, she could look down at two alabaster bowls bared almost to the nipple. "Is there any extra lace? Ribbon? I cannot appear in front of your friends like this."

Julia circled, twitching the scarlet folds into place. "It's a shame to cover you up. You're magnificent. But Cal might be a tad upset if a lot of other people get to see you being so magnificent, too."

"A trifle, yes." Libby shuddered at the thought of what Caleb's jealously might lead him to do. "Quick, Teresa, did you bring some of your tatting?"

A piece of Teresa's thick lace disguised some of the mounded flesh. "Better," decided Libby with a sigh. "Thank you, Teresa." She doubted it would be enough to hide the gown's origins from Caleb. Of course, he had been very drunk the one time he'd seen it before . . .

A burst of music from the courtyard made Julia's face brighten. "That's a piano! Mr. Malloy must have arrived!"

Libby changed her grimace into the smooth, politely delighted expression expected of a guest and followed Julia out.

It wasn't too hard at first to avoid Malloy. Libby purposely focused her attention on the food heaped on the tables, and the wine flowing into deep goblets. Not homemade wine, either, Libby noted, finishing a glass and allowing one of the eagerly attentive men clustering around the red dress to fetch her another. The bubbles of the Champagne region tickled her nose and burst at the back of her throat. Unsettling emotions receded.

A small, fussy man was introduced as a reporter from the *Bulletin*. Smiling vaguely, she drifted to the opposite corner of the courtyard.

Teresa was helping to serve the food. Libby caught sight of Julia, surrounded by admirers. Her sister-in-law looked flushed and pretty, and although Julia didn't speak to Juan, who leaned against a post near the refreshments, Libby saw that when Juan stared down at the fierce shine on his boots, Julia's sparkle faded.

Another swain went to find Libby more champagne. The momentary gap in shirtfronts allowed her a glimpse of Caleb, towering in a sober group of substantial-looking men. Barely remembering to smile an apology to her gallants, she slipped across the crowded courtyard to his side.

His elbow crooked invitingly. Libby tucked her hand in the warm space and leaned against him. His anger seemed gone.

"Gentlemen, it's my pleasure to introduce my wife, Elizabeth." Was that pride vibrating in his low voice, or just the bubbles in the wine? Libby decided not to worry about it.

Drawing her a little ways apart, Caleb was aware of male stares glued to the flutter of lace at her bosom. The bit of netting did a very insufficient job, in his opinion, of veiling her charms.

She patted his cravat and stood on tiptoe to kiss him lightly. At the taste on her lips, his brows beetled. "Libby, are you liquored up?"

"Yes, lord and master."

"Now why would you do such a thing?"

The wine made it easier to share what was in her heart. "I spent the night with a lover," she murmured. "This morning he went away. Then I got kidnapped. Then I rode sixteen miles over very hard ground and forged a creek when I was already . . . *saddle sore*. It's been an extremely trying day, lord and master."

"Er, Mrs. Logan, ma'am . . ."

A young man offered her a glass of champagne. Of course; he'd gone to get it for her. She drank thirstily.

Caleb watched Libby ravish the fellow with a smile and directed a stern look at him. Her admirer backed away. Plucking the glass from her hand, Caleb drained half of it before giving it back.

"Sips," he said firmly. "Small sips."

"As you command, lord and—"

"And don't call me that. I'm your husband."

Her delicate brows dipped. The red satin had a tendency to wash the green from her irises; if anything, they appeared an indeterminate gray, and now they clouded. "Are you? Does one success in bed make a marriage?"

No wonder he hadn't been able to tell their color in the saloon, he found himself thinking, and his scowl turned blacker as realization hit. "What are you doing in that dress?" A tinkle from the piano rose over the noise of the crowd. "Is it for him?"

The wine couldn't protect her from this anguish. "How can you ask? You know how it was for me— before last night."

"That doesn't mean you aren't in love with him. You spent two years with him. No man could resist you that long. He would have tried to get you infatuated with him."

"Your theory would be flattering if it weren't so absurd. Besides, drink unmans Malloy, and he was drunk as often as he could arrange it."

"He seems to be man enough to charm the ladies," Caleb pointed out. Several women, looking like exotically inverted flowers in their tulip-shaped skirts, gathered round the piano. Kingfisher blue flashed in the bouquet. "I'm going to—"

"Logan! Heard you caught yourself some sons of bitches! Good work. Practicing up for the big day in Frisco?" The small, cold smile Caleb gave him failed to dampen any of the speaker's enthusiasm, which he transferred to Libby. "Are you the beautiful Mrs. Logan? Must be proud to be married to one of the men who's going to rid the city of the Hounds of Portsmouth Square."

"I beg your pardon?" Libby asked.

"A leading citizen in the committee of vigilance. About time those Hounds got a taste of their own medicine." The big man staggered. "Going to get me some more of that fizzy water they're serving. It sneaks up on you. First you think it's just like lemonade, and then it hits you with a real nice wallop. Pleasure meeting you, ma'am."

"Some people talk too much," said Caleb, eyeing Libby uneasily.

"Indeed. And some too little. How many times have you let me maunder on about your refusal to meet the Hounds?"

"Now, Libby." He stroked the arm linked with his in a calming way. As if she were a restive mare, Libby thought. It reminded her that she was still leaning against him.

She removed his arm with the gingerly distaste of a woman disposing of a slug that had mistaken her satin for a tasty petal. "Is there a particular reason why you felt safe confiding in that blatherskite and not in me?"

"I'd never tell him. Someone else must have blabbed. He doesn't seem to know anything except in a general way, so it's not too bad. I couldn't say anything to you because—" He took her chin in his hand. "Because you have a face that's transparent as water and a damnable, schoolmarmish desire for heroes who leap before they look. That's not the way I fight."

"Honor—"

"There's more than one kind of honor, Libby. Is it courage to bring a wife and daughter to a new continent and kill one and leave the other to starve? Or is it foolhardiness?"

Libby couldn't look away from Caleb's hard, insistent eyes. "My father cared about me and Maman. He couldn't help suffering from—enthusiasms. And I admired him for them." She freed herself. "Now and then, Caleb Logan, I trick myself into imagining that you—that we—" Her trembling chin firmed. "If I understand you correctly, you don't mistrust my intentions, precisely, just my intelligence. Well, I really do believe I've let you make a fool of me for the last time."

"Where do you think you're going?"

"For more champagne," she answered sweetly. "And then I shall dance with every one of the fourteen gentlemen who has asked me. So far."

Outraged pride took her as far as a gulp of wine, but the unaccustomed fun of getting light-headed had gone out of the evening. Disconsolate, she sidestepped hopeful dance partners. Julia called to her from the piano. "Mr. Malloy says he'll play something you know. Sing, Libby, do."

Performing was the last thing she wanted to do right now. "I doubt I'm in voice. Surely the senoritas Vallejo—"

"No, no." Benicia Vallejo smiled, stately in black. "Please favor us."

Malloy regarded her blandly, short-fingered pianist's hands hovering over the keys.

Pushing a path through to the front of the guests, Caleb couldn't miss Libby's quick consultation with the piano player. The bastard had duded himself up since the last time Caleb had seen him. He'd been hiding a pretty face under the sparse beard. So he'd never physically been Libby's lover? There was something between the two of them all the same. The ease of familiarity spiced with tension, a kind of recognition when their eyes met, as they did when Libby nodded to signal the man to play.

She sounded wonderful, of course. A red-robed angel singing in Italian. Caleb had been stranded in Venice once, with its imposing buildings and stinking canals. It didn't take much of the language to translate *caro mio*. Libby kept her eyes trained on the piano player while she sang—of love.

Suddenly the huge, open courtyard seemed airless, too hot and bright.

The moment Caleb stalked away, Libby's throat tightened, and she had to call on her years of breathing exercises, pushing the last few notes out by main force. No one but Malloy seemed to notice anything amiss. Julia led the applause and the demands for an encore; aware of Malloy's malicious gaze, Libby refused as graciously as she could and tried to slip into the background.

"Ah, yes, Mrs. Logan puts the lark to shame." Malloy's brogue grew louder. "I've seen her hold an audience in the palm of her pretty hand, so to speak. And not a bit above her company, either. Why should she be, when the last place she performed was a waterfront saloon?"

His last words caused so many indrawn breaths they sounded like one huge gasp. Julia stared at her, then Malloy, blinking rapidly. Abandoning his post by the punch bowl, Juan took a quick step toward Julia. Everyone else waited with the greedy faces of those offered a public spectacle—for her to deny the charge, Libby realized—and when she licked her lips and failed to speak, they turned pointed shoulders. Conversations resumed, glassware clinked, someone laughed.

Poor Caleb, she thought. His wife disgraced. Furious with him as she felt, she knew what a blow this would be to his pride. At least now his friends wouldn't wonder why when they divorced. And the social stigma wouldn't be as bad for him as for her; perhaps someday he'd remarry. An annulment would have been a tidier solution, but the most optimistic prophet couldn't foresee one under the circumstances.

The solid row of backs parted. Caleb walked through the resulting dry land, his forehead furrowed until his shadowed eyes found her. Then he lifted his brows in question. Libby shrugged. "Quite like the Red Sea, isn't it? It's a very colorful evening. The Red Sea, a scarlet woman . . ."

"I'm going to kill the next man who gives you anything to drink."

Laughter spurted from her. "I'm not inebriated."

"Then what are you talking about?" he growled.

"Me. They all know. About the taproom. The one you called a kennel. I'm sorry, Caleb."

"Sorry?" It emerged as a roar. "What have you got to apologize for? You were doing honest work to keep yourself, and anyone who says you were doing anything else in that place will answer to me."

A quiver of interest ran through the crowd.

"Caleb," said Libby, astounded.

Julia slipped through the cordon of guests to put her arm around Libby's waist. Juan quietly ranged himself behind her.

Caleb raked a derisive glance over the attentive backs. "I have no doubt a female of less mettle would lay down and die before she sang for pay in public. Well, a dead woman is a purely useless article of goods. I'd rather have a wife with the guts to face life."

"Indeed," came Senora Vallejo's serene second, "such a woman is a valuable acquisition. There are many situations in a woman's life that call for great courage." Her inscrutable glance lingered on Teresa for a moment. Libby looked away. Private hurts should remain private, and too many of them were being paraded at this fiesta.

People shuffled around, their faces friendly again. It took so little, Libby thought in amazement. A declaration—of sorts—from Caleb of his faith in her. Kindness from a near stranger. But what would all of Benicia's guests say to each other at the end of the party? "Guess a Logan can afford to make the best of a bad bargain." And then they'd write letters home, warning their wives and daughters to be paragons of propriety.

Libby's insides knotted with humiliation.

Under the cover of the social noises beginning to rise again around them, Caleb asked softly, "I'll have to square the reporter. It shouldn't be too hard. I—"

"I know. You own a share in the newspaper."

"Matter of fact, I do. Who let out you were singing in that saloon?"

"Mr. Malloy. The person for whom you think I harbor such affection."

He grinned wolfishly. "I'll have a word with him."

But the piano had been silent for some time. Malloy
was gone.

Chapter 22

〰〰

"Padre's here."

The strong light of midmorning blazed through the window of the bedroom in the Vallejo's adobe. The room had been given to Caleb and Libby after the fiesta had lasted so late it would have been impossible to ride back to the Manzanita.

"Did you hear me, Libby? The padre's here."

Aggression put a steely undertone into Caleb's announcement. Libby continued to face the mirror, making minute adjustments to the pins holding her braids in place. She took a good long time doing it, but the hand in the looking glass shook slightly. "Thank you, Teresa," she said when she had finished. "You may go."

Teresa looked disapproving but refrained from comment. Her silence was so eloquent that when she walked out the door into the courtyard and gave a stifled exclamation, Libby spun on her seat.

The general stood outside, visible through the open door. He seemed as startled by Teresa's sudden appearance as the housekeeper was dismayed; his heavy, handsome face went blank at her *"Madre de Dios!"*

Libby jumped up and ran to the threshold, to do what she wasn't quite sure. By the beehive ovens at the edge of the courtyard, Diego glanced up and his face darkened. He threw down his breakfast tortilla and closed in, but Vallejo had been a great man for a long time and neither intercession was necessary. The general smiled, patted Teresa's shining black hair, and strolled on with a vague bow in Libby's direction.

Libby watched Teresa walk straight-backed to the room assigned to Julia. Diego's dark eyes, their liquid beauty frozen for once, trailed her, too. The plump, comely figure disappeared from view.

"I will say this much for you, Caleb," she muttered, "you've never patted me on the head like a puppy you were tired of."

Caleb lay back on the bed they'd shared last night. It was too short for legs the length of his, which wouldn't have mattered had Libby been in a more receptive mood after the fiesta. The hush after they retired had grown awkward and then brittle. Something vulnerable and lonely about the angle of her shoulders had kept him from trying to prod her into speech or lovemaking. So he'd lain there, trying to concentrate on the irritation he felt over the fact that his feet hung over the side of the mattress. Doing his best to ignore how much he wanted to kiss her into submission and bury himself in her warmth.

Caleb could have had her with enough patience and persistence. The quality of her stillness and the weight of her gaze running over him in the half dark convinced him she wanted him, too.

He couldn't order his arms to reach for anything she didn't offer freely. Nor could he let her go blithely off to England. Not after she had given her virginity to him.

Now he hid his thoughts behind lazy lids. "Noticed I'm alive, have you? I said, the padre's here. Come on; he's waiting."

He didn't give her a choice about this. He couldn't. He sprang out of bed quickly so Libby couldn't evade him, and she followed because his hand was tight around her wrist.

"This isn't necessary," she panted when he halted abruptly in front of the smiling Franciscan.

"He's brought his parish book so you can sign it."
Caleb pointed out the obvious, dipping pen in ink and
closing her fingers over the utensil.

"Never. Never ever ever."

"Libby, everything's different. What you want, or I
want, doesn't change the fact that you were—untouched—
before we met, and now you're—"

"Not." The barb in her husky voice seemed to catch
the priest's attention. His uncomprehending smile
faded as she went on, "Don't say anything more,
Caleb. If you do, I won't be responsible for the consequences."

"Damn it, woman, I'll take the blame for the consequences. I know I'm not blindly honorable the way
you want me to be, but I had your virginity and I'm the
man you'll marry."

She looked at him as though he'd slapped her instead
of offering a real marriage. "Blame? We need to ap-
portion blame for what we did?"

"Stop twisting my words. Christ, Libby, we're already
married except for a signature on a piece of paper. You
could be bearing my child—"

"Oh, I was forgetting. You're planning on renting
storage space in my womb."

He nearly did slap her at that. "That's a hell of a
way to describe the joy of bringing a child into the
world."

Her eyes filled with tears, and all he could think of
was drowned emeralds. "I refuse to be the virgin sacrifice on the altar of your nonexistent honor."

The priest interrupted in quick Spanish. "Senor,
senora, there is a problem? The senora cannot write?
She can make her mark instead."

"Thank you, padre," Libby said in the same language between gritted teeth. "The senor considers me
a light woman—despite proof to the contrary. And why
should he not? So does half of California. But no one
has accused me of being unable to write before. I had

not appreciated how low it is possible to sink. You have repaired a gap in my education.''

She dropped the pen, which left a smear across the page, causing the priest to cluck with anguish and grab at Caleb's sleeve. Dashing out of the quiet room, Libby ran head-down for the stable. When she got there, she wiped wetness from her cheeks and looked around impatiently.

Waiting by their saddled mounts, Julia said, ''Libby? Whatever is—''

Libby had put on the simple dress she'd worn yesterday. With a leap that left Julia and the hostlers and guests standing near the stables openmouthed, she flung herself into the saddle. The gelding reared, came down with a jarring impact, and Libby loosened the reins, giving the horse its head.

They flew west, along the track they had used yesterday. After several heart-pounding miles, she pulled up, appalled at what she had done. ''Good boy, good clever-footed boy, you kept us from going down in a rabbit hole, didn't you? Why did we choose this way?'' She answered herself crossly. ''Because it will take us home. Devil take it, Caleb's house is home.''

The chopping sound of hooves biting into dirt neared. Libby squared her shoulders and waited.

Without a word, Caleb leaned over from his mount and took her reins. The grim line to his mouth made her heart give a sick thud, but she returned his gaze with no expression.

He led her horse, and Julia rode watchfully behind. I'm a prisoner, Libby thought, bound by love I never wanted to feel. Julia probably thinks I'm insane. Certainly falling in love with Caleb had been the maddest thing she'd ever done.

Finally, they arrived home. With a subdued ''I'll see to—to something,'' Julia slid off her horse and into the house. Caleb dismounted and held out his arms for Libby. At the fierce light in his dark eyes, she didn't dare try to evade him. His arms closed over her, holding her inches off the ground, until she looked him in the face. He kissed her softly, surprising her with his gentleness.

"That's better," he muttered against her lips.

Desire, clean, sweet, and sharp, cut through her. She tilted her head back and forced herself to speak. "Can we live on lust, Caleb? Do you really believe a marriage can be founded on nothing but carnal desire?"

"Plenty of 'em have."

Libby pushed on his chest. Slowly, so she knew that it was his choice and not hers, he released her. "Not happy ones," she said. "I won't be a party to such an arrangement. What happens when the passion burns itself out?"

He folded his arms and looked at her in something like amusement. "You think ours is likely to do that?"

"I can't judge. I never knew anything about passion until you forced me to learn."

"I didn't mean to—"

"There's force and then there's force. In England they have glass buildings, called forcing houses, where gardeners keep plants and force them to bloom all year by giving them light and keeping them warm. I think you're the sun in my life, Caleb. But you won't accept that. You growl and snap at every inoffensive young man who blunders within a mile of me. I can't defend myself against your imagination."

He knew it; the knowledge that his jealousy had become poisonous enough to destroy his scant chance at happiness with Libby had sent him back to find her at the fiesta. He'd barely been in time to save her socially then, and now the frustration of being unable to settle with Malloy once and for all cracked his resolution to seduce his wife with rationality.

"The way men look at you in that red dress isn't my imagination. I didn't much like the cozy glances you were exchanging with the piano player, either."

"W-with—" Outrage throttled her. All of her reasons for despising her former accompanist jostled at the tip of her tongue, but the memory of the greatest one made her grateful for stuttering. This wasn't the moment to reveal that Malloy had threatened to claim an intimate relationship with her. It didn't matter that Caleb knew it couldn't be true; the scandal would be unbearable. Trying to imitate calm, she said, "I had to watch for my phrasing." The excuse sounded lame, even to her.

Caleb said something rude, and then, "No more love songs with other men, Libby. I wanted to kill him. You know why I didn't go after the bastard?"

She shook her head dumbly.

"It would have made more talk. I'm tired of seeing you hurt. But you have to give me the tools to protect you. Sign the damned book. Admit you're my wife."

No matter how hard she listened, she couldn't hear a word of love in what he had to say. He would protect her because she was his; he would even care for her in a limited way. It wasn't enough. The burden of love she carried for him would drag her down, had already irreparably altered her image of herself. Love wasn't a cheat—she'd never regret the love she'd given her parents or Caleb—but the cost was too high. For her and for Caleb. She wasn't the wife for him.

"It's really quite amusing, isn't it?" she said lightly. "You never wanted me to wife, just to bed. Yet here you are, stuck with this troublesome possession that refuses to be possessed. I'm going h-home. To England."

"Can't you be content with me?"

If she had to consider only herself, she would mate with him, bear his children, and cosset him till she died. But Caleb deserved to love, too. "It's no use. Unless the law attaches importance to the fact I haven't signed the register, I ruined an annulment—" She ignored the quick hand he stretched out to her, and after a pause he let it fall to his side. "It shall have to be divorce after all."

"That'll be complicated and take time. A lot of time."

"We could go away together for a—a wedding trip. I can take ship and you could put it about that I've died of a fever or been run over by a cart. You must have friends in the legislature or the courts. They could put through a quiet divorce, and no one in America need know you're not a widower."

He gave an icy shrug. "I'll be damned if I'll kill you off to save my lily-white reputation. It's not so lily-white anyway. Are you planning to murder me, too? You'll have to claim I'm dead if you mean to pass yourself off as a widow. Decent men don't marry divorcees."

She never wanted to be married to anyone but Caleb—if what she and Caleb shared could be called a marriage. Still, the cold truth in his statement, and his even tone, infuriated her. "You are impossible! I'd do anything to escape living with you. I'll just disappear!"

He went white around the mouth. "Promise me you won't do that! Christ, Libby, if you start wandering, a juicy tidbit for every saddle tramp and pimp in the state, I'll—"

"What?" she asked, hope, like a hydra, rearing another hurtful head.

"I'll hunt you down and strangle you."

The hope died swiftly. He didn't love her. It was as simple as that.

I love her. The knowledge was so sure and instinctual, fit so well with all the crazy feelings afflicting him, Caleb was astonished the discovery hadn't struck him sooner. He would even learn to trust her if the alternative was losing her altogether. *I love her.*

Caleb washed as if he were punishing himself. Cold water, hard, abrasive strokes of the washcloth, soap stinging in his eyes. It could be he'd been so blind because he hadn't foreseen falling in love. There had been lust, respect mixed with dismay at her headstrong courage, bemusement at her gallimaufry of unladylike accomplishments. But something as unlikely as a deep and abiding love that acknowledged and dismissed the differences between them? That had never entered his calculations.

This emotion had nothing to do with the maudlin simpering of poets. It went savage and deep, and the hell of it was, Caleb would have to let her go if showing her that he trusted her didn't work. Giving her up might be the only way to make her happy. Making Libby happy had assumed a disproportionate importance in his life.

Ever since Caleb had run away from the influence of his grandmother, he hadn't thought much in terms of spirits good or bad, but now a devil seemed to sit on his shoulder and poke him with the stinger on the end of its tail. Surely building a life with him would be better for Libby than the isolation that would be hers as a divorced woman. His love was strong enough to bring her contentment in the long run. Surely . . .

Caleb vigorously toweled his face dry. He'd try one more time. He'd tell her. The closed door between his room and Libby's offered a mute challenge. He threw the towel on the floor and pushed the door open.

Gauzy curtains filtered the evening sunshine to an unearthly glow. Kneeling by the window, Libby caught the light and reflected it, hair shining and lovely skin luminous. She was wrapped in something white and filmy—he guessed it was called a negligee—that transformed her into a carnal angel. Her profile was turned to him, and he thought he'd never seen anyone look so forlorn.

In the face of all that beauty and loneliness, he felt big and awkward, his love an imposition. Then he realized that however much the white robe became her, it was hardly the sort of thing she normally wore to supper, and he asked, "Why aren't you dressed?"

She rested her forehead against the glass. "I'm not hungry. Go ahead or you'll be late. Julia will be waiting."

He tried humor. "Your emeralds would go well with that." Her full breasts moved freely inside the material, which wasn't completely opaque in the shimmery light. She must have left off her corset, he deduced, and his groin ached as arousal followed the sudden heating of his blood. "They'd go with it very well," he added softly. "Will you wear them for me?"

"I can't." She made a gesture, and dust motes danced around her wedding ring. "They're downstairs in your desk." Caleb had decided on a small room off the parlor as his office.

"What are they doing there?"

"That's where they always are, in the bottom drawer you never use. The emeralds were a truly generous gift, Caleb, but it makes me feel kept to have them lying about." A tiny sigh escaped her. "I didn't mean to be ungrateful and tell you that."

He knelt beside her, putting his hands around her neck. Inside the circle of his fingers, it was long and fragile. Blue veins lay just under the skin in the vulnerable areas beneath the smooth jaw. Her pulse leaped.

"Don't."

"Why not?" He licked each frantic pulse. "If this is the best way I make you happy, let me do it."

One of his hands slipped into her hair, holding her still for a kiss so tender she forgot to breathe. The other roamed lazily from breast to belly to thigh. A singing ache trailed from his hands. Her lips opened to welcome the hot invasion of his tongue.

Libby meant to say she would allow him the service of her body to ease *his* need, not hers, but then he bunched the robe out of his way and parted her legs, seeking among the short curls until he found the precise spot that made her arch and clutch at him.

The relentless, absorbing pleasure didn't require any explanation. It was its own explanation.

They were *very* late to supper. At the last minute, after both had scrambled into clothes, Caleb insisted on retrieving the necklace and earrings, and fastening them on her himself.

Beyond a significant glance at the clock and amused, raised brows that lent her a momentary resemblance to Senora Vallejo, Julia behaved herself, but her obvious and correct assumption as to what had delayed them grated on Libby.

Her body had surrendered a rapt and violent climax in response to Caleb's lovemaking, and yet the sleepy well-being she'd begun to expect after such sensations had failed to materialize. An unaccustomed state of nerves kept her fidgeting with the green and gold glitter around her neck.

"Are those the stones Cal gave you?" asked Julia with interest. "They're wonderful with your eyes. I'll show you my rubies after we eat. We should have made sure you got to wear your jewels to the fiesta."

"The color would have been wrong with red," Libby said dryly. "Why didn't you bring yours?"

"The blue wasn't right for rubies. My Christmas dress will be perfect, though, won't it? Drat. *You* could have worn the rubies last night. People would have sat up and taken notice! Of course, they did anyway. You were a sight to behold. Whyever did you give the gown to Ascensión? She's cutting it up for petticoats, of all things."

Caleb set down his biscuit. Heat traveled up to Libby's cheeks from the base of her throat; the metal warmed on her skin. "Some wine spilled and stained one of the panels," she lied. "I'd noticed many of the women have bright petticoats." And Libby wouldn't have to see the unfortunate scarlet again.

A small smile played around Caleb's mouth. "Is there anything green in that mountain of stuff you ordered?"

Julia nodded briskly. "Libby liked it, too. Shot silk will make up into a fine ball gown."

"If both you ladies have ball gowns, we'll have to give a ball," said Caleb.

This time Libby steeled herself against hope for the future. "Don't you have some legal business that will take precedence?"

Their eyes met in a silent battle. Libby's fell first, but Caleb said, "If that's your wish. There's something I have to clean up in San Francisco next week; I can talk to a lawyer then. Will that be soon enough?"

"Yes," said Libby sadly. "That will be soon enough."

Wrinkling her forehead, Julia pointed out, "You're not going to be too popular with certain elements in the city, Cal. I heard the county sheriff barely kept some boys from burning down the jail last night with those Hounds in it. Are you sure this is a good time to be gadding?"

The nature of what Caleb planned to clean up in San Francisco occurred to Libby. At her quick, stricken look, Caleb gave her a slight shake of his head. So Julia hadn't been told. It was childish, but the news healed part of the wound to Libby's feelings. Julia hadn't been trusted either.

"The general made me a little bet yesterday," Caleb went on. "He owns most of Newtown, you know. He said flat out the *Red Jacket* can't scrape by the sand-bars in the rest of the slough, and I said that was New-towners' bull. A few of the other directors were there and into the champagne, so the upshot is I'm taking the *Jacket* on Monday next from the city to a brand-new dock being built this very minute in Petaluma."

Julia heaved a sign. "Finally. We've been hauling produce extra miles for far too long. Just keep out of trouble while you're in the Hounds' territory, brother."

"I'll do my uttermost. The reporter who was at the fiesta will be putting a piece about the trip in the newspaper. We had a friendly conversation, and he was glad to trade one story for another.''

Libby shuddered. If she stayed with Caleb, that would be his life. Bargaining with gossip mongers to safeguard her reputation. "He won't be mentioning your name in print, will he?"

Sliding over the question, Caleb continued, "Things should get pretty exciting in Petaluma when the *Jacket* arrives. Reliable transport—" He grinned at Libby's sniff. "Reliable transport will mean a boom. Why don't we throw a party for the town? You can be belles in your new dresses.''

It was such a startling thing for Caleb to say that Libby peeked at him sideways.

"You mean you won't snarl like a big old bear if Libby dances with other men?" asked Julia with cheerful tactlessness.

"Not as long as she saves every other dance for me," Caleb countered. He put his hand over Libby's fist where it clung white-knuckled to the edge of the table.

His warm grasp still sustained her when Julia excused herself to ride over to the adobe. "Juan's escorting me over. I'll stay overnight, and tomorrow I'll hear the children's alphabets.''

"I see.'' Libby understood that from Julia's perspective, the plan had more than one point in its favor.

"Really, you're the one who should be teaching, though, Libby.''

"I? Why in the world?''

"That's just the reason," Julia said. "Listen to you. Anybody else would have said *me,* and never known they—''

"He," Libby corrected with a pale flicker of mischief.

"See? That he was being uncultured. You talk like you were born a schoolmarm.''

"Female teachers don't marry," she objected. "It's grounds for dismissal.''

"Well, I hardly think that's a problem if Caleb is your employer."

In several senses, Caleb was already her employer, but Libby expected to be gone and disgraced before she could teach the children more than "In Adam's fall, we sinned all."

They walked with Julia out onto the porch, where Juan greeted her with a reserved "Miss Julia."

Tiny lines appeared between Libby's eyebrows. "Poor Julia."

"I can try giving Juan a nudge in her direction," said Caleb thoughtfully. "He does seem to be what she wants, and he's smitten as well."

"It would have to be a delicate hint," Libby warned. "He's proud. Perhaps having him to supper regularly, to show him he's one of the family."

"Who'll take meals with the hands? It's the foreman's job to make sure they eat and don't fight."

"Really, they aren't babies. Let somebody else—Diego—do it."

Libby caught her breath. She was rivaling Julia in tactlessness this evening. But instead of pokering up with jealousy, Caleb nodded. "That's an idea." He lounged against a post. "Diego did a good job organizing the team to get your furniture moved."

Her eyes narrowed. "I've been curious. How was that accomplished with so little noise? I never heard a thing."

"You were occupied at the time, as I recall. I had them dismantle the furniture, remove the grates from the outside window, and lower the pieces with ropes over the outer wall."

Libby wanted to scream, to slap the reminiscent grin from his face—even, shockingly, to giggle. So many conflicting impulses attacked her that she couldn't choose among them, and ended by saying merely, "You promised me you wouldn't have the furniture removed."

"No, dear heart. I said it wouldn't be moved until it

went to this house. They brought it here that night. I never break my word.''

''But the other party had better listen very carefully to hear just what that word entails. Devil take you, Caleb. You *are* going to ask the attorney to arrange a divorce, aren't you?''

With his head tipped back against the column and lids drooping, he looked tired to death. His harsh cheekbones stood out against shadows that in a few years would be creases in his lean cheeks. Too much riding to and fro, Libby thought. Too many life-and-death decisions to make. Too many nights of broken rest. ''If that's what you want,'' he said.

Nothing could make her say she wanted a divorce from Caleb. ''It would be best.''

''All right. In the meantime, the sun's going down. Ranchers bunk down early. You're still my wife. Come to bed. You can wear your emeralds for me.''

Too much lovemaking? ''You need your sleep more.''

He pulled her close, pressing her palm into the cradle of his hips. ''Find some other way to insult me.''

Her hand instinctively cupped, caressing in response to the insistent pressure that filled it. ''Is this supposed to happen when you're tired?''

''Well, not if I was too tired.'' He nibbled at her bottom lip. ''I guess my body needs you more than sleep.''

Later, when only her cloak of hair and the emeralds glowed against her skin, she asked softly, ''Will your name be in the newspaper?''

''Doesn't matter.'' He settled over her, joining them with aching slowness. ''We've got one chance. If we don't catch them all in a single—thrust—'' His breath shortened as she lifted her hips to meet him. ''It'll be too late anyway. Oh, God, Libby, put your arms around me . . .''

The days until Caleb had to go away lagged when he was out on ranch business, sped by when he found chores to do nearby. Each day divided itself up into a series of tasks in the kitchen and house, and Libby gave every chore her complete attention as it presented itself to her, refusing to think about the future at all. At night she wrapped herself around Caleb and pretended that the passion singing between them was enough.

It would have to be enough, she reminded herself as she shooed away a maid and packed his valise. When he came back—she wouldn't allow herself an *if*—everything would be different. Once the divorce was in train, she could no longer form part of the household.

Caleb took the bag from her on the porch. He'd already asked her not to come with him to Newtown dock, but she said again, "Couldn't I ride with you at least a little way? In fact, I'd prefer to go to the city with you. I could be ready in—"

"No." The instant refusal was terse enough to hurt, Caleb knew. He was sorry for it, and mitigated the rejection with a kiss. Although it would have been pure pleasure to ride beside her through the early morning freshness, he'd decided to spare Libby a prolonged farewell. No matter how skillfully he made love to her, or how long he held her into the night, the sadness never faded from her eyes. He'd get her her damned divorce—but Caleb wasn't taking the chance that his reluctant bride would book passage on an outgoing vessel if she could find one and disappear from his life without a trace.

Her lips parted under his. Resisting the invitation, Caleb shifted his head, planting a light kiss on her cheek instead. Her mouth was already red and pouting from making love last night and again this morning; she gave and gave, he thought incoherently, without noticing the toll it took from her. The only thing she wouldn't give was her consent to remain his wife.

He'd been to England. Filthy skies, rowdy ports, crooked lanes teeming with poor. There were nice spots as well, but he'd rarely gotten to see them. What drew her . . . oh, well. The lure of the Manzanita seemed to escape Libby, too.

"I'll slay some dragons for you," he said. He felt the quick shiver that rippled through her, and put it down to cold. "Here, inside with you."

"I don't care about dragons." He waited for her to say she cared about him. Instead, she looked at him with eyes like mountain lakewater, green and still and sad. "Goodbye, Caleb."

Chapter 23

The committee had decided not to strike at night when they would possibly be expected, but instead during the supper hour. Caleb's arrival at the wharf was the signal for bands of heavily armed men to gather and move into positions pinpointed by the volunteer spies.

"You'd know I'd end up here," said Caleb. He regarded the front of the dingy waterfront saloon without favor.

Beside him in the lee of a building, Jacob Klein's long beard split in a smile. Each huge fist grasped a rifle whose butt rested on a barrellike thigh. "Not a promising locale. But pearls may be found in the lowliest oyster."

"I found gold," Caleb said, thinking of Libby. "And I'm in the process of letting it slip away because I don't know how to hold it."

"That does not sound like you, my friend." When Caleb shrugged irritably, Jacob went on, unperturbed. "A treasure is on its way to me, also—"

Word passed down the line. Time to move.

The men ambled across the narrow wooden street, footsteps echoing. Caleb had chosen a knife with a long, wicked blade in addition to a rifle. He held them lightly, lovingly, and few pedestrians in this rough-and-tumble quarter gave him or any of his friends more than a glance.

The group split at the saloon doors, more than half going to the entrance to the attached bordello. The warren of sordid little rooms would be harder to search. Caleb waited until a protesting yell burst forth, then shouldered open the swinging doors.

At the first barrage, aimed toward the ceiling unless the man shooting recognized a Hound he could bring down, men and glass went flying. Most ended on the floor, where ropes hog-tied the saloon customers into place until "the grain could be sifted from the chaff," said the reverend, who looked very happy with a pistol shoved into the waistband of his black clerical pants. The women found under the debris blinked when pulled out into the last rays of the dying sun. Raddled and tawdry out of the kinder setting of candlelight, they accepted the minister's sermon on the evils of their profession with bowed heads, which Caleb privately judged had more to do with shock than repentance.

"The priest is taking a considerable while to release those poor women from his eloquence," said Jacob disapprovingly.

Just then the reverend sketched a vague blessing, and the recipients dragged away. The forlorn air that clung to the displaced prostitutes reminded Caleb, just a little, of Libby. Unlike her, they were an unsavory lot, but—did they have anyplace to go? Alive to the absurdity of it, he wondered if Libby would expect him to find sleeping berths for as unpromising a collection of whores as he'd ever seen. "Maybe I should—" he began.

Several members of the committee of vigilance darted after the contingent of soiled doves. Face stiff with the effort to suppress a bark of laughter, Caleb looked at his friend. "Looks like they'll make out all right. You—" Oh, hell. "You don't have a particular reason to be concerned about any of the girls, do you?"

"I?" Jacob's broad chest shook. "No. My concern is more general. By gracing San Francisco, all such ladies have done me a great favor."

A steady glow emitted from Jacob, which Caleb had put down to excitement over the action. "Sarah," he said in realization.

"My Sarah," agreed Jacob. "She is coming to join me."

And Libby, no matter how many times she let Caleb make love to her, seemed at a further distance every time he touched her. "How did you convince a lady as—as—"

"Finical," Jacob supplied.

"—fastidious as Miss Sarah to leave civilization and New York?"

"A feat, is it not? Letters. Long, lugubrious letters, filled with my love for her and scenes of life in San Francisco. I tell her of the beauty of the bay and the prices charged by tailors, so my shirts remained unmended. I describe fog drifting like eiderdown and how I lose strength because it fills the store and I cannot find my pans to make a simple meal."

"She may question that one." Caleb poked Jacob's solid midsection.

"You interrupt. I write movingly about how lonely I am and about the plague of prostitutes swarming over the town. More than the locusts that covered Egypt, I say." He sighed contentedly. "It worked. So now I will have my Sarah."

Jealousy. He'd tried so hard to smother it in himself—my God, he'd even made Diego assistant foreman to show Libby he trusted her—and it had never occurred to him what a potent weapon it might be brought to bear on the object of his affections. Golden, muleheaded, increasingly sad-eyed Libby. Beautiful Libby, who'd tossed him out of his own bed when he'd made the tiniest, least offensive remark about the inventive whore from Marseilles.

She had even fantasized a name for her rival. What was it? Ah. Marie-Rose. A slow smile crossed Caleb's face. The last time he'd been in his office, the ship's model had been secreted in the darkest corner. The

Mary Rose. Marie-Rose. Mary Rose? She'd asked him about a Mary Rose before. What had Libby fabricated out of that chivalry-fed imagination of hers?

The alcalde made an appearance, after all the shooting was safely over and done with. Caleb found himself hailed and delegated into a temporary administrative post. A tally of names was thrust into his hand. He settled onto a stoop to study the list in the last of the light when one name caught his eye. William Ainsley Smith.

The Hounds had overflowed San Francisco's inadequate calaboose and were being penned in an abandoned merchantman out in the bay. Waiting for William Ainsley Smith to be hauled up on deck, Caleb shook his head over the decline of a perfectly fit ship. Its owners would probably maintain it out here until the bay-filling projects caught up with it, and then claim the new land. They'd sack the hulk for its fittings and burn the remains. A waste.

"Mr. Logan, sir? Got the prisoner you wanted."

Smitty had lost his cockiness along with his front teeth, but malevolence still curdled the air around him. He spat blood at Caleb's feet.

"I rowed out here for the pleasure of beating your face in," said Caleb conversationally. He watched the pink liquid spread and mingle with other stains on the unswabbed boards. "The hell with it."

Smitty spoke suddenly in his new lisp. "Married that thlut Elithabeth, did you? Detherve each other, I thay."

A cur with its teeth drawn, Caleb thought, and waved to the guard to return Smitty to the hold. Libby had been right. All it had taken was a little backbone, and the village bullies were defanged. "I hope so," he said to himself. "I hope I deserve her."

Smitty shouted at Caleb's calm back. "You think we're finithed. Ith not over yet!" His shrill laughter rang out over the water.

* * *

"Aren't you coming to meet the steamer?" Libby asked.

Libby was aware of irony. Julia should be saying the words to her; after all, if Libby had any sense left in what passed for her brain these days, she'd be avoiding the slightest contact with Caleb Logan. But the chance to see him, whether in victory or defeat, to touch him, perhaps even dance with him before the legal separation began, was too tempting. Once more, she thought, and then was disgusted with herself. Just one more little minute—that's what Marie Antoinette had said when faced with the guillotine. Libby was just as bad. Just one more little minute to live, to breathe the happiness of being close to Caleb.

Julia pushed nervous fingers at her switch. "No, thank you. I have an engagement."

"With someone more important than the arrival of the *Red Jacket*?"

The younger girl didn't meet her eyes. "With Mr. Malloy. Don't worry," Julia rattled on, "I'll be there for the party. He can escort me."

Libby took Julia by the shoulders. "Why? You can't like him. Juan is—"

"Juan won't come near me! But he looks—especially when Mr. Malloy is around. Aloysius has visited several times while you've been busy. Lately I've wondered if I'm not an idiot for squandering my chances waiting for a man who'll never make a declaration. Aloysius has his points. He's—he's biddable."

"Weak-willed, you mean."

"So, I'm too strong-willed. Men don't seem to appreciate that in a woman. Aloysius I could boss around. And he's handsome and charming. His only interest may be the Logan fortune, but at least I'd get entertainment for my money."

"You'd be content with a husband like that?" Libby asked disbelievingly.

"There are lots of different kinds of marriages." Julia pulled away to fluff the parlor pillows with brutal little shakes. "I've learned from you and Cal not to put too much store in love. It surely doesn't lead to happiness."

"Don't settle for second best. You should have more. So should Caleb."

Satisfied at last with the fatness of a bolster, Julia dropped it onto the window seat. "You're not calling yourself second best, are you? Men fall down and grovel for one of your smiles."

"I'm an ill-famed woman," said Libby unanswerably. "You saw what happened at the fiesta. If Caleb and Senora Vallejo and you had turned your backs on me with the rest, I would have been done for. I can't expect Caleb to bear with the sidelong glances forever. I'm leaving him."

"Jerusalem crickets, Libby. How blind can you be? Cal won't wilt because of a few mean-spirited comments."

"Men talk about women with reputations. Tell me Caleb won't consider every overhead remark a challenge. I once saw him almost kill a man who said something—ugly—about me."

"So he'll fight," Julia said impatiently. "My brother's been in and out of scuffles since he was in short pants. Someday he may outgrow them, but if he doesn't, it'll have nothing to do with you."

"It would have everything to do with me." Libby looked into a bleak future. "Caleb should be able to be proud of his wife. When a gentleman loses his pride, he dies inside."

"Cal's not a gentleman. He's a scrapper. Who did you know who died from a few insults?"

"What?"

"I said, who taught you that a real man backs away from other people's opinions?"

"My father. That's not a fair way to put it. People said horrible things about Maman. She gambled, you see. So did Papa in his way. He couldn't bear to stay in England and be less than Squire Owens when we had to sell the manor. He lost his home, his country—his sense of who he was. Trying to win them back cost him and Maman their lives. But he was brave; they both were.''

"Just not about what people say. None of that kind of stuff is going to bother Cal. You can't leave him.''

"He doesn't love me." Libby smiled at Julia's blush. "Does he? Have you ever heard him say it? I want him to have the luxury of loving his wife. And he'll never have that as long as he's tied to me.''

"If you can be stupid and whistle Cal down the wind, then I can be practical and take Mr. Malloy.''

"You can't trust him farther than the fencepost! Julia, he stole money from me. He betrayed me to all those people at the fiesta. The man's a drunkard!''

Julia relaxed and laughed. "Now that's an out-and-out lie. I was nearly believing you for a minute. There's never been a sign of drink on him. And he explained about the fiesta. He meant it for a compliment—professional musicians look on these things differently,'' she said eagerly.

"Neither of us was very professional. We were just survivors.''

Libby sat with a thump. Those years of traveling and singing, singing, singing . . . How she'd hated that life. Caleb had made it possible for her to sing again for no other reason than that it made her feel good.

"Aloysius Malloy was drinking himself to death in a Hudson's Bay fort when I found him," she said. "His family had shipped him to Canada to keep him from doing so on their doorstep. He trapped for furs until he got between a sow bear and her cubs; that's where the limp came from. He could play several instruments; we became partners. Professional? By definition, I suppose so. But successful? Hardly. We made it to San Francisco with barely a hundred fifty dollars in profit to split between the two of us. He drank up everything else we earned.''

"If he's conquered his habit, then that's a point in his favor." Julia crossed her arms stubbornly.

"The man's still full of malice." Libby could tell she'd gone about this the wrong way, but she didn't know what to do except repeat the truth. "He's weak, and the weakness lets evil in."

"But you see," said Julia, "if Juan won't have me, and I can't have Aloysius, then I'll be alone."

"Is that so bad?" Empty nights stretched ahead of Libby into eternity.

"I'm used to male companionship. Whatever—accommodation—you and Cal come to, Cal's attention isn't going to be on me anymore. I want a husband."

"Then for heaven's sake, let's get you Juan!"

"I won't take a man who isn't willing to come out and say he loves me." Libby could hardly argue the point. Julia's lips twisted. "That's not a problem with Aloysius."

"How many times have you met him?" Libby demanded. Without waiting for Julia's answer, she went on, "Then both of us will miss the *Red Jacket*. I'm not leaving you with no one but Aloysius Malloy. I hope Caleb understands." He wouldn't, she knew.

"Going to play duenna?"

"Amusing, isn't it? The saloon singer shall chaperone."

The specially sprung wagon which was to carry the ladies and their finery during the two-hour trip to Petaluma creaked up outside. "I'll tell the driver he'll have to wait," said Libby coolly.

She dressed as quickly as Ascensión would let her. All the help would be attending the festivities in town, and the maid's bright calico skirt had been lifted into deep scallops to reveal the red silk underneath. Libby compared Ascensión's sparkling anticipation with her own haggard face. The new gown with its tiers of sea-green flounces was the loveliest dress Libby had ever owned, but not even it could give her a party glow.

"Senor Malloy is here." Teresa's voice from the doorway was cool.

"I don't care for him much, either," said Libby frankly. On impulse, she added, "What are we going to do? Senorita Julia—"

"It is known." The bow of Teresa's mouth became more pronounced. "Sometimes when there is more than one stallion in the corral, the situation resolves itself."

Libby thought. "Who?"

Surprise raised Teresa's eyebrows. "Juan, of course."

"But—" Libby searched for the right word. "Will he . . . perform?"

"He will be spoken to. Pardon, senora. I must see that Senor Malloy is detained."

It was only after the housekeeper bustled purposefully away that Libby remembered that corraling two stallions together usually left one of them dead.

Chapter 24

Julia's foot in its kid dancing slipper tapped. "They said Aloysius was here. Where is he?"

Libby played with a flounce. "If you can't even depend on him to escort you to a dance . . ."

"Stop trying to make up my mind for me." There was a light knock on the parlor door, then it opened. Julia ignored it. "I'll choose my own husband, thank you!"

"Not if it's that mincing fancy man," said Juan grimly. Julia whirled to face him, jaw dropping. He pulled her into his arms. "Shit, Julia, if you want somebody who's not good enough for you, take me."

He kissed her long and hard. Julia's arms wavered, then stretched around his waist.

Biting her lips to keep from smiling, Libby turned and looked through the curtains. Teresa was leading Malloy in a stately fashion up the steps. "Perfect," Libby murmured.

The newcomers halted on the threshold at the sight of a dusty wrangler and a woman in a shimmering blue ball gown locked in an embrace. Teresa bobbed her head in Libby's direction, directed a glare at Malloy, and said quietly, "The rest of us go to the dock."

The Manzanita's employees with beds in the old adobe had long since left, Libby knew. Just as softly, she asked, "Is someone escorting you and Ascensión?"

339

"Diego." Her black eyes glistened, but all she added before she left was, "Your driver waits in the kitchen. Do not let the senorita and Juan tarry too long or the driver will eat all the food for breakfast."

"Thank you, Teresa," said Libby dryly.

Juan finally broke the kiss. He stared into Julia's bemused face. "I couldn't believe you'd really consider marrying a pitiful nance like that piano player. Teresa told me, and I came to put a stop to it any way I could. *Madre de Dios*, Julia, what's the matter with you? I used to think you had some common sense."

"Juan!" said Libby in a warning undertone.

It was too late. A slow, unpleasant grin adding character to his looks, Malloy strolled into the room as Julia gave Juan's chest a hearty shove. "Well, I have too much sense to hug you again! How dare you kiss me out of pity!"

"I didn't—"

"Parceling out your kisses to save me from myself! Who do you think you are? Of all the insulting—"

"All I said was—"

"You know, there are etiquette books to help johnnies so clumsy they trip over their own tongues," Malloy put in helpfully. "You might be reading one or two. Or three. That is, if you can read."

Juan started for him.

"He wants you to hit him!" said Libby sharply. "Then Julia will be angrier with you."

A patter of Spanish accompanied by fading laughter washed through the window. Diego, Ascensión, and Teresa were on their way.

Juan looked from Julia's crimson cheeks and heaving bosom to Malloy's pleased smirk and Libby's frown. " 'Scuse me, ma'am," Juan said, bowing to Libby. "Looks like I've strayed into the wrong part of the house. I'll go saddle a horse and join the servants now. The company is better."

Julia's hand came out hesitantly, but Juan didn't glance in her direction. Tears filled her eyes and fell one by one as she put the hand to her mouth. Still grinning, Malloy moved forward and brought her fingers to his own lips. She shuddered as he pressed a kiss on her knuckles.

"I can't," she said in tones of discovery. "He's a horrible, stupid fool, and I can't marry anybody but him. I'm sorry."

Malloy drew a long, hissing breath. "It's sorry I am, acushla. I've come to be fond of you, I have, and I counted on carrying your beautiful self off to the altar."

In response to Julia's conscience-stricken silence, Libby interjected, "You counted on spending her beautiful dollars."

"Yes," he went on with a judicious air, "it hurts me to bear bad tidings to a tender maid like you. Now Libby here, she's got a hard blow or two coming." He smiled and pulled a pistol from his coat pocket. "Or should I say a bullet?"

"We carry guns, too," said Libby through stiff lips.

Malloy laughed. "Do you now? In gowns the likes of those? Not likely, I'd be thinking. Ladies wouldn't want to be spoiling that fine silk and lace and such. But if I'm by way of being wrong, by all means show your big, wicked firearms and we can all shoot each other dead. No? Then, you, Libby, over next to Julia." The barrel waggled as he pointed.

Julia gripped Libby's hand. "Bad tidings?"

"You can't trust anything he says." Malloy had changed, Libby thought. The spite in him made him formidable now that he was sober. Not knowing what else to do, she tried the old trick of disdain. "I must say, you were actually a more pleasant companion when you were drunk."

He settled himself into a wing chair. Something avid and desirous jumped behind his bland malice. "And you've always been a sharp-tongued bitch. How did Logan bear with you, I wonder? Whatever poor sport you offered between the legs couldn't make up for the horror of your nagging day and night."

Past tense. She clutched at Julia so hard she felt bones grate in both their hands. Caleb—past tense?

"Too bad it is," Malloy said expansively, "that our little heiress has discovered she suffers from such low taste. I was willing to cross my own employers for the sake of her delightful person, I was. My orders were to spread the tale that I'd had you, Libby—many, many times, and under an intriguing variety of circumstances—but I held off, I did, to win Miss Julia's favor. It was a gamble I lost. I'll be needing funds to take leave of the fair state of California. The Hounds are not understanding men." He regarded the women's white faces with smiling ridicule. "Nothing to say, Libby? A red-letter day."

"Do you expect it to surprise me when beasts run in the same pack?" Could Caleb and his friends have moved against the Hounds last night and been defeated? News traveled so slowly. Was it possible that her love was dead and her insensate heart had stubbornly gone on beating? How could blood be pumping through her veins in slow, painful rushes if her reason for living had already been blasted into eternity? *Oh God, why didn't you take me, instead? Take me, and bring back Caleb.* Her shoulders remained straight and her head proudly poised, but her knees gave way and she sank onto the settee. *He's more valuable, more loved, more important to so many people than I am. Take me.* Blackness rose all around her. *Please, don't make me live without him.*

Julia sat down and put her arm around Libby. Satisfaction made Malloy's mouth cruel. "Hit by this, aren't you, ladies? It's tit for tat, you see. If it hadn't been for Libby here, spurning Smitty and setting him afire to take her down a peg, I'd be happily minding my own business and not bothering you at all. But she did, and he is, and so the Hounds, they come looking for me, denying me the comfort of a dram now and then, using me like—" He swallowed. "You can't be blaming me for wanting my wee bit of revenge."

"Are you going to rape us?" asked Julia bluntly.

Distaste sharpened his features. "I've more pressing concerns than what you two keep under your skirts. Thank you, Miss Julia, but I'll be denying myself the pleasures of rape."

Libby heard them through the curtain of black mist. Hoarsely, she said, "What has happened to Caleb?"

"That information will cost you," Malloy answered. He lifted the gun. "Those pretty baubles around your necks, for example. And the earrings and rings. On the table."

Dropping the emeralds next to the heap of gold and crimson flashes formed by Julia's ruby jewelry, Libby clenched her left hand protectively. Malloy noticed. "That swaggering dullard you married turned you sentimental, did he, Libby? I never thought I'd be seeing the day you toss away emeralds as if they were dishwater and make your stand over a bit of trumpery."

"This is my wedding ring. You may not have it."

Malloy's eyes were on the small fortune glowing against the mahogany. "I'm feeling generous, I am. Keep it. I'll think of you mooning over the beggarly thing, pining for a man you'd not have spat on had you met him in England."

The mist didn't go away, and she welcomed it, because it kept her from feeling much of anything. "Where is Caleb?"

Gun in one hand, he pulled a square newspaper clipping from his coat with the other. "Why, aboard the *Red Jacket*, I suppose. Your blockheaded husband doesn't seem to have meant it to be a secret. The Hounds may not know their letters, but there are plenty who do to read to them."

The bold print fluttered as Malloy flicked the article toward Libby and scooped up a handful of jewels to stuff into a pocket. "Ho, for Petaluma!"

Julia sat forward. "Then my brother's all right? He's—"

"In perfect health, as far as I'd be knowing." Malloy

paused to admire a ruby cut like a teardrop. "At least he will be till the bit of tinkering the Hounds did on the boiler causes the dear thing to blow up. The relief valves are so delicate, you know. Just a tiny increase in the pressure is all it takes."

Facts added up laboriously in Libby's brain, and the fog of shock lifted. Malloy was corroded by hate clean through; if Caleb were surely dead, he would tell them to enjoy the sight of their pain. So that much of what he'd said was probably true—unless the boiler had exploded already, Caleb was alive. Libby took a deep breath, so her body flooded with the life that suddenly seemed to fill the air. The curtains stirred, a finger of breeze touched the pendants of the chandelier and startled a chime of music and rainbow glimmer from the crystal.

Color splashed across Libby's silk, giving the yellow-green threads of the warp and the blue-green threads of the woof a liquid sheen.

Liquid.

It was, after all, Malloy's most easily exploited weakness. Libby knew that sometime in the future—if she had a future—remorse would overtake her, but just now she didn't have time for it.

"It must be thirsty work, becoming a rich man in a single afternoon," Libby said. Out of the corner of her eye, she noted Julia's quick glance. Julia's cheeks, even her lips, were still dead white, but her eyes blazed with a red light in their black depths. Libby risked a short nod. Then she deliberately shifted her gaze to the Vallejos' silver goblets, which decorated a side table.

Rising, Julia wandered to the table and picked up one of the tiny, exquisite things, rolling the cup in her hands as if to warm it. "Did you really once drink to excess, Aloysius? I don't believe it."

"It was always a matter of opinion," mumbled Malloy, his attention distracted from the gems. He watched the flash of silver between her palms.

"Cured, Mr. Malloy?" asked Libby. The hope blossoming within her made it difficult to hit just the right note of contempt. If Malloy thought she was doing anything but taunting him, hatred might keep him from that first, crucial sip, despite the craving that almost visibly crawled beneath his air of calm superiority. "Take care. Are you sure the bottle won't be your downfall yet?"

He pushed the last piece of jewelry into his pocket and ran a hand that quivered slightly over the lower half of his face. "I'm sure, bitch. In fact, I'd say this moment calls for a wee celebratory drink. No," he said stridently, "you stay where you are. Julia can get it for me. You'd poison the best whiskey just looking at it."

There was a bottle in the sideboard, kept there for company; Julia uncapped it and poured, standing back when Malloy motioned her away with the gun barrel and grabbed the goblet. Some of the amber contents slopped over his wrist. He tossed off the rest, sucked the drops beading on his sleeve greedily, then drank straight from the bottle.

He lowered the now quarter-empty container and cradled it to his chest. "A fine brew. Your hospitality, Miss Logan, Mrs. Logan, is of the best. It pains me, it really does, to ruin such a pleasant visit and bring up the subject of money—"

"You've got stones and gold worth thousands of dollars bulging out of your pockets. What else do you want?" demanded Julia.

"Security, let's say, for me old age." The Irish lilt had noticeably intensified. "A pension, if ye will."

Julia borrowed a word from the stables. Malloy guffawed. "Ah, Libby, me girl, what genteel company ye've landed among. It does me soul good to see it. It's like this. I have a hankerin' to be movin' on and leavin' me current associates behind. The way I intend to live will be costin' a pretty penny. Sure and your reputation is worth a small sum every quarter."

"Blackmail," breathed Libby.

"A mutually advantageous business transaction. Your

money for me silence. Otherwise letters—very detailed, explicit letters—will be arrivin' at every newspaper in the state. Broadsheets will be printed. Your face and figure would look well on a broadsheet. That husband of yours can lurk in the background, wearin' cuckold's horns—'' He chuckled and drank again. "Of course, he'll no longer be among the living, and what he'll look like if you find enough to bury is anybody's guess. A boiler's a mighty tricky thing. When one blows, the heat can melt the skin right into a person's clothes, so it comes off his bones when the undertaker undresses the dead man to put him in his good suit . . .''

The level in the bottle went steadily down. Malloy passed from self-congratulation to sleepy combativeness faster than Libby would have expected; the period of abstinence must have reduced, rather than increased, his capacity. When only an inch remained in the bottle, and his eyes were agate slits under drooping lids, she sidled close and reached stealthily for the gun.

He raised it to her face, opening his eyes unnaturally wide. "Thought you'd take advantage of ol' Aloysius Malloy, didja, Libby, girl?'' The words slurred badly.

"I tried,'' she admitted, standing full in front of him, waving her fingers imperatively behind her back. Julia took the hint; Libby heard quiet steps, a faint rustle, then the sounds ceased altogether. She didn't dare look over her shoulder to confirm that Julia had sneaked away.

Relief made her generous. Julia would get a warning to Caleb—if it weren't already too late. Hastily, she shut that thought into a mental storeroom. Julia would warn Caleb, and her beloved wouldn't die . . . "Let me bring you another bottle, Mr. Malloy.''

The sooner he drank himself into insensibility, the better she'd like it.

But Malloy had only begun to make inroads on the second bottle when the amount of liquid he'd poured into himself required relief. "Find an outhouse,'' he muttered, lurching to his feet. The pistol bobbled so wildly that Libby felt her first shiver of real fear for her own safety.

"Miss Julia can show me—where'd she go?" His expression grew ugly. "Run off? Won't be doin' her any good. Nor you either, Lady Too-Dainty-to-Piss Logan. Come on. Stay where I can keep my eyes on you. Where's the outhouse?"

A short hall at the back of the house opened onto the narrow walkway. It was uncarpeted, magnifying every sound along its length. Walking ahead of Malloy, Libby was aware of the *shhh-shhh* of her wide silken skirt brushing the walls, and the uneven rhythm of his stumbling footsteps. Her throat constricted and her stomach hurt. He was drunk enough to shoot her in the back without meaning to.

The sursurration of silk, two sets of footsteps . . . It seemed to her she heard nothing else for a thousand years, and then a soft scrape interrupted the meter. There couldn't be anyone ahead—no one remained, except the driver in the kitchen, too far away to hear, and perhaps Julia. But, no, she must have hurried away toward the slough a good quarter hour ago . . . Despite reason, Libby pressed herself against the wall.

"Go ahead. I'll wait here."

"Are you thinkin' I'm a fool?" Malloy's bleary gaze sharpened. "You'll run like that other bitch."

"Well, you can't expect me to go in there with you. I couldn't in any case. Both of us won't fit."

"Damn all crinolines," grumbled Malloy. "All right, you wait in this prissy gallery. The door stays open," he added, shoving past her and pulling on the latch.

Libby's muted gasp warned him. She couldn't help the startled, indrawn breath; she hadn't really expected anyone to be hiding behind the door.

Juan lifted a heavy, efficient-looking shotgun and took aim. But Malloy was already in clumsy motion, gripping Libby awkwardly by her short, dropped sleeve to pull her forward as a shield. His hand touched the sensitve skin of her inner arm, and the flabby wetness made her jerk away. Hitting the wall, she slipped and began to go down. At the same time, a memory of Caleb snaking out an arm to trip Smitty, so vivid it eclipsed what was actually happening, flashed across her brain.

She twisted, jackknifing her legs so they bridged the width of the walkway.

Malloy went down with a satisfying thump.

Lowering the stock from his shoulder, Juan said disgustedly, "I suppose you'll let out a squawk if I shoot him now that he's knocked himself out?"

"Don't tempt me past my limitations. He'd be considerably less trouble dead. Oh, God, what are we going to do with him? We have to get to the *Red Jacket*—"

"Julia told me. She's saddling horses. I couldn't leave you two women alone with a piece of manure like Malloy," he explained. "Help me with this rope I brought."

The knots Juan used looked sturdy and painfully tight. Libby nodded in approval. "Turn him on his side so if the whiskey comes back up he doesn't choke to death. Hurry!"

Three horses waited in front. Julia was already mounted, blue skirts and white petticoats frothing around her in wild and attractive confusion. Somewhere she'd lost her switch, and her chopped hair fluffed out around her face like a black nimbus. "Sent the driver to warn the sheriff. Let's ride!"

Tossing Libby into the saddle, Juan vaulted onto the last horse and stormed toward the east. With barely enough time to link her knee over the pommel of the sidesaddle, Libby gave her mount its head. It thundered close behind Julia.

They pushed the animals as hard as they dared, but after twenty minutes slowed to a walk to keep the horses from foundering. Already wavelets of lather discolored the glossy hides. These weren't thoroughbreds, or even the strong, ugly Californio ponies, but the bigger, still-unconditioned stock Juan was breaking to riding. Libby had to bite the inside of her cheek to stop herself from screaming at Juan to quicken the pace. Continuing the punishing speed would accomplish nothing and be death to the horses; either they'd burst their hearts and fall, possibly rolling on the riders, or the thin bones of their equine legs would snap in an unseen burrow.

They'd gone five miles, and had at least five more to go.

"Julia and I could trade horses," she said suddenly. "That would rest this one a bit."

Juan gave the beautiful skirts a disparaging glance. "Might if she had on her normal clothes. In all those ridiculous fol-lals, she must be hauling thirty extra pounds. The weight difference between you isn't worth the time to remount. Forget it."

"What I'll forget is any notion of you." Julia urged her horse to a trot. "Why do you have to be so disagreeable to Libby? She's worried sick."

"What did I say?" he asked in astonishment.

"That we look ridiculous! You insulted our taste in—in companionship and our intelligence! You—"

"I never said all that to Libby."

Julia clapped a hand to her decolletage, smearing her upper chest with gray dust. "Women only dress this way to please men and how do you reward us?"

"I kissed you," he pointed out. His heels dug into his horse's side, forcing a pace to match Julia's. "How much more of a compliment do you want?"

"Bend your mind to it."

"How am I supposed to guess what—"

Edging by both of them, Libby put in, "She wants you to love her."

"*Libby*," Julia wailed.

"At this rate you two will squabble away the summer while Caleb needs us!"

"You're a fine one to talk!"

Libby shrugged and encouraged her tired mount to canter. Juan followed suit, hands and knees automatically competent despite his obvious confusion. "Julia knows I love her. I told her—"

"No, you didn't," Julia contradicted.

"Well, I meant to. I'm telling you now." He glared at her. "I love you."

"I've loved you since the first year I came to California," answered Julia.

"I can beat that. I've loved you since the first moment I ever saw you. You were sixteen and skinny and still green from being seasick, and I wanted you then, but I knew it would be taking advantage and Cal would never allow you to go to a mixed-breed bastard with nothing."

"You might ask him," suggested Libby, "assuming we get to the steamer in time."

They cut through the hills until they came out on a crest with a wide view of the estuary. In the north squatted Newtown. The water was here green, here brown, meandering peacefully across the valley.

Julia squinted. "It's nowhere in sight! Jerusalem— no! Wait! Do you see?"

Still miles to the south, a boxlike shape made steady headway through the reeds. Libby let out a sob and put her horse down the slope, careless of rocks and wicked little holes hiding in the grasses.

"Libby! Libby, not that way! The bank is too soft!"

The horse hit marshy ground in one last burst of speed and slithered. It stumbled, drenching Libby to the thighs, then recovered, heaving itself upright and standing stock still.

From the top of the knoll, Julia and Juan peered down anxiously. "Are you all right?" called Julia.

"Fine," she shouted back. "Ride along the crests and try to get their attention aboard the *Jacket*."

They began the race south. Libby watched them for long minutes, conning over the little she knew of steam boilers. The valves through which steam escaped were particularly delicate and prone to failure. Caleb had sworn the *Red Jacket*'s boiler was dependable, but that was before the Hounds tampered with it. If Malloy had been telling the truth. How could she separate the real from the lies, pretense from a possible kernel of fact? Malloy would say anything in his desire to hurt her.

Caleb, too, had stretched the truth in his dealings with her, even if, as he claimed, it hadn't actually snapped. And every time the big barbaric American had been trying to protect her, or to help her learn about herself as a woman, or to save her from what he fondly believed to be her infatuation with Malloy. For the first time, Libby smiled at that particular delusion of Caleb's. He'd find out better when he saw Malloy roped and tied heel and wrist to the outhouse door.

If the homely little *Red Jacket* could just make it another mile up the stream.

The riders disappeared into the fold between two hills, then reappeared as suddenly. Libby murmured to her horse and turned it toward the bank. She had to get it out of the stream before it drank itself to death or caught a chill. As the horse heaved them both up onto drier ground, her sopping skirts didn't even flap. They were too saturated with cold salt water. The clinging weight glued her to her mount.

The clatter and chug of the steamer reached her as distant thunder, shaking the birds and frogs into silence. Juan and Julia were almost abreast of the boat now; they stopped and Libby could see Julia, a flash of blue, jump to the ground. Juan waved his arms, and after a moment a large white flag billowed into the air over Julia's head.

One of Julia's petticoats.

Too wrought up to laugh, Libby stared hopefully at the *Red Jacket*. Someone would have to notice so much motion on the hilltop, even if the sound of voices didn't carry over the noisy wheel. Someone would have . . .

But apparently no one did.

The steamer pushed steadily past Juan and Julia.

"What's the matter with you?" Libby demanded fretfully. "The time I rode on you, you went aground every ten minutes. Where is the silt today?"

Either it had shifted or another pilot was directing the helm. She straightened in the saddle. A lean, familiar figure, growing larger by the moment, bent over the snub-nosed prow.

"Caleb! Over here!" she called.

He continued to gaze intently into the water. The boat was even; it was drawing away. None of the scurrying men aboard heard her or saw her. Drops flung by the paddle wheel struck her in the face. Fighting the drag of her skirts, Libby stood up in the stirrups and used her full operatic volume.

The scream deafened even her. She screwed up her eyelids, holding her seat on the startled, rearing horse by instinct, and screamed until the effort burned up enough terror for her to remember to draw a sobbing breath.

"Libby! For God's sake!" Somehow, instead of being in the prow, Caleb was there, drenched to the waist but next to her, and pulling her from the shaken, demoralized horse. She went into his arms and clung. "What's happened?"

"Get everyone off the boat. The boiler—"

He didn't wait for the rest. "Abandon ship! All hands!" His bellow carried easily now that the wheel was stilled.

Men boiled over the side and waded toward them.

With Caleb holding her and people moving to safety, Libby let the weakness of reaction wash over her. And—oh, God, what if Malloy had been lying and there was nothing at all wrong with the relief valves?

Big, gentle hands lowered her to the grass. "Tell me, Libby."

Hounds, boilers, and Malloy tied up with his pockets bursting with rubies and emeralds tumbled out of her. Caleb rubbed the back of his neck. "We beat the Hounds, dear heart. As for the piano player—" She waited for a jealous explosion. His lips twitched. "It sounds like he'll keep."

A brawny fellow in a greasy shirt said diffidently, "I suspicioned she was running hot, sir. But you'd checked the gauge when you came on board, and I kept my eye on it. I'll swear it was holding steady."

Caleb and the engineer studied the innocent-looking steamship warily. "Gauges can be meddled with. And I can think of three ways to fiddle the valves just off-hand. Only way to tell for damned sure is shut down and take each valve apart." He glanced at the man who'd leered at Libby when she'd traveled on the *Red Jacket*. "Agreed, Captain Zachary?"

Zachary was pale and sweating. "Aye, sir. I'll take care of it."

"No, you watch out for Mrs. Logan. Keep the men together. I can handle it. I sure don't want to lose that bet with the general."

Caleb knelt and tilted Libby's face to his. "My sweet wife," he said, and kissed her hard on the lips, then tenderly on the forehead.

The ground rumbled underneath them. For a moment, Libby connected the vibration with Caleb's kiss, shaking their private universe. The drumroll swelled, though, even after he raised his head to look over her shoulder. Earthquake? But it was Julia and Juan, forcing a last burst of speed from the spent horses.

"Juan. Good. Help keep order here. Julia." There was a hug for his sister.

Caleb waded to the boat and climbed to the deck. Gallons of river water poured off him, making his trousers fit indecently close over his narrow hips and the bulge between his legs. Libby looked, and ached, and met his dark eyes. He gave her a brief, tight grin and went below.

The engineer was explaining to the newcomers what Caleb was doing. Juan's voice rose. "And you let him get back on board that deathtrap?"

"He's one of the owners." The captain shrugged.

Libby struggled to her feet. "What do you mean? The danger's over, isn't it? Caleb will check the valves—"

"Sure, Libby," said Juan. "There's nothing to worry about."

Embarrassment made his eyes wince away. Julia's mouth had become small and firm, but her chin trembled. Everyone else stared frankly at Libby as onlookers might inspect the widow at the scent of an accident.

"I have to know what kind of gamble Caleb is taking," she said quietly.

Reluctantly, Juan mumbled, "He has to get all the steam out of the boiler before he can touch the pipes or valves. Until the pressure goes down, the *Jacket* could blow any time."

Picking up her skirts as if they weighed nothing at all, Libby ran toward the *Red Jacket*.

Julia clamped arms around her first, then Juan, and then several of the men. She shrieked until a sweaty hand muzzled her. She bit into the tough, salty skin, making someone curse, but the hand didn't go away. So she fought viciously and silently until Julia hissed in her ear, "Stop it! Just stop it, Libby. You can't help Cal. You'll get in his way and keep him from what he has to do!"

Libby pulled her elbow out of the belly where it was planted and halted her foot in mid-kick. The hand and arms holding her released their grips cautiously.

"I won't try to get on board again," said Libby wearily. She didn't bother looking at her well-meaning captors, just at the steamship. "Oh, devil take you, Caleb Logan, for being a hero. Devil take you straight to hell."

Chapter 25

Coal fire roared beside him. Caleb ignored it, except to bat absently at his waterlogged trousers as they steamed in the terrific heat.

It was the steam in the boiler that concerned him. The engineer was right; equipment was definitely running hot. With his gut, he could feel water boiling, steam churning, pressure building. And building.

No time to curse the idiot who should have reported the oddity, gauge or no gauge. No time to waste precious seconds blaming himself for not noticing the suspiciously gleaming surface of the dial, as if somebody had recently handled and wiped it. A single twist would unscrew the plate from the back to reveal the vulnerable spring that could be set so the marker would refuse to swing above any pressure one pleased.

His hands worked the handle that controlled the first relief valve. Steam whistled breathily up the pipe and out into the open air. The second valve gave the same almost human sigh.

The third made no noise at all.

Once the boiler had emptied itself, the pipes cooled enough to touch despite the furnace. Contracting metal gave off weird, hollow clangs. Mopping sweat from the back of his neck with a shirtsleeve, Caleb discovered muscles knotted into hard balls.

He rolled his shoulders. With the boiler now dead, there was no need to feel tense. The engine couldn't

explode. But Libby might. Libby was a different proposition altogether. No telling what she'd do when she
found out he hadn't been to consult with any lawyer.

Using the engineer's tools, Caleb set to work taking
the third valve apart and unearthed the round, flat piece
that ought to pivot when pushed from below by excess
steam. Small but heavy filings held it fixed into position. He swept the metal bits into his hand. "Too bad,
Smitty," he said. "You gambled again and you lost.
Again."

His Libby had been too much for the Hounds twice.

Smiling, Caleb reassembled the valve. Either the
Hound who'd done the damage had been interrupted
before he could add extra weight to the other valves, or
he'd believed blocking one out of three would create
sufficient pressure to cause a disaster. It could have,
Caleb thought with the lightheartedness of a narrow
escape. But it hadn't. Boilers were strange animals. He
patted this one affectionately and sprang up the ladder
to the upper deck.

Libby had sat, cold and numb, her gaze unswervingly on the captain and engineer. Once long, contin-
uous streamers of white steam began to rise above the
boat, they relaxed their stiff stance and chatted with
Juan or swore genially at the deckhands milling on the
shore.

The emergency was obviously over. Caleb would
live. They would all live, like it or not. And with her
emotions strung precariously between sharp joy and dull
despair—Caleb was alive, and she would have to leave
him—Libby wasn't sure she did like it. The one great
benefit of being dead must be that a person didn't have
to make all these harrowing decisions. Paradise, assuming she was allowed in after knowing Caleb Logan,
sounded like such a nice, peaceful place. In heaven,
she wouldn't have to turn her back on love for her lover's good. She imagined it as a shining city, rather like

London but better cleaned, and surrounded by perpetually gray skies.

Caleb was suddenly on the deck of the *Red Jacket*, waving emphatically. A cheer went up. Rough, kindly hands hoisted her aloft, and passed her from man to man over the muddy bank and gurgling water to the side of the boat.

"Can you manage the ladder, dear heart?"

Libby looked away from the sailor who under Caleb's eye was holding her, very properly, as if she were a parcel, although the man was sweating freely. The clear California sun struck Caleb's face, turned down toward hers from the deck above. It picked out the strong nose and chin, illumined the good lines of cheek and jaw, sprayed sparks through his black hair, and reflected in his dark eyes.

What a ridiculous moment, she thought, to understand that gray and tasteful England was as far distant as some pallid afterlife. Life was here, in the white sunshine that burned away the past and left . . . Caleb. Long years of laughter and fighting and loving were meant to lead to a heaven that would be anything but colorless if Providence allowed her to share it with her turbulent love.

It made no difference, of course. She still had to leave him. But the vision of what life could have been released a cleansing flood of anger. Her temporary husband looked so calm, so superior, as if he hadn't just scared her nearly to death for something as unimportant as a boat, or a bet. Oh, he was brave—stupidly, thoughtlessly, insanely brave.

"Dear heart? I'll come get you."

"Please don't bother," she said distantly, and reached for the first rung.

Juan wouldn't let anyone carry Julia but himself. Laughing, they and the others crowded around Caleb with noisy congratulations. Retiring to the lounge, Libby wrung out her clothes and tried to tell herself she cared about the three-foot-deep watermark and streaks of mud.

After a while, the engine built up a large enough head of steam to push the paddle wheel again, and it slowly began to turn. Arm in arm, Julia and Juan sauntered in to join Libby. "The captain's ordered an ounce of whiskey for everyone," Julia said, waving a glass in the air. "To stave off chill. Do you want some?"

"No, thank you." Libby absolutely refused to ask where Caleb was.

"I hoped you'd toast our happiness." Julia lifted a glowing face to Juan.

He looked sheepish. "Asked Cal if he had any objection. All he said was 'About time.' "

"And so it is." Her genuine pleasure at the news put warmth into her reply, but even so, Juan gave her the kind of glance a man might award an unpredictable animal.

"Cal's put himself on duty in the engine room," he offered, explaining the caution. "He said you'd better not visit, because it's too dirty in there for ladies."

Libby directed an ironic look at her bedraggled skirt and flicked at a strand of her hair, which was coming down piecemeal.

Juan barely hid a grin. He eased out of the lounge while Julia sat beside Libby. "Go ahead," Julia said. "You might as well use some of that spleen you've got stored up on me. I'm so happy, it'll just roll off my back."

Libby jumped up and began to pace. "The Hounds could have killed your brother today. What did he risk his life for? An idiotic wager!"

"There was the boat, too," put in Julia fairly. She picked up a deck of cards and shuffled them inexpertly. "It turns a tidy profit."

"You'd trade Caleb for a *boat*?"

"No. If he'd asked me, I'd have told him to let the infernal thing blow. But he didn't ask me. And he didn't ask you. Rankles, doesn't it? Cal is always going to choose his own risks for his own reasons. It's part of being the man he is.'' Julia tried to tuck a lock of hair behind an ear. The cards fluttered back onto the table. "Besides, what do you care? You won't be around to put up with it. You're divorcing him, remember?''

Unable to meet the challenge in Julia's eyes, Libby scraped the cards into a neat pile. One of them had gotten crumpled; picking it up, she saw the jack of hearts with his cap bent awry. She smoothed the crease.

The steamer ran aground. Jarred almost off the bench, both women went out on deck to watch the men work the poles. Afloat again, it chugged by a group of twenty or so on the wharf at Newtown. Some people waved, some jeered, then they all bolted for horses and wagons that stood ready to race along beside the slough.

Caleb brushed by her, murmuring an apology. "I won't touch you." He showed teeth that were startlingly bright in a smeared face. His once-white shirt was covered with soot, as were his trousers. The boiler room was indeed dirty.

The shot silk dress was long since ruined. It was a matter of complete indifference to her. "As far as presentability is concerned, we're a good match."

He looked at her searchingly. "We are a good match."

Libby shrugged.

"What have you got there?" he asked.

"This?" She knew she blushed. "Just a playing card. There's a pack in the lounge."

Anxious to be rid of it, she started to toss it over the side. Caleb's hand clamped on her wrist and he gently pried her fingers back from the betraying piece of cardboard. "Jack of hearts. Don't throw him away. I have a fondness for him. He saved my life once, you know." He hesitated. "Damn, I have to pilot now. If I leave it to Zachary, we'll be wallowing in mud the rest of the day."

"Go," she said.

"Libby—"

"Go on." A smile wouldn't come, but she wiped a smudge from his cheek with gentle fingers that were at variance with her dangerously level tone. "I know it's important to you."

"Yes'm. We'll settle up when we reach Petaluma. I can tell it's hard for you to wait to tear a strip out of my hide."

The phrase echoed Malloy's gruesome description so exactly that she shuddered.

The narrower channel kept passengers and crew alert. Every time the vessel dragged against the bottom, causing the white spume to turn brown with mud, a collective groan went up. Libby paid tense attention, although she turned away self-consciously when Caleb spared her a wink from his station in the prow. Julia had been right. She wasn't supposed to care.

To Libby, Petaluma looked identical to Newtown, except that there was more of it. Raw buildings, a wharf, dirt streets. A larger crowd spilled across the dock, clapping and cheering as the *Red Jacket* approached. High-pitched whoops punctuated the more genteel clamor. A few guns went off, fired into the air.

The moment the ropes were tied, Caleb started purposefully toward Libby, but a mob of sailors intervened, hoisting him onto brawny shoulders and carrying him down the gangplank while hundreds of hands reached out to shake his.

Libby hung back. Finally, everyone else had disembarked into the laughing, excited throng. The deck provided a good view. Caleb was allowed to jump down, but his commanding height made him unmistakable. So did his soot-darkened face. The black head bent over Vallejo's. For a man who had just lost a wager, and whose investment in a more southerly port had become worthless the instant the steamer docked, the general seemed cheerfully resigned.

Vallejo would lose it all, Libby saw with unaccustomed foresight. The broad acres, the fabulous fortune.

She looked at him and saw her father. Neither was like Caleb, a man who knew how to hold on to his own with both big fists. Like the general, her father had come from a more courtly, less harsh world. A world that no longer existed except in memory or imagination. A place forever closed to Libby.

"Goodbye, Papa," she whispered.

Juan was coming in for a lot of backslapping and Julia for courtly bows. Teresa parted the well-wishers and seemed to give Juan a lecture; even from her lonely corner, Libby could see the straight, strict line of her brows. Diego smiled indulgently and pulled the housekeeper away, dropping a kiss on her braided hair. Teresa seemed to ignore it, then looked up at the handsome vaquero with shy pleasure.

Folding her arms, Libby curved her back farther into the corner. Teresa and Diego, too? Everyone had paired off except her. From the number of wide skirts circling Caleb, despite his filthy condition, it wouldn't be long before he found consolation.

Now that the time had come for her actually to leave—not just plead, or threaten, or plan—but to go, seeing Caleb busy with a life that no longer included her was too hard to bear. Libby retreated into the lounge.

She tried to slam the door, but it caught on her skirt. The small frustration was one too many. She began a slow, careful, meticulous litany of every bad word she'd ever heard on two continents.

Caleb's jaw ached from smiling, and his tongue stumbled over itself trying to find another polite phrase. Pumps primed by free-flowing whiskey and a lemon punch originally intended for the ladies which had been improved all out of recognition by the discreet addition of several ladlesful of rum, the crew had inflated his deed into an act of daring so extravagant he barely recognized it. The result was this covey of females made up of the girls in the county too young to be married.

They pelted him with questions, and Caleb couldn't tell any of the adoring, unformed faces apart.

Where the hell was Libby?

A signal from Diego gave him an excuse to escape. Wiping his forehead, he grimaced in disgust at the smudge his action transferred to his knuckles. Diego handed him a kerchief.

"It'll never be the same," Caleb warned.

"Please. It will give Teresa something to fuss over. She will like that."

"If you say so." Caleb scrubbed vigorously. "Any better?"

"You are my employer, so I will say yes. Senor Cal, this is perhaps not the place, but—may I ask a question?"

"If one of those glasses you're holding is for me, you can."

Diego was balancing two cups in one palm. He passed one to Caleb, and they drank. The unwatered whiskey burned going down, and Caleb breathed deeply. "Another?" offered Diego.

"No." No doubt Libby would be showing up soon. "I've got to keep my wits about me. What's your question?"

"It is this. The old family rooms in the adobe are empty. Teresa and I were wondering if you would object to our moving into one of them."

"You and—"

"We have already talked to the priest." Diego looked into his glass. "I had never seen her that way—as a man sees a woman—until . . ." His gaze touched the general and came back to Caleb. "I wanted to protect her, but she needed no protecting. A brave and a strong woman. I will give her many reasons to nag, and we will both be content."

"Of course you can have house room in the family quarters. Makes sense. Juan's moving to the big house, have you heard? Good luck! Teresa's a woman worth having."

"As is the senora. She does not join you?"

"I've misplaced her. Temporarily," Caleb added. He might have buried his unreasoning jealousy, but there was no point taking chances around a self-confessed lecher like Diego. "Julia! Where's Libby?"

Hair sticking straight out and gown streaked with mud, Julia paused in the act of being gracious to a group of dignitaries from Sonoma. "Do you know, I can't recall her getting off the steamer. Caleb? Where are you going?"

His jaw had hardened. "To retrieve my wife!" he called over his shoulder.

He heard her the minute he boarded. It was a wonder the rest of the county didn't, too. His well-bred wife wasn't making any attempt to keep her carrying, upper-crust British voice subdued. "Damn and blast and cow chips and bloody, bloody, bloody hell!"

The door wasn't quite closed; he entered and remedied the omission. There was a simple lock, and he used it. The snick of the bolt being thrown brought Libby around to face him.

Her golden river of hair had fallen completely out of control to flow down her back. Tear tracks smeared the dust on her cheeks.

"Hello, dear heart." His gaze devoured her. "You look so good to me."

"Since the defects in my appearance are solely due to my efforts to keep you from being blown into small bits—an endeavor in which I must say you gave me not the slightest assistance—"

"I wasn't mocking you, little one," he interrupted. "I was just telling the truth."

"You always do, don't you?" she asked bitterly. "Except that you leave out snippets of information. Like the fact the boiler still could have exploded."

"I didn't want to burden you."

"Perhaps I wanted to be burdened! Perhaps I deserve the right to worry about you. I've paid a high price for knowing you, Caleb Logan. At the least I've earned the courtesy of proper notice when you're getting ready to—to turn yourself into sausage meat!''

"I'm sorry." He lifted her hand and, to her surprise, kissed the finger that held her wedding ring. "I'll be more forthcoming next time."

He knew it took her an effort to pull her hand away. Her chin jutted, but a bruised look clouded the green of her eyes. "And there will be a next time, won't there? You like danger—"

"Now be fair." His mouth remained grave, but he sounded as if he were laughing at her. "You got all in a tizzy because I didn't want to take on the Hounds. You thought I was some kind of yellow coward."

"I didn't know what to think! One moment you were leaping into a battle and the next you were dragging us both away from one."

"Didn't like the odds. I only fight to win, Libby. It's the safest way. I wouldn't go and get myself killed for no reason. It was you convinced me to join the committee of vigilance." He took her hand again, and this time she let him. "Justice can't always be enforced at the end of a gun, but some fights have to be fought. They're everybody's business. And—I wanted to impress you."

"You did," she said. "I hated you for becoming so important to me."

"Still? You still hate me?"

She let out a tiny, broken sigh. "No."

Relief loosened the tight muscles in his neck, and a small measure of confidence flowed back into Caleb. She didn't want to leave him. Maybe, just maybe . . .

"But I'm angry, seriously angry with you. You didn't have to risk yourself to save this stupid boat. It was a crazy gamble and completely unnecessary."

"Of course it was necessary. I have to be responsible. I'm the cap—"

She raised her brows. "Oh, no, you're not. That what's-his-name is. You may have been captain on your sailing ship, and you may be captain at the ranch, but here you're nothing but—but the owner.''

"So I'm supposed to pay other people to take the chances? Libby, listen to yourself. You'd never love a man like that. Admit it.''

"I—''

"If it makes you feel any better, I'll apologize for not being more of a coward. But I have to tell you something, dear heart. You're sounding just like a wife.''

She went a fiery red visible through the dust. "That's a state of affairs that will be rectified in the near future, I trust.''

Caleb looked at her, and wanted her. The sadness in her eyes had been replaced with dangerous emerald fires. Although not cut anywhere near as low as her infamous scarlet dress, the neckline of the seagreen gown hinted broadly at the loveliness of her full breasts. Even bound, the peaks had stiffened—with fury, probably—enough to push visibly at the silky material. Her petticoats had been drenched and mangled to the point where the skirts couldn't completely hide the shape of her hips or tapering lines of her legs.

Yes, he wanted her crushed to him, holding him tight inside her legs as she forgot herself in passion for him. But mostly he wanted her to admit that she belonged, not *to* him—he knew too much about her independence to believe that anymore—but *with* him. They belonged together. One flesh, one heart.

"So beautiful,'' he murmured.

She laughed. "I'm blowsy as a slut. The slut you were sure I was.''

"You look like a woman who can give a man what he needs,'' Caleb said with a touch of roughness. "What would I do with a wife who was nothing but icicles and seven layers of corsets that never came off?''

"At least your neighbors wouldn't snicker at you in private and feel sorry for you in public!''

Brown eyes snapped at her. "I don't give a rat's ass for public or private opinion. Who's the coward here?"

"I'm trying to stand up for your interests, since you're too blockish and male and stubborn to do it yourself!" she blazed.

"Then fight for me!" he said urgently. "Don't let me go, Libby."

Uncertainty softened her voice. "But—it's all settled. You talked with the lawyer, and I'm going to England." The soft note disappeared. "You did speak to a lawyer, didn't you, Caleb?"

The wooden bench couldn't be called a very inviting piece of furniture, but Caleb slumped onto it and stretched out his long legs in what comfort it provided. He fingered the battered deck of cards idly.

"You sound very much like a wife," he repeated.

He figured he owed her dishevelment and spitting rage to the piano player. It would be a distinct pleasure to deliver him personally to the sheriff. No one would question Malloy's condition as long as he was breathing, and Caleb meant to make sure the man was breathing often and painfully. God, what he'd put Libby through being jealous of that worthless piece of . . . One thought led to another.

"I've been meaning to answer something you asked me once," he said. "About Mary Rose."

Libby's heart stopped beating. It started again almost immediately, but she felt she'd already died. She could stand anything but to hear that she'd only been a substitute for Mary Rose.

If Caleb didn't count one notable exception, everything he and Libby had done in bed had been straightforward. Would accounts of perverse pleasuring drive her wild with jealousy? Would they merely disgust her? Or—would she know what he was talking about? She probably thought herself a woman of the world. But under her regal air, she was still an innocent, and would be, he predicted, till judgment day. Filled with innocent ideals, aglow with innocent warmth, generous with her sensuality in a way only an essentially innocent woman could be.

It was that innocence he was appealing to now. He didn't want to destroy it; he loved it. And the quality was his best chance of winning her. He needed to come up with a story that made Libby so out-of-her mind jealous she'd sink ladylike talons into him and never let go.

The steamer rocked gently as she knelt on the deck beside the bench, putting her face on a level with his. Under the dirt, hers was pale and serious. "Caleb, whoever—whatever—Mary Rose has been to you, I don't see how she could possibly have loved you as much as I do."

Caleb lay back and closed his eyes. At last. At last.

"It's no blame to you if you don't want to hear me say it. But I love you so. Perhaps Mary Rose was nobler than I am, or prettier or—or better in bed. The one thing she couldn't have been is more in love. I'm drowning in love. No matter how I tried, I couldn't save myself, and I'm so far gone now I'm not even sorry about it. You are a wonderful man. I'm proud that you were my lover."

"Libby, I love you."

"You don't have to say that."

"Have I ever lied to you?"

She smiled faintly and shifted to rise. Caleb gripped her elbows and held her fast.

"You hanker after England that much?" he asked.

"Oh, not anymore. I did. I was going to go back and be a little girl again—live in someone else's house, let society dictate all my actions so I could have a rest from the responsibility of deciding them for myself. Well, I won't make those mistakes, but—it will be best to have an ocean between us, Caleb."

"Do you really despise the Manzanita so much?"

"I don't fit in. There's no place for me."

"That's the craziest thing I've ever heard you say. Who's going to keep us all from dying of scurvy and teach the school? Who's going to be company for me at night? I get lonesome, Libby." His hands slid to her face, cupping it so she couldn't evade his gaze. "Same as you."

"The problems with our marriage haven't changed," she protested weakly.

"No. Only we've changed. Tell you what. Take these cards." Releasing her, he held them out. "I'll make you a bet. I know you don't wager, but you won't be able to resist this one."

"I possess more powers of resistance than I've given you reason to believe," she said with a resumption of some of her usual spirit.

"Cut the deck. If you win, I'll sail you straight to quayside in London myself. There are likely ships rotting at anchor in the bay; I can buy one and outfit it and have you at your uncle's tea table inside a year."

"That's hardly—"

"But if I win, you stay at the Manzanita. We move my bed into my room, which will then be our room. With our bed. You will sign the goddamned parish register in front of as many people as I can find to witness your signature. God willing, we'll have children and grandchildren and great-grandchildren."

"Caleb—"

"We'll populate the whole damned state. And if you threaten to leave me, it won't be for some asinine reason like your thinking we don't care enough about each other to weather a few storms. You say you love me. I know I love you."

Her tongue flicked over her lips, leaving them pink and moist. Caleb forced down the impulse to kiss her and looked at her sternly instead. Libby asked, "Wh-what about Mary Rose?"

"You can forget Mary Rose. If you trust my word at all, accept this. You're the only woman I want for my wife."

It was certainly true. Sweat broke out along his spine at the thought of what Libby would do if she ever found out Mary Rose was the name of the mother of the bored sailor who'd whittled the model ship and presented it to his captain at the end of a long voyage. That—what had she called it?—snippet of information would be worth his life, Caleb reckoned. Maybe it would be safe to tell her after thirty or forty years of contented marriage. Maybe. If she chose to stay with him . . .

The pack sat in his hand, tempting, seductive. Edges frayed and surfaces wrinkled, as easy as an alphabet for Libby to read. She'd touched those cards. The pads of her fingers remembered the nick in the upper left corner of the two of spades and the thin spot in the crown of the queen of clubs.

Never take a little flutter?

Never.

Caleb's brown fingers curled around the deck as he pressed it into her palm. "Cut, Libby. Choose for me first."

Slowly, her fingertips danced over the individual edges, separating, identifying. The one she sought wasn't there. Oh—of course, she'd tucked it into her bodice for lack of another place after Caleb had handed it back to her outside.

Eyes holding his, she made no attempt to hide the motion as she plucked the only card that would do from between her breasts. His bright, dark eyes took on a deeper glow. Her palm shielded the card from him.

"For you. Jacks wild," she said, looking into Caleb's face. She turned it over without glancing down. "Jack of hearts wins."

Libby wasn't sure what she was looking for in her husband's expression until the muscle beside his mouth pulled his lips into the grin that had infuriated her on the saloon stage the night they met. Now it filled her with joy.

"We win," he said, pulling her to him. They collided in a flurry of hands and mouths and tangling limbs. The buttons of his shirt were too much bother, so Libby simply pushed it up so it wouldn't hinder her as she stroked and licked and bit the smooth skin of his chest. The hundred or so hooks that held Libby's bodice together made Caleb curse briefly, then he took the thin but resilient silk between his strong hands and ripped. The fabric gave with a loud, shocking sound.

The noise startled both of them into freezing for a moment. Libby disentangled herself and breathlessly stood to strip off the torn material and untie the laces at her waist. "This gown is not fated to be worn again," she remarked, green eyes growing huge as Caleb peeled away his clothes with equal rapidity. "How are we going to get off this boat in some semblance of decency?"

He made a loose mattress out of the ruins of her softer petticoats. "Juan and Julia know where we are. They'll be around eventually. Not too soon, I hope. Are you worried about the appearances?"

To Caleb, her carefree laugh sounded like music. "Mrs. Caleb Logan? Why should I be?"

She shook her hair so it fell like a golden net that waited to trap him close to the ivory body gleaming through the marks of adventure and exertion. Where he wanted to be.

He held out his arms. "Then come and be my wife."

If You've Enjoyed This Avon Romance— Be Sure to Read. . .

THE MAGIC OF YOU
by Johanna Lindsey
75629-3/$5.99 US/$6.99 Can

SHANNA
by Kathleen Woodiwiss
38588-0/$5.99 US/$6.99 Can

UNTAMED
by Elizabeth Lowell
76953-0/$5.99 US/$6.99 Can

EACH TIME WE LOVE
by Shirlee Busbee
75212-3/$5.99 US/$6.99 Can